THE DEATH FACTORY

"So it's bombs Fra___ O'Donnell said, sniffin___ dollar for every time ___ hideaways where terro___

"I wouldn't expect ___ Cause like yourself ___ Geraldine responded.

"I don't play amateur games with explosives," he said.

"You underestimate us," the tall, red-haired beauty said. "We have two lads in our cellar who have Bachelor Degrees in Chemistry. So when you say—"

"I have no time for chatter," Liam interrupted. "I'm here for my son." Jerking the cellar door open, he hollered down, "Ambrose O'Donnell! Get up here on the double!"

After a moment, Ambrose stumbled up the stairs. "See here, Pa," he said. "What they're teaching me is—"

"Not a word out of you," Liam ordered. "I want you out of here, on the double!"

As his son left, Liam turned again to Geraldine. "I want a word with Boyle," he said firmly.

"However you like it," she said. "But be warned that Francis has lately found it prudent to carry a revolver, and—"

Her sentence was cut short as the universe erupted in one shattering, deafening roar. The walls of the building seemed to rise and waver in mid-air before starting to cave in. Timbers crashed and glass shattered. Suddenly the whole night was orange. Flickering. Crackling.

And for Liam O'Donnell, the world went black . . .

The O'Donnells
An Irish-American Saga

a Waltz on the wind

ian kavanaugh

A JAMES A. BRYANS BOOK
FROM DELL/EMERALD

Published by
Dell Publishing Co., Inc.
1 Dag Hammarskjold Plaza
New York, New York, 10017

Dell TM 681510, Dell Publishing Co., Inc.

ISBN: 0-440-09487-9

Printed in the United States of America

First printing—April 1983

BOOK ONE

VERONICA

1

At her desk in the library's bay window, overlooking her gardens and twenty wooded Connecticut acres, Veronica signed the last of her morning's checks to worthy charities. Her pen swept through the customary final flourish which had characterized her signature since, a year ago, she first had adopted the hyphenization embracing the names of both dead husbands. Veronica O'Donnell Tyrone-Quinn was actually on the threshold of her eightieth birthday. She herself stoutly refused to feel old and allowed no quiver in her firm script, nor any trace of unsteadiness or uncertainty.

Despite a pesky pinch of arthritis which, during the past year or so, did have the impertinence to plague her, Veronica was able to stuff each contribution into its proper addressed envelope with a sharp little thrust. Her name stared up at her for an instant before it vanished from view. *Tyrone-Quinn*; a false touch of elegance perhaps, but both her husbands had been fine men. Tyrone was a solid and respected banker, and Quinn was equally top-of-the-heap in his world-renowned pharmaceutical congomerate. Neither deserved to be dropped from her life. She honored each.

"Yet I think I miss Vincent more. A few years younger than me, agreed. But what a high time we had together," she said aloud, lifting her gaze for a moment from the orderly desk. This past year, alone in the big Connecticut house, with little company except for visits from the vast O'Donnell clan into which she had been born, she had taken up the habit of conversing with herself. She found that she made quite satisfactory company for herself, and that generally she had more interesting things to say than what she could elicit from many she could mention.

"Vinnie was a heller. Not half so proper as Rob Tyrone. Still a kid on his seventieth birthday. Forever whipping around the globe to visit this plant or that lab where some new drug was being developed. Always wide-eyed about tomorrow. Just mention some new adventure to Quinn and he was off like a shot to be part of it. Which, of course, was why . . ."

Her sentence broke, its frayed final word dangling. Careful, Veronica. No self-pity. Each mortal soul has to finish his run sometime, early or late, And with Vinnie it certainly wasn't early. So watch yourself, old widow lady.

It was still too soon to believe he was gone. It was only a little more than a year since the day when the miracle Zeppelin came floating in like a huge silver swan across serene skies over Lakehurst, New Jersey. Only a small bouquet of months since the awed, cheering crowd below—herself among them—had watched the queenly cylinder burst suddenly into its devil conflagration, rigid struts crumpling like tissue paper, internal hydrogen gas cells blazing as the wounded monster began its horrifying plunge.

"I knew how excited you'd be over that incredible Atlantic crossing, Vinnie. I knew how you'd itch to tell me every detail of your latest romance with the unknown. That's why I drove in from Giant Oak with Joe when he took the Packard down to meet you. I knew how full of it all you'd be. And then . . . and then . . ."

Was it already a year ago? Really?

At night she often caught herself listening for his step on the stairs, coming up from some late radio news broadcast detailing events he found too fascinating to switch off. And his step, if not taking the risers two at a time as he'd done in the earlier seasons of their marriage, still would be firm. When it didn't come, despite all her listening, she often found herself puzzled, bewildered.

"Enough of that, Veronica! You'll be mewling like a stray kitten in a rainstorm."

With a businesslike straightening of her shoulders, she riffled the envelopes on the surface before her into a tidy pile, ready for Joe to take down to the post office. From the desk's top left-hand drawer she extracted an envelope of a more personal sort, engraved in one corner with a likeness of the huge tree for which the property was named. Next came two matching sheets of the almost transparent pale blue notepaper she favored for family correspondence. *Miss Norah O'Donnell*, she inscribed in a authoritative hand, and then signed a crisp check for a hundred dollars which was already made out and lying ready for enclosure. Below Norah's name she wrote the Manhattan address of her favorite nephew, Jim O'Donnell, Norah's father.

As always when Veronica thought of the pair, parent

and daughter, a faint smile of fondness stirred her age-thinned lips. Had he lived to see how these two were turning out—his son and his granddaughter—her brother Patrick would be proud. In their separate ways, Jim and young Norah both were determinedly carrying out the family's passion for ancient Irish music. The clan's founder, the first Liam O'Donnell, who'd crossed from the old country in steerage—Liam, the Sligo fiddler, her own father, and Patrick's as well—would have rejoiced in them too.

> *Darling Child:*
> *Your affectionate Great-Aunt won't be able to come to town for your Sweet Sixteen party on Thursday after all. A tiresome but inescapable meeting of one of my political committees up in Hartford conflicts. I've had private information that my arch-enemy (a real jerk but dangerous) is planning motions to thwart an absolutely necessary project. I must be there to overturn his apple cart . . . Therefore, let the small gift accompanying this note of good wishes bring my kiss with it. I shall be thinking of you every time I rise to call a point of order. Observing the dismay on my adversary's face will seem small consolation for not being with you . . .*

The note and its offering were sealed together and added to the stack for Joe's attention. Flexing stiff fingers, Veronica pushed back her chair and rose with a sigh, reaching as she did so for the silver-headed cane she sometimes secretly wished she might wield as a shillelagh at such gatherings as this up-coming Hartford meeting.

Limping only slightly, Veronica crossed to the long French windows and thrust one of them open before her.

May sunlight washed the terrace bricks with watercolor softness, outlining each crack and scar. They were old bricks. Once she and Vinnie had bought the pre-Revolutionary property, starting a new phase of their lives together which each confidently assumed was to last for decades, the terrace had been Vinnie's first Giant Oak project.

The material for the house had been trucked across five states, from the site of a small tannery Vinnie had pulled down to expand one of his regional enterprises. He and Veronica had wanted nothing new on the land. Its sense of outlasting time—as did the mammoth tree towering above it—was what had appealed to them so strongly on their first visit here. It had lured them to Connecticut from a perfectly comfortable New York brownstone.

Squatted above a rose rootling at one of the floral borders, Alex glanced up when he heard the crunch of Veronica's step on the gravel. He grinned respectfully and Veronica smiled back.

Like the house, like the terrace bricks, like loyal Joe, like herself, her gardener bore a patina of long association. Every employee at Giant Oak had served her practically forever. They had even been willing to uproot themselves when the Quinns had made their move. The cook had been with her even back to the days of Rob Tyrone, and despite her long career as a militant suffragette, and then in the burgeoning feminist movement, Veronica valued these people as part of her settled order and established roots.

"The garden should be lovely, come summer, don't you think? Even more than last year?" Veronica asked.

"If the rest of them perennials we ordered come soon enough for proper setting out, ma'am, you won't never

have seen the like. We'll have a show place to bug folks'
eyes.''

"I'm not especially anxious to impress the public, Alex.
But I do want it pretty for the children if they come for
summer visits, as they always seem to."

"That Miss Norah, she looks like she'd grown on some
rosebush herself."

"Her brothers, Shane and Brendan, aren't exactly
gargoyles, to my way of thinking. Nor their second-cousin,
Miss Madge, either."

"No, ma'am. Everything does seem to blossom along
with the garden when the young ones are here, that's a
fact. But somehow it's Miss Norah that most puts me in
mind of a rose."

Moving on along the path, Veronica felt oddly caught
between two disparate worlds. Her own world was scarcely
the world of youth. Sometimes she found herself wishing
for a magic elixir which could waft her back to being
Norah's contemporary, or her granddaughter Madge's. There
was still so much work to be done. She'd hate to leave any
of it unfinished. The proper place of women in the scheme
of things would not be achieved within her lifetime, and
well she knew it, but perhaps her only child—her daughter
Bernadette, Madge's mother—might outlast and outfight
the political and social forces arrayed against their shared
determined efforts. But she herself, no. Glory be! When
she herself was the girls' age, veterans of the Civil War
were still running national politics!

Under her sensible well-polished oxfords the gravel path
changed to a flagstone walk as Veronica rounded a corner
of the big white house. Before her spread the gently
sloping sweep of the front lawn. Early in the season
though it was, Alex already had manicured the grass to
perfection. Not a blade of it seemed unattended.

The cane's ferrule tapped a firm accompaniment to her progress up the flagging—and then checked as she came to a halt, studying the mighty oak just ahead.

For Vinnie, as well as for herself, that venerable tree had meant much. It had become their shared totem, its majesty carved not by clever hands but by Nature. It was pride. It was strength. It was all those qualities that America itself had offered to her emigré father Liam, so long ago.

Veronica moved toward it slowly, until she was close enough to reach out and touch the tough, runneled bark. It seemed curiously similar to the skin of her own extended hand.

God alone knew how far back into the miasma of time the monster oak traced its biography. When it was young, wolves and Indians must have roamed the hillcrest where it had taken root. The *Mayflower* probably still lay at anchor off Plymouth. Salem Witch Trials doubtless waited in a yet unimagined future. George Washington's grandfather was still a diapered baby in some distant English nursery.

"You're a survivor, old man," she murmured fondly, as to her oldest friend. "Like me. In our separate ways, we've outlasted a lot. And we're not finished yet."

Along the smooth driveway from the garages, out of sight behind the house, the Packard Limousine rolled almost as soundlessly as a passing ghost. At its wheel, Joe caught her glance and touched the visor of his chauffeur's cap. He was on his way to the village with the cook's grocery order and her letters for the post.

She watched for a moment while the grey car veered into traffic at the foot of the low hill. The memory of letters had brought back a thought of Norah's party.

"There'll be others to take over when it's time for us to

go," she said, this time not quite sure whether it was to the oak or only to herself that she spoke. "Good blood. O'Donnell blood. I wish I could give Jim's girl that kiss in person."

By the appointed hour Jim O'Donnell's comfortable though far from splendid apartment near Murray Hill was ready and waiting. Silver gleamed. Crystal sparkled. Masses of food stood by, set for serving. The vase of florist's out-of-season peonies, sent by Jim's only surviving first cousin, Bernadette, made a beautiful centerpiece for the dining room table. Paper streamers hung in multicolored profusion from every walnut door frame.

Admiring the festive effect, Jim marvelled mildly at a notion which briefly flicked his mind. Where had he read or been told that fettuccine, his favorite pasta, had been created to honor the flowing ringlets of Lucretia Borgia? Ah, what true Irishman would waste a thought on Italian food?

He heard light footsteps behind him, and turned, recognizing the sound of them. There Norah stood in the arch from his small private office. Something seemed to swell unbearably in his chest as he looked at her. Almost a full-grown lady, now, was his Norah. Wasn't tonight's celebration a sort of tacit admission of the fact?

You never noticed the water gliding under the bridge and suddenly, too almighty suddenly, the little ripples were miles downstream from you, twinkling in some far land you had small knowledge of. Norah sixteen? Shane eighteen and Brendan only a year behind him? Why, he and Sheela both had whispers of silver in their hair! Another decade and they well could be grandparents. Yet here on the bridge it had, until tonight, seemed beginners' territory.

"Daddy!" Norah whispered, coming to him quickly. "You've bought a new suit for my party! My, but you're handsome in blue serge!"

"The least I could have done, my darling. You wouldn't want me in rags, now?"

"You'll be the most elegant boy at the whole affair. You're going to cut the cake with me, aren't you, when the time comes?"

"Isn't that a chore for your current young man—whoever that happens to be this week? You should be beaued by some proper Prince Charming, an event like this."

"You've always been my Prince Charming, Daddy. You know that, don't you?"

For a moment they stood looking at each other, the fondness of all the years Norah could remember shining on both their faces. Then she leaned forward and kissed Jim lightly on the cleft of his freshly shaven jaw. Her voice, already showing signs of the training it had lately been receiving at the convent school, seemed to quiver fleetingly.

"Besides," she said, "there isn't any current young man this week. There hasn't been one for several weeks, in case you didn't notice. I haven't time for boys right now."

"Whatever in the world? And you a spinster of sixteen?"

"I need so much time for my practicing. I want to be really good, Daddy, *really* good. Sister Ernestine says I show promise of a true singing career."

"And Sister Ernestine is a sibyl of careers?"

"She had one of her own, you know, before she entered the convent. She even sang opera for two seasons in Berlin, Daddy, before she came to America and became a nun. So maybe she knows."

"Is it opera you're aiming for, honey? And cold-shouldering the boys to get there?"

"There'll be plenty of time for flirting later. But I've got to find out first if I've any real talent. Oh, not for Puccini and Verdi. Nothing so high-flown. But the kind of music you care about so much yourself."

"The old Irish music?"

"And newer things too. There's a lot being written that people ought to hear sung the way only people with Irish tradition in their bones can offer it. If I could ever do that decently, well . . ."

Out in the hall, the front doorbell shrilled, cutting across their moment together. With a grin, Jim heard his elder son Shane going to answer it. He had been appointed butler for the evening, and evidently, he was taking his duties with a proper solemnity.

"Hello," a lilting feminine voice was saying just beyond view. "I'm Norah's classmate, Agnes Moran. You must be one of her brothers. Shane? Brendan? I've heard her talk so much about both of you."

"I'm Shane."

Suddenly it seemed to Jim that all his tall son's recently acquired sophistication had suddenly deserted him. That forgotten squeak which had plagued Shane's voice during the months it was turning seemed to have surged back once again. The boy actually sounded dazed. Could this new arrival have kicked him in the shin?

"Am I the first to get here? Oh, dear! But someone has to be first at every party, I guess. May I come in, please? Perhaps there's something I can do to help Norah."

"Oh! I mean . . . sure . . . please come in. I d-didn't realize I was blocking."

Footsteps crossed the foyer parquet, light to match the words of Agnes Moran, classmate and friend. With a joyous giggle Norah swooped out to greet her. Jim followed more slowly, aware that parental rituals must be observed.

He didn't know quite what he was expecting, in the light of his son's audible disintegration. Some latter-day Theda Bara, possibly. Or one of the newer femmes fatales, like maybe Marlene Dietrich. Whatever the pre-image, it crumbled even before Norah could introduce her.

"Daddy, I want you to meet my very best friend at school. Her name is Agnes, and we share a gym locker together, and I'd be *lost* in Chemistry class without her."

Agnes was a pretty girl, all right—a *very* pretty girl, if you didn't mind a few freckles, which Jim certainly didn't. But she was definitely no siren. Her smile was friendly and frank, yet in no way puppy-alluring. Her handshake was firm but not clinging. Whatever glamor she might have picked up at Constance Bennett movies had failed to register.

"Hello, Mr. O'Donnell. Norah talks about you so much I feel I already know you."

"Hello, Agnes. Glad you could make our big evening."

The bell began ringing with increasing frequency as the next quarter-hour eased on. This, if Jim were any judge, was a mixed bane and blessing on the part of Shane. He seemed grimly unwilling to quit Agnes Moran's side for long enough to answer each summons; yet, in her presence, as mute as a village idiot.

Brendan appeared from his own quarters, freshly scrubbed and properly suited, and was perfectly at ease and in no way ruffled in Agnes's presence. And Sheela too finally emerged plump and smiling from last minute touches to the buffet table. Only Shane appeared to be shaken. As for Agnes? If she were as expert at chemistry as Norah claimed, at least it didn't appear to include *that* kind of chemistry.

Among those who arrived were members of the clan who had been able to accept the invitation. Bernadette and her husband, Eamonn McHugh, had their attractive if not particularly vivacious daughter Madge in tow, but Bernadette's son—the younger Liam O'Donnell, named for the family's founder, Bernadette's grandfather and Jim's own—arrived slightly later and unaccompanied even by his very recent bride.

Jim had always privately believed Liam II to be a difficult lad, although one had to make allowances for a child with an unorthodox history. Liam's father and Bernadette had been engaged when the World War broke out. Jack Sandford, the young hero, had died in the front line trenches soon after his arrival in France. Not long thereafter, it had become obvious that their final farewell had been somewhat more loving than society condoned.

Aunt Veronica, Bernadette's mother, would have made whatever private rescue arrangements Bernadette selected, even an abortion, and that in the face of the Church's prohibition, but defiant in the memories of a lover who would never return, Bernadette had insisted upon giving birth and raising her son quite openly in her own home.

If Liam, now pressing twenty, showed signs of wildness, perhaps this was understandable. Jim, having fought in that same war himself, would have been the last to censure.

His brother, Terence, outwardly the most successful grandchild of Liam O'Donnell, reached Jim's door somewhat late for the gathering. With him came his second wife, Hilda, clinging somewhat distractedly on his arm. Terence still walked with the faint limp he had acquired from a beating received while in the process of reaping his dubious Prohibition days fortune. But Hilda's unsteadiness stemmed from a less physical cause. Shortly after their arrival, she drew Jim aside to explain it.

"We went around to pick up your mother. Terence intended to bring her with us, and he'd gotten her down from Newburgh as far as a suite at the Plaza. It's Mother Margaret's own granddaughter's party, after all. But . . . but when we got to the hotel . . ."

"Again?" Jim murmured. A more appropriate term, he knew, would be, "As usual?"

"The maid who'd come down to the city with her informed us she's been passed out cold on her bed since late afternoon. She did intend to come to Norah's party, Jim. You must believe that. A party dress was all laid out and matching shoes and her favorite fan."

"But there was an empty whiskey bottle on the rug beside her."

"Well, it was gin, but otherwise, yes. Please, please try to understand and don't let Norah be too resentful. And don't be hurt yourself. She . . . well, Mother Margaret *tried*."

"I know," Jim said quietly. "Margaret is my mother, too. As you just mentioned."

Hilda plucked at his sleeve. "Terence is furious. It's partly a guilt thing, I think. For so many years he was . . . well, a playboy. Never making any effort toward the brilliant sort of career she'd set her heart on for all her menfolk—your father Patrick included."

"Poor Mother's dreams!"

"If Patrick had become a senator, which she always yearned for, maybe she'd never have started drinking at all. Or if her efforts had succeeded to turn you that same way, instead of toward your music. Or if Terence had blossomed earlier. But now . . ."

''Now Mother's comfortably asleep in her own bed at the Plaza and the rest of us are here at a pleasant party.'' Gently, Jim clasped the fingers which held his blue serge. ''The kids have tuned in Benny Goodman in the front room, Hilda. They're dancing up a storm. What say we oldsters drop by and show 'em how?''

Long before refreshments time, it was well established that Norah O'Donnell's party was a five-star smash. It might not have been staged in one of the fancier Fifties ballrooms, as many such parties were, but it was Norah's own.

Someone from her class at the convent school started insisting she sing. When Norah was herded protesting to her father's piano, a sudden hush fell on the room. For the next half-hour, it was much as though a young nightingale had flown in through an open window. Grouped around the walls on sofas and chairs, they lifted silent faces toward her and simply listened. Shane squatted absorbed, one hand clutching Agnes Moran's. Even Norah's cousin Liam, drink clutched in hand, quieted down and abandoned his wry cynicisms.

Standing in the doorway, one arm loosely around his wife's waist, Jim listened with the others—and wondered if anyone else in the apartment understood as he understood what they were hearing. There was a mating of voice and music here which he had, despite his pride in Norah, never anticipated. He must talk with this Sister Ernestine. A miracle was happening right here among the paper streamers. He had to find out more.

Glancing briefly away from Norah, he happened to notice a look on his younger son's handsome face. It was an expression for which his startled recognition could find no explanation; yet he knew what it was. Brendan was light years too young to be wearing it, or to be feeling the feelings that had to lie behind it. It was an expression of withdrawal. It was the sad, sure closing of a door.

And the boy was only just seventeen.

Jim felt his heart cry. He wanted to reach out and let a hand fall on his son's shoulder. Never in his life had he seen anyone who looked so utterly alone.

However much he loved them, did a man never truly understand his children?

2

Summer's mid-season green flowed serenely past the windows of her mother's Packard as its grizzled chauffeur, Joe, drove Bernadette O'Donnell McHugh from the Stamford railroad station toward Great Oak.

Once free of the suburban city's scruffy outskirts, the Connecticut landscape assumed a tranquillity far from mirroring the disturbed thoughts plaguing the woman who viewed it. Comfortable country estates replaced commercial bustle. Well-tended lawns prefaced dignified houses shadowed by ageless trees. Stirring uneasily against soft grey upholstery, Joe's passenger found herself almost resentful. All the world should be allowed this calm that Veronica and her dead second husband had searched out for themselves.

It was a strange thought for the Bernadette O'Donnell who usually itched for a place in the front ranks of battles for social progress!

Where her still vigorous mother had led, Bernadette always had eagerly followed. And despite semi-rural retirement, the family matriarch was still a force to be reckoned with. New York's loss had been Connecticut's gain—although that was scarcely the word many old-line Hartford politicians would apply to Mrs. Tyrone-Quinn. "Dragon" was the one Bernadette had encountered most often when people described her mother.

Bernadette was coming out from town that day in hope of a taste of that same guidance she had grown up depending on. How many mothers in war-weary 1919 would have supported a rebellious child's stubborn determination to bear and raise the illegitimate baby of a lover killed in action before marriage vows were taken? And supporting her child had cost Veronica dearly. The Nineteenth Amendment stood on the brink of ratification then. How much political support for it in Veronica's district was sacrificed because of her unflinching acceptance of a bastard grandson? Bernadette remembered well.

In a sense, she was coming from New York today seeking defense of Liam II again—grown Liam, this time. Twenty his next birthday, prematurely married, against all family opposition, and still a problem.

"You feeling okay, Mrs. McHugh? Anything I can do for you?"

For the first time, Bernadette grew aware that Joe had been studying her in his driver's mirror. She marshalled a smile to meet the patent concern in his eyes.

"I'm fine, Joe, thanks. Maybe a little tired from the train trip."

"For a minute there you had a look like a pain was deviling you."

"I never felt better, honestly. It must have been hunger

pangs. Anticipating one of those lunches my mother always spoils us with.''

Moments later, the Packard turned in at the driveway, and mounted a gentle rise toward Great Oak. The mammoth tree for which the house had been christened spread its shade over the house's white facade. The stately front door was flung hospitably wide. Veronica stood waiting on the top step, trim knitted suit impeccable, hair white as duck feathers and smiling.

For an instant, descending into dappled sunlight, Bernadette felt almost like a schoolgirl again—here was mother, now everything would be all right.

Luncheon, served at an iron lace table in the coolness of the rose terrace, was everything she had predicted to Joe. Iced melon veiled in wafer-thin prosciutto, a soufflé lighter than the breeze teasing the wisteria tendrils overhead, and a sherbet concocted of fruits not readily identifiable yet surely gathered in Eden before the Fall.

Her maternal worries about Liam were not automatically set right, of course. Once that nostalgic surge accompanying her arrival receded, Bernadette had mocked herself silently for any childlike hope of miracles. The real world was the real world. She had been well aware of that for most of her forty-three years. Mothers—even Veronica— were only human.

The steadying quality of their discussion of her troubles was not failing her, however. Practical good sense was, in its way, an anodyne.

''There's no real reason to assume your son is damned by his cousin Kieran's old obsession, Bernadette. Poor, misguided Kieran cut a romantic, dashing figure in his day. But the Easter Troubles were fought and lost three years before Liam was born. Liam never actually *knew*

Kieran. So Kieran couldn't infect him with that hot-headed Fenianism.''

"Sometimes," Bernadette answered quietly, "ghosts wield a power living men can't match.''

"Imagination is a potent drug, granted, but Liam can't help noticing the changes taking place in Ireland. Only last year, the new constitution was introduced. Eire is now an independent nation within the British Commonwealth. De Valera's a sensible prime minister if ever there was one. Deep down, Liam must recognize all those changes.''

"He doesn't think change is coming fast enough.''

"He's still a child, Bernadette. You know the young don't live on patience.''

"He's nineteen, within a spit of twenty. Despite all our protests, he has a wife. That's not a child. I watch him daily. He's burning inside. Even these recent goings-on in Germany, the rise of this madman Hitler, events as remote as that, cry out to him of Ireland's total freedom.''

"What can a German wallpaper hanger have to do with Ireland?''

"Liam keeps talking of a possible second war between Germany and England. He actually prays for it. He sees such a tragedy only as one more chance to rid Ireland of England—not as Armageddon.''

"He's a romantic, just as Kieran was. But the times have changed, darling.''

"Romantics never change. Not at the core. They're forever dangerous men.''

For a while the two women sat silent, gazing out across the riot of blooms Alex had brought to life in the beds below them. Another manifestation of the romantic spirit, Bernadette thought. Why could her son not have discovered some gentler form for his obsession to bring perfection to the world?

Not that she and Eamonn, his stepfather, would want Liam to spend his future grubbing in garden soil, like her mother's Alex, but there were so many ways a young man could dedicate himself to quieter visions. Their cousin Jim's preoccupation with the motherland's music, for instance. But Liam hadn't a musical bone in his body.

"As a mother," Veronica was saying, "I'd be concentrating more on this girl your son has married. You've told me her name, but I've forgotten."

"Evaleen. Née Cowrie," Bernadette answered. "She's a rich uncle's ward. The uncle is in building. He's put up several of the new office towers in Manhattan."

"Well, then? Isn't that a dream of a different sort for someone young to latch onto? Erecting splendid spires instead of bombing old ones into rubble?"

What might have resembled a smile twisted Bernadette's lips. "Not for those two. Not for a moment. The girl seems to regard Liam's violent notions as the aspirations of a knight in shining armor. I try to listen sympathetically when they come to the house. But the revolutionary drivel they spout . . ."

"When you were young, dear, how often did you think or speak against the dreams of any young man you held hands with? Poor Jack Sandford? Or, later on, Eamonn McHugh? In your youth, a World War was brewing. Jack used to talk of a 'war to end war'. Now, it's twenty years later. Do we think his war accomplished that? Do we still believe what he died fighting for was achieved?"

A mist had settled upon the gardens, so that Bernadette suddenly could not make them out clearly. "That was different. That was for good, the whole world's good."

"To young Liam, there's no difference at all. It's the boy's father, Jack, speaking in him, every bit as much as it is his cousin Kieran. Try to understand that, Bernadette."

"But it's all such a *waste*!" Liam's mother protested fiercely. "I ought to know. I was left with a baby by one such dream, and without a husband. I don't want Liam shipwrecked!"

"Perhaps he won't be. This Cowrie girl may turn out to have just the practical streak in her, underneath the starstruckedness, that can hold Liam in check. Her uncle must be a practical sort, making his success in so tough a business."

"She's as scatterbrained as Liam! Children aren't carbons of a preceding generation."

Veronica chuckled. "That's not what people used to say about you and me. Peas in a pod, they used to say. Still do, if I'm not mistaken. I'd dive head-first into whatever needed doing for women's causes, and you'd be so close at my heels we were practically abreast."

"I know." After a silent instant, Bernadette repeated softly, "I know."

"Truth to tell," her mother murmured, "I'm more concerned right now over Jim's Shane than I am over your Liam. For very different reasons, of course. Shane's as level-headed a boy as you'll find anywhere these days. Following right along in Patrick's footsteps with his interest in politics. Maybe Shane dreams of changing the world, or at least one country of it, as much as Liam does. But with the ballot box, not terrorist bombs."

"Shane belongs on a pedestal. So do Norah and Brendan. Jim's a perfect father. If my boy's own father had lived, maybe . . . Well, my husband tries his best, but he's only a stepfather."

"Don't think Jim's children don't worry me, just because Jim's a model parent. What if his Shane isn't gung-ho for anarchy, like Liam? Actually, it's Shane's very stability that has me worried."

"How could anyone possibly worry about *Shane*, Mother?"

"The boy comes across as just what he is—honest, bright, hard-working, devoted . . . and appealingly handsome, naturally. Don't think your late Cousin Delia's one-time gentleman friend, Desmond Molloy, hasn't made note of all that."

Bernadette stared down at her empty dessert plate.

Even death had not dimmed the family's memories of Delia O'Donnell. Spoiled beauty, actress, heroine of far too many flamboyant adventures with prominent men, Delia had passed her years in a blaze of public notoriety. That had not, however, lessened her special private cubbyhole in the clan's affections. Des Molloy had been one of Delia's more persistent pursuers. How successful his campaign to bed her might or might not have been was still one of the many riddles Delia had left behind her.

The lingering problem about Molloy was that in the process of wooing Delia he had also, in quite another way, wooed various male members of the O'Donnell family.

His connections with the powerful Tammany political machine, true masters of New York, had never been explicitly defined. But that his connections wove tentacles into many unsavory quarters of the city had always been obvious to the family. No O'Donnell had ever mistaken him for an angel.

What had he in mind, then, for Jim's boy Shane?

It was a matter which had never commanded much of Bernadette's attention, concerned as she was with the dangerous development of her own Liam. Yet, being an O'Donnell, Bernadette was anything but indifferent to whatever affected any member of the family. Like snips from a movie newsreel, bits of the family's past history flicked across her memory while she sat silently with her mother.

Patrick's failure to become a senator, for instance, may have been substantially contributed to by Molloy—once he realized that Patrick was not a man to be bought or intimidated. And what of Patrick's wife, Margaret? Nowadays, she was hopelessly declining into a drunken near-senility. Her condition could be directly traced to her failed ambition, after Patrick's defeat at the polls. How much had Molloy contributed indirectly to her troubles?

And there was Terence, Patrick's and Margaret's second son. Terence had not taken politics, or anything else, seriously enough for Molloy to sponsor him in city or state affairs. Terence's one ambition had been to spend more money than he earned, and he never would have worked doggedly enough to win any public office. But though Molloy must have spotted this weakness, it was known that he had been a supporter of Terry's bootlegging adventures during Prohibition, though exactly what role the man had played behind the scenes was very unclear to Bernadette.

And what of Jim himself? Pressed by Molloy, Patrick had always wanted Jim, his steadier son, to follow him in politics. What webs had Molloy been weaving for Jim behind that false, jovial smile and the blue haze of his cigar smoke before he faced the flat truth that the music of Ireland was the only future Jim aspired to?

"So now it's young Shane, Mother? You think Molloy's after Shane?"

"He wants a personable candidate to develop and control." As they did so often, Veronica and her daughter had been following identical lines of thought. Neither needed to spell out hers for the other. "A stooge. A straw man. God knows how he'd bend the boy, once he hooked him."

"Shane's always been the right target for Molloy, hasn't he? Shane's the one who truly *cares* about government affairs. He's Patrick reincarnate, and he's so young, too young, if Molloy started molding him now, to even realize he was putty.''

Veronica stared out blankly across her rose gardens, far into the distance.

"Desmond Molloy is only another name for the Devil. If the man tries to spoil Jim's boy, Bernadette, I'll find a way to stop him. Even if I have to kill him myself.''

Through odd coincidence, another O'Donnell was, at almost that very moment, discussing the same matter some sixty miles south and west of Veronica's terrace. Terence, immaculately garbed, as was his custom since Prohibition profits had both enriched and partially crippled him, sat facing Desmond Molloy across a corner table in the Plaza's equally impeccable Oak Room. He twirled his martini glass, studying reflected pinpoints of light in its pale contents, as he listened to the smooth, honey-drenched Irish voice of the man opposite.

"So Jim's lad is about ready to start a career, wouldn't you say?'' Molloy was murmuring.

"Shane still has college ahead of him, Desmond. Only just begun at Yale.''

"Of course, of course. He'll have to finish there, including law school. But you can't stick a toe into the political waters too early, Terry. A young fellow benefits by paddling around and getting the feel of the waves. It'll become almost second nature to him before he's ready to really launch into the big time.''

"With you to launch him? Is that what you're leading to?''

Molloy's smile was angelic. "I can be of help, here and there, maybe. I've always been a true friend to the O'Donnell family, as well you know.''

"We have plenty of reason to appreciate your friendship, Des, that's for sure. You were always at Cousin Delia's shoulder, right through her career."

Molloy's pseudo-candid eyes narrowed perceptibly, as if the remark had hit a nerve. "I was very fond of Delia, Terry."

"For a long stretch there, I thought you'd talk her into marrying you. That was what you wanted, wasn't it? I always thought so, watching from the sidelines."

"No man who ever knew Delia didn't want her." Now Molloy's forthright grin deepened. "She's gone now, bless her. That sweet chapter's closed. But I still feel a great warmth for you O'Donnells, man."

"That's well on record. Your support of my father when he aspired to the Senate . . ."

"Patrick should have made it. He was a good man, a capable man. Only skullduggery on the part of the opposition edged Patrick out."

"You tried hard for him."

"And I'd have tried the same for your brother Jim, if he'd given me the slightest encouragement."

Terence lifted his glass and touched lips to its rim. "Jim's like my Grandfather Liam, Des. Music's the only reality in his world."

"To my disappointment, so I discovered. Jim makes it very clear he wants no part of Desmond Molloy. Still, I always try to do him good. Never understood why he resents me."

"That's an O'Donnell for you. Each one makes up his own mind on a thing, follows his own course. Jim's my brother, as you say. But I never could budge him an iota. God knows how often I harangued him about the doors you once eased open for me in business."

"I always did my best for you, Terry." Molloy spoke earnestly.

"And it was much appreciated."

"It was no affair of mine when you were set upon and manhandled by those hoodlums. If I'd had an inkling any violence was in prospect, believe me you'd have had warning in good time to duck it."

"I know that, Des," Terence answered. "You only wanted good for me, that I've never doubted. But some of the family take it different. Aunt Veronica, for instance."

Despite himself, Molloy's grin tightened.

"I'm afraid Mrs. Tyrone-Quinn mixes me up in her mind with Mephistopheles. If looks could kill, that fine old lady would have put me in my grave long, long ago. I'm sorry for that. I've always admired her."

"You put your finger on it, though," chuckled Terence. "Aunt Veronica mistrusts your motives. Nothing you could do would sway her. I wish I had a dollar for every time I've heard her call you The Devil. And she turns Lady Macbeth as she says it."

"A shame I never could get her into politics here in New York. Tammany could have used the iron in her. But it's Shane my eye is on nowadays, Terry. I like the kid."

Empty, the martini glass was returned to the table. "I don't know how Shane feels about you, Des. He listens a lot more to his father. Jim never much appreciated your well-meaning efforts to help him follow in Patrick's bootmarks. But then, he hated politics, while Shane is the spit of his Grandfather Patrick. To tell the truth, I haven't much idea what young Shane O'Donnell does think of you."

"Precisely why I invited you for this little chat today." Molloy's look across the table was almost mesmerically sincere. "Sound the lad out for me, will you, Terry? Find

out as much as you can about the boy's image of me. I
want to be his friend.''

"If Shane wants to climb the Tammany ladder," Terence answered, "no man in this city could help him more.
I want him to have you behind him. Sure, I'll ask him
what he thinks of you. I'll put it to him next time he's
down from New Haven.''

"Not *ask* him, Terry, not outright.'' Molloy said, shaking his head. A thick mass of silvering hair gleamed under
Oak Room lights. "We need a little subtlety here. You
might just drop a word marking some kindness I've attempted for one or another of the O'Donnells in the past.
Then note the boy's reaction. Then say what you can in
my favor.''

"Little enough return for your friendship to the family,''
Terence said.

"Shane may be the very one I can help the most. So do
what you can, eh?''

Late Spring laid its hand on the Yale quadrangle with an
unusual benevolence. The grey surrounding walls seemed
gilded with May sunshine. In the established trees, birds
twittered at their nestings as if singing Hallelujahs. The
year's classes were all but over, and the bleak sweat-out of
final exams loomed dead ahead. Beyond that stretched a
long, voluptuous summer with infinite possibilities.

Jim O'Donnell drove up from New York to treat his son
to a last evening spree before he burrowed into intensive
study sessions.

An Irish singer named Colm Kinsella, freshly trans-
Atlantic for an American tour, was appearing at one of
New Haven's cozy bistros. With his passion for the music
of the O'Donnells' native heath, Jim was almost as eager

to hear how this new arrival handled the ballads as he was
to give the boy a breather from his books.

They arrived at the small, crowded room in good time
for dinner. Every table was taken, evidence of Jim's wis-
dom in telephoning from out of town for a reservation the
moment he first learned Kinsella would be singing. Irishmen
from half of Connecticut had descended upon New Haven.
They were like children drawn by a piper who was one of
their own, and well before the singer appeared, the stucco
walls were ringed with those for whom there were no chairs.

When he stepped up onto the low platform, guitar in
hand, Kinsella seemed to Jim the very personification of
the land from which he had travelled. He was a giant of a
man, broad and red-bearded, wearing faded denim and an
open-throated shirt. He looked more like a longshoreman,
able and ready to knock heads together, than he did a
wandering poet. Still, when his splayed fingers touched
guitar strings the room fell still.

The Bonny Bunch of Roses, which dealt surprisingly
enough with the adventures and final defeat of Napoleon
Bonaparte, was familiar despite its subject matter. It drew
warm applause. Listening along with his rapt father, Shane
found the text dealing more with Yale and that night than
with remote historic events in Europe.

> *One pleasant ev'ning in the month of June*
> *When all those feathered songsters*
> *Their liquid notes did sweetly tune . . .*

Shane's thoughts returned to his window overlooking
the quad. His books were spread out on a scarred desk-top
before him but he ignored them in favor of writing his
nightly letter to Agnes Moran. He poured out everything
within him, as he had been doing since very shortly after

meeting Agnes at his sister Norah's birthday party. The birds outside seemed to orchestrate his words.

"Agnes . . ." they seemed to sing.

He was called back to the present only when a storm of handclapping faded and *The Kerry Recruit* began. This was followed by *The Wreck of the "Mary Jane"*, with its account of a ship that never reached Timbuctoo. It was late when, as a second encore, Kinsella played *Grá-Mo-Chroí, I'd Like To See Old Ireland Free Once More*.

> *Cold is the heart that does not love*
> *Its own dear native land,*
> *When her sons are far beyond the sea*
> *All on a foreign strand.*
> *By land or sea where'er they be*
> *They love their fertile shore,*
> *It's Grá-Mo-Chroí I'd like to see*
> *Old Ireland free once more.*

Jim leaned toward Shane and murmured, "That's the sort of ditty your Cousin Liam would relish. Fire in it. More fire than good sense."

Shane grinned.

"Liam would strum the hell out of it, if he'd ever troubled to learn the guitar. Did great-grandpa Liam ever fiddle it, I wonder?"

"I don't remember that he did. The sentiment would fit my Cousin Kieran better."

"Or Kieran's daddy, blowing himself up in the act of trying to assassinate Queen Victoria." Shane glanced toward the bearded hulk on the dais. "There's hot pepper in such singing. Still, wouldn't a man's devotion belong first to the country that gave him shelter, not to the one he'd left behind him? Great-Aunt Veronica always says so."

"Aunt Veronica's a scrapper, like all us O'Donnells. But, yes, she's always fought her battles for America. Women's Rights on this side of the ocean are her cause, not routing the British out of Ireland. Veronica's every drop American."

"That's how I feel, too, Dad. I really want to get into working for good government, once I'm through law school. I think I'd have something to give. Agnes says she thinks so, too."

"If it's what you want, Shane, it's what you'll go after. I hope you get it."

Now we can't forget the former years,
They're kept in memory still,
Or the Wexford men of ninety-eight
Who fought on Vinegar Hill. . . .

Kinsella's spirited strains followed them as they shouldered out into the New Haven night. At the edge of campus, Jim bade his son goodnight and headed southward toward Manhattan. Climbing dormitory stairs to his own bailiwick, Shane was still thinking of his father. It had been a good evening. He and Jim had been close.

On the top floor the hall telephone was shrilling. Someone answered, and presently shouted, "O'Donnell? A call for you!"

Loping past the stair landing, Shane picked up the dangling receiver. "Hello? Shane speaking."

The voice which answered was not, as he had briefly hoped, feminine and heart-stilling, but masculine and mellow. "Ring you too late, young fellow? It's Desmond Molloy."

"Oh." Shane choked back disappointment. "Good evening, Mr. Molloy."

"I'm calling with a proposition. You've a summer vacation facing you, haven't you? Your Uncle Terence tells me you're headed toward politics."

"Well, yes, sir, I think so. But that's a good way off as yet."

"No time like the present to try a sample and make sure. How would you like to put in time in my office through July and August? The pay is fair, considering it's only a vacation job. There's a lot you could learn about how the wheels go round."

Shane hesitated, taken aback by the abruptness of the offer.

"Well, gee, Mr. Molloy, I'd been planning to put in time at Great Oak as my great-aunt's assistant gardener. She suggested a couple of weeks ago that Alex could use me."

"There's little political knowledge you could extract from Mrs. Tyrone-Quinn's rose bushes, bless the darling lady. Nor is it just the pay. It's what the job can teach you. My offer will stand open, young fellow. Give it some thought, eh? Some serious thought."

3

An unseasonable hot spell came in mid-September. Fortunately, the end-of-summer weather actually prolonged the riotous beauty Alex had coaxed out of Veronica's gardens. Still, the temperatures somehow managed to vex her. Perhaps, Veronica reasoned, this was because the emotional temperature inside her was likewise out of kilter.

Thank the Lord young Shane was at last safely back again at his Yale classes.

All through July and August, the awareness that the boy was reporting daily to Desmond Molloy's substantial offices had been a thorn in her side. Terence was openly delighted. He no doubt himself had a finger in that unwholesome pie. Even Jim, who cherished no fondness for Molloy, had agreed that probably it was a good idea for his son to pick up a bit of early experience if politics was to be his career.

But to Veronica the whole thing was an unmitigated disaster.

Norah had been her only solid supporter when she tried to dissuade Shane, although they were ill-armed for the battle, to be sure. The advantages of an active learning experience could scarcely be overcome by her offer of garden time-killing under Alex's guidance. Fond of her though Veronica knew Shane to be, what weapons had she? Dawdling at Great Oak scarcely could take precedence for an ambitious young man who had a girl he wanted to marry, when he finished school.

"And how could I convince Shane that Molloy is evil?" Pacing in the shade of the huge tree on guard before her house, Shane's great-aunt muttered aloud. "It's more of a sixth sense warning me than any solid evidence. I stand idle and watch a net settling over the boy's shoulders. There's not a damn thing I can do to cut the strands."

Once, to be sure, she had vowed to Bernadette that if need be she would personally murder Des Molloy to save Shane from him. But that, of course, had been bravado.

Veronica was a woman well rooted in respect for the law. The altering of laws she considered harmful had been her life's great preoccupation. She had O'Donnell fire in her, but in no way did it encompass violence. Once possessing proper evidence against him, she would joyfully have hauled Molloy to court. She itched to drag him through any mire. But personal murder? That was beyond her. What would her dead father have said to it? Not to mention the Church?

"Bless you, Norah, for speaking up when Molloy pressed his offer!"

Having the dear child at her side in the doomed June discussion had been a benison, however futile in the end. Norah's outspoken disfavor of her brother taking the job had been a Gibraltar. The girl was wise for her tender age. Either she sensed intuitively that Molloy's assumed friendliness had menace behind it, or else she had caught onto something tangible, somewhere, somehow, that spelled out the man's true character.

If it were the latter, Norah had been unwilling to divulge it, which suggested it might have something to do with the girl's dead Cousin Delia. As a tiny child, Norah had been bedazzled by Delia. Suppose she knew of something Molloy had done to harm her goddess?

Pondering the possibility, theoretical yet not absurd, Veronica found herself glancing Heavenward almost as if in search of Divine assistance.

The sky overhead had assumed a curious brassy quality she had never seen before. Still shining brightly, the sun had taken on a metallic glint. The low hilltop which Great Oak dominated, usually so safe and reassuring, had without warning drawn an almost sinister ambience about it like an invisible shawl.

"And such a wild notion is where plottings and suspicions will lead you, woman. The most every-day things in your life will suddenly absorb the evil you're pondering."

Still, the day did seem uneasily different. As if a demon had possessed it. Squinting upward, Veronica stepped out from the giant tree's shade.

The sky really did look different, although she could not exactly pinpoint how. Had she been a superstitious woman, she might have imagined Molloy's evil aura hovering overhead—determined to restrain her from something she ought to be doing.

"And what in the world would *that* be, Veronica O'Donnell?"

Having asked herself the question, she glimpsed half an answer—*Delia*. Once she connected Delia with Norah's opposition to Shane's having any connection whatever with Desmond Molloy, Veronica turned to old memories. Certainly, there once had been a widely recognized affair between Delia and the politician.

Back then, the clan had more than half expected them to marry. Veronica's own reaction had been one of dismay. Younger, handsomer, exuding sex appeal, Molloy was even then a man she mistrusted.

Memory begat memory. Suddenly, almost like a crap-shooter, she snapped her fingers.

"I'd forgotten," she said. "But they're upstairs some-place!"

Delia's sad and premature death, all that comet bright-ness fizzled out too early, had left behind it the usual snaggle of loose ends. In respect to paper work, Delia had always been a pack rat. Every fragment of writing that drifted into her days had been squirreled away and saved. School report cards; press clips of her acting career, even dating back to the early years when the plays in which she appeared were amateur theatricals; old drug prescriptions; discolored cards which had accompanied flowers once adorn-ing stage dressing rooms—all of these were kept.

"And letters. *Letters!*"

When Delia died, her closets had been choked with a melange of cardboard boxes and cartons stuffed with hoarded junk. The family hadn't wanted to heave it out, not until someone had time to sift through it properly. So the whole mess had been transported to Great Oak's roomy attic, where an accumulation of decades could easily be stored. There it still lay, all Delia's yellowing trivia.

But need it all be trivial? Among the bits and scraps, there must be clues to real events of Delia's personal life.

Why had Delia's liaison with Molloy never ended in the expected wedding bells? Could she have stumbled upon something about her lover so unsavory that their torrid affair had shattered? Had Norah, not much more than a baby then, somehow caught on to the reason and hidden it away ever since? Loyalty, blind loyalty, might gag the child even now.

"Ifs and suppositions, Veronica. Only ifs and suppositions."

Still, at the very least a possibility existed. Her hypothetical "something" would have to cast a shadow on Delia, as well as on Molloy, in order to seal Norah's young lips. What that might be Veronica could not easily imagine.

But her thoughts were racing.

An out-of-wedlock baby fathered by Molloy was one possible answer. Delia had often been away on theatrical tours for months at a time. Suppose on one such absence she had given birth? And Molloy had refused to marry her? And Norah knew this?

Or could Molloy have been jealous enough of Delia's several other passionate admirers to have viciously damaged one of them? Even perhaps arranged a murder? And had Delia discovered this and broken off the relationship?

Questions swarmed after her like a hive of hornets as Veronica hurried indoors and began the climb to the attic.

She took the stairs like a woman years younger, scarcely touching the curving rail at all. If there were anything in that jumble of odds and ends that could bring down Molloy's hopes to dominate Shane, she meant to discover it. Yes, and use it wherever it might hurt him most.

The sky over Manhattan had also turned metallic.

Trouble was coming, and Jim felt it keenly in his middle-aged bones. Something seemed different about this gathering weather. Tropical storms, even hurricanes, had ripped through the islands of the Caribbean and the Florida Keys since his boyhood, and doubtless for centuries before that. Gulf states had been pulverized. Rivers had swollen to torrents. All this was seasonal, an accepted reality of nature—but not for New York; not for Long Island; not for New England. And now there were thorny radio predictions, growing more alarming by the hour. Was it even remotely possible that this disaster recently ripping up the southern coastline would indeed hit home territory? The doomsayers in the news studios seemed determined to convince everyone of it. What then? In all nature did there exist a turbulence so devastating that the steel and granite towers outside Jim's windows could not withstand it?

Working at his desk on a batch of time-frayed Gaelic ballad sheets, correcting the verses of several bowdlerized modern versions, he nonetheless left his radio turned on low. The room, so comfortably impregnable in its shabby informality, seemed to hum with forebodings.

Once, uneasily, Jim rose from his chair and looked out the windows. His sanctum filled a corner position of the family's second-and-third floors apartment in a somewhat run-down remodeled brownstone. From the front window, Jim could see a stretch of pavement with facades almost the clones of his own. From one side window, there was a view of narrow alley and a corner of the cramped back garden on which the alley opened. When the house was new and occupied by only one family, there had been stables in the rear. The alley was meant to let horses through. In recent years, Sheela's green thumb had been at work there.

From what he could see, the day was not ideal for gardening.

A wind had risen. Trash—discarded brown paper wrappings from a parcel, sheets of unwanted newspaper—whirled along the gutter like tumbleweed on an unprotected range.

Overhead, harsh blue had turned to rough black. The sky reminded him of the hide of some jungle animal.

Two houses down, a neighbor was putting up storm windows—working fast. The ladder on which he teetered shook as the wind manhandled it. The toiler must have been taking the recent radio news bulletins to heart.

". . . worse threat to local shipping in many decades," a disembodied voice droned at Jim's shoulder. "Many shops in the area are taping their display windows against shattering glass. Businesses of all descriptions are closing early, so employees may reach home before disaster strikes. . . ."

Disaster? Here am I, Jim mused, snug as the proverbial bug, and my Norah's literally safe as a church, attending auditions for the choir at the cathedral; Shane's cozy at his college; Brendan's upstairs studying. And their mother, bless her, is off relishing Errol Flynn and David Niven in *The Dawn Patrol*. Come, come! What disaster?

Briefly, a sound like distant thunder rolled down the curb along with the tossing refuse, but Jim recognized its true source. A train was passing on the Third Avenue elevated tracks a block to the east. So long as those massive support girders stood, Manhattan was in small danger. The news hawkers did love to stir up a bit of Doomsday.

He turned back to his desk, adjusting his work light to cast a stronger glow across the topmost sheet on the stack of precious ballad sheets.

The Much Admired Song of the Young Maid's Love was the title of the ditty. In distant times, one awarded a compositon its full majestic title. Jim could remember his grandfather fiddling this one, bow dancing, catgut fairly throbbing. But these old verses, a good span senior even to his father's father, seemed to carry a variety of verses ill-fitted to those Grandfather Liam once sang. Had his words been the true ones or distortions?

> *Some marry for riches but it often brings woe,*
> *Others for beauty—for my love's sake I'll go.*
> *But if ever I marry I'll marry for love*
> *And I'll be as true as the sweet turtle dove. . . .*

The door from the hall burst open and Sheela stumbled past it to sink gasping in the nearest chair. At the sight of her, Jim sprang to his feet and hurried to her.

"God's grace, darling! You look like a drowned ghost! What's happened?"

His wife was struggling to quiet her breath.

"I didn't think I'd make it home from the movie, James, honestly I didn't. As I rounded the corner, the wind hit me so hard I went down on my knees. I had to hang onto the fencing to lift myself back on my feet."

"But you're soaked through!"

"Who wouldn't be in a downpour like this? I'd sooner take a shower under Niagara Falls."

For the first time, Jim realized that while he was working, it had indeed begun to rain. Rain? That was a flimsy word for what was hammering at the windows. They seemed almost submerged under a sea which swept across the glass in appalling waves.

"Wow!" The only word which came to him seemed grossly inadequate.

"It's a running river out there. And rising every minute." Sheela began wringing water from her flowing hair. "I've never seen the like of it, Jim. Never."

"There was a lot about it on the radio, but it all sounded just too impossible."

"You weren't really listening to the warnings, were you? You were a million miles away, sorting out new from old in whatever manuscript you're working on."

"Well, maybe. Who'd believe all that stuff about a hurricane in New York, now?"

"I would, for one. I've been out in it, and it's a terror."

"You're soaked through to the skin, Pet. Better run upstairs and get yourself into dry clothes. We don't want you coming down with the sniffles."

"Run upstairs, the man says! I haven't the strength to crawl up those stairs on my hands and knees, Jim O'Donnell. It was like having a truck roll over me. Run? Just let me sit here."

"If you're that spent let me carry you up. I used to. Remember?"

"I remember very well indeed. And if you're thinking what I think you're thinking, James, you ought to be ashamed of yourself—with me so bruised and battered."

"No such idea crossed my thought," Jim denied piously.

A roaring of wind filled the street outside. The house seemed to shudder. Rain struck the panes as if a giant was hurling buckets of water at them. Stepping across the little puddle that had dripped from her onto the carpet, Jim swung Sheela up into his arms.

Umphhh! She'd put on a pound or two, since the last time he attempted this maneuver—or maybe it was the weight of her soaked clothing.

Half-way across the hall, Jim froze with panic. A ghastly rending, splintering sound reached them above a lull in the storm's howl. It sounded so close that at first he thought part of their apartment wall had caved in, but then he remembered that the drug store on the corner was half-way through a remodeling. For the past three weeks, there had been a skeleton framework up around it. Not much would be left of it now.

"Jesus, I hope no workmen were on that scaffold when it crashed!"

"Don't blaspheme, James O'Donnell. What blithering idiot would be up on a platform in the face of this? It's the end of the world, Jim, the end of the world."

They were half-way up the stairs when, as if a black hand suddenly smashed the sun out of the sky, their lights went out. Darkness swooped on them like an attacking bird.

The storm was not a sort Veronica cottoned to. Under ordinary circumstances, she might have been worrying about damage to her roses, but here in the attic, crouched above a growing heap of litter, she was too absorbed to notice.

The vast slant-ceilinged cave atop Great Oak had never been wired for electricity, so Veronica had brought a kerosene lamp with her. Set on the floor beside her, it cast a restricted circle of yellow which defied the deep shadows gathering on beyond.

Well before rain began to slap at the small, dusty windows, she had hauled out the collection of Delia's memorabilia from under the low eaves. Carton after carton, box after box, she carefully picked through. Occasionally, she came upon some memento which caused a quick stab of memory. She had known her sister Bridget's beautiful daughter for all her life, and most of Delia's triumphs had been parts of Veronica's own days as well.

Thus far, however, any hint of what she was seeking still eluded her. Not even a Christmas card carried Desmond Molloy's signature. It was unthinkable that there had been none—the family magpie would have preserved some souvenir of so serious a lover.

Hands filthy with dust and cobwebs, Veronica was drawing near the close of her search. The hope which had flared high a few hours earlier had begun to gutter and fade. There never had been a real basis for her hopes. She didn't *know* there was any dire secret against Molloy. That had been only a premise, a possibility, a one-in-a-hundred long shot.

Wind was rising outside the house's thick walls.

Once, briefly, Veronica arose to stretch her punished joints and took a look out the window. The wavery glass of century-plus panes was running rivers. Beyond the deluge she could make out a skyful of towering sable clouds, dark as midnight but far more ominous.

Below, trees were tossing wildly as they bent in the eerie convolutions of some savage dance. Even the great oak was in writhing hysteria. The lawn seemed ankle-deep in stripped leaves, and Veronica thought how poor Alex would have to work late hours the next day, cleaning up the mess.

She sighed and returned to her labors.

The wind's howl followed her, higher and shriller by the moment. Her father had regaled her childhood with tales of shrieking Irish banshees back home in Sligo where he had grown to man's estate. This was the way the evil spirits must have sounded, pouring out their fury.

Squatting anew, she plucked at frayed string holding together another pasteboard shoebox. Few containers were left to be investigated, and she would finish the job, just to make absolutely sure. Then she'd limp back downstairs, every muscle aching, and soak for an hour in a blessed hot bath.

The old string was giving her a battle. She jerked at it impatiently and felt a fingernail snag. Damn!

The knot then gave abruptly. The string slithered from its battered container like a garter snake seeking refuge under a garden rock. The box sides collapsed, spilling contents into her lap.

More correspondence. Bills for the hats and shoes Delia had purchased for her role in *The Cat And The Canary* when she took to the road with the national company. An advertisement for a skin cream. Two match covers from nightclubs long vanished. A ragged recipe for quiche, clipped from a newspaper column.

And a slim upside down packet of envelopes, held together by a bit of blue lingerie ribbon. Weighing these between soiled hands, Veronica paused a moment before turning them over.

"No reason to get excited, Veronica. Letters can be from anybody. Lord knows there were men enough along Delia's path. They flocked like flies to honey."

Still, for some reason her fingers were shaking. Did she recognize the grey, almost square envelopes from long ago? Or was it wishful thinking? Thousands of men must have ordered this stationery in its day. Tens of thousands. Common as milk cartons.

She turned the bundle over and from the upper lefthand corner of its topmost envelope a return address, boldly written, leaped up: *Mr. D.X. Molloy, Hotel McAlpin, 34th Street at Sixth Avenue, New York* . . . The tiny words seemed to jiggle before her.

A world gone berserk hammered at the roof just above her head. With anguished shrieks nails gave way as shingles were ripped from their moorings. A thin trickle of water began to hit floorboards close by, splashing attic dust.

Veronica never noticed.

The first letter, when she clawed it open and devoured the contents, was disappointing. Molloy was obviously a lover firmly in the saddle. His endearments were confident. His tone was that of a man who was getting what he wanted.

The second letter was more of the same. Apparently, Delia was out of town touring with *The Girl In The Limousine*. Left behind because of a primary campaign for some budding aspirant to the city council, Molloy longed to be with her. He was arranging a quick trip to join her in Baltimore, when the show played in that city. If the passionate phrases could be believed, all between them was serene, even idyllic.

Veronica's hopes plummeted. Nothing anywhere of something unsavory Norah might have known; some reason for the child to detest and mistrust Molloy, as very obviously she did.

Somewhere not far off, on Veronica's own property, a tree gave up its fight against the raging onslaught of wind and rain. Slipping a third letter from its envelope, Veronica heard the sickening death cry that was a melange of roots torn loose, trunk splitting, branches crashing. It seemed less real than the line shimmering before her on grey paper:

Darling, you must let me explain how it happened. I didn't intend it, I had no notion, I can't account for what came over me. . . . Eyes wide, Veronica followed the desperate lines. Here! Here, in the very next paragraph, it lay boldly spelled out.

This was it!

This was what Norah, since infancy, had somehow known about the man. And if publicized, it could even now polish off Desmond Molloy once and for all, as far as any public career was concerned. She, Veronica, had only to confront him with this long waylaid confession.

No, with a photocopy. It would be unwise to meet a man like Molloy in private with such material—unless he realized its original were safely locked away in a bank vault. Given her new knowledge, there'd be little he wouldn't attempt to silence her.

"He'll back away from Shane O'Donnell now, God Almighty!"

The instant she gave him a choice—exposure or withdrawal—he'd give up whatever self-serving plans he was nurturing for Jim's son. At her grim command, he would slink away from the whole O'Donnell family like the jackal he was.

How soon could she arrange a meeting?

Not tonight, obviously, with this insane weather pinning her down and Molloy miles off in the city. How long was the storm likely to hold? Until tomorrow? Next day? The pounding of it overhead now was like a whole phalanx of war drums being assaulted by maniacs. Her hilltop seemed a target for annihilation.

The other sound, when it came, was even more fearsome. A long, wrenching roaring like that of an express train gone mad in a tunnel. The great crash of it enveloped her, dazed her. The end of time, surely! Nothing less could rend the very heavens.

Staring up in horror at the rafters close overhead, she watched it happening.

The roof collapsed, crumbling like tissue paper, and through it surged the top branches of the great oak, sweeping away timbers and shingles and insulation like so much tissue paper. A broken giant thirsting for a death revenge—

after centuries of benign protection. Frankenstein's monster was turning upon its human masters.

"The big oak! Vinnie, we always loved it! We always thought . . ."

She began to scramble on hands and knees through the debris around her, frantic to elude descending destruction. But it kept on coming.

4

On the second anniversary of Veronica's funeral, Bernadette felt a shroud of depression enfolding her, very much as it had done twelve months earlier.

Most of the time she was able to master these waves of remembrance. Either she summoned the busy events of a full life to erect fences between herself and her grieving, or she channeled thoughts of her mother toward happier times. They had shared so much that was meaningful and productive. They had shouldered successes and failures together, and had fought for the full women's partnership in society which both of them advocated so believingly.

It usually wasn't difficult to remember those good times and relive them comfortingly, but with September, her thoughts of hurricanes grew nightmarishly strong.

News broadcasts throughout the season frequently centered in disasters striking one or another of the Caribbean islands. Newsreels at the movies were inclined to feature

photographs of tropical storm wreckage; emergency soup
lines feeding battered victims, streets of houses turned to
rubble, trees stripped bare, lost animals and children rov-
ing hopelessly. And each time she saw or heard these
things, that awful night in '38 toppled over her again,
flattening her soul as that monstrous ruined tree had flat-
tened her mother's body.

At night, in her dreams, the phone would start shrilling
again and it would be Brendan's gentle voice—boyish and
hesitant, yet filling her bedroom like a great scream.

"Cousin Bernadette? This is Brendan. Dad asked me to
call you. He's just caught the midnight for Stamford. The
highways are all flooded. He can't move his own car. But
Joe promises to get the Packard through to the station
somehow and pick him up there."

Still half asleep, her own voice mumbled. "Why on
earth is Jim going up to Great Oak? Does he think Mother
needs someone to hold her hand?"

"There's been an accident. The big old tree was uprooted.
It fell on the house."

Alarm twisted her insides. "My mother, Brendan? Was
she hurt?"

"It's worse than that, Cousin Bernadette. Joe called
Dad as soon as they found her. Apparently, she'd gone up
to the attic to hunt for something without telling anybody.
She was up there when the tree came through the roof.
She's dead, Cousin Bernadette."

She's dead, Cousin Bernadette . . . those awful words
were always the end of the nightmare, the crashing
crescendo. Bernadette would waken with them still ringing,
her body pouring sweat, her heart pounding like a trip
hammer. *Dead . . . Dead . . . Dead . . .*

And for nothing. Whatever Veronica had been after up
there in the attic, when she should have been snug down-

stairs where the servants could look after her, it could be nothing but a whim, an impulse.

Bernadette herself had caught the first Connecticut-bound train leaving town that next morning. The great white house on the hill seemed almost cleft through. The huge oak sprawled across its facade like a drunken lover bent upon rape. The lawns were a garbage dump. The gutters still ran rivers.

Joe had carried his long-time employer down to her own bedroom even before telephoning Jim. Lying on the wide bed she once had shared with Robert Wilson Tyrone and later with Vincent Quinn, one could imagine that Veronica was only asleep. A flowered silk coverlet had been tucked in around her—Joe's tender work, or maybe Jim's. Only when it was drawn back could one see the mangled, crushed mid-section where the oak had struck.

Later on that grim morning, Bernadette had gone up to view the attic.

Water had poured in, although the wide old floorboards still fitted so precisely that little damage had been done to ceilings below. Someone—Alex, perhaps—had cut away the tangle of intruding branches with a chainsaw. Floating in a shallow pool were the contents of the scruffy old boxes Veronica evidently had hauled out and was scrabbling through. For what daffy reason, Bernadette could not imagine. They seemed to be nothing but the junk carted up here after Delia's death. Worthless. Trash.

Teeth chattering from a cold that had nothing to do with temperature, Bernadette stumbled back down to the library and let a solicitous Joe fetch her a cup of hot broth from the kitchen. Power lines throughout the area were still down after the hurricane, but somehow the capable chauffeur managed.

"Sorry you went up yonder, Mrs. McHugh," he

muttered, hovering over her. "A real mess up there still, ma'am. No time to tidy up after Alex cut away the tree-sections."

One of those strange shafts of thought which sometimes pierce a numbness such as Bernadette was feeling struck her now. "How did he use the saw? There's no power."

"It hadn't gone out yet when we found Mrs. Tyrone-Quinn, ma'am. Blackout didn't hit us here until later on, thank the Lord. We wanted that weight hauled off our poor lady."

She stared up at him. "Was my mother still alive then, Joe?"

"No, ma'am. We figure she didn't live much after the oak come down on her. Maybe she didn't even know what hit her. Could well be the end was that sudden."

"What in the world was she doing up there instead of down where she belonged? If she'd kept out of the attic she'd be alive and safe this minute."

"Hard to say what she was after, Mrs. McHugh. She'd told nobody nothing."

"Well, I saw what she must have been grubbing through. A mess of worthless discards. I want it out of the house." Suddenly, Bernadette's tone was savage. "Have it all carted away. Burn it."

"Yes, Mrs. McHugh. What about repairs to the roof, ma'am? Greak Oak will be yours once the will is read. Whatever you want, just you tell me or Alex or the others."

"I never want to see this house again. I'll arrange in New York for fixing the damage and putting the hill on the market. But one thing I do want, Joe."

"Yes, ma'am?"

"Call someone in to pull down that tree. Have it cut up

to firewood lengths. Then you *personally* see to it that every last twig is in ashes.''

Two long years later, her recollection of that implacable order still remained clear as still wine—*two years ago to the day*. The world had kept turning, not at all in the right direction, and Bernadette had begun to believe that civilization was becoming sodden and worthless, like those fragments of Delia that Mother had senselessly died over.

God in Heaven, what next?

Last year it had been the pact between the Nazis and the Reds in Russia. Then the Germans invaded poor, weak Poland on blatantly trumped-up charges. Then Poland's allies, Britain and France, honored their pledges by declaring war on Hitler, and to top it off, there had been a ruthless partition of Poland between Berlin and the Soviet.

Even on the local scene, those same twelve months had been a major fiasco. Take the absurd turmoil erupting out of a radio show in October. *The War of the Worlds* was based on an old story by the English author, H.G. Wells. A group billing itself The Mercury Theatre had put it on; a mumbo-jumbo about Earth being invaded by enemies from Mars. The whole eastern seaboard had collapsed in hysteria. Thousands jammed the street, screaming in terror as they fled the paste-up ''invasion.'' The story had been accepted by the general populace as Bible truth. America's critics abroad must have had a good laugh.

The present was not much better. The war supposedly raging in Europe seemed as phoney as a three-dollar bill. Russia had moved to take over Finland, and been stopped in its tracks. No one knew what would happen next.

Certainly Bernadette's own Ireland-besotted son was little help in trying to make sense of it all. Her conversations with Liam, when he dropped in at home from his threadbare little Greenwich Village flat, usually ended in

quarreling. Twenty-one, married and legally a full-grown
man, she'd have expected some glimmer of sense from
him. His Evaleen still seemed to regard him as some sort
of Playboy of the Western World, but in his mother's
opinion all that he ranted was blither and blather.

"It's like I said to Uncle Jim and Aunt Sheela years
back, Ireland will never go fighting to bolster the British
tyrants. Look how she's remaining sensibly neutral."

"Do you want the Bolsheviks and Nazis to gobble down
the universe without a protest?"

"I'd be the last to support bloody England against them.
Maybe democracy's had its day, Ma. Maybe it's time for
someone else to have a try at running things."

"So it's not enough that a man three generations American has to pretend shamrocks still grow under his fingernails?
Now you'd be a bearded Russian bear? Or toady to that
silly little popinjay with the mustache, flaunting his
swastikas?"

"I never said I took much stock in either," Liam
answered. "I admit they're not to my taste. But, damn it,
neither is a pack of British murderers. I'd sooner see *them*
go down."

"Would you, now? You're a numbskull, Liam O'Donnell.
And don't swear at your mother."

If it weren't for her husband and his mild good sense,
Bernadette sometimes thought she'd go crazy listening to
Liam. Sound business man that he was, Eamonn was her
bulwark against her stormy son's 'Free Ireland' rantings.
Bernadette sometimes, although not often, went so far as
to weep on the fine man's shoulder. The way Liam was
turning out, after all the love and protection she'd invested
in the boy, was a caution to snakes.

"Thank the saints there's no such gibberish pouring out

of our Madge, Eamonn. She's a sweet girl, thoughtful and good-mannered. She'll marry top drawer.''

"Not quite top drawer, my dear. At least, that's not likely. We Bogtrotters have boosted ourselves a good many rungs up the American ladder, this past near-century. But I've yet to hear of one in the White House—not to mention any overflowing of us in the Social Register.''

"Our Madge will—''

"Madge will marry some good, worthy young Irishman. Just as she should.''

"Why not the top? I'd not curtsey to any dowager on Fifth Avenue, myself.''

"And good for you, dear! But the world's way is the world's way. Don't set your sights too high for Madge. Be content with whatever she picks for herself.''

Bernadette grimaced, half angry, half fond. "You do exasperate me, Eamonn McHugh. Have you no desire to outstrip those who'd look down their snouts at us? What makes *them* so mighty? This Vanderbilt girl who became a fine Duchess—an old, proud title to boot—what did her protestant family have to set them so high, except a boodle of money?''

"Old New York money, love. Ours is new Irish money. There's a difference.''

"It's a difference your wife fails to see. A dollar is a dollar.'' But Bernadette never could argue long with Eamonn. He was too easy-going—and too sensible—for battles.

"I wonder. What do you suppose our other child would be like if he were with us still? Would he be Liam over again? Or would he be like you?''

"Which would you rather?'' Eamonn murmured, and received a warm kiss for his answer.

* * *

With the clan's acknowledged matriarch, Veronica, four years in her grave, Terence O'Donnell strongly fancied himself as Head-of-the-Family. Self-selected to the position though he might be, he felt nonetheless secure in it. And his second wife, Hilda, certainly made an entirely satisfactory First Lady.

Other possible heirs to the throne gave the hypothetical position so little thought that it was virtually a matter of no contest. Jim was so dedicated to his Irish music that he actually remained unaware anyone was supposed to be "Number One." Shane and Brendan and Liam were, of course, too young to rule. Bernadette was a woman, which, despite her lifelong militant stand on the subject, seemed to disqualify her.

It was a deeply satisfying thing to have emerged as a patriarch. Because lucky investments had left him with no need to work for a living, Terence had considerable free time in which to enjoy his fancied crown. Still it did encompass a few dreary responsibilities.

His mother, particularly.

Margaret O'Donnell was by now so far gone with drink—as well as advanced age—that there was no pretense of including her in family gatherings. "Companions" came and went so rapidly at the old house in Newburgh that sometimes Terence could not even remember their names. Maids were hired for her less because of any impulse toward tidiness than for their ability to pick her up from whatever carpet she'd collapsed on and tote her to her bed. Visits to her seemed in the nature of punishment. Drawn curtains, smashed antiques and the reek of whiskey were all that was left to a once beautiful Edwardian estate.

Terence enjoyed being cock of the O'Donnell walk. He assumed the right to present young Shane and Brendan with fatherly pronouncements, and he never hesitated to lecture his cousin Bernadette on her mismanagement of the fortune she had inherited from her mother.

"Bernadette should never have sold Great Oak. I've often thought it," he informed Hilda at late breakfast on the morning after Thanksgiving Day. "Actually, Veronica had no moral justification to will the place as she did. By rights, it should have come to us."

"Bernadette was her only child, dear. You were only one of two nephews."

"Jim would have no use for a big country place. You and I might have continued it in the style Aunt Veronica and Vincent Quinn began it. A place where the O'Donnells would gather on occasions—well, like yesterday, for example. There was room enough at Great Oak to put up every member of the family over a fine weekend."

"I don't think some of the relations would have liked that. The young folks have their own circles of friends. Liam couldn't have brought Evaleen with him, considering how soon now she's expecting this baby. And probably you'd have asked Desmond Molloy to join us, so Norah would have refused. You know how she detests him."

"Norah, my dear, is young and giddy and quite unreasonable. What objection she has to a senior family friend like Molloy is quite beyond my comprehension. You'll note the child never has a sensible objection to raise whenever I mention Molloy to her."

"She has one, though, Terry. You can see it in her eyes whenever they're in the same room. She looks as uneasy as if he were something wild escaped from the zoo."

"Sheer nonsense, Hilda. Jim has spoiled her." As a man with no children of his own, Terence felt he could have written volumes about child-raising. "I'd have taken a belt to her long ago, if she'd tried to come over so hoity-toity with me."

Hilda smiled placatingly across the table. "Now, Terry, you know that isn't in you. You'd never strike a woman, even a child. You're the very soul of kindness."

"I try to be, my dear, I try to be. Well, Great Oak is gone. No use weeping over spilled milk. But I still do my best to give my family a proper sense of unity."

"Perhaps another Thanksgiving you can find some way to . . ."

"Yesterday was a disaster. O'Donnells scattered to the four winds. I think we must mend that. We'll gather here for family cocktails. Next Sunday's the first one in December, the seventh, isn't it? That should suit very well. Not close enough to Christmas so they can plead holiday engagements."

"Terry, you know December schedules are always crowded."

"Just make it clear when you call to invite them that I'm expecting everyone to come. I think that should do the trick. After all, I'm not without some influence."

December seventh was a crystal Sunday. "Halcyon" was the word Bernadette chose for describing it, when she and Eamonn emerged from their taxi in front of Terence's Park Avenue residence. As they crossed the sidewalk, crisp sunlight washed it like a thin spreading of gold leaf. The doorman, who might have been an ambassador for all his uniform braid and dignity, bowed them inside as if acknowledging minor royalty. Occasionally, Bernadette attempted to figure the probable size of Terence's Christmas gratuities. It would be substantial, based on the staff's behavior as tipping season drew closer.

The rest of the clan had gathered before them.

As they left their coats on the pile already littering Hilda's bed, they could hear music spilling from the living room—drawing room, Terence preferred to call it—at the far end of the long hall. Jim was playing the accordion, which was but one of the several instruments on which he was proficient. Norah was accompanying her father on the piano, a handsome polished Steinway which must have been installed to create an impression, since neither Terence nor Hilda played it. Others were singing.

> When winter was brawling, o'er high hills and
>   mountains,
> And deep were the clouds over deep rolling sea,
> I spied a wee lass as the daylight was dawning,
> She was asking the road to sweet Carnloch Bay . . .

Moving in the direction of the congenial sound, Eamonn slipped an affectionate arm about Bernadette's still-slender waist. He liked his relations by marriage, at least most of them, and fitted inconspicuously but solidly into the O'Donnell circle. As he crossed the threshold, he added his baritone to the casual choir massed behind Norah's stool.

> You turn to the right and pass down by the churchyard
> Cross over the river and down by the sea;
> We'll call in at Pat Hamill's and have a wee drop
>   there
> Just to help us along to sweet Carnloch Bay . . .

Leaving her husband to his caroling, Bernadette gently detached herself and moved quietly around the semi-circle. Even Shane was part of it. He had come down from Law School in New Haven for the holiday and was stretching his vacation to accommodate his Uncle Terence's somewhat pompous summons. Agnes Moran stood beside him, and they were holding hands as they sang. A different Shane altogether from the shy boy who had been dumbfounded when he first met Norah's classmate!

But it was Shane's brother Bernadette was seeking. Brendan, as darkly handsome as ever, stood a tiny bit apart from the rest. In recent months she had often observed this tendency in him. It was now definite knowledge among the clan that he felt a vocation and was headed for the priesthood.

"Hello, Cousin Bernadette," he murmured as she paused beside him.

The smile was warm and sweet; yet there seemed a quiet sadness in it. She watched his gaze move from her again, across the circle to where Shane and Agnes stood. It was not upon his brother that his look settled, but upon the girl—so vivacious, so attractive in a way of which she herself seemed quite unaware. The expression in Brendan's eyes, before he turned them away again, was to Bernadette unmistakable. It held loneliness in it—and longing.

Was Brendan certain about his future in the church? Absolutely *sure*? For a moment her heartbeat altered as she contemplated the horror if he were making a mistake. Irrevocable tragedy would lie ahead for the boy, and she wanted a good life for him, just as she wanted one for Shane—and for her own Liam.

Liam himself had arrived at the party well before his parents. As he added his slightly blurred tenor to the general chorus, he clutched a glass in one hand. The amber liquid in it tilted perilously. For once, he had not brought Evaleen along. Bernadette found herself actually sorry for that. The girl did have a restraining influence. But the baby was coming, a new O'Donnell, and perhaps Liam's careless devotion to her was not altogether a disaster.

The tune from Jim's accordion veered toward another

old family favorite. Norah's skillful fingers on the keys danced after it, and the voices of assembled O'Donnells, even Hilda's, followed along.

> When first I came to Ireland, some pleasure
>   for to find,
> It's there I spied a damsel fair most pleasing to
>   my mind.
> Her rosy cheeks and sparkling eyes like arrows
>   pierced my breast.
> They called her lovely Molly-O, the Lily of the West. . .

It was fascinating to watch how Terence unbent after a few of the old tunes. Slightly flushed, his imposing claret velvet host jacket flapped open informally as he bellowed the ballad along with the others. The family's unelected leader had become more a real O'Donnell than a self-conscious kinglet. There was more of Old Liam in the man than Terence himself likely suspected. He who would go to all lengths to mask from outsiders the fact that his grandfather had started out no more than a penniless fiddler out of Sligo, was singing all the old songs.

They were just starting on *The Suit of Green* when Bernadette heard the doorbell jangle.

She glanced about the room in faint surprise. All the family who were likely to heed Terence's imperious summons were already assembled. Certainly poor old Margaret was not expected. Madge, off at Wheaton, had not even come home for Thanksgiving. Yet, Hilda showed no surprise as she moved to the door. Evidently some addition to the group was expected.

In from the hall strode silver-haired Desmond Molloy. Bernadette felt her heart sink and glanced swiftly in Norah's direction. At the piano, Jim's daughter had broken off in mid-chord. Her face had frozen, her shoulders had stiffened. If her father's cousin knew the girl at all, in another minute she would spring to her feet and quit the gathering. This was not the first time Bernadette had observed Norah's strange hostility to Molloy.

Yet Terence felt no frost in the atmosphere. Once more the Lord of the Manor—suave, though a bit servile in his new arrival's almost venerable presence—he strode forward with hand outstretched. His claret jacket was properly buttoned again.

"Ah, there, Des! I'm delighted you could rearrange your schedule so as to include our little gathering. I know you're anxious to catch Shane on one of his rare law school lapses. But that Tammany confab you mentioned . . ."

For once, however, Molloy was not greeting them all with his expansive smile which always reminded Bernadette of the Cheshire Cat. His aging face was granite hard. He had stopped dead in the archway, ignoring Terence's outstretched hand, taking them all in one by one.

"You've been having one of your O'Donnell songfests, so you haven't had the radio turned on." As he spoke, something in his voice branded them all as inferiors.

If my mother were here, Bernadette thought, she'd slap that superior sneer from the snotty old bastard's face. Veronica had despised Desmond Molloy ever since she could remember. She wondered why, and found herself wishing her mother was still alive, just so she could ask her.

Even Terence seemed for once to be shaken by Molloy's patronizing tone. He could barely maintain his usual subservient jovial manner under the undeserved attack brought on by so bijou a matter as their not spending a family gathering clustered about a loudspeaker.

"Why, no, Des, no. No radio. Fact is, we like our own music better."

"So you haven't had the news," Molloy said as he faced the silenced circle. "The Japanese attacked our Navy in Hawaii an hour ago. There's a battle raging right now at Pearl Harbor. This time tomorrow, America will be at war."

BOOK TWO

IMITATING TIGERS

5

This time, "the girls" were meeting at Madge's, which meant her parents' Sutton Place duplex. Nowadays both Bernadette and Eamonn were so often absent on their separate war missions that sometimes for weeks at a time Madge and the two maids were the only householders in residence. The four young women, each one of them so busy herself, were making a small tradition of gathering every second week in one or another's living room to share rationed, almost sugarless coffee and news of their menfolk off at various fighting fronts.

Agnes had christened them "The O'Donnellettes," as the bond that bound them together was entirely O'Donnell— for Madge, her mother's blood; for Agnes, the modest diamond Shane had slipped on her finger a year earlier, just before departing to boot camp; for Norah and Evaleen the clan into which one of them had been born and the other married. So the unofficial title was not inappropriate.

Today only three of the "members" were present. Norah's rapidly developing vocal talent had impressed a young show organizer named Martin Kenny, and she was off on a USO tour singing the Irish songs for which she was becoming increasingly well known. She kept in touch, sending post cards from various stations along the Pacific coast, and she was expected home again within days.

As it was with almost everyone else in America, war had taken over the attention and labors of each of the three now sitting in Bernadette's comfortable sitting room.

Two of then, Evaleen and Agnes, wore well-deserved American Women's Voluntary Service uniforms. Evaleen had earned her uniform by processing sets of fingerprints by the hundreds in the drive to prepare the city in case of a bombardment. Agnes earned hers by serving with the AWVS food wagon in Washington Square, dishing up pre-dawn coffee, doughnuts and comfort to departing draftees.

When home, Norah toiled nightly at the Stage Door Canteen singing the ballads every Irish-bred doughboy on leave clustered around her piano to cheer. Madge faithfully labored on the day shift of a small automotive parts assembly line across the river in New Jersey, then returned home barely in time to scrub off the machine grease and go out into darkness on Air Raid Warden patrol.

"How you do what you do, Evaleen," Madge asked, minimizing her own full schedule, "is a miracle. Nine-to-five at your office desk, and Danny still a toddler."

"No problem. At least, not too much of one," Evaleen answered, shrugging lightly. "I take the bairn right along with me. Stick him into an outside wastebasket alongside my chair, toss him some scrap paper to wad up and coo over, and get to my clients—if that's the right word for people with appointments to have their fingerprints taken."

Agnes set aside her empty cup. "Is it a glamourous place to be working?"

"Ninth Street between Broadway and University? Are you kidding?"

"I was talking to that old politico who seems to take such an interest in Shane's career. Molloy, isn't that his name? He turned up in the Park one morning a week ago along about sunrise. We were just opening the canteen and the draftees were lining up. All of a sudden, there the old man was along with the rest of them."

"Aggie!" Madge gasped. "You can't mean the army's drafting men Desmond Molloy's age?"

"No, no, of course not. But he edged up to me and started chatting. I can't recall just how we got on the subject of where you're working, Evie, but when I mentioned the address he was full of information or misinformation on the building."

"Like what?" Evaleen wondered aloud. "It's just another old crumbling brownstone. AWVS probably rented it only because the rent is peanuts."

"Did you never hear that it was once the town house of the notorious Lillian Russell? She lived there when Diamond Jim Brady was courting her. Wasn't she supposed to have been the most beautiful woman in America?"

"I've seen pictures in one of the old theatrical albums of Norah's—I guess she collects them because they also include occasional mentions of her Cousin Delia. Yes, the woman had a lovely face, but there was certainly quite a lot of her underneath all the feathers and flowers and frills."

"A chorus line was called a Beef Trust in those times, wasn't it? A man liked a lot of woman for his money then. Anyhow, Mr. Molloy was full of lore on the house."

"It's certainly no prize package now. When the war's

over, I can't think what the owner could do with it but tear it down for a parking lot. What else did you pick up on my office-cum-nursery? Any rumors that Lillian stashed her diamonds in a hollow wall?''

"Nothing like that. He soon veered off the subject and onto Shane. I got an impression that was really why he had trotted down to the square at the crack of dawn—to find out what I'd heard from Shane lately. He's always been very interested in Shane. Even wanted to admire my engagement ring. That was the only real diamond in our conversation.''

Madge wrinkled her nose, "There's something very odd about Desmond Molloy. Have you girls sensed it too? I can't put my finger on it exactly.''

"So far as I can see," Evaleen said, "he's just your average political antique, with a finger in every profitable pie at City Hall. I never did like him much. But despite the difference in their ages he seems to be one of Cousin Terence's closest friends. Liam's never had a great deal to say about him. But then, Mr. Molloy never paid much notice to Liam.''

"I guess Liam's political views never jibed with Tammany's.''

Evaleen colored faintly. There had been a time when her young husband's flaming devotion to the Irish cause had received moral support from her. Perhaps he wouldn't have fallen in love with her without it, but a slight increase in maturity had given her second thoughts on the subject. She could recognize that her own eager participation in protests and anti-British demonstrations had been largely sparked by a rebellion of her own against the harsh and deeply conservative uncle who had raised and disciplined her after her parents' deaths. That, and the fact that a dashing and very attractive young Irish-American revolutionary found her enthusiasm attractive.

"Liam doesn't mention Ireland half as often as he used to, in his recent letters," Evaleen said finally. It was a fact she wanted the others to know, although neither of them had ever, at least to her knowledge, belittled their cousin for his rather noisy stance.

"With Japanese artillery banging away at him," sighed Madge, "my errant brother must have other things on his mind. I guess there's not much about those Pacific islands to bring an island due west of England front and center. The problem is staying alive."

"For all of them," Agnes agreed. "I had a letter from Brendan last week—I guess because he's lonely. He has nobody much to be writing to except his parents and Norah. Men friends, of course, but they're all away fighting, too. Sometimes a touch of womanly sympathy can be a help, even for someone committed to the priesthood."

"Has he ever run into Shane?" Madge asked. "They're both in Europe."

"No mention. Europe's a big place, after all. And then there's the censorship. Some of my letters from Shane have so many lines snipped out they look like paper lace for a Valentine. The 'Powers That Be' wouldn't want some spy sniffing out where one unit was, *vis à vis* another. No, Shane and Brendan haven't crossed paths so far as I know."

"Two in Europe, one in the Coral Sea. God, when will they come back?"

For a while the trio sat in silence, each with her ears reverberating with similar if separate echoes of the question nearly every woman in America was now asking in her silent heart. Outside the McHugh windows the almost normal breathing of the city was faintly audible. Tugs on the river. Cars on the quiet residential street. Children playing. A barking dog.

When will they come back? But no answer was forthcoming.

On her nights with the Air Raid Patrol, Madge, too, was in uniform—at least of a sort. The armband made little difference, but her father often told her the white hardhat, worn at a tilt over her burnished curls, was surprisingly becoming. Unavoidably flattered, she tried to pay no attention to the compliment. One wasn't doing one's war bit in search of praise for one's looks. Besides, Eamonn McHugh was prejudiced.

Her partner on the rounds, however, tended to echo Eamonn's opinion, and that was rather a different matter. Despite earnest efforts at various enlistment centers, Barry Sullivan had been unable to join the services. He suffered from a mild though tricky heart condition which deafened all military doctors to his pleas and persuasions. He was illogically bitter about this, blaming himself instead of unlucky fate.

Tramping along at her side as they circled the darkened blocks, tall young Mr. Sullivan often let his bitterness boil over. Madge suspected that he actually yearned in secret for the dramatic moment when they would come upon a Nazi terrorist team planting a midnight bomb. He tingled for violent action—and just possibly for a bit of public applause. Well, after all, Madge thought, Sullivan was an Irishman.

"All I have against a bomb," he'd growl at her as they trudged along, "is that *you'd* be put in danger if anything *did* happen. I wouldn't want you hurt, Madge."

"We won't be running into any enemy bomb squads in

this area, Barry. It's all quiet upper-middle-class residential, without even a Chinese restaurant or a shoe repair shop to break up the apartment facades. What would the Axis want to demolish here?''

But Barry refused to abandon the dream. ''Who knows where some of our big shots in government live? Perhaps there's a war-supplies tycoon asleep in that very complex across the street. It wouldn't have to be any obviously war-related building.''

''Barry Sullivan, be sensible. The worst crime you and I are likely to run into is a window where someone's forgotten to pull down his shade and is violating the blackout. We're no longer really expecting a Luftwaffe surprise raid, although of course the bomb shelters have to stay ready and disaster supplies kept up to snuff.''

Barry glared down at her. ''You sure know how to prick a fellow's balloons, don't you? I would have thought you too pretty for a sadist.''

''I try to be a realist.'' Madge answered, blushing, and hoping that in the dark her companion wouldn't notice. ''I don't mean to belittle, Barry, honestly I don't. Since it frets you so, I'm as sorry as you are about that new turndown by the Merchant Marine last week. But we'll have no pitched battle on Sutton Place.''

''All right, all right. While other guys are off having the real excitement, I'll just shut up and go on taking moonlight strolls with some cute dumb dame.''

''Thanks a lot for the extravagant praise! The Irish are wizards at blarney.''

''Oops! For a minute there, I forgot you're Irish, too.'' He reached for her.

Still angry, Madge jerked her hand well out of reach.

''None of that on the rounds, please, Mr. Sullivan. You're on official business, whether you dislike it or not, and that certainly does not include pawing cute dumb dames.''

As the weeks passed, they both discovered that nights when they were not on duty seemed to drag longer than nights when they were. There began to be a change, but Madge was unable to remember which one of them had made the first move. Had Barry asked her to go to the movies before, or after she suggested that her family would both be out of town over the weekend and she was planning to make an omelet for her supper and it would be just as easy to make two? Since the same idea had blossomed in both their minds, and almost simultaneously, there was little point in solving the riddle.

Barry assumed at first that their new relationship would lead to the bedroom—hers or his, he didn't much care which. Madge had rather a different idea.

In the full glow of apartment lights, Sullivan was every bit as delectable as he seemed on patrol under a night sky. In face and in body he was, Madge decided, like a Celtic god. Naked, he would be . . . but she banished such imaginings. The important thing was that they got along so amazingly well together. And he didn't seem at all impressed by his looks, or even much aware of them.

One of the nice things about Barry was that he didn't take her own talent at the drawing board with any corresponding levity. From that first evening in her parents' apartment, the one in which she had made them omelets, he had revealed a genuine admiration for her talent. Actually, his first critical comment on a framed pen-and-ink she had done of Bernadette was a long drawn-out whistle.

"Hey, lady, did you really *do* this? I've run into Mrs. McHugh a couple times down in the lobby. This drawing of her could walk right off the wall and speak."

Burning with pleasure, Madge struggled to look modest.

"You really handle the blarney bit very well, Sullivan, when you aren't insulting a girl."

"Why didn't you ever tell me how good you were, honey?"

It was his first spoken endearment. Deep inside, she hugged it to her.

"I wonder if I'll ever really be good enough someday. I was just lucky with that sketch of Mother. I know her so well I could have almost done it blindfolded."

"There's only one reason why you won't really be good enough someday," Barry said as he looked directly into her lifted eyes. "That's because you're already there. In spades. Hey, I've just had the idea of the century. Why don't I peel and why don't you study my gorgeous naked carcass? Maybe you'll want to draw me, too." His light voice dropped a notch and richened. "Or something."

"Barry . . .," Madge whispered, as her heartbeat quickened. "Please, no."

"Of course, I'm sort of shy for a city boy. Retarded, maybe. I'd feel a lot more comfortable posing if you'd sort of drop your draperies too."

Her face was flaming. She could say nothing, only keep on mutely shaking her head.

"Aw, Madge, you must know I want you. It's not just fun and games."

"Let's n-not, Barry—not yet. Try to remember that I'm only a cute dumb dame, anyway."

"You and elephants have the god-damnedest memories!" he sighed, but he did not press the matter.

The same moon that Madge and Sullivan patrolled under in Manhattan shone nightly over a tiny village in the extreme south of France. Here Brendan had been billeted for several nights, awaiting a message.

During daylight hours, he was compelled to remain well hidden in a hay-mounded barn loft that belonged to the rugged farmer who was concealing him. But in the pre-dawn hours, even after German patrols had given up sur-veillance of the rutted back-country roads, he dared venture out only a few yards from the rancid building for long enough to clear his nose of the straw dust that tormented him in his hiding place.

His besetting terror was that one day he would sneeze while an enemy soldier was within earshot. That would be the end of Brendan O'Donnell. Far more seriously, it would be the end of his mission to spirit an important piece of information across the Pyrenees and into yet another waiting hand in Andorra. The message was vital to the lives of a truckload of doomed French Jews waiting to be smuggled onward to Spain.

A tree stood so close to the ancient barn that its branches all but brushed the bricks. Brendan had no notion of its species, yet it had become a friend to him. It offered shade too thick for moonlight to penetrate, and late hours there were almost as safe as earlier ones up in the loft. Yet, the tree reminded him of his boyhood and the mighty tree at Great Oak. In the end, the oak had proved a traitor and had taken Great-Aunt Veronica's life. Was this French tree a Judas also?

"When will the message come? Why is it already so delayed?"

Nerves drawn tight as an archer's bowstring, he sweated out the dusty days as best he could. He had a pad of cheap paper with him, and a small phalanx of pocket pens. His supposed cover was that he was an itinerant journalist covering the final death spasms of France for his newspaper in neutral Dublin. They had rehearsed him first in other roles, but his school-boy French was so faulty that no local impersonation could have fooled anyone. But he could coax a Gaelic lilt onto his tongue by remembering Grandfather Patrick's speech. He even recalled how Cousin Delia had been able to give the brogue to a stage part. His past made an Irish characterization the wisest.

Thus far, it had worked.

Cooped up out of sight, Brendan choked back the vomit of panic while lorries bearing helmeted Jerries wheeled in and out of the muddy farm courtyard below. They were there for a number of reasons, but most were looking for an American agent—himself—known to lurk near the town.

Even worse were the visits of French traitors, adhering now to Vichy. These men were spurred not by some brute loyalty to Hitler but by plain monetary greed. Let one of that breed of well-paid headhunters suspect who crouched overhead in the hay and there would be only one way to silence him. Brendan dreaded the possible moment. For if it came, would he be able to kill? Even to save those poor, huddled victims in the van?

For long hours at a time, however, there would be no such threats. He filled such hours by writing letters to Agnes Moran. They were never to be mailed, and with the coming of dark he always destroyed them—ripping them to shreds and dripping each fistful of scraps into the leaky barn cistern. But pretending he was talking to Agnes was often the only way he could survive a long day's apprehensions.

Agnes—his brother Shane's beloved promised wife—he knew with every sinew of his being how wrong this dependence on memories of her was. She belonged to Shane and always had—always, since the night both brothers first met her. The younger brother, himself, had never even raised a finger in competition. How could he, being already as good as betrothed to the Church? And she had turned toward Shane from that earliest hour, almost as naturally as a sunflower turns toward the moving gold in the sky.

Agnes was not for the younger O'Donnell brother, nor he for her. But oh, if by some Divine magic things had been different!

It was sin enough, no doubt, to be writing these letters to her at all; these epistles never intended to be sent, and dutifully destroyed in the same day each was entrusted to paper. If there had been no war, he would already be deep into his studies at the seminary. The path so clearly marked for him would already have his early footprints on it. It could betray a man as sure as any Vichy headhunter to have his intended progress cut off from him, shoved away into refrigeration, while matters never dreamed of took over.

But for this little while the need to exchange thoughts with Agnes was overwhelming. It made the hours of loft dust endurable. She would never know and if that were not so, Brendan never would have written a single word. But a farm village in France was not on the same planet as a great, brawling city in America. Probably, quite different angels watched over the two. Only its God was certain to be the same.

> . . . *so yet another day is all but over, Agnes, and the messenger who is to fetch me the instructions to carry on to the next stop still has not shown himself. Has he met with some disaster? Will he never arrive here? Have the Nazis waylaid him?*

One would find it difficult to believe that such a fate could be God's plan for the mission. Thirty blameless souls marked for butchering surely merited no such abandonment. Yet one looked across the world and saw so many other instances of the incomprehensible. During the past year, flushed with triumph, Hitler's legions had swept all the way into the Caucasus. Japanese victors were spreading like spilled ink over Southeast Asia and Indonesia, while the Pacific ran crimson with blood. All France had fallen, with only its varmints surviving the collapse—and Britain seemed doomed to be next.

> . . . *that it is often very difficult, Agnes, to find God's reasons. How many souls before Brendan O'Donnell must have puzzled that, do you suppose, along the corridors of Christian time? There's no great originality in it. Only a weakness; not a faltering of Faith exactly, but certainly a faltering of Understanding. I wish I might see you face to face and talk with you. I have this strange feeling in me that you could set my thoughts clearer* . . .

It grew too dark in his cramped quarters to keep on writing. He put his pen and pad aside—first extracting the few sheets and ripping them into the customary ribbons, the ribbons into confetti such as had littered the floor at home on the night of Norah's party.

He settled back in blackness, remembering the party as he had remembered it every day. He remembered the doorbell pealing and Shane loping to answer it. He remembered the voice from the doorsill, and then, most clearly of all, he remembered seeing Agnes Moran for the first time.

Only when the moon was low and the farm erased to nothingness did he dare swing down the rickety loft ladder. Outside, a cool breeze stirred the tree's branches. There was a tiny sound in the stillness, but Brendan recognized it as the minute dripping from a crack in one of the decaying cistern's planks. He lifted the wooden lid and fished the letter scraps from his pocket. He then dropped them on the surface of the unseen water, and as they soaked they would sink, and like others before them be lost forever.

Out of the deeper shadow beyond, a vague form materialized without warning—still so dim it had no real shape to it. Brendan recoiled, heartbeat quickening, trained muscles flickering. The dour, dependable farmer? No. This one he did not know.

He groped at his side for the sheathed knife that was part of his emergency equipment. And even as he groped, he wondered how he could force himself to utilize the weapon. God made life, and only God should take it. But there were thirty innocents whose lives were endangered by this implacable German or Vichy toad who had tracked him down . . .

"It's a long road to the Pyrenees." Why, it was a woman speaking. Or did it only seem to be? Only fools were ever certain. This was a world of lies and cold pretendings.

"It's longer to Andorra," he answered as his superior had instructed him to.

The woman stepped closer. Perhaps a hair too close? She plunged one hand into a deep coat pocket. Brendan felt his own wet fist clamp hard about his knife hilt. He sucked in a breath and said a silent prayer: *Please, God, don't have this decision rest on me. One life? Thirty lives? . . .*

She removed her hand from her pocket. In it, she held a folded paper which she handed to him.

"This is what you are supposed to take with you, O'Donnell. The Commandant is pretty sure now you are somewhere on this farm. So leave at once, while you still have three hours of dark. Two fields along the road, you'll find a bicycle hidden in the ditch. It should get you to the border before sunrise. May luck ride with you, American.''

6

Sometimes, her relationship with Barry Sullivan seemed like the one real anchor for her daily existence. Tuning in to each morning's radio news was almost an exercise in masochism.

Blackness seemed poised like a tidal wave to engulf everything good. Axis forces, massed in Africa, were preparing a pincers movement to crush the little countries of the Near East. France lay in total submission. England's back was to the wall. Belgium and Holland were in chains, Denmark and Norway overrun, Poland and Finland destroyed. And the Nazi ally, Japan, had the whole Pacific by its throat. Even with America now firmly in the battle, it appeared all but hopeless that the tide could be turned.

Barry's indomitable optimism was often, in these grim months, the steel in her own spine. Instead of trying to coax him out of his personal blues, as she had first done, Madge found herself leaning almost helplessly on his reas-

surances of eventual victory. Barry might still endure peri-
odic seizures of self-pity, but as to America's ultimate
triumph he never suffered the slightest passing doubt.

"How could we possibly lose the war?" he demanded
confidently, as they made their nightly rounds together.
"Look at the facts, girl. We're Americans!"

"We O'Donnells, and you Sullivans too, were Irishmen
once. A lot of good that ever did us, though we've fought
the fight ever since Elizabeth Tudor was Queen."

"Ireland's a different proposition. The spirit's there, but
not the mighty natural resources. Sure, it's taken this
country a year to mobilize its strength. But we're getting
better organized every day. Once we hit with full force,
you'll see Hitler begin to crumble. And the Mikado, too.
And those comic opera Italians."

"There hasn't been one hopeful sign since Dunkirk,
Barry. That operation broke the English land force out of
the Nazi trap, I know. But it was still a retreat."

"It gives them time to regroup, that's all. They'll be
back on the continent again, you'll see. And now they
have *us* to back them up. How can they fail?"

Madge had to chuckle, however ruefully. "Was there
ever an Irishman who wasn't a braggart?"

"We're supposed to be handy lovers, too, according to
the legends. When are you going to give in, honey? Admit
that you want me, just like I want you."

"I do, Barry. I've never denied it. But until the time for
us is right . . ."

"What you really mean is, until I've put a gold ring on
your finger. What is it that scares you, Madge: Not your
parents, surely? Not your awesome relatives?"

"I don't think so. It's just something deep inside me."

"Sure, I know what ought to be deep inside you." The
earnestness with which he said it somehow robbed his

words of any hint of vulgarity. "What are we waiting for, darling? Must we wait until we're doddering over the hill to the Old Folks Home?"

Madge quivered, feeling the mighty pull of his yearning. "Until . . . until I *know*."

Barry had become such a symbol of strength to her during their night-long vigils that it seemed almost unthinkable he could have mortal weaknesses—aside, that was, from his deep-rooted fear of marriage and its chains. But one evening when she reported to Headquarters for the start of their regular tour, Barry wasn't waiting there for her, as usual.

"Called in sick," Walter Hardwick, who ran their sub-station, informed her. "That head cold Mr. Sullivan was fighting all week turned into something a little worse. He's under doctor's orders."

She felt herself stiffen. "When did this happen? Is it serious?"

"Sullivan assures me not."

"It *must* be, to make Barry skip a session. I'd better call him and see what I can do."

"I was instructed to tell you not to worry, Miss McHugh. He was very specific."

"Still, I'm worried. Do you think one of the other teams could sub for us tonight? Then I could go to his hotel and make absolutely certain . . ."

"He was very positive about that over the telephone," Hardwick said. "You were to go on as usual and not give his skipping a patrol a second thought. The only problem is, none of our regular substitute partners is available. I've been calling around, but without luck."

"I don't need a substitute, Mr. Hardwick. Ours isn't exactly a hard crime area. I'll be perfectly all right with only my flashlight. But this isn't *like* Barry."

"The best of us can't outbox a determined germ. Well, then, if you are sure you'll be all right. I'd go with you myself, but tonight we're extra short-handed. I've no one to take the incoming messages."

Madge had not anticipated the sharp-edged loneliness which moved with her along the dark blocks she and Barry usually walked together. Walter Hardwick need not have been in the least concerned about her. Unsavory characters had vanished from the Universe, along with almost everyone else. One darkened car to a block purring past her created a virtual traffic jam. The pavements were peopled only by shadows. If she listened only a trifle harder, she ought to be able to hear the stars wheeling by overhead.

This was how the world ought to sound after it had come to an end.

She caught herself straining for the fall of Barry's step, like an echo of her own. When it didn't come she looked up, frowning, to find out what had become of him. Germ? What germ? There was no epidemic rampant in the city, none that she knew of. He hadn't mentioned feeling poorly, although Hardwick seemed to have been aware his subordinate wasn't in top form.

I should have seen it sooner than anyone. I'm the one who loves him. . . .

Her thoughts kept her company. Lacking Barry's hand to hang onto, she clung to them. It was almost a year now that she had been denying him. The man's patience was extraordinary. He must care a great deal for her to put up with her at all. He'd talked of their growing old together while she still said 'no.' But what if they had no chance to grow old? What if while they were still young he was suddenly gone?

It can't really be all that serious a germ. It can't be. It mustn't.

A man on foot swung around the last corner, a third of a block behind her. Even before she picked up the rhythm of his footfalls, quicker than her own and paced to a longer stride, she had realized he was coming. He was whistling the tune that everyone in the city seemed to have on his lips these war days. Her own began to frame the words: *I'll never smile again until I smile with you, I'll never smile again . . .*

Nothing to be concerned about. No citizen bent on evil went about his business whistling. The lilt of the music astern of her suggested that the follower himself was lonely and needed the tune for company. He'd have made out her white helmet already, even in the dark. Perhaps as he passed he'd say something about the quiet night, just to hear a few human syllables in reply to his comment.

Almost certainly, the tempo of those footsteps had quickened. The tune broke off.

For the first time, a ripple of uneasiness flickered along her spine.

The man behind her had cut down the distance between them considerably. It was as if he were trying to catch up with her. But why would he possibly want to do that? And why had he stopped whistling? Only one likely answer suggested itself. She clutched her flashlight desperately, ready to wield it as a weapon, and spun around.

"I thought it was you, Miss McHugh," he said, stopping dead. "Good evening."

She gaped at him. "Why, you're Mr. Molloy!"

"Of course I am, my dear. At least, I always have been until now. What is a pretty young woman like you doing out on the streets alone at such an hour, might an old man inquire?"

"I'm on patrol duty." Her breathing was still a trifle ragged.

"Yes, I see that. I recognized the gear even before you turned, my dear. But shouldn't you have a partner with you? I thought you were supposed to travel in pairs."

"My teammate's sick tonight. We had no one to replace him."

"Then, if you'll allow me, I'll accompany you myself on the rest of your tour. I'm a good friend of the O'Donnell family, as I'm sure you know. Allow me a little worry."

"It's very kind of you, Mr. Molloy, but it really isn't necessary. I'm quite all right."

But the still quickened throb of her pulse made a liar of her. In the instant she whirled to face him, she *had* been afraid. The night had suddenly sharpened, honed by a presence at her back. She had wanted Barry beside her desperately, wildly, with all the primeval need that her mother so scorned in her militant feminist speeches.

"No doubt the need for a male escort went out with the bustle, Miss Madge. But we men cling to it. We like to feel needed. So unless you'd rather that I don't . . ."

"Why, I'll be glad for the company. It's a very quiet evening, isn't it?"

Molloy fell into step beside her, matching stride to stride. They finished the dark block in silence, negotiated the crosswalk, and started down on the next row of blank, still houses.

"As a matter of fact, my dear," Molloy said pleasantly, "I've been aware for some time that you and a young co-worker have this particular patrol. I've passed this way at night before, several times. But usually in a taxi, so I never could speak."

"If you'd waved from your window, sir, we'd probably have recognized you. It isn't exactly a teeming neighborhood in the small hours, is it?"

"I would imagine many a desert island to be more

heavily populated. You'd have recognized me, would you? From just the few times we've encountered each other at your Cousin Terence's? To my remembrance those are the only times I've met you.''

''I think they have been. My parents don't entertain too often.''

Which was a falsehood, because both older McHughs were gregarious. But now that she thought about it, Mr. Desmond Molloy had not very often crossed their threshold. Without knowing why, she sensed that her parents didn't much like the man.

''You're a very old friend of my uncle's, aren't you Mr. Molloy?''

''And of your Grandfather Patrick's before him. You O'Donnells hold a very special niche in my heart, young lady. There isn't one of you I wouldn't be proud to turn a favor for. Right now, for instance, I have one in mind for your Cousin Shane.''

''But Shane's a thousand miles away, sir. Somewhere in Europe, fighting.''

''Somewhere in Europe? I was hoping you could place him a bit more exactly for me.''

The words seemed innocent enough. What was it about the underlying tone that put her off? Again without knowing why, Madge found herself suddenly on guard.

''We never know exactly where Shane or Liam or Brendan are, Mr. Molloy. They aren't allowed to say. Government regulations forbid it.''

''But Shane *is* in Europe. I've found out that much myself, a good while back. If I'm to pull a string or two and bring him back home, I'd like to know more.''

''Bring Shane back home?'' She stopped in mid-stride, facing him. ''What do you mean?''

''Wouldn't you like to see one of your handsome young

cousins safe back on this side of the Atlantic, now? No girl's happy knowing her kinfolk are being shot at.''

"I'm sure that none of the O'Donnells who are in uniform would want 'strings pulled' to get them out of the fight before we've won it,'' Madge said flatly. "Shane is certainly no coward.''

"Of course not, my dear! I wouldn't even suggest such a thing! But there might be more valuable work he could do for his country right here. And I might have the very pass key to let him in on it. So if you or your family have some private news of his whereabouts . . .''

"We know nothing that we're not supposed to know, Mr. Molloy, I'm sure.''

"But if you happen to stumble on such, Madge, my dear—if a little bird should twitter it, passing by—you'll be a darling and pass it along to Uncle Desmond, won't you now? Shane hasn't a firmer friend on earth than Desmond X. Molloy.''

"Then Shane would be the first to tell you where he's stationed, wouldn't he; provided it were proper news to pass along? This is the last corner of my beat, Mr. Molloy. Thank you for keeping me company. And a good evening to you, I'm sure.''

She was on her way before he could speak again. If she heard those quick footfalls behind her again, she knew she would run. Just what she found so frightening about the old man's quiet pressure she could not have said, but one thing she did know—whatever his purpose, it was not for Shane's benefit but his own. If he had indeed glimpsed her on patrol before tonight, it had been because he was spying on her—and never until now had found her alone, without Barry walking beside her.

Why her parents mistrusted Desmond Molloy was their own affair. But so did she.

*   *   *

Bernadette always felt a sense of relief when one of her cross-country War Bond tours was finished and she could get back to Sutton Place again. She was no longer as young as she had been when she and Veronica took to the road on their Women's Rights campaigns. That had been exciting, stimulating work. She had been keyed up to impatience each time, eager to be up and off, but nowadays it was heavy going.

Not that for a moment she would have given up doing what she had been asked to do. She appreciated that she had been approached by men high on the ladder, who might not have agreed with her feminist principles but who had learned over the years to respect her skills and dedication. Every dollar she could lure into the Country's war chest was a special dollar. It might buy the bullet with which Liam defended himself against some Jap bent on his destruction. She'd have toiled forty hours a day for that, and felt herself lucky for the opportunity. But sometimes she'd been so exhausted she had forgotten in which city she was making her determined speech, on which dais she stood on to plead, or to what audience she urged, *"Give, give, give!"*

These past several months, she had also been worried about Madge. Leaving her girl alone with only the maids was, she felt, not being much of a mother. And she felt especially bad when Eamonn had to be away from New York even more often than she, supervising the shipments of medicines being produced for the fighting men. Madge— and Bernadette was certain she was not imagining this— was in love for the first time.

As she rode in the taxi from the airport, she sank back against the cracked leather of her seat and watched the blur of city-bound traffic. Others were sharing the ride, that was the way of it now and no one objected, but she was too tired to really register their faces. Once the cab reached Manhattan streets, they began to get off at this door or that corner bus stop. She closed her heavy eyes and recognized each shadowy departure only as an increase in her share of air to breathe.

Sutton Place, being a backwater, was the last stop on the driver's schedule. She must have been dozing for the last block or two, because she fancied herself to be on her way to Great Oak to talk about Madge and ask her mother's opinion.

"Last stop. All out. That's three dollars, fifteen cents, lady."

Her eyes opened, and she was slightly disappointed that it wasn't dependable old Joe who stood with door open and hand held out. The Packard's upholstery had been soft as the clouds of Heaven and never the hint of a crack to scratch at you. She messed about in her purse and paid her fare. Soon she was walking through the apartment house lobby.

Home. Why this was home. No speech to give. No haranguing. Just—home.

The key to their own suite was for a moment recalcitrant. She tried to force it, found she was using the wrong one among a dozen on her ring, corrected her error, and felt the front door swing open. Lights were burning discreetly in the foyer. Well—all right, the room had no windows, nothing for Madge to chide her about. Or were the black-out regulations relaxed now? She couldn't remember. Madge would know.

She paused before the old gilt-framed French mirror that once was supposed to have reflected the Marquise de Pompadour. Someone with dark circles under her eyes stared back out of the specked glass. Dear Lord, she looked as if she'd taken to the boxing ring and been given a couple of shiners.

"Hard to find good make-up nowadays. I look my age. A million."

On the little marble table under the mirror a single envelope lay waiting. Madge—or Eamonn, if he were back in town ahead of her—must already have taken care of the accumulated mail. All but this one item. She stared down at it wearily.

Mrs. Eamonn McHugh—She read no further. She had recognized the writing.

Her hand shook and she ran a fingernail under the flap. It had been left here where she'd be certain to find it the moment she came in. *Oh, thank you, God! It's from Liam!*

How she got to a deep chair with a decent reading light beside it in the curtained library was a matter of indifference. The important thing was that she was holding the quivering pages before her and his words were leaping out at her. *Dear Mom: Guess what!* (Guess what . . . How long ago had it been since she'd heard him use that awful phrase? If all the things she had been asked to guess about over the years were laid end to end—Oh, Liam!)

> *Here I am on the beach in Hawaii. Shipped back for two weeks on R and R, sort of combing the gunpowder out of my whiskers. It must have hit the news a while back. I guess they'll let me write a little about it. The Japs sure know, so it's no big secret. The battle was off these islands they call the Marshalls, Mom . . .*

So Liam had been part of that ghastly conflict. Bits and pieces of it, citizens back home already knew. She hadn't slept a peaceful hour since, wondering the rest. And now,

yes, he *had* been part of it. But he'd come through. He
was all right. He was safe in Hawaii.

*The Nips had things pretty much all their own
way, up till that afternoon. We'd just been trying to
hold them back, keep a thumb in the dyke like that
Dutch kid you used to read me about when I was
little—what was his name, Hans Brinker? No, I guess
Brinker was the one with the skates. Anyhow, we
hadn't been doing so hot. But wow!*

*We'd been mixing it up with them for a good while,
that morning. It was going pretty much their way,
too. Thirty-five of the forty-one torpedo planes off our
carriers—The* Hornet, *the* Enterprise *and the* York-
town— *had been shot out of the sky. But our bombers
still zeroed in on their own carriers for a big surprise.
Was it just luck, or was the good Lord with us? Either
way, their air cover was at low altitude because they
were braced for one last torpedo attack. The air
above them was only lightly defended when we hit.
They weren't expecting us.*

*And were they ever vulnerable! There were gas
lines open on their decks. Instant-contact bombs meant
for an attack on Midway itself lay around like fallen
apples in an orchard. Our American dive bombers hit
them like swooping falcons. The* Kaga *and the* Soryu
*were smashed by bomb blasts, with fires sweeping
their decks and the loose bombs going off as if it was
July Fourth back home instead of June Fourth in the
South Pacific . . .*

Bernadette looked up from the page, the picture of
violence still seared on her eyes, and saw her husband
standing across the room quietly looking at her. She had

no notion of when he had come in, or how long he had been standing there.

"It's from Liam," she said. "He's been in a battle."

"It came this morning," he said. "I thought you ought to be the one to open it. After all, the boy addressed it to you. Is he all right?"

"In Hawaii. On leave. Combing out gunpowder, as he puts it."

"That's fine." She had seldom noticed, these past several years, how soft her husband's voice could be. "So go on reading then. I'll wait my turn."

Bernadette turned her attention back to the letter.

> *Luck or God, Mom? Which? Anyhow, some of our fellows spotted a Nip destroyer streaking hell-for-leather to rejoin its carriers. Gas almost gone, our dive bombers off the* Enterprise *swarmed down on it. Down to Davey Jones' well-known locker we sent them. And then we blew the* Akagi *right out of the waves with a bomb that dug into stored ammo below the carrier's flight deck.The torpedo planes and bombers that had been massing there for a strike at our own carriers were blown to—well, Mom, you don't like cuss words.*

> *After that, their* Hiryu *was the only Nip carrier still in commission. By then, she had hurt the* Yorktown *so bad it later had to be abandoned. But her number was up, all the same. Four thousand-pound Yank bombs did for her; them and their own bombs, which we ignited. Wish you could have seen that night, Mrs. McH. Burning carriers—Japanese ones—lit up the ocean for miles around. It was curtains for Admiral Yamamoto, sure enough. We've still got plenty of fights ahead. But it's them who'll be on the run now.*

*So here I sit under a palm tree at Waikiki, waiting
for a coconut to fall on me. If one doesn't brain me
before then, they return me to my outfit next week. I
can hardly wait to get back in action . . . .*

She deciphered the bold, oddly boyish signature and
silently passed the letter into Eamonn's waiting hand.
While he read, she sat looking off into space—her eyes no
longer glazed with weariness, her face almost as youthful
as it had been when Veronica first led her into battles of
their own. Eamonn scanned the last page, folded it in with
the others, slipped them into their envelope, set down the
envelope on the fireplace mantle.

"It was mailed over a week ago," he said. "Which
means . . ."

"That Liam is back with his outfit by now. No more
Hawaii. No more coconuts."

"That last could be a good thing. He may be hit by
nothing worse for the rest of hostilities. With a bit of luck,
the boy should make it right on into Tokyo Harbor."

Liam's mother stood up and moved toward the greying,
dynamic man who faced her. "As you read the letter,
Eamonn, did you have the impression of an echo?"

"Echo?"

"That was a *happy* young man speaking to us. Liam
still aches for a fight, doesn't he? Never mind he's a
married man with a wife he loves, never mind he's the
father of a son he's never seen, what still holds him is a
rousing good battle. He *loved* it."

Eamonn smiled widely. "And why not, he being
Irish?"

"You're right. That's what I was remembering. Will he
still be like this when he comes back to us? Back on the
ramparts again, howling about freedom for Ireland? I don't

guess we'll have a very peaceful time hereabouts, even when the Japanese surrender.''

"And, heaven forbid, he's an expert now at handling weapons!''

"I know. When this war's over, the poor British may never know it.''

"Where are you going?" Eamonn asked as she headed for the hall.

"To call up Evaleen and Danny. I have a sudden yearning to talk to them. One of the bad things about world conflagrations, darling, is that they make a person forget she is a mother-in-law and a grandmother. Oh, Lord, and a mother too. Where is Madge, Eamonn? I haven't heard a peep from her. Oughtn't she to be home from patrol duty?''

"Home an hour ago, changed, and off again with her young man. It's some sort of midnight show Norah's doing at the Stage Door Canteen. They were determined not to miss it.''

"I thought the young man was laid low with pneumonia. Wasn't that the latest?''

"A remarkable recovery, dear. With our own answer to Florence Nightingale hovering over him, pneumonia hadn't a chance. Bernadette, I'm afraid this is for real.''

"Either it is or it isn't. But to my knowledge he hasn't yet asked Madge to marry him." For an instant, a shadow crossed Bernadette's face. "He'd better, the bastard. But to me, Mr. Barry Sullivan doesn't seem like the marrying kind.''

7

As was becoming more and more the rule on her public appearances, a small ovation followed Norah's final exit from the band stand. That night the crowd was posher than most because it was an Opening Night. Her encore had been *The Last Time I Saw Paris*, and now that Allied forces were plowing their dogged way inland from the beaches of Normandy and the freeing of France's great city seemed imminent, the tune generated a new enthusiasm with listeners everywhere.

Applause rose, crested and faded, dwindling to a tinkle like that of the crystal chandeliers ablaze against the ballroom's arched ceiling. As the velvet curtain to the dressing-room corridor fell behind her the sound was silenced altogether. She had been called back for two bows, and that was enough.

Norah's personal cubicle was so small that, standing, she could touch the wall on either side. But there was room enough in it for a makeup shelf, a mirror, a folding chair and a rack on which her costumes could be hung with reasonable neatness. No producer was mounting Norah O'Donnell's name in lights yet, but she had been signed, only weeks ago, as female vocalist with a band successful enough to rate national recognition. Terence was insisting she would be the family's new Delia. Her parents made no rash claims, but obviously were proud as peacocks of her successes. She was on her way up.

That night, as she had done often lately, she was heading to a small, dark bistro on the far West Side. She and Dennis both favored it. Perhaps it was like a hundred others in the city; candles stuck into wax-streaked wine bottles, checkered table cloths, thick crockery, dim booths, and some really good French Provincial home cooking, but for the two of them *Les Bouffons* had a special meaning, a private flavor.

Dennis Gallagher! Would she ever have met him at all if there had been no war? If there had been no North Africa landings in which he had been badly enough hurt to be permanently out of the fighting forces? Had he not been shipped home to take up anew his former work as a music arranger, they might never have come face to face as they had done a few short weeks ago.

They had met, not quite by accident, in the businesslike office of Martin Kenny, who had undertaken to serve as manager to each of them.

Crouched before the mirror, scrubbing away her stage makeup with remnants of cold cream from an almost empty jar, Norah tried to imagine what the world had been like with no Dennis in it. But memory faltered. Love her parents and two brothers though she did, her world had simply begun turning that first afternoon in Martin's waiting room.

Dog-eared magazines on the reading table, some of them dating back to before Pearl Harbor, had failed to intrigue either of them. While they waited for their separate appointments, idle conversation had been the only alternative, except that after the first few minutes it had not been idle, not for either of them. When the unimpressive door to the youthful manager's sanctum opened, neither had even looked up. Martin had to clear his throat rather noisily to secure their attention.

"Dennis? Norah? You did come here on business, didn't you?"

Dennis flushed and sprang to his feet. Norah blushed and remained seated. But it was she who spoke. "Hello, Martin. Mother gave me a message you'd called and wanted to see me. Another Service show? Will we be going out of town again?"

"Nothing so temporary as that this time, I hope. It concerns both of you kids, so you'd better come on inside together. This is a two-birds-with-one-stone sort of thing."

Seated in the inner office, they had been told what was cooking. Buddy Disston of the Starlight Serenaders had just lost his long-time arranger to a heart attack, and on Tuesday had fired his female vocalist after a date in Cleveland where she had fallen off the stage in a drunken daze. Quick replacements were needed, and Martin Kenny's office had been contacted.

"It's a good outfit. You probably both at least know of it. More and more deb parties are hiring The Serenaders. They're playing big college homecomings, fairly important nightclubs, even Government dates in Washington. Buddy is queer, but he doesn't mess around inside 'the family' so that needn't worry you, Dennis. Most importantly the pay is aces."

Had it really all happened so quickly and with such little maneuvering?

Now, these few weeks later, Norah found herself almost unable to remember the exact details. Contracts had been drawn up, Martin had approved them, she and Dennis had signed where Martin indicated they should. Then they had gone off together for dinner, to celebrate.

"Anywhere special you'd like us to go, Norah?"

"Wherever you say. Just so long as it's a place I can let off a little steam before I explode, Dennis. Can you believe we're both really *hired* by Buddy Disston?"

"There's a place I kind of like in the Forties. *Les Buffons*. French, but not too."

"Oh, yes, *Les Buffons!* I know it. Some of us used to wind up there on late evenings after the Stage Door Canteen. The beef stew is from Paradise. Let's go there."

Which they had done, delighted to discover yet another addition to their long list of shared affections. After that first dinner, it had been *Les Buffons* almost every evening Disston's band played Manhattan. In Denver or San Antonio or Milwaukee, settling for some perfectly adequate substitute, they had grieved together for "home"—meaning a special corner booth, a special checkered tablecloth with a darned spot in one square, and a special lopsided candle dripping stalactites.

Tonight they were going "home". It was the first evening back in New York for The Serenaders. Norah worked fast at removing her stage paint and the sequins in her hair. Scrubbed clean, the family-featured face in the mirror did not remind her quite so much of Delia—and that night so long ago when, if Delia had not flown in fury to the aid of a small and terrified child who shared her O'Donnell blood . . .

Ready for the street before her, Dennis knocked at her door.

"Coming, Dennis. In a jiffy. Have the boys finished?"

"Just through the last set. They're packing up their instruments."

Norah thrust aside the curtain and emerged into his waiting embrace. Time for one long kiss in the empty back-stage corridor. His arm circled her waist as they went out through the stage door into another humming New York night.

With their last show finished, it was so late that the city too had removed most of its glamour makeup. Down the block, marquee lights at the theatre where Frederic March was starring in *A Bell For Adano* had already darkened. The sidewalk was deserted, except for a prowling cat who glared at them as they strolled past. Nearer the corner, at another playhouse, a less successful show had posted its notice after only a week's run. A truck was backed up to the curb and burly semi-shadows were loading scenery flats into it for carting to Cain's Warehouse. The workers seemed like graveyard ghouls as they labored in sweaty silence.

Snug in their corner at *Les Buffons*, they ordered their usual onion soup and smiled into each other's eyes across the flicker of the haphazard candle. Often at such moments they were completely quiet. What each of them was thinking crossed the table without words, and was joyously understood. But that night what they had to discuss demanded articulation. Dennis was first to break the silence.

"So we're back from the road. You'll be in your own room at your parents' place tonight, instead of pigging it at whatever Class C hotel Buddy has booked us into."

Norah knew how much more the comment meant than it

ostensibly said. It really was a question. The most important question a man could ask a woman.

"I know," she said softly, and waited.

"Well? Isn't it the time to tell them you'll be moving
out for good soon? Unless they find objections to me as a
son-in-law?"

"It's going to be hard for them, Dennis. Oh, not to fall
in love with you on sight. I don't mean that. Who could
resist you? Certainly their daughter didn't."

"What do you mean exactly, then, honey?"

"With both boys still overseas, I'm the only chick left
in the nest. I'm so afraid they'll feel abandoned. Especially my father. All my life, Jim's treated me like some
sort of princess. He's pretty used to being 'Head Man' on
my list."

"If he really loves you, he'll know this is the time to
move aside."

"He'd do anything in the world to make me happy. But
he thinks of me as someone special. And he doesn't quite
believe that anyone else could look after me the way he
always has. Nothing against you would be implied. It's
just the way he is."

"So you're telling me I have to wait, Norah? How
long? Until the mess in Europe finished and your brothers
come home? Will your folks take me better then?"

The whisper of despair underlying his steady question
twisted Norah's heart. "You know better than that, Dennis
Gallagher. They're going to love you from the first minute
they meet you. And we're going to be married as soon as
Father Shaughnessy can arrange it, not one day further off.
I just want you to help me get them over that first little
wave of loneliness, that's all."

His face across the candle flame seemed one gorgeous
sunrise. "I'll be good at that, my darling. I'm an instant

expert at loneliness. Just now, while I was thinking you meant to put me off for God alone knows how long, I lived through a whole lifetime of it.''

"Dennis . . .'' she whispered. ''Oh, Dennis, neither one of us is ever going to be lonely again. I promise you that. Do you promise me?''

He reached for her hungrily across the little table, thrusting aside the winking candle to clear his way.

As Shane strode across the field's tarmac on his way to chow, tension throbbed in the air like raw electricity. "Somewhere in England" was as close as censorship allowed his letters home to describe this base of the 121st Airborne.

Long ago, he had discovered that he truly loved Britain—which doubtless was cause enough to render him comtemptible in the eyes of his fiery cousin Laim. But be that as it might, Shane felt an ever-growing affection for rolling green hills and unshakeably courageous people. With many of their cities in ruins, with their backs pushed against the wall, the English had fought like tigers. And now at last the tide had turned for them.

Easing into a place at a long table in the mess hall, Shane was still thinking of the simile—tigers. What was the bit from Shakespeare? He nudged his memory and the lines drifted back.

> *In peace there's nothing so becomes a man*
> *As modest stillness and humility:*
> *But when the blast of war blows in our ears,*
> *Then imitate the actions of the tiger,*
> *Stiffen the sinews, summon up the blood . . .*

Well, that was what they had all been doing these past years—he and Brendan and Liam, in whatever corners of

the wide-flung fight they found themselves, the women
and the older men accomplishing what had to be done
behind the lines. Tigers, one and all. What was true of the
tiny personal cosmos called O'Donnell was just as true of
whole nations.

Amazing that on such a high noon a man could sit
spouting Shakespeare silently to his own remembering ear.
The very munificence of the menu marked this day as
special. Steak and mashed potatoes, fresh vegetables in
profusion, ice cream, decent coffee, milk. Eating, he con-
centrated on anything, even *Henry V*, to ignore the reason
for the feast. Many of the division, as they well knew,
would never taste another such meal.

Since an early hour, the camp had been barred to all
outsiders; no one was let in or out. Around the hangars,
the ground crews were laboring like colonies of goosed
ants. Men readied weapons and equipment, or wrote home
what might be their last letters, or carefully packed away
small personal treasures with instructions as to where they
should be sent if their owners did not return to claim them.

Laughter was boisterous, if hollow. Tempers walked a
tightrope. Even Top Brass were awarded only dull stares
instead of brisk salutes. It was on everyone's taut lips that
it didn't much matter where they were headed because a
crumbling Germany was narrowing down each day and
there couldn't be many miles between a landing and shaking hands with the advancing Russians. A picnic, this was
going to be. A piece of cake.

A light drizzle began to fall just as the first of the great
transport planes rolled out at the far end of the strip.
Propellers began to spin, Men fell into line for their assigned planes, heavy packs of gear hugging their shoulders.
The whine of motors seemed to suck them vacuum-style
into the cavernous interiors of the waiting giants. Here,

Shane among them, they sat in close-packed rows, eyes glazed, jaws set as if nailed into position.

On the dot of 1705 hours the lead transport plane roared down the strip and climbed into the sky. The other planes followed one by one, with a mechanical precision which—when he had watched similar maneuvers from ground side—had always brought to Shane's mind the flawless performance of a Rockette line back home at Radio City. From other fields, meticulously timed, other fleets would even now be rising. When it rendezvoused, the whole Armada would be a giant winged monster. This was no hit-and-run raid. This was a major operaton.

They were crossing the Channel before Shane found his breathing half-way returned to normal. The gleaming water so far below was already taking on a gloss of evening, its surface rumpled like metallic lamé. A fair-sized fishing trawler rode the silver like a crawling ladybug, and men stared upward, marvelling at this sudden infestation of their peaceful twilight.

Water vanished and land replaced it. The false sense of peace continued. Years of destruction might have ripped those scattered towns asunder, but from this height, evidence of devastation was scarcely visible. One by one the leagues slid past.

Far front in the cabin, a green light in the fuselage began to blink at them like a dragon's eye. They all knew what the signal meant—"*Stand up and hook up!*" Like robots the silent men obeyed, and even as they followed one another, Hell broke loose in the air below. German anti-aircraft installations had opened up with everything they could hurt aloft. The transport shivered from the swarming violence. Christmas-tinted tracers, red and green, floated slowly in the dark like cruising swans.

The plane had lost altitude and was gliding no more than

a thousand feet above Jerry soil. This was the DZ—the drop zone. They were over target.

"Ready to jump!" their Captain barked.

As a sergeant, Shane had been appointed jump leader. He was already braced in the cabin doorway when the order came. At its final word—*Jump!*—he flung himself out into empty space and began his count. The night tore past him, howling, roaring.

Like bits from a broken kaleidoscope, he glimpsed the mass of raiders moving overhead. Here and there a unit had been hit and was spewing flame along its underbelly, but the Allied formation held. Implacably, the transports droned on course.

The earth shook beneath him. The sky screamed around him. *This was it.*

Shane yanked hard at his parachute cord.

What had been drizzle in England was a harsh pelting rain in Germany. Shane hit ground on the sharply inclined bank of a small stream and rolled over and over until he lay panting half in and half out of the murmuring water. Encumbered by weeds, he struggled to shed his parachute and loosen the grenades circling his waist.

Paratroopers higher on the bank were already speeding past him, but they seemed to be members of other outfits. He recognized no one from the 121st as he stumbled to his feet and began to climb. Orders were to move forward with all possible speed, and he joined the anonymous runners.

He had twisted one ankle in landing, but the stabs of pain from it were not enough to slow him. Machine guns opened up ahead, jabbering like berserk demons, and shadow figures in the lead spun and crumbled grotesquely. Shane flung himself to the ground, hit the dirt already rolling, and crawled frantically out of the line of fire.

The stench of battle, and the din of it, engulfed him. The rain beat down on him as he started once more creeping forward. One grenade, and then another, hit the machine gun nest. The deadly greeting of its weapons were cut off abruptly. He smelled his own warm urine adding to his wetness.

As boys, he and Brendan used to discuss old Father Shaughnessy's lurid Sunday admonitions and ponder whether or not the Hell so frighteningly described was real.

It was. And this was it.

By shortly after sunrise, the attackers had secured the particular village assigned them for capture. What was left of its pitiful streets in the wake of the bombers still smoked with fites. Here and there a fragment of a still standing wall collapsed into rubble. The dust of destruction shimmered in the air, replacing the rain of yesterday. Through the drifting veil, a jaundiced sun seemed too inert to penetrate.

On sentry detail before what was left of a Town Hall—wide stone steps, twin marble column stumps shattered near their bases, gnarled wreck of a brass door sagging on twisted hinges—Shane watched the citizenry returning to what had been their town.

They crept silently out of cellar holes and from under the pyramids of debris. Ghosts more than people, Shane thought. They were the enemy. Their Führer had sought to set the world aflame. Their countrymen had sought to kill him, yet he found himself pitying them.

A woman who might be young, yet would never look young again, wandered dazedly past. The pinched mask of long near-starvation made her features all but skeletal. Her skin was the dead white of porcelain brought home by

Great-Aunt Veronica from Dresden before that city's famous potteries had been blown off the earth's surface.

Moved by her emaciation, Shane struggled with a deep and unexpected desire to offer comfort. He knew little German, only a smattering of common terms, so he spoke in English as she trudged past.

"Good morning, fräulein. Are you all right?"

She turned blindly, as inhuman as a moving form on a music box. To his surprise, she seemed to understand him. "I am alive at least."

"Was your home hit in the bombing?"

"This is not our first bombing. My home is now a tree. I live as do apes."

"I'm sorry, fräulein." What else was there to say?

"We are all sorry. No house. No food. No hope. *Ach, der Lieber Gott,* what is to become of us now? What have we been led into? Where can we turn?"

The sudden bitter outburst took Shane by surprise. There was venom in it that he had not believed could burn in such a downtrodden person. Until he had heard her words he had only half-believed that she was really alive. But now he knew. Crushed she was, like her village. Beaten. Desolate. But fire still guttered in the ashes.

"Why hasn't your Führer given up? Why have you all been reduced to this? He must know by now that there's no longer any point to it."

Her gaunt face twisted. She hugged the few rags which still served for a shawl more tightly about her. Could a body be so scrawny and still contain all the essential organs?

"Führer!" she spat. "Führer, Führer, Führer! I spit on the Führer! May he burn in the fire of the Devil. It's where the rest of us have roasted long enough!"

When she went on her way, moving like a figure put

together of sticks. Shane stared after her for a minute before resuming his measured pacing—back and forth, back and forth, before the litter half-burying the Town Hall steps.

What had been a respected building was little more than ashes. Ancient cobblestones underfoot spoke of centuries of strength and perhaps even grandeur. The hooves of horses carrying mailed knights to the Crusades well might have passed over them. Yet, on this wan morning, they divided only twin rows of wreckage which had been busy shops.

Shoes and harness had been the chief products of the place and doubtless this had been the center. Now the buildings within his view, those that had not been completely destroyed, were burned-out hulks. What windows were left in the scarred facades were boarded up and blank.

At a corner of the stair flight, Shane wheeled smartly and began his measured return. Faced as he now was, he had a panorama of the fields beyond the town—and the quiet sheen of the Rhine beyond the fields. Out of uncut grass, the arthritic framework of a Focke-Wolfe plane jutted upward like some barbaric tombstone. *Hic Jacet Hitler. Hic Jacet Nazism.*

Surprised at this, Shane realized that suddenly he was thinking of Desmond Molloy, back in Manhattan. It was men like Molloy—always so gracious about offering aid to Shane's infant career in politics—who really pulled the strings. Molloy had not held any elective public office since almost before Shane could remember; yet the power in him was unquestionable. If such men wanted things to happen, they happened.

Once the job in Europe was done and Shane was back again at the base of the ladder he itched to climb, he would take this up with Molloy, his family's long-standing friend.

Surely, that was the way to start wheels moving. How else could miseries such as those spread before him here be coped with? The tsars at the top seldom felt the crushing weight of their own juggernauts. But oh, how the faceless masses down below them suffered!

"When I get home . . ." The rest of it was lost in uncertainties. But it was nonetheless a promise, a vow, a dedication.

In his mind, as he paced, he began to compose a letter to Desmond Molloy.

8

Dangling from the jaws of Victory, or so Bernadette often nowadays fancied, she could see torn remnants of losses upon which the dazzling beast had fed. Death had become the master of some dull treadmill on which she plodded endlessly, doing her duty, peddling her War Bonds, and watching horror after horror snatch away too many of those she most loved or admired.

Her own Eamonn had been first to go.

Rugged, forceful male that he had been, he had seemed to his wife immune to destruction. In middle of life, he was still flaunting the vigor and staying power of someone half his years. War needs had doubled the output of his pharmaceutical factories, and Eamonn had been at the helm every yard of the way—building a new plant here, stretching the facilities of an older one there. The conglomerate he had joined as a younger man—his talents early recognized by his stepfather-in-law, Vincent Quinn—had mushroomed dramatically.

And then to have the one childish strain in him bring him low!

Since the very first days Bernadette had known him, her husband had been a circus buff. Let the name North or Ringling or Barnum and Bailey first flash across the amusement page of the *Mirror*, and the man could not rest. Nothing but war duty took precedence until he had ordered a box for the McHughs and friends at the advertised seasonal opening. He'd be out at the freight siding hours before sunrise to watch the show unload. He'd tramp through the dark city streets clear to Madison Square Garden, following the camels and elephants.

That July of '44 had begun so well. The family was still basking in the afterglow of Norah's simple wedding to Dennis Gallagher, who seemed to the whole O'Donnell clan to be precisely the right young man to make their darling happy. There had been more reassuring news from Liam, off in the Pacific, and Eamonn's successful conclusion of long dickerings to absorb a trucking fleet which would vastly improve his shipments to both coasts made everything look fine.

On the glorious Fourth, celebrated with special fervor, because the war in Europe was so obviously nearing a hard-won triumph, Bernadette and Eamonn had treated the whole O'Donnell crew to a celebration picnic at the place in Newburgh which her Cousin Patrick, now dead, had purchased for his bride Margaret in days when it was expected that very shortly he would become a United States Senator.

Even the sad aftermath of those golden anticipations had not cast a shadow over the picnic. It was almost forgotten by the converged O'Donnells that up in one shuttered bedroom of the mansion an emaciated residue of a once-regal Margaret O'Donnell lay unaware of their collective presence, attended by her latest nurse-keeper, muttering soddenly against her pillows.

Evaleen was proudly displaying her son to the others. Small Danny was well able to toddle and was possessed of an inexhaustable curiosity which had him into everything. Madge had persuaded her young man, Barry Sullivan, to accompany her despite his talent for eluding anything resembling a family outing. Jim and Sheela, although still exhausted from their daughter's wedding, had never looked happier. Even the bride and groom themselves—having just substituted a ten-day tour with their Starlight Serenaders for a honeymoon—were newly back in town and able to come up the Hudson with the others.

"A marvelous occasion!" Those were Eamonn's words for it as he drove Bernadette back across Bear Mountain Bridge on their return to the city.

"I think they all enjoyed it," Bernadette agreed. "Considering how many of us are still scattered to the four winds—Liam, Shane, Brendan."

"It's a pity to see the holiday ending," Eamonn said as he swung their car into the southbound lane of Route 9. "We haven't taken even a mock vacation since Pearl Harbor, honey. What do you say we sneak a bit of one now? Nothing spectacular. Just a mini-week together."

Her eyes lit at the thought. "What had you in mind?"

"The circus hits Hartford two days from now. We could just laze around the apartment tomorrow, go out for dinner somewhere romantic and maybe have a dance together. Then on the sixth we might sneak off to Connecticut and catch the Greatest Show on Earth again."

"You not having laid eye on it since March, when it

played Manhattan?'' Bernadette jeered good-naturedly.
''When will you ever grow up, McHugh?''

''Who wants to?'' he challenged. ''I'm doing fine being
a teenager, thanks.''

''It's a pure miracle you didn't grow up on the high
trapeze or putting the lions and tigers through their paces.
Did you truly never run off with the circus, in your school
days?''

''Never even once, I hadn't the talent, or maybe the
daring. And I hadn't the brawn to get work as a roustabout.
No future ahead of me whatsoever.''

''You haven't done so badly, considering your sad lack
of qualifications.''

''Ah, well. A man's ambitions change. What do you
say about our playing hookey, lady?''

Bernadette had her business-like self back under control
by now. ''You know I have that speech to give in Dallas
on the sixth. It's too big to ditch, Mr. McHugh.''

''The war's already won, Bernie. We rate a little time
off, just to be *us*.''

''The war's not won until that murderous Hitler comes
crawling on his knees to beg an armistice, and well you
know it. You wouldn't be gamboling off now if the truck
deal weren't firmly signed, sealed and delivered. I'd love
it, Eamonn, but I can't.''

He accepted her decision with only a sigh. ''I tell you
what. Let's split the difference, then. Tomorrow we'll
share. I'll put you safe on your plane at the end of it.''

''And you'll sneak up to Hartford and watch the clowns
and the trained bear act. I wish I *could* go along, I
honestly do. If only to buy you your pink spun sugar
goodies, Infant.''

So they'd had their July Fifth together; romantic dinner,
reminiscent dance at the Rainbow Room, and all. True to

his word, and with no further attempt to dissuade her from what she saw as her duty, Eamonn had ushered her aboard the Dallas plane early the next morning.

The speech had been a fund-raising success of impressive proportions. Oil wells had lately been coming through in the area with increasing frequency and her audience included several drillers with patriotic money in their dungarees. She had gone to bed at the hotel exhausted but satisfied. Not until the next morning, when a bellhop delivered a newspaper along with her coffee and croissants, did she discover she was a widow.

FIRE DESTROYS CIRCUS BIG TOP IN HARTFORD 168 DEAD.

The smaller print undulated before her disbelieving eyes as she read on. The sudden flames . . . the crashing canvas . . . the screams . . . the stampede . . . the horror . . .

Much further along, part of the runover on an inside page, came her real horror:

> Among bodies recovered was that of prominent industrialist Eamonn McHugh, said to have been in the city expressly to attend the performance. An outstanding figure in war-relief circles as well as in the pharmaceutical world, Mr. McHugh's widely recognized contribution to the war effort. . . .

The paper, sliding from Bernadette's hand, overturned the tray. She clawed aside the coffee-soaked bedding and dashed for the bathroom door. She was miserably sick.

"Eamonn . . . my darling . . . Eamonn . . ." It was an absurd place to say goodbye to her love, down on her knees on the tiles in front of a toilet. The little boy at the circus. Oh, God, the wide-eyed little boy.

*   *   *

There had been many mortal shocks before and since. The deaths stretched back to her mother's sudden crushing at Great Oak on to the killing of sons of O'Donnell friends during the unexpected last savage German flare-up at the Battle of the Bulge. But, at least thus far, no O'Donnells had been killed in battle. No Liam. No Shane or Brendan— although lately there had been no word whatever of Brendan, off somewhere in the trenches, and Jim and Sheela were growing uneasy.

But again, the purveyors of the passing scene had done it to her once more.

She had missed the first scattered advance reports on the radio. She seldom dared flick on the news shows these days, rather, she would wait in dread for disaster to seek her out. Tragedy was never shy about making itself known.

Today was no exception. She sat at her desk overlooking Sutton Place's select passing traffic, writing the requisite family note of congratulations to Sheela on her coming birthday—and abruptly there was Madge in the doorway, *Times* trembling in hand.

"Mamma, haven't you heard? It's been on the street for a couple of hours."

The dragon of fear chained inside Bernadette stirred, growled. "What has, darling?"

"He's dead. The President is dead. A massive cerebral hemorrhage."

Words from the crumpled front page sprang across the sunny room, their huge type obliterating distance. *ROOSEVELT SUCCUMBS* . . . The rest of it was hidden. There need be no "rest". The essential fact, and Madge's face, were more than enough.

Bernadette half rose to her feet, then sank back slowly into her desk chair.

A mass of memories swept over her, as relentless as lava from an erupting volcano. The sweeping election campaigns in which she and Veronica had played their notable, if local, roles, the buoyant, reassuring voice of the Fireside Chats, the tilt of the cigarette holder that had become so familiar through newsreels and front-page photographs. Even that silly little dog called Fala, whom he seemed to cherish. *"Nothing to fear but Fear itself . . ."*

"Mamma! You look awful! Shall I get you something?"

"Nothing, Madge, thanks. I'll be quite all right in a moment."

But would she be? Ever again? She peered down at her hands and they were a stranger's, agitated by the tremors of palsy. She looked up at the wall directly ahead and, although it was far from the largest object in the collage on display there, the framed photograph signed *With Sincere Appreciation, Franklin D. Roosevelt,* was all she could make out clearly.

"You ought to go upstairs and lie down for a while, Mamma. It's been a shock."

"No," Bernadette said, her voice low but under control. "No, I think what I'll do is go out for a breath of air. Just a stroll around the block. Coming along, Madge?"

"Barry said he might be dropping by," Madge said. She looked uncomfortable. Plainly, she thought she ought to be ashamed of putting such a matter ahead of a President's death, yet she had no real intention of doing otherwise. "I don't think I'd better leave just now, Mamma."

"I see. Well, I shan't be gone long, anyhow. Make yourself pretty for him, darling."

A light wrap flung about her against the April coolness, Bernadette let herself out of the duplex. Sutton Place stretched empty, as if dreaming of Spring on its way rather

than of national tragedy. She headed west, toward First
Avenue and then Second, walking briskly.

A few windows along her way stood open. Occasional
scraps of newscasts spilled from them as she passed. ". . .
*White Sulphur Springs, where a new portrait was being
painted . . . so close on the heels of his return from Yalta
in obviously poor health . . . messages of commiseration
both from Churchill and Stalin, the two with whom he so
recently . . ."* Why did newscasters, whatever names
they went by, all sound so endlessly the same?

On someone else's brownstone step, an old woman in
garments suggestive of a mission barrel sat sobbing her
heart out. Tears smeared her baked-apple cheeks until it
was impossible to tell which lines were tear streaks and
which were age furrows. She was rocking as a younger
woman might when she held a baby, and wiping her nose
on the back of an unclean hand.

At the corner of Lexington, two men with attache cases
had halted in passing to congratulate each other.

"Never thought we'd get the so-and-so out of the White
House, not even with a time bomb. Four terms, can you
believe it? Even Egypt only had its plague of locusts for
seven years."

"First time I was old enough to vote against him was
the Wilkie campaign. But I knew what was about to
happen to this country all right back when he defeated
Hoover. I tell you, when I first heard we had him off our
necks at last . . ."

Bernadette walked faster, afraid she might wheel back
and offer a comment. It was a free country. No one could
tell anyone else who to love and who to hate. But the raw
joy in those two voices set her on edge. No matter what
their opinions, had they no *decency*?

Poor man, whatever else he had done, good or bad,

however you looked at it, he had worn himself out with the cares and responsibilities that he had carried on his shoulders. The Yalta Conference alone would have buried a far stronger man, and he in his wheelchair. Before that there'd been Teheran and the mobilizing of a giant country for war, and decisions on all the strategies of waging it; there'd been co-ordinating his fight with that of Britain, of the Soviet. Who wouldn't have collapsed, even a well man?

She turned right, uptown, on Madison, intending to double back.

A shop carrying the latest and fanciest in lingeree also had heard the news. Long enough ago, evidently, to have provided time for a quick change in window dressing.

At dead center of the new display, a large framed likeness of the late President stared out benignly from its easel upon passers-by. Clustered about him, on wax models, on stands, on suspension rods, hung what might well be every piece of black lace in stock; panties, bras, filmy peignoirs, marabou-trimmed half slips.

Stopped in her tracks, Bernadette stared at the collection unbelievingly. A small crowd, similarly checked, was gathering. There were snickers. There were giggles. Only one voice, coming from behind Bernadette so she couldn't identify it, hissed in outrage: *"Disgusting!"* She hungered to applaud. But applause might be interpreted variously.

Walking much faster, she made her way back to Sutton Place. Upstairs, from her desk, she drew out a monogrammed sheet of note paper and a matching envelope.

Dear Eleanor, . . . She wrote that much and her pen faltered. These past two war years, they had become closely enough connected during campaigns and committee meetings and private consultations to have progressed from "Mrs. Roosevelt" and "Mrs. McHugh" to "Eleanor" and "Bernadette". But even with memories of her own Eamonn's loss pressing hard, what could be written that might ease the sudden desolation?

Dear Eleanor, . . . What in the world was there to say? Except: *I understand.*

The farm truck bucked down a rutted farmcountry road and crossed the Spanish border. Brendan stood where it had left him, looking after it for as long as it remained in view. Something he scarcely recognized as a substantial part of his own heart was leaving the wild, lonely hilltop with it.

Months could be years if one lived them as he had lived these past eleven; a year could be a whole separate lifetime. The European phase of the war was now ended. Only a crumbling Japan remained to be attended to. Well before that was accomplished, he himself would be gone from this remote mountain pass forever.

It seemed incredible that he might ever feel homesick for Andorra once he left it. When Brendan had first been transferred here to replace the man before him, who had been discovered by the roadside with a dagger in his throat, he would have disbelieved any notion that he might develop affection for this rocky scrap of nightmare. Now he knew better. He would remember the place always. And with the love of a native.

Andorra!

You could drop the whole scrap of a nation into the smallest of the forty-eight United States—small, spunky Rhode Island—and Andorra would simply disappear from sight. Come looking for it a week later and no one would remember where it had been filed. Tucked into the remotest fastness of the Pyrenees, with the untamed mountains of the Spanish province Lerida half-embracing it, Pic d'Estats towering westerly and France bracing its backbone, it was—well, the right word was probably *Nothing*.

Yet what a Nothing, after one knew it! Once one had hidden in its forest caves while determined enemies ransacked the town—enemies none the less deadly because they were never a proper invading force nor in identifiable uniform—one began to appreciate Andorra. Nothing became Something; something daily more precious.

Brendan had lost count of the hundreds, more likely thousands, who had passed through his hands with death and torture snapping at their heels—hotly pursued to the ultimate inch of French soil, still pursued as they were spirited up along the crags and ravines where only four-footed wolves were supposed to prowl. A dozen times and more he had felt certain he would lose one or another of his escape parties before he could smuggle them down the Spanish slopes. His work had been difficult, often bloody, because not everyone escaped the enemy. The chase, even when it went underground, would never cease until its quarry reached some free port in Portugal.

Now it was over.

Germany had collapsed like a great gas bag pierced by the spear of its own evil. Berlin lay in ruins. In his own pet rat hole, Hitler and his woman had committed suicide. Back home, the only President Brendan could clearly remember lay dead, and a faceless man named Truman had caught up the falling reins.

The world was far from being the world out of which Sergeant O'Donnell had quite literally vanished. But it was the world to which he would very soon be returning. Once again, he found himself thinking of Agnes—had she changed, too?

The truck, now receded to a faint motor throb in the deep gulch below, was toting with it all the army material which had equipped the tiny shack whose warnings and orders had been received and transmitted. There was little left behind but his sleeping bag and the small tinned food supply to sustain him until the truck returned two days later to start him on his own long trek back to civilization.

Light had receded altogether from the untamed valley and now lingered only on the higher reaches of the taller mountains. Brendan turned slowly from the road's unkempt edge and moved back through near darkness to the outthrust of rock where the shack clung like an eagle's nest to its cliff.

Doubling down to the dirt floor, he rocked on his haunches and listened to the silence. Andorra also could mean the essence of aloneness.

He must have fallen asleep, must have been dreaming, for when he opened his eyes again there was a sliver of moonlight gleaming along the sill of the east-facing window. Agnes was no longer seated here beside him as she had seemed to be, telling him how matters went back home. Brendan shook the last of a phantasy from his mind. He stretched cramped muscles. He froze.

That small crunch—was it a repetition of another like it which had aroused him? He knew from experience what had caused this one: the shift of weight as a cautious foot crossed loose shale outside.

Moving with the fluidity of an eel, Brendan was once again on his feet. He took a catlike step backward, which carried him out of range of the moon beam. Sucking in breath, he watched the battered door which he had closed only loosely behind him. Despite all the reports which had come to him while he still had a radio to command, perhaps the war—his war—was not yet quite over.

After a long moment the sound came again. Beyond question, a human footstep.

The loose shale surrounding the tiny cabin was there by
no mere accident. Loose rock, gravel really, had been
spread for a purpose. Through the months, Brendan himself had raked it over at regular intervals to keep it from
compacting. It had to give warning if anyone attempted to
approach with a surprise attack in mind.

Whoever was out there had reached the door frame. The
moon lay at his back, and shadows of his movement
showed through cracks in the planking. Slowly, very slowly,
the panel began to slide inward. Behind it, the man who
eased it further ajar stood revealed.

A silhouette only, cut out of blackness. It was listening.
Brendan listened too.

"Sergeant?" The whisper was so soft it scarcely crossed
the tiny room.

Brendan slid his pocket light from its habitual resting
place in his belt, positioned it, and flipped the switch. The
narrow beam pinioned a face like tanned leather, eyes that
could be bits of ebony, a tattered woolen poncho—and the
naked knife in his caller's hard grasp.

"Chombo!" he gasped in recognition.

"It is really you, then, Sergeant. I could not be sure."

"Come in, come in. What on earth were you doing
creeping about out there?"

"I knew there was someone inside. I did not know for
certain that it was you. If trouble were coming, I wished it
to be I who had the advantage. The chance was fifty-fifty,
eh?"

Chombo was the Basque sheepherder who had worked
alongside Brendan almost since his arrival in Andorra.
Ostensibly looking after his flock up and down the slopes,
the man was in a perfect position to smuggle arriving
refugees up to the crest. His reason for being on the

mountainside made him almost as inconspicuous as the rocks themselves.

"Who else but me could possibly have been here tonight, old friend?"

Relaxing against the doorjamb, the shepherd chuckled. "I saw the truck heading down, at dusk. You could have been with it. Then, later, a figure crossed the road and slipped in at the door. Who? I asked myself: the Sergeant?—Or a Nazi renegade?"

"Chombo, the Nazis are all gone from these parts. Their war is over."

"Perhaps. Perhaps not. Their great, bragging visions were always crazy ones, eh? Some of them must still nurse their mad fantasies. Until yesterday, they may even have hoped against hope. Their Japanese rivals might somehow reverse affairs in the Pacific and work a miracle victory for their Axis. So they hid, many in these very mountains, and waited."

"You said until yesterday. What happened yesterday, Chombo?"

The man grunted. "Did you get no word on the cell radio?"

"I had it dismantled and packed up, ready for the truck. I no longer had use for it."

"A pity. You would perhaps be parading your American flag through the town even now, joining the celebration, if you knew. Your President authorized use of a devastating new American weapon, *amigo*."

"New weapon? What new weapon?"

"It is called the atom bomb. Three days ago one was dropped on the city of Hiroshima. Today a second was dropped on Nagasaki. In their terror the Japanese have surrendered."

"Two bombs only? But for years now we have been hurling bombs by the thousand."

"This bomb is unlike any the world has ever seen before, Sergeant. When one falls, a great cloud shaped like a mushroom rises, and a whole city is nothing but a hole in the ground. A whole population simply evaporates—men, women, babies, dogs, cats, everything living."

"Such destruction can't be possible!"

"Even those from a distance who come with assistance, even they are doomed. The radiation is so great that the earth itself breaths death. No one survives."

The torch in Brendan's hand wobbled suddenly, fell to the floor and blinked out. Gagging, he sagged back against the wall. He was trembling as if from a fever.

"What's wrong with you, Sergeant? Are you not happy? You have won the war."

"Will God ever forgive us?" Brendan whispered. "We humans have poisoned his Universe. And I thought, idiot me, that I was going home to Civilization."

BOOK THREE

BERNADETTE'S QUESTS

9

In the midst of her own growing sense of isolation, Bernadette watched the increase of O'Donnells all around her with a mix of pride and ruefulness.

1945 was certainly the year of family blossoming. Liam was scracely back from the Pacific two months before Evaleen confided in her mother-in-law that another grandchild was on the way. Norah had already beaten them out on the schedule with her Dennis, and was plainly showing. And Shane and Agnes, quietly married within weeks of Shane's debarkment from his military transport in New York, were looking as smug as the cute little animals juvenile illustrators drew for their picture-books.

All of this was welcome evidence of the clan's sturdy continuance, but Bernadette wished that the ledger of happy mothers-to-be included her own Madge. She hoped that Barry Sullivan would soon give up his bachelor lifestyle and marry Madge. The poor girl did look so wistful sometimes, when the other young women of her generation babbled on about morning sickness and shopping expeditions to assemble layettes.

Perhaps she could sympathize with her daughter in a somewhat special way because she herself too often succumbed to feelings of another sort of deprivation. Bernadette despised the weakness in her, yet it too often persisted. Twice, she had lost the man she most loved—long ago it was Jack Sandford, and now Eamonn McHugh. It was far from likely that such warm closeness would brush her again, she being a matron with nearly half a century lying behind her. She would be by herself, in that sense for the rest of her life.

She was frequently quite sharply aware of this.

"The end of the war brought the end of my usefulness with it." Of late, she realized, she had taken up her mother's old habit of talking aloud to herself, as though she, alone, had a companion also named Bernadette in whom to confide her concerns. "Who needs me now? Just when I need outside matters to keep me too busy to think, they've up and left me."

Oh, people kept remarking about the busy, busy role of the grandmother—the joy of baby-sitting with the kids while their parents were out on the town having a ball. All well and good, but Veronica O'Donnell had not raised a daughter to believe in such fulfillment as a be all and end all. Her mother had died under a falling oak at well past seventy, yet Bernadette could not recall a single instance when the indomitable Mrs. Tyrone-Quinn had volunteered to coo over a playpen. She had always been too busy following her own vigorous career to think of herself as a cozy nursemaid.

"Which is exactly what you ought to be doing yourself,

Bernadette, my girl. There are no more war bond drives to exhaust you. So find something else."

Ever one to emulate Veronica, even to carry Veronica's projects one step further, she could look back to those years when her mother and Vincent Quinn had just acquired Great Oak. Reshaping the handsome old house to their liking, creating brand new country lives for themselves after years as city mice, those two had been as busy and happy as any two young honeymooners. No, Granny never built her life around Liam or Madge.

"Go thou and do likewise, Bernadette!" Yes, but how? Where?

The growing answer centered upon another house. True, she was alone. She had no Eamonn to share the adventure, but this did not mean there ought not to be the sort of preoccupation which had filled Veronica's later days so abundantly.

"Mother had political struggles to spur her, too, after she lost Vinnie, but she was every bit as fascinated with her labors over Great Oak. I'm out of the political swim, true. In New York, to edge back into that stream I'd sooner or later have to make contact with Desmond Molloy. I do detest that man. But a house would be different."

More and more, the idea grew in her. Sutton Place was all well and good—convenient, comfortable, packed with contented memories, but in the end it was rented turf. She couldn't to any great extent brood over the advisability of knocking down a wall to throw two rooms together; rebuild a kitchen from the floor up; replace a row of windows with French doors. What she called "home" belonged to someone else. A co-op committee really owned it.

Well, suppose she did make the leap? She could hang onto the Manhattan quarters for as long as she wished—while Madge needed a base, or while Bernadette herself was testing the waters to make sure she'd done the right thing. She was what Wall Street would consider a wealthy woman. Eamonn had seen to that, leaving her his shares in the medical conglomerate if not his own old role on the throne of the Empire. Whatever she wanted she could afford. The trick was, really, to *want*.

"If you do it, Bernadette, then where? What sort of Xanadu?"

Certainly not in Connecticut. Even so long after Veronica's death, memories of those green and gently rolling hills with their handsome historic Colonials hurt far too keenly. She could not even consider another Great Oak, nor any property that reminded her of it. Florida? That was for ladies in retirement, who had *really* given up the ghost. California? Build your hopes over the St. Andreas Fault and watch an earthquake topple them. Arizona? But she disliked deserts and was mortally afraid of rattlesnakes.

Someone at an otherwise boring charity concert mentioned Maine. Not at all like Connecticut, the woman assured her; which Bernadette herself remembered, from those wartime bond tours. There was probably nowhere else in the world quite like that strong, rough, rock-corseted coastline.

"You could at least poke about a little, Bernadette. Take a look here and there. What can that cost?"

She made inquiries as to the names and locations of responsible realtors in Maine, and very shortly thereafter put through a long distance call to an agent named Rockwell, who operated out of Kittery.

Otis Rockwell was a man of considerable discernment and even greater patience. From the first Tuesday she hired a car and drove to the Maine border, via Boston, Bernadette learned a respect for him which gradually developed into trust and liking. On subsequent trips north, in response to a note or phone call advising her that a property she might find of interest had just been added to his statewide list, those feelings deepened. And she was grateful that Rockwell was not a man who wasted her time—or his own, for that matter.

Almost without exception, every house he showed her had definite qualities to recommend it. The only trouble with them was that Bernadette herself did not yet know what she was looking for. There was no explosive love at first sight. There was no wild leap of the heart such as Veronica had described to her, when telling her of the Quinns' original confrontation with Great Oak. These were simply fine buildings, nothing more.

Maine itself, however, was a different matter. She knew within weeks that this was the place for her. After each journey to Kittery, her descriptions of what she had seen to Madge, who appeared to be not overly interested, were like those of a true movie buff attempting to get across to a neophyte the particular quality of young Laurence Olivier in *Wuthering Heights*.

"If you like Maine so much, Mother, why didn't you buy the house?"

"Well, it wasn't so much the *house*, you see. It was perfectly all right, quite handsome really. But I just couldn't picture myself settling into it. It's too, oh, I guess 'Tory' is the word I'm groping for. Too stiff. The place seems to wear kid gloves. Opera length, at that."

"The one you went through last time wasn't grand enough, as I remember. Too much like a fisherman's shack with elephantiasis, you said. Just what *do* you want?"

"I'll know when I see it, Madge. I'll know the right one."

She did know.

Without eliciting a sigh of frustration on Otis Rockwell's part, she had very nearly run through his available listings. York had given way to Kennebunk, Kennebunk to the Casco Bay Islands, Casco to Bath and Wiscasset, as they worked their way north along the coastline. Still, *the* house had not appeared. With every disappointment, Bernadette grew obstinately more certain that "her" place was waiting somewhere just around the corner. Somewhere. But where?

Then Rockwell's office called, asking her to meet him on the coming Thursday morning in Bar Harbor, on Mt. Desert Island. The death of the last heir to a substantial summer dwelling there was about to put the property on the market. Once others knew it was for sale it would not remain obtainable for long. True, Bar Harbor was a fair distance north of the area in which Mrs. McHugh had shown interest, but this house did seem her sort.

Her trust in the agent was by now implicit. Bernadette was where he had asked her to be at the suggested hour, an overnight stay in Castine at a charming little inn which overlooked the harbor and had once been a sea captain's house making the early contact possible.

Although the legendary name Bar Harbor—that summer Eden for many of the nation's wealthiest and most socially prominent—held a sort of second-hand magic for her, Bernadette herself had never visited the place. From the moment she crossed from Bucksport by the ferry, she had a dreamy sensation of being on her way to Samarkand.

Rockwell and his Pierce Arrow met the ferry. As he taxied her along celebrated Ocean Drive, his client stared out at the great swells pluming against majestic cliffs and felt a growing sense of recognition. Could this sea-sweep be like some special corner of Grandfather Liam's Ireland that he'd taken away from home with him? Why, she was *remembering* it!

"The house I'm taking you to is called 'Scrimshaw,' Mrs. McHugh. The family who built it, Foxworth, were old whaling money. Gone Boston social in the last few generations, I'm afraid. By then they no longer had to work for their livings. Prudent investors."

"I hope this Scrimshaw isn't *too* elegant, Mr. Rockwell. That's not exactly what I'm looking for, as by now you must know all too well. Remember, I'm third generation steerage."

"I think I do know what you're seeking, Madam. That's why the office phoned you when Scrimshaw came up available. Beyond saying it's in top condition, sturdy as Gibraltar, I'll not try to describe it to you. Just look at it as you have the others, then make up your own mind. That's your way, isn't it? And I like it."

When they reached the place, Bernadette was all but taken by surprise. The car turned in off the Shore Drive between matching gateposts of local stone. On one of them a metal plate, cemented in, said SCRIMSHAW. But it seemed they were then driving through an untouched forest of pines. Somewhere in the near distance, the rumble of rolling water could be identified. The shining air was a concoction of salt and evergreen. Unseen gulls were close at hand, for their raucous shrieks slashed the stillness with excitement. Rockwell heard them, too, and lumbering down the path beside her, he grinned.

"They've spotted a school of herring in the bay," he said. "Did you know that gulls are divers?"

"I know very little about the Maine seacoast's fauna, Mr. Rockwell. At least as yet."

"You'll get a fine vista of ocean from Scrimshaw's banks of windows. The open veranda was tacked on as an observation station. We follow the path right here, Mrs. McHugh.''

Not scorning the hand he offered to lead her across crude steps cut into the live rock sloping seaward, Bernadette moved along beside him. She drew a deep breath and the incredible perfume of the cliff filled her lungs. The path took a right angle and with no warning whatever they were upon the building that awaited them.

It was low and comfortably situated, looking not so much that it had been constructed as that it had grown there. Part log, part shingle, part stone, its ells spread out like wings in flight. From the spread of the rooflines it was not far short of princely; yet there was a simplicity to it, a quality of welcoming.

Morning sunlight dazzled the rows of windowglass. Wind off the water below tossed branches of the close-crowding conifers until they moved like the plumes of chariot horses. The gulls, wheeling down-cliff, shrilled vituperation. A marine bell somewhere clanged.

To Bernadette's utter surprise she found herself racing toward the low walls, stumbling on uneven ground. Her arms were flung wide. Her heart was hammering. And, incredibly, she seemed to be weeping.

"What deposit will be sufficient?" she asked as the Pierce Arrow idled back toward town. Mansions that might be termed nothing less than stately lined their route, but she was scarcely aware of them. "I brought my checkbook with me, just in case."

"There's already another offer in on the house," said Otis Rockwell, shifting gears for a hill. "You mustn't set your heart on Scrimshaw, Mrs. McHugh."

"But I already have! It's mine! I simply must have it!"

"We'll do our best, of course. I wouldn't have asked

you up here if I didn't think there was a chance. I know a few strings that can be pulled."

"Who is this—this pirate who wants to steal my house?"

"A rubber king from Akron. I don't even know his name. Someone in my Frenchman's Bay branch office overheard a scrap of gossip just before I headed to meet you."

In her adjoining seat, Bernadette turned on him with a savagery which might have better become her burning revolutionary son, Liam.

"I want one thing positively understood between the two of us, Mr. Rockwell. I am to have that house. Not perhaps. Not maybe. I am to have that house."

"As I just left off saying, Mrs. McHugh, we'll do our best."

"It better be a successful best, sir, or . . . or I'll . . . I'll . . . *I am to have that house.*"

Scrimshaw—she had decided to keep the name—required very little in the way of repairs to make it snug, and a house that was both spacious and snug was by way of being a miracle. During the weeks of delicate minuet-dancing before the Akron man finally withdrew to lick his battle wounds, she had begged Brendan to pray his best prayers for her. The prayers must have worked, either through an angel or the shrewd Mr. Otis Rockwell.

Never had a man more deserved his commission. To Rockwell's other sterling qualities Bernadette added, reverently, inflexibility. With his lesser representative, the loser hadn't a chance, but during negotiations, some skittish moments had arisen. If her champion had seemed to falter, she might have offered to marry him to spur him on. Fortunately, Rockwell had no such thought in mind— McHugh money or no McHugh money. He was devoted to his client's cause, but the devotion held no scintilla of lust or avarice.

All that first Bar Harbor summer, Bernadette lived in a joyful whirlwind. Furniture had to be purchased, or old pieces included in the sale price re-upholstered. But it was a happy few months she spent on her sudden merry-go-round. She felt almost young again.

"Mother's really pulling out of the blues for the first time since Daddy's death," Madge reported to Sheela, stopping by Jim's apartment to inquire about Norah's progress. "This Bar Harbor toy of hers is as invigorating as a new lover."

"The house in Maine; you mean. Have you been up to see it, Madge?"

"Not yet. I only know it from pictures. But a million of those, Cousin Sheela. Mother even bought a new camera and enrolled for a series of lessons. She *adores* Scrimshaw."

"What a funny name for a house. I always understood scrimshaw was something old-time sailors did at sea. Carving on walrus tusks or the like."

"Whale-bone, actually. The earliest Foxworth was a whaling captain, I've been told. The rooms were full of that old handiwork when the executors sold out. But the scrimshaw collection had been willed to a museum in Boston, so eventually it had to go. Mother was desolate for weeks. Then she decided to replace the missing with her own scrimshaw collection. Nowadays a German panzer division couldn't keep her away from any auction where carved bones are coming up."

Sheela smiled benignly. "I'm so glad Bernadette has something to spark her interest again. Eamonn's death was such a blow to her. Jim and I have really worried."

By October, when Maine was a bonfire of scarlet foliage blazing against serenely dark pines, the "settling in" had been fairly well accomplished. Bernadette had no thought, however, of facing winter on her proud cliff, alone in the colony with acres of empty, shuttered cottages— many of them as regal as late Victorian chateaux. The caretaker she had hired drained the water pipes and put up winter shutters—double ones on the side of the house facing the ocean. Bernadette returned to Sutton Place, weeping quietly all the way south.

The winter brought its own unlooked-for discoveries.

There had been the shock of Veronica's passing to outlive. On the heels of that tragedy had come war, and for that long stretch private lives had been in abeyance. Then Eamonn's sudden, horrible departure from her daily realm. And lately there had been the dizzying round of small missions required by the house. Now all that was over.

Yet the clock went right on ticking. The days each still held twenty-four hours to be filled, each one of them. The clan still loved her, but each member had his or her own paths to travel. Madge now lived in a little rented studio on the West Side, taking up her painting again or just possibly making love to Barry Sullivan. Jim had his music, Terence his clubs and theoretical good works, Shane and Brendan their very different fledgling careers, and Norah her tours with the Starlight Serenaders. Moreover, all the girls, with the exception of Madge, were in a traditional flutter over babies.

Which left Bernadette keeping company with a clock and a calendar.

Her morning mail basket was still as full as it had been during the war years, but now the heavystock envelopes contained a paucity of invitations. More often, they encased appeals for contributions for this worthy charity, or that urgent cause, all hopeful for a generous sprinkle of

McHugh money. Even the more exclusive fund raisers
seemed to have forgotten there was still a living Mrs.
Eamonn McHugh around.

"A bunch of thin-blooded snobs. Ignore them, Bernadette."

But the sting remained, however wisely she counselled
herself. An empty appointment book still stared up at her
from her desk each morning. The silent telephone still
mocked her. It had been her willingness to work herself to
the bone, not any other quality in her, that for a while had
kept the wheels humming. They had used her, not valued
her.

The knowledge came slowly. She acknowledged it
reluctantly. In common with the other second and third
generations of O'Donnells with whom she had grown up,
she had supposed that the family's rise out of meager
beginnings was a generally admirable progression and one
deserving respect. In this, she now began to see, she had
been mistaken.

The blue-haired dowagers with names out of Knicker-
bocker history had welcomed her to their committee meetings and bond-selling campaigns. Like her dead mother,
Bernadette McHugh had a proven track record for accomp-
lishment. But now patriotism no longer required acceptance.
The discreet doors silently shut, she was left on the outside.

As this new awareness seeped in, Bernadette was at first
only bewildered and hurt by it, but because she was not a
stupid woman, the bewilderment did not last long. The
pain lasted longer. It hurt to have to keep up pretenses
with those closest to her, especially her daughter.

"I'm off to the studio, Mother. I'll be home late. What
are you doing today?"

"Why, I'd been planning to go to lunch with two
friends I made on the last bond tour. We were just going to

get together and rehash old times. But I woke up with one of those nasty little headaches. I think I'll cancel and just stay home, Madge."

"Darling, you worry me. You never used to have these headaches. Shall I stay home today and keep you company? Maybe you'd like me to read to you."

"Don't be ridiculous. I'm perfectly all right. Just been overdoing things a bit lately, I suspect. You run along now. Get back to your drawing board."

"If you're sure, then. Isn't it marvelous to have the war over at last, so we can all get back to our normal ways? For so long we were just chained to seeing the fight through."

What sort of day was it that one had to begin with playing games, telling lies? Bernadette was not even sure that Madge really believed the pretenses. A forthright woman by nature, she winced at every fabricated "headache". Inventing other veils to hide a simple ugly truth grew thin as an indoor sport.

The real source of the trouble, as did the source of so many of life's major bumps, revealed itself in the guise of a small accident. A new show called "The Horse In Art" had opened at the Metropolitan. Intrigued by what she read of the prestigious opening, Bernadette pulled herself together one early afternoon and went across town to view it. Alone, of course, as none of the 'Blue Book' ladies who once had served on war committees with her had telephoned to suggest that she come along.

The show was well displayed. Bernadette moved thoughtfully from case to tall case, lost in study of their contents. Reading up on art because it was Madge's commercial field and she wanted to keep abreast, Bernadette had soaked up considerable knowledge. Her interest in what she was seeing was informed and genuine.

Here was a plaque of quadriga and a bearded charioteer, wrought in Asia Minor probably near the time of Christ; the galloping energy of the four straining horses astonishing, the determination to win of the driver unmistakable. Opposite this stood a caparisoned terra cotta T'ang Dynasty steed, contrastingly placid, its enameled colors exquisite, its subtle musculature exquisitely stylized.

A head-high case, deftly lighted, held a bronze cart pulled by two pairs of horses. The deliberately elongated proportions of the beasts' legs and bodies, grotesque yet graceful, seemed ultra-modern. Yet the card alongside them was lettered: *Greek, circa 750 B.C.* Bernadette had paused to admire them when from the far side of the case she heard some familiar voices.

"We need someone with a real numbers flare as our treasurer," one was saying. "I'd thought of Candace, almost asked her to serve, but she can't balance her own checkbook, my dear. She calls in her husband's secretary once a month to add and subtract."

"Why not invite the secretary?" the other woman was saying, but obviously in jest.

"The trouble is, nobody wants to do the nuts-and-bolts desk work. Everyone wants to be hostess at the gala, receiving guests in her latest from Paris."

"Julia! I've just had a thought. That woman who chaired the ration stamps finance committee, remember? She was smart as a whit and a tireless worker."

"Mrs. Eamonn McHugh, you mean? *Darling!* Her grandfather once lived in a cold water flat over a butcher shop on Avenue A. I took the trouble to check her out, of course, since back then we had to see so much of her. She herself was raised there, I believe."

"Still, Julia, she was terribly capable. She might be just the one we need."

"A little bog-trotter from nowhere? I don't think we're *quite* that desperate."

Bernadette's cheeks were flaming as she turned from the Greek wagon. The next case housed a strongly molded Japanese funerary war horse, again in terra cotta, with a card identifying it as from the First Century. She bent closer, seemingly fascinated, while twin sets of heels clicked off on the naked marble flooring. But she did not even see what she seemingly studied. A searing red haze jittered before her, obliterating the treasure on display.

Bog-trotter from nowhere! Something had to be done about this.

10

The pure rage of her afternoon in the Museum did not ebb, but as the next weeks followed, Bernadette found her anger crystalizing into something else. This newly emerging emotion was harder, colder. It even seemed to have elements of logic and common sense to it.

Those females on the far side of the display case had been typical of their breed. Not having laid eyes on them, she still could have drawn accurate word portraits of them both. They were arch-types of the same women who owned the neighboring summer places in Bar Harbor. The house she had bought and refurbished with such devotion was still, to her, perfection. But living in Scrimshaw was going to be a lonely business for any "bog-trotter". Mt. Desert's vacation folk were not exactly the democratic kind.

"Coming to Maine on visits," she told herself, setting it all straight, "isn't going to be the same thing for Madge or Norah or Shane or Liam, nor for their children, that visits to Mother's Great Oak were for us. We'll be isolated and left strictly on our own. The clubs, the parties, the casual droppings in—forget them!''

Unless, that was, the stigma implicit in those Museum voices was dealt with.

What made the women of that rarified social super-plateau feel so damn superior? It wasn't hard to figure that one. Money was part of it; but Eamonn McHugh's widow had as much of that as all but the very top few. Devotion to one's country or to public service? They'd have said so, no doubt, but for the most part they'd have lied. Berna-dette McHugh had fought for American victory as steadily as the best of them, and well they knew it.

No, what made the difference was the color of the blood in one's veins; the hypothetical color. Red was the right tint when a fight was to be won, but that changed after Peace came. Now, the nearer to sky blue the better. Turquoise, at the very least, was a requisite.

''I didn't fall in love with Scrimshaw, nor sink my money into it, just to have my grandchildren ostracized and tagged as pariahs when they come to stay with me. One snubbing like that and the hardiest of my lot would invent reasons why they needn't take a second dose.''

Talking it out with herself was the best method she knew for putting a matter into focus. Marching up and down the living room on Sutton Place, she did a lot of such talking.

''What makes them so high and mighty is their knowing that one ancestor or another—nothing *they* need take credit for—was a General or a President or carried some inher-ited title in some foreign kingdom. Even Germany or Italy is all right again, now that the Big Ruckus is finished. It's the packaging, that's all. The seals and ribbons.

''And the further up the tree the title, the snippier the

angle of the chin's set. A deposed King is aces. A Duke isn't much behind. A Count, a Marquis, a Baron—anything.''

It was bound to drop onto the fallow ground of her reasoning eventually, that little acorn from which a mighty tree could grow. In the way of acorns, her idea prospered.

"Grandpa Liam came over steerage, yes. As I remember him, he never did much bragging. But that's not to say we O'Donnells have nothing to brag about. Which of us has been back to Sligo looking into what we were there before the famine?''

Jim and Sheela once had gone over, yes; but seeking only for old music. Liam, the younger, had cared for nothing but the holy revolution. And the same held true for her Cousin Kieran, whom she still well remembered; and for Kieran's father, her uncle, who had blown himself to Kingdom Come while trying to sneak his dynamite under Queen Victoria's fanny. Not one of those American O'Donnells who had trod the old sod again had been in search of identity.

"It might be proved our line could trace direct to Brian Boru himself, or to the Earl of Kildare or the Earl of Desmond. We may be so blue in our guts the jaybirds would pale out white alongside us.''

The idea was amusing, but more than amusing. There was a new stir of excitement in her. A fiddler crossing steerage didn't give you much to hang the notion on, but suppose it were true? Suppose somewhere up the ladder of the years there sat just one of the sturdy O'Donnells who hadn't been quite such a bog-trotter as smelled bad to the grand ladies?

Her acorn was sending out rootlets already.

"High time certain matters in this family were attended

to, Bernadette. And who better than yourself to do the attending? Call it taking out a bit of social insurance.''

A few days later she paid a visit to Norah Gallagher to inspect the newly arrived baby. His formal name, when he was old enough to get to the church for christening, was to be Anthony, but his parents had already shortened that to Tony. On what Anthony before him had the same fate not fallen?

The apartment was small, but pretty, on one of the low numbered streets just off Fifth Avenue. Both Norah and Dennis were doing well enough with their popular dance band to afford a little cream with their coffee, and Norah would be going back on tour with the others as soon as Tony could be left in other hands. She was still as beguilingly pretty as she ever had been, now that her slim figure was returning. For Bernadette's dollar, Norah was still the real darling of the crew; more so than poor, giddy, spoiled Delia ever was.

"He's a handsome scrap, that's for sure," she said as she bent over the bassinet approvingly. "God help the women, once he has a bit more size to him."

The compliment was abundantly true. Already Tony knew how to look up out of his deep, deep blue eyes in their tangled sooty lashes, both inherited from his mother, and coo and gurgle and turn a visiting older relation's heart to mush. He'd be a devastation, twenty-odd years later and Bernadette wondered if she would still be around to see it.

"It's so good of you to come and look him over, Cousin Bernadette. Dennis will be thrilled to know you approve. He seems to be a little partial to Tony himself."

"And what right-minded father wouldn't be? I'll bring the lad a shamrock when I get home from my trip to the old country. His first whiff of Ireland."

Norah's eyes widened. "You're going abroad, Cousin Bernadette? To Ireland? Really."

"A week from next Thursday, darling, on the new Cunarder. I haven't talked it up with the others yet, my plans being unsettled, but you might spread word for me."

"But how exciting! Buddy Disston is always talking about taking our band overseas, now travel is safe again. But I don't suppose it will happen. Oh, Cousin Bernadette, *Ireland!* If I could ever hear the music sung the way it was born to be sung!"

"Spoken like your father's true daughter. You'll be there some day, Norah. But it's my turn first. Maybe you and Dennis will be taking Tony."

"None of us suspected you'd be going. What made you decide so suddenly?"

Bernadette turned her face to the bassinet again. She was never very good at masks.

"Just a sort of business thing. Something that needs looking into. I'll likely be back before anyone has time to miss me."

Being the woman Veronica had trained and the one whom businessman Eamonn McHugh had married, Bernadette did not leave home without first firming up details at the other end. The most competent travel agent Eamonn's old office could locate for her arranged her coming. In Sligo, a local family named Lynch took in paying guests. Aside from the Imperial at the center of town, which was nearly two centuries old, there was no Sligo hotel he would recommend. Aside from this, Bernadette had a feeling she would do better with a less formal place. A private family might be prone to dredging up leftover gossip, once they found their guest was an O'Donnell.

Eamonn's deferential agent prepared her in every other way possible.

"You'll find the weather chancey along the west coast where you're visiting, Mrs. McHugh. Forty degrees Fahrenheit is as cold as you'll encounter, but the rain is a caution. Be sure you take light rain gear with you. And carry it along on your rambles, no matter how blue the sky is when you start out."

"And aside from that?"

"Take what you'd wear here for a November chill with moisture in the air."

"And what about transportation once I'm there, Mr. Barsotti?"

"If you plan to be driving about yourself, Ma'am, you can rent an economical vehicle in Dublin for the rest of your journey. If you plan to explore the Sligo country afoot, it's three hours and a little from Dublin by bus or train."

So Bernadette arrived in the country that Grandpa Liam had deserted, her suitcases packed with tweed suits and her head as organized as it could be ahead of time. She did indeed hire one of the small Dublin cars Barsotti had recommended, and drove the rest of the way. There was no time for any feelings of loneliness and not since the day of her first acquaintance with Scrimshaw had she felt this young, suspenseful eagerness surge within her.

"The mountains there are purple," she could remember her grandfather telling her when she was a child and her mother took her to call on him. And purple indeed they were. Lying in the distance, drawing ever nearer, they seemed indescribable in their capes of heather. Beyond waited the craggy coastline and the deep inlets of Sligo Bay, and almost before she was prepared for it, the bustling little town itself lay in view. Her foot on the petrol instinctively increased its pressure.

Something about the busy shopping center at the core of the ancient huddle of buildings seemed to reach out to her and draw her in. Sligo was built along both banks of the shimmering Garavogue river. The streets were narrow and handled streams of one-way traffic.

The tourist office stood on Stephen Street. She found it with no difficulty and the pleasant clerk on duty was happy to provide any information she requested, and, if wanted, a good bit more.

"Sure, Dunlavin Grange—that's the Lynch place, Madam. It's no great distance from here at all. You take the main road on past town and make a turn just beyond toward Ben Bulben. That's the fine distant mountain you must have noted on your way in, Ben Bulben is. Past your turn, the Grange lies at the foot of the first real rise."

"Thank you very much." She said as she turned toward the door.

But the young man seemed unwilling to let her depart with so little information. "Will you be stopping with us for a good stay, Madam, or are you just passing through?"

"I'll be in Sligo for a while. I don't yet know quite how long."

"Likely, you've heard the beauties of the region touted, else you'd not be intending a worthwhile pause. Most folk coming this way are en route either toward Donegal or Connemara. But Sligo has its own allurements. We ain't to be passed lightly by. Sligo is Yeats country, Madam. Did you know about that?"

"William Butler Yeats, the poet? My grandfather used to read about him when Yeats was only a rising youngster. He took great pride in the man's success."

"Then your grandfather was a Sligo man? Were you raised with us also?"

"Grandfather came to America during the Famine. None of us has been back to Sligo since, though some have touched base in Ireland. I'm the first."

"And more than welcome surely. Might I inquire the name?"

"My own? It's McHugh. But Grandfather was an O'Donnell. Liam O'Donnell."

"Fancy that, now!" The young man, whose own oddly-spelled name, from a small sign on his desk, appeared to be Micheál Hanifin, beamed upon her. "There's still O'Donnells to be found scattered over the countryside like confetti. Some few even christened Liam."

Bernadette's breath caught. "How have the kin Grandfather left behind here fared since he went away? Are any of them prosperous? Even . . . well, top of the ladder?"

"I'll tell you for sure, you've no cause to feel shame for the name. But top of the ladder, now? That depends. Our O'Donnells are mostly honest folk and hard workers. Farming. Fishing. A school teacher here and there. The souvenir shop down the block is run by Nellie O'Donnell. You'll find your kin respected and clean. They'll admire to welcome you."

It was not exactly what she had come over to Ireland to hear, but Bernadette left the tourist office not altogether disheartened. She had not expected the ghost of King Brian Boru to be awaiting her with keys to the ancestral castle, yet this didn't mean that somewhere in the line she'd not unearth a Sir or an Honorable. As she drove out of the town, she found herself with plenty to ponder.

Hanifin's directions were as easy to follow as they had been explicit. Dunlavin Grange stood so precisely where he had said it would that one could not possibly miss it. It was a random-looking structure, most of it two stories tall and put together with rough fieldstone. In sections, grey stucco had been slapped over the rocks. A short lane led to it, lined at both rims with neat stone fences. Beyond these low barriers spread rugged pasture land. The signs all suggested that Lynch was a working farmer as well as host of a hostelry.

She parked to one side of the lane and jerked at the bell-pull. After a moment her summons was answered by a smiling girl with carrot braids. She was shy enough to keep her bright blue eyes downcast and her voice was as soft as the stack of freshly laundered towels she had to set aside before gesturing Bernadette into the house.

The upstairs bedroom to which the Grange's new guest was ushered lay along a series of connected upstairs halls flanked by numbered doors. Her own, eleven, seemed to be the highest number; which indicated the maximum possible guest list, although Bernadette had no way of knowing how many of the other rooms they passed might be occupied.

Number Eleven was not much larger than was required to accommodate a comfortable double bed, a wash stand and the armoire which served as a clothes closet, but it was immaculate. Effie Lynch and her two daughters obviously did not stint on housekeeping.

Having hung up the tweeds and their simple accessories, Bernadette drifted over to her window, and gazed out at the green pastureland that sloped gently upward. Her room was at the back of the Grange, and far up on the rise she could make out a male figure—John Lynch himself, perhaps—herding black-and-white cows towards the barn.

The mountain itself, rising out of humble beginnings,

took on a certain grandeur as it ascended. A symbol, perhaps? Wasn't it at least possible there might be a connection, a comparison?

She slept well in her snug quarters. When she came downstairs next morning to the big square family dining room, Bernadette felt as crisp as the day outside. Clad in the oldest but one of the prettiest of her tweeds, mauve with a touch of paler pink to it, she was ready for her first day's work in Sligo.

There were at least a dozen places to search in town—the County Library and Museum seeming to her to be the most promising. Liz Lynch, the second daughter, had mentioned to her while serving dinner the previous evening that the library contained a collection of all Yeats' literary works, his Nobel Prize medal, much of his correspondence and a variety of other keepsakes. It was, therefore, logical to assume that other local memorabilia would be on file there as well. No reason to assume that O'Donnell and Yeats data were equally regarded hereabouts. Still, if the O'Donnells were well rooted in the neighborhood, there might be some clues awaiting excavation.

The dining room's furnishings consisted of three round tables and their circles of plain wooden chairs. One table was fully occupied by the Lynch family. There seemed to be endless Lynch youngsters to feed, although the only one besides Liz whom Bernadette could identify by name was the eldest boy, Mickey.

The second table was momentarily occupied by a couple from Rosscarberry with their three identically spectacled small daughters, and a frigid-looking spinster in mannish serge whom Bernadette heard addressed as Miss Penny-pickle—a name which secretly delighted her. So it was to the third table that she herself instinctively gravitated. Here only one chair was already taken—by a young man somewhere in his early thirties, blond, lean, intense-looking and altogether resembling some rumpled, careless godling.

"May I?" she asked, gesturing vaguely toward a seat across from his.

Instantly, he was on his feet, around the table and pulling out the chair for her. Manners, then. The sort she never had been able to mold young Liam into, despite many an attempt. Liam had never once bothered to pull out a lady's chair, not in the whole of his life.

"Good morning," he said, with a smile which seemed to reflect the sunlight. "Are you staying here too? I hope so. I was feeling quite lonesome."

"I'll be at the Grange for several days, I expect. And you?"

"Perhaps. Perhaps not. I'm Cornelius Shaara, and they say if I work at it I may turn into a fair artist. So I'm on tour, so to speak, toting blank canvases about and finding out if I can fill them with anything acceptable."

"And that brings you here?"

"Sligo is very paintable."

Bernadette warmed instantly to his almost puppylike friendliness. "You're really an artist, are you? How interesting. So is my daughter, Madge, back home in America."

His innocent blue eyes widened in disbelief. "But you can't be old enough to have a child already launched in a career. It isn't possible."

"It's more than possible. It's an accomplished fact." But she felt a small surge of pleasure at the naive compliment. "Madge must be very close to your own age, Mr. Shaara."

"Tell me about her. What kind of work does she do? Has she settled on something?"

"She's primarily an illustrator. Mostly of children's books, since that's where the most money seems to lurk. But she occasionally works on projects a bit more ambitious."

"Has Madge ever painted her mother? I hope so. You have a marvelous face, Mrs. . . . . ?"

"McHugh. I'm Bernadette McHugh. No, Mr. Shaara, she's never done anything of me beyond a few quick sketches. But my husband liked one of them well enough to hang it. In truth, it's far from a finished work. I doubt I much interest Madge as a model."

"Your husband? Mr. McHugh's in Sligo too?"

"My husband died some months ago." Almost for the first time, she found herself able to speak of Eamonn's death as though it had been a natural thing. "In a fire."

"How dreadful! I'm so very sorry. Were you with him when it happened?"

"He'd sneaked away to a circus. He was a child about circuses, Eamonn was. Perhaps your papers carried the story of the fire. It was a major disaster."

Shaara nodded sadly. "I do recall the tragedy. It was in an American city called Hartbury, wasn't it? Did you and Mr. McHugh live there, then?"

"The city is Hartford, and no, we didn't live there. We're New Yorkers. Eamonn had slipped off to his beloved Big Top the night it . . . it . . . ."

"You needn't talk about it, really. I can see how it upsets you. I shouldn't have been so snoopy, popping all those impertinent questions. Forgive me for asking."

"There's no need to apologize, Mr. Shaara. How could you have known?"

"When you mentioned your husband's name, a lot more of the fire story came back to me. Was he the McHugh who headed that American pharmacology outfit? McHugh is a brand name in medicines even over here in Ireland."

"We're the same McHughs, yes. But Madge hopes to make us known as the Madge McHughs."

Liz, arriving with a breakfast tray, briefly interrupted them. The meal set before Bernadette was of a heartiness she had not encountered for many a year; creamy porridge, brown bread thick with marmalade, delectable scrambled eggs, strong Irish tea. For a few exotic moments her attention was sidetracked from Cornelius Shaara.

But not for long. As Bernadette finished her last delicious mouthful and set down her fringed linen napkin, she discovered that the young man across the table had not really turned his green gaze—yes, green and not blue as she had thought at first—from her. He sat studying her closely, yet not unpleasantly. The artist making the assessments of his calling, she told herself. She had seen Madge similarly analytical.

Shaara grew aware that she had caught him out in his preoccupation, and had the grace to flush. "Sorry, Mrs. McHugh. I don't wish to seem rude."

"I'm not in the least offended, but I can't make all that fascinating a subject for the brush, and much less now than when Madge sketched me. Few women profit from the passing of time."

"You have, I think," he said, buttering his own last scrap of brown bread. And then, as if aware that further comment on the subject might indeed give offense, he veered to other matters. "You're staying on in Sligo for a good while, I hope? And here at the Grange?"

"It depends. I'm here doing some research. I don't know how long it will take."

"Research. That sounds like the business of an author. Are you one?"

"Not in the least. My family comes from hereabouts. I'm curious to find out who they were and are. I'm told the Sligo Library has extensive local records."

"That's where you're headed this fine morning, is it? With a sky like that one outside the window, what a pity to bury yourself in dull archives."

"If I find what I'm looking for, Mr. Shaara, the archives won't seem in the least dull."

He smiled naively. "I wish you'd call me Cornelius. 'Mister' sounds so depressingly formal. And I hope we're going to be friends."

"I hope so, too—Cornelius." Bernadette pushed back her chair.

Instantly, he was on his feet again. Fleetingly, she wondered how his mother had managed to teach him such manners.

"I can't remember when I've enjoyed a breakfat more, Bernadette." Her name slipped from him so easily that neither of them took much notice of it. "I only wish you were coming along with me, instead of heading in to town on your dusty chores."

"Where are you going that would improve me more than the library?"

"I'm going up the mountain to paint. Will you join me?"

"No," she said firmly, smiling as she said it. "But thank you."

All the way into Sligo, guiding her rented car around the ruts in John Lynch's back-country lane, she half regretted her decision. Cornelius Shaara was an uncommonly attractive young man. She liked him. More than once during her morning hours with stacks of crumbling old records, green eyes and golden hair came to mind.

She had learned that one O'Donnell at the beginning of the last century had indeed risen to the office of Reeve in this county, but that was considerably less than a Lordship, and his small glory was balanced against another O'Donnell who had been hung for stealing cattle.

She wondered what Cornelius might be painting, up on the mountainside.

11

On the following morning, Bernadette's "No" was considerably less authoritative than her first one, and by the third morning, with most of the pertinent Sligo records examined, she decided to join him.

But this third morning was not the crystalline concoction their first breakfast had ushered in. Clouds like layers of grey chiffon enrobed the peak where Cornelius had climbed to paint. In tatters the ghostly garment drooped down the stone ribs and drifted restlessly in every gully. As she dressed to join him in the dining room, Bernadette heard the brisk patter of rain on the roof. The sound was like that of leprechauns dancing a reel across the shingles.

"No mountaintops today," Cornelius bemoaned, when they were seated as usual at the corner table. "My canvas would sog."

"It's a day for indoors. What a pity my indoors search in Sligo is finished."

Cornelius lifted his gilt mane, one strand of it persisted in tumbling down over his square forehead, making him seem even younger than he claimed to be. "What next?"

"I haven't quite decided. Several items I've seen indicate that my O'Donnell branch moved here from the Dingle Peninsula. Perhaps I'll go there and root about a bit."

"Leave Sligo? Leave me? You couldn't be so cruel!"

"I'm sure you'll survive, Cornelius. This time before yesterday, we hadn't even a nodding acquaintance. My going would have no effect on you whatsoever."

"I'd be devastated, Bernadette, and I'm reasonably sure you know it."

The implication could not be seriously meant, of course. She laughed. "We both have our missions to see to. They come first, but I admit, it's been great fun getting to know you."

"What are we doing sitting here and talking about goodbyes?" Suddenly, he was infused with energy. "The important thing is that neither of us is packing to depart. You just admitted your day is open. So I'm going to make it mine. We're going places."

"In this rain, Cornelius? What conceivable places?"

"It isn't all rain. There've been smidgens of sunshine in between. The clouds may very well vanish altogether. Besides, we both have rain gear with us."

"You'd deliberately forsake the comfortable, dry Lynch fireside to venture out into that weather?"

"Wouldn't you, if it meant an adventure? We're going to have one together, Bernadette. We're going to discover the Lake Isle of Innisfree."

That was probably the easiest recognized of any verse Yeats had written. She knew it well. She could have recited most of it without prompting, and softly started doing so.

"I will arise and go now, and go to Innisfree,
And a small cabin build there, of clay and wattles made;
Nine bean-rows will I have there, a hive for the
*   honeybee,*
And live alone in the bee-loud glade. . . ."

Cornelius grinned across at her. "Good girl! Go up and get your rain things."

They drove into town together in her rented compact with the rain pelting the windshield. The weather was clearing a trifle by the time they had parked on Quay Street. The wet sidewalk had a satin sheen as they tramped along it, shoulders almost touching.

At the souvenir shop which Hanifin had identified as belonging to Nellie O'Donnell, Bernadette was taken with an impulse to send a picture postcard to Madge at home. While Cornelius prowled the piled side shelves aimlessly, she selected one, and scribbled on it with a pen borrowed from the large woman behind the counter.

I'm having such fun. There's a delightful young gent
name of Cornelius Shaara who doesn't mind chaper-
oning me around, and we're already fast friends. Oh,
darling! If only you were with me!

"The dock is this way, not very far along," Cornelius said, as they quit the shop together. "It's an easy hike for two healthy kids like us. Come on, come on!"

"What dock?" she wanted to know. "Why are we going there?"

"It's where we board the *Countess of Kildare*, Milady. Unless you've mastered the art of walking on water, we have to catch a boat to Innisfree."

The dock stood at the rim of the Garavogue, and their craft was readying to cast off even as they raced the last few yards to it. A young first mate, sporting a full red beard, pulled Bernadette aboard. She was still struggling to regain her breath as they began to move upstream in the direction of Lough Gill. A fine mist pursued them.

The *Countess of Kildare*'s deck was enclosed and she could carry some fifty passengers, but on this mid-week run not more than a dozen peered shoreward through the quicksilver shimmer. Leaning her forehead against cool glass, Bernadette sighed contentedly.

Presently, as the lough was reached, a taped lecture on passing points of interest began to blend with the throb of the engines. The voice seemed exactly right for its undertaking. It had a lilt to its rich brogue which sometimes suggested it was about to break into song. Grandpa Liam would have approved the melodious near-poetry.

The shores of the lough seemed almost virgin forest, cathedral still; and beyond the woods rose the mountains, shouldering sable sky. Having paid the Captain their fares, which he insisted must come from his own pocket, Cornelius quietly rejoined her. They stood side by side, watching the silver world of the lakeside glide past. Bernadette felt very aware of his silent presence.

"Yonder, then, you'll be feasting your eyes upon Cairns Hill," the disembodied commentator informed them. *"Tis that rounded promontory coming into view a bit off in the forward rail. History places graves of two great chieftains there. And underneath it lies what's called Tobermault. That's where in the bloody times of the Penal Laws against Catholics secret masses were celebrated . . . ."*

Bernadette glanced up at her companion.

"It's a whole other world, isn't it?"

"Listen to the Professor and you'll hear more snips and tags of Yeats quoted than the average ear can hold. I hope you're partial to the poetry. In Sligo you can't escape it."

"They treat him like some ancient god, don't they? And he's been gone only half a dozen years."

"They'll get the man home again yet. When he died in '39 in the south of France, he was put under the sod in Roquebrune. But it was Drumcliffe churchyard he himself wanted for his resting place, close by Ben Bulben. Once his own great-grandfather was rector there. In his last year, Yeats set down his own preference."

"Poor poet! His remains must resent foreign clay."

"Romantic Innisfree, when it was within sight ahead of them at last, seemed at first oddly disappointing. It was a little island, roughly the shape of a griddle-cake, and lay too close to the lake's eastern shore to seem at all isolated. It was not more than a hundred feet across, Bernadette estimated. A small spot indeed for a man to row to on private days and indulge in lonely contemplation. An odd island to be immortalized.

The *Countess* half-circled the wooded island and then dropped anchor. Lake water slapped lazily against the hull. The shore seemed almost close enough to touch, and the sense of peace was extraordinary.

"I think I'm happy," Bernadette thought. It was the first time such a notion had touched her since Eamonn's fiery ending.

The mountain behind Dunlavin Grange was called Knocknarea. It stood between the coastline crags and Sligo town, its flat top a keystone seemingly set in place to support the sky. Bernadette and Cornelius had decided to climb to the summit.

Deep in a purple sea of heather which lapped against her shins as she climbed, Bernadette followed Cornelius' erratic path up the mountain. He seemed to take the steep slope with ease, with energy and enthusiasm, as if leading a charging army. In his wake, she was panting. Usually, being with him thrust back the years for her until she felt almost his contemporary, but this scrabbling up a mountainside was making her feel her age.

She was gasping for breath as they reached the final level plateau where the monument had been erected.

It was obvious that the Irish notion of a monument differed dramatically from that of those men who had peppered Central Park and much of the rest of New York with equestrian statues. This Sligo monument, a towering pile of crude rocks that was four score feet high at the least, was widely believed to be the burial cairn of the legendary sixth-century Celtic warrior Queen Maeve.

If the legend were true, thought a winded Bernadette as she stared aloft at the balanced rocks which seemed about to topple, the dauntless lady had a great weight pinning down her bones. She studied the pile until Cornelius came to stand beside her.

"It's not much like Westminster Abbey where they bury their royals in London, is it?"

"Not at all. Are they really sure Queen Maeve lies here?"

He shook his head. "Who can say? The site has never been excavated, so they can't substantiate what's deep inside. But there's got to be some basis for the story. I've been told a crock of gold lies hidden close by the coffin. Maybe so. In olden times they buried Kings and Queens with their worldly possessions."

"You'd think someone would dig for the gold, Ireland being so lean a country."

"Oh, no! Anyone who digs here will die within twelve months. Or so it's said."

Cornelius moved a trifle closer. His strong young hands fell on her shoulders and turned her from him until she was staring out across the world unfolded below them. Bernadette could not suppress a low cry.

Those spreading miles at their feet were all green and gold. The majestic Ben Bulben, rose to the north so beloved of Yeats and thousands of other Sligo men. To east and south the countryside was a vast patchwork quilt of fields and whitewashed cottages like sugar lumps. West of them swept the shining trackless sea.

Cornelius spoke close behind her. "How many O'Donnells must have stood exactly in this spot over the centuries, do you suppose? Can you feel their ghosts alongside you?"

She had been thinking so much the same thing that her surprise made her turn toward him. Not since days when her mother was still alive had Bernadette experienced this sense of uncanny communication. Yet Cornelius Shaara shared none of her blood at all.

"Maybe none whatever," she managed. "They may all have been Lowlanders."

"I doubt it. The ancient Kings and Generals favored high ground for their forts and castles. The heights gave a view and the slopes a defense against enemies."

Abruptly, she was trembling. "Why do you fancy any O'Donnells shared the lots of the mighty?"

"Because I've watched you this past week, Bernadette. I think I've come to know you well. There's a seeking look in your eyes sometimes. Bernadette, they're what you really came here seeking, aren't they—the Kings and Generals?"

"I . . . why, really . . ."

"You've a feeling in you that some of those personalities were ancestors."

The challenge would have been impossible to deny. Yet she didn't want him to think her an idiot. "I guess it's possible. But I've found no evidence of it at all."

"It's here to be found. A man has only to look at you to see a throwback to a Queen or a Countess. Let me search with you, Bernadette. I think I might be useful."

"It's kind of you to want to help. But without any special knowledge of the O'Donnells . . ."

"Possibly I even have a little of that, my dear. Months back, I was painting in the neighborhood of Drombeg over in County Cork. Off the coast there's a lost road almost gone back to grass. I'd followed it afoot because no car could master it. The road ends at a crumbling wall with a stile in it, and beyond lies a ritual site."

"If you're about to connect that with my ancestors, Cornelius, it's no use. We O'Donnells didn't hark from County Cork. Not that I ever was told by anyone."

"Listen a bit before you cut me off. The site is a circle of upright stones, a circle maybe twenty feet across. Could be, it was some sort of antique calendar or a spot where sun-worshippers gathered. I've read since that archeologists believe so."

"But what could all that have to do with—"

"Deep in the grass, one stone had fallen over and stretched flat. That was why I took note of it. I turned it over. On the underside I found a portrait scratched into the surface. What they meant for a portrait in those remote times, anyway. A stick man, spreadeagled, dead-looking. A line meant for a spear jutted out of his chest. A crude crown circled his head."

"Cornelius, I'll ask it again. What possible connection . . ."

"I was intrigued enough to ask questions when I got back to Rosscarberry. Every native there knew the story of the stone, it seemed. An almost prehistoric chieftain had been murdered in the circle, millenia ago. Run through with his enemy's lance. And, here's what I was getting to,

he is remembered in local history as King Seáinin O'Donnell.''

Bernadette was still staring up into his earnest young
face, mesmerized, then the first splatter of rain slapped her
cheek. A perfect example of Irish weather had overtaken
them on their expedition. Caught up with the matter they
were discussing, neither she nor Cornelius had taken note
of black clouds gathering over Sligo. The ominous canopy
had rolled toward Knocknarea as if an invisible racing
engine propelled them. Within seconds, all vibrant light
was wiped from the valley. The pelting sound of the
downpour seemed to beleaguer the rooflines of Dunlavin
Grange, far down the slope.

There was no shelter here on higher ground except the
massed rocks of Queen Maeve's cairn, and the violent
downpour was upon them like a lunging beast.

Without thought, or so it seemed, Cornelius dragged her
down into the seething heather and fell protectively across
her. His back took the brunt of the storm, but savage rains
still pelted across her face and tugged at her loosened hair.

Frightened, she clung to him.

The heather where they lay seemed to shrink from the
onslaught. Bernadette felt herself recoiling in imitation.
No attack so wild had ever caught her this defenseless.
With an inevitability quite divorced from intention, Cornelius lowered his drenched golden head. She knew what
was about to happen, and so did he.

His free hand was already at the buttons of her blouse
when his mouth came down. His weight shifted, growing
heavier atop her. The rain's knifetips were pricking naked
flesh now, stinging her to a faint moan of resistance.

''No . . . Cornelius, please no . . . It's absurd, it's
wrong . . . we mustn't . . .''

''I love you, Bernadette. I love you.''

"But I'm so old. My son is your age, or almost . . . I'm old and you're so young . . ."

"Whatever age we are, it's the same age. Lie still now, my dear drenched darling. Be happy, Bernadette. Just love me back."

They still lay in the sodden heather when the hill storm passed as swiftly as it had arrived. Cornelius held her close against him, stroking her wet hair. Beyond his head as she stared up, the clouds began to fragment and splinter apart. The sun tore through like plunged knifeblades plated in gold. The heather became a field of unset amethysts, glittering, glittering.

"You aren't sorry, are you, my darling?"

She closed her eyes slowly. "No, Cornelius, I'm not sorry."

"And you know that it was right, what we've just shared?"

"It was right."

His room at the Grange was number Nine, with only a single door between it and number Eleven. Mercifully, number Ten was unoccupied. Still plagued by the ethics her mother and the Church had taught her, still unable to quite believe in the passion with which she had responded to his hunger on Knocknarea, Bernadette walked a tightrope of conflicting responses.

A respectable middle-aged woman and a beautiful boy scarcely out of his twenties? What kind of a union, in God's name, was that? It was a quintessence of absurdity. She knew this perfectly well. Yet when she so much as thought of never having him again, never giving herself to that rapture of the mountain, her heart felt it was cracking.

"Eamonn McHugh," she found herself whispering, as she lay in bed waiting for a light knock at her door on that first night. "Why did you go off and desert me, Eamonn? If only you'd not taken yourself away to that half-witted circus, none of this would have happened. Either I'd have stayed home where I belong, or it would have been you viewing cairns with me."

But hers was too balanced a mind to dump the blame on Eamonn. Her husband had been a worthy and well-loved companion all their years together. He had done handsomely by her, not only in material matters but also in the marriage bed. They had bred two sweet babies together; a son who died, a daughter who lived. Eamonn had not been at fault, nor had he intended to leave her unprotected to her own confused devices.

"Come back, Eamonn. Be here when Cornelius knocks. Send him away for me."

But when the light, eager rap sounded on her door moments later, she was, of course, alone, and nothing within her rose in her defense. Aroused by new needs—or old needs reawakened—she lay desperately wanting. Wanting a man. Wanting *this* man, young and vital, with the look of a mortal angel.

Wanting her lover.

"The door isn't locked," she called unsteadily.

It was hard after that miracle on the mountain to maintain her decorous American facade.

Without feeling at least foolish about it, Bernadette was young again when Cornelius was beside her, but she did not want the bustling, friendly, hard-working Lynch tribe, all so eager to please their guests, to suspect the nightly visits. She was determined to be circumspect, yet all too often she wanted to dance and burst into song.

When she wrote home to Madge, it was not quite possible to keep the suppressed elation under wraps. Things

kept creeping in between the lines which surely must
puzzle her daughter if they were noticed. Thank goodness
Madge was not fundamentally the noticing sort. What was
more, return letters from Sutton Place indicated that the
younger McHugh was absorbed in a problem of her own.

> *In fact, Mother, I have stopped seeing Barry
> Sullivan. I am still in love with him. I'm almost sure
> of that. But when I discovered he's been sleeping with
> this Lois Davis person and has been for at least six
> months, how could I let him go on coming here? No
> matter my feelings for him, there's fundamental pride
> to be considered.*
>
> *Oh, Mother, I'm so mixed up and miserable. This
> all must really be my own fault somehow, mustn't it?
> I've been so firm about our not going to bed together
> unless we were married, and Barry is such a physical
> type. But he really is afraid of the idea of marrying
> anyone—not just me. The days seem so empty without
> him. I wish the war were still going on and we were
> on patrol together. Is that wicked of me?*

What in the world would poor Madge have to say about
her mother if she even remotely suspected what went on
every night in Dunlavin Grange's out-of-the-way Room
Eleven? Madge with her ideals, and Bernadette with her
youthful lover?

"You must leave here soon, Bernadette. You're the
child's mother, wicked or no. She needs you, and that's a
mother's job. My own mother never left me in the lurch,
God knows."

Walking her little room, looking out on the slopes, she
tried to steel herself, but the other side of the coin was
Cornelius. Cornelius and Bernadette. What about *them*? It

would all be clear-cut and manageable if there never had been a climb to visit Queen Maeve's cairn. She could just pack her bags and go. But they *had* gone up Knocknarea together. The rain *had* caught them. They *had* lain down, embracing in the heather.

"And now how could you contemplate just walking away from Cornelius, Bernadette? Yet you can't dawdle here while Madge needs help. God, but it's a sorry business just trying to go from day to day and do what's to be done!"

Cornelius, apparently, had no notion of the rioting inside her. It seemed that if one were young and uncomplicated, the path ahead could be roses, roses all the way.

He greeted her at breakfast each morning with the same simple joy shining in his eyes that had shone there while he'd pressed against her in her bed, brief hours earlier. The only thought in his head seemed to be how they'd spend the coming day together.

"There's a pub on Old Market Street in town where they sing the old Irish songs like the hymns in Heaven. Let's go listen, darling. And after we've downed a pint or two I'll take you on for supper at an arcase I know off O'Connell Street. There's always a quiet corner to be found there, and I've something I want to say to you."

Bernadette rather dreaded that quiet corner. He obviously had some scheme in mind—no doubt that they were to take off together for County Cork or some such spot where the nobility of a long-dead O'Donnell might be verified. Having discovered this was her purpose, he was coming up six times a day with handsome suggestions to please her.

But at the pub where the songs were sung, he never once mentioned one of his junkets across-country. He seemed to be content merely to sit beside her on one of the long wooden benches, holding her hand with an imperial disdain for whether or not any of their fellow listeners noticed. The music was Irish indeed, sometimes lilting, sometimes sad. It put her in mind of her Cousin Jim. Like the elder Liam, Jim would have loved it.

Earlier than she would have thought, Cornelius stood up and pulled her after him and they were off to the arcase of the quiet corner. It was a short trip and they walked it. He never once let go of her hand on the brief journey. Whenever their eyes met, he smiled, but this apparently was not one of his talkative days. Silence seemed to suit him. The meal he ordered for them was an unexpected astonishment. Smoked salmon on crusty brown bread first, for an appetizer. Then a fish curry, peppery on the tongue and hot and satisfying. The cook turned out to be a true talent.

Just before the lemon tart was presented, Cornelius fished deep in one jacket pocket and dredged up something which he held out to her. When Bernadette saw what lay cupped against his palm, she stared at it in disbelief.

"It was my grandmother's engagement ring, darling," he said simply. "She loved it to the very end. Will you love it too, I wonder?"

The setting was gold, heavy and Victorian yet oddly appealing. The stone was an emerald, not very large but with quality to the sheen of it. It was the color of its present owner's eyes, which she had once thought blue. She looked up from green to green.

"I can't accept such a gift, Cornelius. You know I can't."

"Why not? The gold band that's to go with it is still in a safe box in Dublin, but they're sending it on from the bank. I've already written instructions."

"You mean a wedding band? Oh, Cornelius dear, if I'd

dreamed you had any such sweet, impossible notion in your beautiful head . . ."

"Why impossible? We've been husband and wife for a week now, Bernadette."

Darling, unthinking Cornelius! What was coming over this new generation? Why, he was as much a Puritan as her own Madge back home. Their ideals matched precisely.

"But, our ages, the generation dividing us—some day, some girl your own age, Cornelius . . ." she was stammering like a flustered girl.

He scowled ferociously. "Let me slip the stone on your finger. You're to be my bride, Milady, not my mere bedmate. I'll stand for no arguments. And as for our ages, that's pure nonsense. We'll not discuss it further."

BOOK FOUR

BRENDAN AND MADGE

12

A fellow seminarian loped up all four flights from the dormitory's reception parlor to inform his classmate that some young lady was down below waiting to see him.

"Young lady?" Brendan asked, looking up from the study papers spread on his scarred desk. "Who would that be? I don't have young lady callers. Only aunts and cousins, Tim. Like it is in that Gilbert and Sullivan operetta about the good ship *Pinafore*."

"This one says she's a cousin. For sure, she's a pretty one. But she doesn't look very happy, Bren. Her eyes are red and she keeps mopping her nose with a soggy handkerchief."

All his way down the steep stairwell, Brendan struggled to think who it could be. Norah? But she and Dennis were off on the road with their band again, leaving their adored Tony for the week with Jim and Sheela. Madge, then? He hadn't seen much of her lately, what with his studies and her obsessive painting at the studio; but so far as he knew she was dealing with her split from Barry Sullivan pretty well.

Nobody much was left but his brother Shane's wife Agnes, whom Brendan had worked hard to keep out of his mind, or his Cousin Liam's wife Evaleen. One of those two, then, surely.

Never once had he seen Agnes weep in all the years he had admired her secretly from a distance. She simply wasn't the sort for soggy handkerchiefs. Perhaps her very coolness had sparked his once devastating infatuation. Sympathy, yes, kindness, always, but tears, never. She took everything calmly. Well, anyway, he thought, she'd not call herself cousin but sister-in-law. He breathed a sigh of relief, because he knew that it would still be difficult for him to see her. It had to be Evaleen, he decided, who was no weeper either. Whatever had upset her—unless something were awry with young Danny or younger Ambrose—would have to do with Liam, her husband, his own cousin.

Liam had come home from the Pacific almost as much an Irish firebrand as ever, although perhaps a touch more mature in his ways of handling the blaze. Clearly, he had relished the violence of that naval war. Clearly, he still saw gunpowder as the cure for all such ills as Britain's unbearable presence in his beloved Ireland. Brendan had talked with him recently, the day after his mother, Cousin Bernadette, had announced her intended trip to Sligo. Liam had been writhing with envy.

What mess had he gotten himself into now, then? It had to be serious, or Evaleen wouldn't be after advice. On the ground floor Brendan turned under the parlor archway still pondering the possibilities when, springing up off the utilitarian oak settee, a slim female figure hurled herself upon him.

"Madge!" So Liam wasn't deep in debris of his own wrecking, after all.

"I just didn't know where else to turn, Brendan." Her thin hand clutched at his black sleeve as though it were a drowning person's spar. "Liam would only blow up like one of those demolition bombs his precious terrorists are always messing with. Norah's out of town and so is Shane. Ambrose has mumps, so Evaleen's quarantined. Anyhow, you're the sensible one."

"Not always. But sometimes. What seems to be the trouble now, Madge? Barry?"

She shook her head violently. "I don't see Barry nowadays. It's *Mother*."

Brendan was already developing the quality of comforting that he would need when he became a priest. He had begun that tutelage in Andorra's mountains, where imperiled border fugitives had sorely needed reassurance. His hand fell on her shaking shoulder lightly, yet at the touch she seemed to tremble less.

"Cousin Bernadette has always seemed well able to paddle her canoe without much outside assistance. Take it easy, Madge. She can't be in water too deep to handle."

"She's lost her mind, that's what she's done! She's gone completely crazy!"

Cousin Veronica's capable daughter? This wild collapse seemed unlikely. "Suppose we sit down together then, while you tell me all you can about it."

Sinking down alongside him, Madge still seemed poised on the edge of flight. It surprised Brendan that Tim Murphy had realized she was pretty. She didn't look that way now, her mascara streaked, her face like cold ashes, her eyes brimming over.

"There was a cablegram this morning. From Lake Leane,

somewhere in County Kerry. She's *married* the creature, Brendan. They're on their honeymoon.''

Now this was not what could be regarded as light news. Whatever the rest of it meant, clearly Cousin Bernadette had taken herself a fresh husband. And just as clearly, Madge knew, or believed she knew, some fact which made the union a disaster.

''You'd best fill me in on a few details, dear. Just who is the 'creature'? From the sound of you, he's a demon direct from the far side of Hades.''

Madge's voice, edged until now, went flat and still. So did her face.

''He is one of the most handsome criminals in Ireland. I've managed to discover that much. His name is Cornelius Shaara. He's a slimy, conniving, unscrupulous fortune hunter.''

''Ouch! Truly that bad?''

''He's known to have tried luring at least three rich widows into marriage before now. And at last he's managed to haul in his fish. Namely, my unsuspecting mother.''

''Slow, now, go a bit slower. How did you learn all this, in so short a time?''

''Oh, today's cable wasn't the first I'd heard about precious Mr. Shaara. Almost from the day she reached Sligo, Mother's been writing paeons about him. It seems he was a fellow paying guest at some Grange where they both were staying.''

''And he set his cap for her?''

''Without hesitation. He must have wormed it out of her right off how important Daddy was, and how well fixed he left her.''

''You actually know all this, dear? Not having been on the scene?''

''Very simply, Brendan, I smelled a rat. Mother's very

first postcard gave him away. She'd met this charming man, she wrote. Much younger than she. Close, in fact, to Liam's twin. He was being incredibly attentive, beauing her around. It simply didn't add up.''

Brendan frowned. "Weren't you just possibly thinking of Barry Sullivan, Madge? Transposing one man's flaws onto another?''

"Barry a *fortune-hunter*?'' Madge's laugh was short and sharp, bitterly mocking. "Barry always knew that Daddy left me a generous trust fund of my own, but he wouldn't have married me, not if I'd been wearing the Hope Diamond in my navel. Money doesn't matter to Barry. He wants his freedom too much.''

"Then he isn't why you took your scunner to what's-his-name—Shaara, you said?''

"Cornelius Shaara.'' She spat it back at him. "No, Brendan. It was Mother's praises. Clearly, she'd gone in off the deep end over him from the very first, even though she herself didn't seem to realize it. She needed protecting.''

"So you've set out to protect her?''

"Daddy would have wanted me to. It seemed almost as though that were the reason he left me my own inheritance. So, well, dislike it though I did, I got in touch with Shane's sponsor, Desmond Molloy.''

"Old Mr. Molloy? Why on earth him?'' Brendan's brows travelled upward.

"I knew he'd be the sort who could put me in touch with some reliable detective agency in Dublin. Politicians always know such things.''

Brendan studied her quietly. "And did Mr. Molloy oblige?''

"Of course. He never seems to fail, if it's a favor one of us O'Donnells needs done. Within twenty-four hours I'd hired the firm he suggested and wired them a retainer. I've had two reports on Cornelius Shaara already. Very detailed ones.''

The cheerless reception room, with its brown walls and ill-assorted discards of furniture, seemed to vibrate with Madge's anger. She was no longer tearful. The blaze in her eyes burned sorrow and confusion away.

"The point is, Brendan, what can be done with the information. There'd be no question of Mother's ability to handle her own affairs, no matter what witless thing she's gone and done. I couldn't haul this Shaara into court. I can't apply for an annulment. I'm not her guardian.''

"To convince any judge of Cousin Bernadette's incompetence would require all the proofs you could assemble. And then the intervention of at least a dozen angels.''

"But we can't just stand aside and let this monster rob her blind!''

"Are you really sure that's his intention, dear? Your mother's not without a great attraction, you know. Cousin Eamonn adored her, all their years together.''

"My mother's a darling. But you know her age. Her bridegroom was twenty-nine his last birthday. And she's the fourth rich widow he's openly gone after.''

Brendan examined his shoe tips. "It doesn't sound good, I'll grant you.''

"So what do I do next? Let him get away with it? I'll never do that!''

Unpleasant though it was, Madge found herself dialing Desmond Molloy's home telephone again an hour after returning home from Brendan's Seminary. As always when an O'Donnell called him, Cousin Delia's long-ago admirer was glowingly cordial. He invited her to meet him at the Pierre for tea.

All the way across town in her taxi, she wondered

whether her intended appeal were folly or not. His relation-
ships with her relatives—Cousin Terence particularly, and
just lately Cousin Shane—had always been cordial, even
devoted. Why, then, did she tend to mistrust him? Was it
only because Norah seemed to detest him so intently?

Or was it because of that night, back in wartime, when
he had followed her along her patrol route and tried to
coax Shane's military address out of her. She could remember having backed away from him and hurrying all the
lonely way home, ready to break into a run if he followed.
She had been afraid of Desmond Molloy, that night. Why?
What instinct prodded her? Surely the man was the
O'Donnells' good and proven friend?

He was waiting when she arrived at the hotel entrance,
thick silver hair just so, pearl grey suit immaculate, dapper
cane in hand. He guided her solicitously to a choice table
in the cocktail lounge. He ordered their drinks with a flare
which suggested he might be her most ardent young admirer,
happy at her condescending to a date with him.

"A most delightful opportunity to get to know you a
little better, Miss Madge. If I may say so, you've always
been the young relation of Terence's I've most whole-
heartedly admired."

Madge let an old puzzlement prick her. "That's nice of
you to say, Mr. Molloy. But I can't think why. I'm so
much quieter than Norah. She's generally the admired
one."

Was it only imagination, or had Molloy's eyes frosted
suddenly at mention of Norah's name? Had a glint of panic
chilled them? No, surely not; for he was smiling at her
now like the prototype of all generous, devoted courtesy
uncles.

"Norah is undeniably charming. And talented—oh, yes,

talented. But then, my dear, so are you. I've seen several of your gallery paintings lately. I'm truly impressed.''

"Thank you.'' But she had to look away. That flash of reptilian wariness had frightened her.

"And now, Miss Madge, what is it I may be privileged to do for you? An old fogey like me can't have inspired your charming call without some reason.''

She still could not face him. "I don't know quite how to say this, Mr. Molloy.''

"Is it something about the Dublin people I recommended? Have they proven unsatisfactory?''

"Not that at all! They've done a very thorough job for me, thank you. No, it's the facts they've discovered for me. Mr. Molloy, my mother has just remarried. In Ireland. To a man young enough to be her son.''

For the merest instant Molloy seemed to digest this. "And the young man is more interested in what Eamonn McHugh left her than in the lady herself? Is that it?''

"That's it precisely.'' She had to lift her head now. Across from her, he leaned forward, keenly attentive. "You know my mother. You've known her almost all her life. She's never played the fool before. This Cornelius Shaara has mesmerized her.''

"They can't have been acquainted long, I judge. Tell me about it.''

All the while Madge sat filling in details, she fought a miserable conviction that she was playing Judas; betraying her own and closest into untrustworthy hands. But once begun she could not stop. Her desperate worry fed on his listening.

"And so, you see, he must be planning to bilk her. All those other rich older women must have seen through him in time. Why didn't Mother, too? She's usually so shrewd.''

"The smartest of us can have our blind spots, dear

young lady. As you say, I've known Bernadette for decades.
She is anything but silly. This may not be what you think
at all.''

"I wish that were possible! I'd like her to be happy. I'd
like her not to be so alone anymore. But the man's record
speaks for itself. Four wealthy widows in a row!''

Molloy sipped thoughtfully from a frosted glass. "How
detailed were the agency's reports to you, Miss Madge?
What sort of description of Shaara did they furnish?''

"A most adequate one. He's very handsome. Thick
mane of blond hair which he wears in a deliberately boyish
rumple. Green eyes that look as guileless as pots of
shamrocks. Tall. The body of an Adonis. An artist, or so
he pretends to be. And he can charm the birds off trees.''

"That, I think, will give me enough to go on.''

Madge tensed slightly in her chair. "For you to go on?
Go on *how*, Mr. Molloy?''

"Dear Miss Madge, you haven't chosen me for your
confidante merely to hear yourself talk out your problem.
Of course not. You sensed that I might be the friend best
equipped to take action. And fortunately, you're quite
correct. I am.''

"In what way?'' Alarm flicked her, whiplash quick.
"You wouldn't do anything to harm Mother, would you?
Make her look ridiculous, I mean? Make her a laughing
stock?''

"Could you seriously believe I might? My devotion to
all you O'Donnells has been proven before now, I think. I
admire Bernadette, as I admired *her* mother before her.
There will never be a whisper suggesting she behaved—ah,
ill-advisedly.''

"How else could you break up this ghastly marriage,
sir, except by dragging her through a public scandal?
Courts and charges and counter-charges?''

Molloy smiled back at her. It was intended to be a benign smile, yet somehow it wasn't. "You mustn't worry your pretty head about routine details, Miss Madge."

"But I want to know what you intend to do, Mr. Molloy. I *have* to know."

"There's nothing at all for you to know that should fret you. Leave the problem in your Uncle Desmond's wise old hands, child. Give it no second thought. I guarantee you this cad Shaara will vanish from your life, and from Bernadette's, as painlessly as a bad dream at sunrise. That's really all that matters, isn't it?"

Brendan, too, nursed a deep concern over his Cousin Bernadette's surprising departure from intelligent behavior, but never in a thousand years would it have occurred to him to discuss the matter with Desmond Molloy. But he, like Madge, had his advisor.

Monsignor Harrigan, administrator of the seminary, was a man for whom Brendan had developed the deepest personal respect. Small, balding, pert as a chipmunk, his superior still seemed to the younger man what Shakespeare must have meant when he wrote the line "the noblest Roman of them all."

The old priest saw now in his rather threadbare study facing out on treetops in the close. Far below, clergy and students passed along the transverse walks on their silent errands. But the Monsignor paid them no heed. As always, his full attention was focused upon the matter immediately at hand. Deep-set eyes under sparse brows watched Brendan unwaveringly.

"So then, Brendan, it's a question of a possible annulment you're raising?"

"I guess that's it, Monsignor. I don't really know. My

cousin is usually a clear-thinking person. But this younger man she's married seems to have bewitched her."

"Bewitched. There's a word no man of the cloth should be using lightly, my son. It conjures up a credence in pagan things no one of us believe. But to the present point, does your cousin desire such a voiding of her union? Has she herself asked you to come to me? Has she tired of this second marriage so speedily?"

"No, Monsignor. No to all three. It's her daughter, my Cousin Madge, who's come to me. But I've loved and respected her mother all of my life. If this chap is really out to get his hands on her money—and, sir, there's a great deal of that . . ."

"Tell me the circumstances of the wedding," Monsignor Harrigan interrupted.

"I truly don't know them. She was off in Ireland on a journey when she met him. Two weeks later Madge had a cable saying the two of them were married. They were off on their honeymoon when Cousin Bernadette sent it."

"Then you don't know even whether banns were posted. But no, of course they weren't, considering the speed of the affair. Was it a proper Church marriage?"

"Cousin Madge wasn't even certain as to that, Monsignor. We'll only know when the two are back here. The message did say Cousin Bernadette intends to open her summer place in Bar Harbor, near to September though it is. She's taking him up there immediately. But they'll be in New York on the way."

"That doesn't exactly sound as though the bride were eager to break off the relationship, does it? Planning to go off with him alone and all but by-pass her family?"

Brendan sighed. "I'm sure that's a matter of her actually by-passing family censure, sir, not the clan as people.

She must know there'll be a furor, the age difference considered.''

"Is it a family's place to criticize the decisions of one of its competent adult members, then? She's middle-aged. He's not a child. Can't they make their own decisions?''

"If it were only the age thing, Monsignor, but if we have proof this Shaara means ill by her—and the record looks definite as to his true purpose with her . . .''

"Still, it is not they themselves who have come to us. Brendan, think a moment of this word *Annulment*. What definition does the dictionary give it? An invalidation. That is the erasing from existence of something which once did in truth exist. But this is not the meaning our Holy Church accords to *Annulment*. We must use it while remembering the admonishment of the Lord God Himself. *'Whom God hath joined together, let no man set asunder.'* That's what our Church remembers.''

"Even though one of the parties enters the relationship with indecent purposes?''

"Even so. The pledge they take together remains insoluble. The obligation stays in force until Death do them part. In that light, there can be no annulment in the sense a dictionary encompasses. When we of the Church use the term as regards to a marriage contract, we cannot mean that we revoke a valid pledge mutually given. It can only mean that for substantial reason there was no marriage in the first place.''

"Then Cousin Bernadette is chained to this—this adventurer forever?''

"Was her husband already married to another wife, Brendan?''

"I don't think so, sir. He certainly never hid the fact he was pursuing a rich wife. He'd not have done that with a legal one lurking in the wings.''

"One would think not. Then had he ever been married in the past, but had obtained a civil divorce? A divorce the Church could not recognize?"

Brendan scowled, trying for a sound answer. "I don't believe he could have been married and divorced, although he may have. He's very young for that still. If he's spent much time wooing these previous candidates, it seems unlikely."

"Lack of mutual consent, then? Duress unimpeachably proven, as in the famous case of the Duchess of Marlborough? Do either of those conditions apply?"

"Certainly not on Cousin Bernadette's part. Madge's postcards overflow with her delight in him. And Shaara, of course, was just as eager—if for a less loving reason."

"Then you'll have the Devil's time trying to pry them apart, so far as Canon Law's concerned. There are good reasons for the stand it takes on this. Ponder them, my son."

Dejected and feeling rebuked, Brendan closed the study door behind him and stumbled down the several stair-flights to the close. For him, this green acre had long ago become the most isolated place on the earth. Although others passed and repassed frequently, one could meditate under any of its ancient locusts far more truly removed from the world than ever he had been on a mountaintop in Andorra.

There was one tenet the Monsignor had not brought into their discussion; and as he sat there, Brendan considered it.

Ratum sed non consummatum. Could Cousin Bernadette and this fortune hunter possibly have gone through a wedding ceremony as some sort of lark, and then never gone to bed together? That might be cause for the Church's declaring the marriage had not truly existed.

If Bernadette somehow could be persuaded to swear to such a situation. . . .

Hope flared in him and waned. He called back descriptions of Cornelius Shaara that Madge had quoted from her mother's fond accounts. He remembered how the stunning cablegram had originated at a honeymoon inn. Lust after his mature bride or no, Shaara scarcely would have failed to pleasure her between the sheets. It took time to persuade a wife to make over stocks and bonds, re-write a will, alter title to a lavish Bar Harbor mansion and an even costlier Sutton Place condominium. Scratch *Ratum sed non consummatum*!

Someone had halted beside him, casting a shadow on the gravel path. Brendan looked up to find a secretary from the Seminary offices teetering over him.

"There's a telephone call for you, Mr. O'Donnell. In the outer office. You can take it at my own desk, if you'd like."

He arose, disinterested but dutiful. "Thanks, Rosemary. Lead the way!"

Whoever was tracking him down, it could not be for any purpose likely to divert him from his family problem. Cousin Bernadette's disastrous marriage weighed on him like a stone. Because he had always been warmly fond of her, because she was his father Jim's favorite among the cousins as well, because this mess she had brought upon herself was so ugly, lesser matters were not likely to displace her.

He picked up the receiver Rosemary had left dangling. "Hello?"

The instrument began to crackle excitedly. He had difficulty at first in making out Madge's voice in the stumble of words engulfing him like water from a broken dam. "Is it you, Brendan? Listen, something's just happened. I'm not sure if it's good or bad.''

"You've had new word from Cousin Bernadette?"

"No, not a peep. But listen! I called Desmond Molloy again, after you and I talked. I couldn't think what else to do, but I had to do *something*."

"I don't think you should have called Molloy, Madge, but Terence would probably disagree."

"I know, I know. Anyhow, I did call him. He asked me out for drinks, he called it 'tea,' of course, I being so young and virginal. I was really on the rack, Brendan. He'd helped me once about a detective. I just thought he might somehow help again.''

"Are you starting to tell me he refused you? And you an O'Donnell?"

"No, no, it wasn't that at all. He told me he'd take care of Cornelius Shaara and Mother would be rid of the man and I wasn't to worry at all.''

"Well! That sounds as if you'd landed in clover. What does your White Knight propose?"

"He didn't. I mean, he wouldn't tell me. But somehow the way he looked and the way he sounded—all velvet on the surface, all steel underneath. I'm worried, Brendan.''

"So am I, Madge," Brendan said, hanging up. For a moment he stood staring over Rosemary's untidy head and out the nearest wide window. Tree branches stirred in the breeze. Typewriters clicked and clacked. In the distant chapel, an organist was practicing a *Te Deum*. Beyond, city traffic murmured.

"Right, Madge," he said to himself. "So am I. If Molloy was like you say he was, I'm worried as hell.''

13

The bridal couple's Manhattan-bound liner nosed into her dock on a crisp Wednesday morning in mid-October.

At their high railing, Cornelius' arm around her shoulders, Bernadette had been watching the unfolding scene since shortly after sunrise when they had moved majestically through the Narrows. Staten Island slipped past them to the left and Governor's Island to the right. The harbor was alive with plying ferries and chugging tow tugs. Miss Liberty lofted her torch in steadfast welcome. The towers glittered with light from the east. Gulls circled and screamed.

"So this is your America!" the tall man pressed beside her marveled.

"Only one part of it, Cornelius. We'll be seeing a lot of different Americas, by and by. But the New York skyline isn't bad for a curtain-raiser, is it?"

"It is enough to take the breath away, Mrs. Shaara. And to think it's your home town!"

She looked up at him, suddenly shy. "I hope you're going to like it, darling."

"How could I not, with you to show it to me?"

The North River piers were crowded, a liner or freighter fitted neatly into almost every slot. Puffing fat beatles of craft shunted their own luxurious ocean queen into her particular, close-fitting resting place. Horns tooted and whistles pierced the eardrums. The long platform, awash with its crowd of greeters, lengthened beneath them.

Bernadette began to scan the nearing throng of lifted faces, searching impatiently for the one she most wanted to see—Madge's, of course.

The message that had been delivered at their Lake Leane hotel was the only word she had from her daughter since wiring her the glowing news. And that terse line had scarcely suggested outflung arms and trumpets of rejoicing. *News received, family informed.* Not much of an outflowing of congratulations. She hadn't shown the yellow slip to Cornelius.

"How do I recognize my new relations, love?" he asked, grinning, the pressure of his circling arm increasing. "Are they all folk as handsome as my wife?"

"I'm the family's Ugly Duckling. Wait until you see Norah. And my Madge."

"I'll be her stepfather, won't I? And Liam's, too. The thought's just struck me. Until now I've been too occupied rejoicing that I'm a husband."

No Madge in the waiting crowd below. No Liam, either. Bernadette prayed that Cornelius had not noticed her slight stiffening as he pressed beside her. Not one of the clan stood down there waiting to greet them, not a single one. She felt as though an unseen hand had slapped her. Just as she had felt a week ago at Lake Leane.

"Where are they, Bern? Point me in the right direction, so I won't be waving back to strangers."

She braced before she turned to him; to his ingenuous smile and the anticipation shining in his eyes. "Oh, Cornelius, didn't I tell you? We'll be seeing them all later. The men-folk in the family all have to be plodding their assorted treadmills by this hour in the morning. The women mostly have nurseries stocked with bairns demanding attention."

"What of your Madge, dear?"

Bernadette bit her lip. "Madge is, well, rather a special case. Being a painter yourself, you know how it is when something's tugging you to your easel."

"And Madge is into a picture too engrossing to let her take an hour off?"

"It's a portrait commission. For a sitter who can only come to her studio mornings before lunch. He's a symphony conductor, I think that's what Madge wrote, and has his musicians rehearsing all afternoon and concerts booked for evenings."

"I was looking forward to meeting them all." Cornelius shrugged lightly and bent to kiss her on the ear. "Well, all in good time. I've got the real jewel of the family right here with me, anyway. Come along, Bern. People are going ashore."

In a taxi loaded with their luggage they rode across town. Cornelius was like a small boy, staring out his window as the city spun past. He was intrigued by the crowded West Side avenues, teeming with their mix of nationalities. He was open-mouthed with wonder at the cloud-piercing summit of the Empire State Building. He was like an urchin at Christmas, taking in the glitter of Upper Fifth Avenue's glamor shops when the cab veered north on the way to Fifty-Seventh, where they would head east again.

"Is all this real, Bern, or am I dreaming? The city must be inhabited only by millionaires. And every block is packed solid with them."

"Window-shopping, mostly," she answered as she patted his cheek. "But it's true the avenue gets more congested every year. A day will come when City Hall will pass an ordinance ordering one-way traffic to control the mess. And when that happens, some way or other Desmond Molloy will find a way to reap a profit from it, though I can't imagine how."

Cornelius still studied the teeming sidewalk, fascinated. "And who is this Desmond Molloy?"

"A friend of the family. A friend of my Cousin Terence, mostly, although I hear he now is taking young Shane under his political wing. Myself, I can't say I cotton to the man. Nor do Madge and Norah. Nor did my blessed mother in her heydey."

"I'd detect he isn't what you'd call a ladies' man."

"Oh, plenty of women seem to admire Molloy, even now when he's well into his sixties. Maybe it's some lack in the female O'Donnell genes. We just don't seem to function on the same wavelength, although I've no real notion why. He was set to marry my Cousin, Delia once, but it blew over."

"If he's as powerful hereabouts as you were hinting, is it wise not to be friends with him? I gather that Terence and Shane don't shy off him."

"No," she stated flatly, trying to sound neutral. "Well, you'll doubtless meet Molloy soon, along with the others. Make your own judgment. And here we are, home at last, darling."

Showing off the duplex to him, watching his obvious

delight in it, dulled the bitter taste on her tongue during the next hour. She needed her happiness to counter her sharp disappointment at Madge's absence on the pier. The string of evasions and even outright inventions to which she had been forced, rather than hurt Cornelius, had not been the homecoming she had anticipated.

Granted, her mother's sudden remarriage must have taken Madge by surprise. Granted, she might feel some resentment at seeing her father replaced so unexpectedly in the big master bedroom. Still, she owed a little common courtesy; and courtesy demanded some show of welcome. Madge had no right to damn Cornelius, sight unseen. It was brat behavior. It was utterly unfair.

Of everything in the spacious apartment, Cornelius was most overwhelmed by the marble master bath, with its gold-plated swan fixtures and its draped shower almost the size of the entire number Eleven room back at Dunlavin Grange. Examining it, he was exultant.

"Speak of magnificence! Who but a King would ever dare wash here?"

"You, for one. Me. In fact, the two of us exclusively. Why don't you try a shower now?"

"And you with me? I'll soap your pretty bottom for you, Bern."

"Not now you won't. I've been away from home close on two months, and Madge is no housewife. I have a few things to attend to downstairs. You soap your own bottom, Mr. Shaara. The towels are in that closet yonder with the cupids painted on it."

Making her way down the awe-inspiring spiral stairs, she could hear a rush of water from the shower. A fond smile flickered on her lips. Turning in at the baize door to the pantry, she found Marie polishing silver. The maid Bernadette had brought from Great Oak was of such vintage that she actually bobbed an arthritic version of a curtsy.

"It's good to have you back, Madam. All of us have missed you."

The true reason for Bernadette's descent wasted no time. "Apparently, Miss Madge wasn't too lonely for me to meet the boat. And she's not here to greet us. Where is she?"

Marie reddened miserably. "Why gone, Madam. I thought of course you knew."

"Exactly what do you mean by 'gone', Marie?"

"She moved out bag and baggage, Madam, the day she received word you and Sir were coming. She's set up quarters in the studio Mr. Eamonn rented for her. She lives there now."

"*Lives* there? But that's absurd. There's only a single big room and a tiny bath."

"She already had considerable refixing done. A kitchenette and the like. I believe she partitioned off a bedroom and a living room for her painting space."

Bernadette breathed slowly, sucking in air, fighting the hurt and the fury which struggled for possession of her.

"In other words, she's been making arrangements for this move for considerable time. It was no sudden impulse. How long, Marie?"

"I wouldn't know that, Madam. About the time we first heard your happy news, I should venture. If I might make a guess, Miss Madge probably wanted you and Sir to have the apartment to yourselves for a while. Being you're still on honeymoon, so to speak."

"That's not why she's gone. She's done it to spite me. To throw an undeserved insult in Cornelius's face. To be as disagreeable as she possibly can be. But she has no right to think my marrying in any way demeans Eamonn or

my love for him. It's a cruel hurt to my Cornelius, who's
done nothing to deserve it. I'll not let her get away with
it.''

The revamped studio had been made over so recently
that a smell of paint and sawdust hung almost tangibly on
the air. The paint had no connection with Madge's working tools. She had not touched a brush since that ghastly
cablegram from County Kerry brought her familiar world
tumbling down around her.

She sat now at one of the windows of the very new
living room, already made sketchily presentable. She had
taken out of storage the few pieces of fine old furniture
that she had asked for from Grandma Veronica's house
when it was broken up. She had treasured them, imagining
them as someday being mainstays of the home she and
Barry Sullivan would share. Now, against the pale green-
grey walls so hastily constructed, they at least gave the
place some tinge of familiarity. She did not feel altogether
alien in this space so drastically altered as to retain few
evidences of its former self.

The street she looked down upon, at least, was no
stranger.

Visible if one leaned forward only a little, the west rim
of the Park was still green; silent and bronzing as it waited
for full autumn. The block was a quiet one, lined on either
side with once substantial mansions built in an era with no
great reverence for conformity. A diverse block. A block
with character. She had painted it from this same window
more than once; in spring, when the light seemed so young
that one ached, in winter, when snow lay like ermine on
the corbie gables of the brick facade across the way.

Madge felt no urge to paint it now. She felt, at the
moment, almost nothing. Unpacking her suitcases and hang-

ing her dresses in her new bedroom closets had drained her, if only temporarily, even of hatred for Cornelius Shaara.

Mother's thief would be ashore by now she thought. Already taking over the rooms that had been Daddy's. Striding about like the owner he must fancy himself. First payment on the silken future he had won by dazzling poor Mother.

Terence's friend, Desmond Molloy, had made her mighty promises as to severing the unscrupulous Shaara from his profits. But had she ever really believed in the old politician's ability to carry through? After all, nothing the detestable imposter had done could land him in the jail cell he deserved. Unencumbered, he could marry. Unencumbered, Mother could take a new husband. No law forbade it, and all Mr. Molloy's influence was no mightier than a butterfly.

Brendan had told her as much, following his own consultation with Monsignor Harrigan.

Even after she had outlined for him her new stepfather's previous career, her cousin had held out little hope. Clearly, they both were right about Cornelius Shaara. He was a miscreant. Also very clearly, the marriage was valid in spite of this. The Church had no remedy. If one hired a lawyer, even a sharp one, the Law would do no better.

A sense of loneliness had settled over Madge like a tombstone. Daddy gone, Barry gone, and now that last and closest prop, her mother. She sat in the chair she had drawn up alongside her present vantage point almost like a rag doll replica of her usual self—feet set primly together, hands folded in lap, back too stiff, an unconscious copy of wallflowers at Mr. Willie De Rham's dancing classes when she had attended them ten years ago.

At the curb below a yellow cab was sliding to a halt. Dull leaves of the tree set out to shade the house's entrance

half-obscured the passenger who emerged and crossed the
sidewalk; but suddenly Madge was quivering.

Her bell pealed demandingly.

It was bound to happen. She had known all along it was
inevitable. Yet now that she actually faced it, she felt
sickeningly unprepared. She was back at square one, when
the cablegram was first delivered, and all the hours of
thinking since then had been wiped out. She wasn't ready.
She knew what she felt, and how passionately she felt it,
but the words wouldn't come. She had never been one to
stand up against Mother; especially on a life-and-death
matter such as Cornelius Shaara.

The bell rang again, this time with a note of determination to it.

Madge rose slowly and pressed her door buzzer just as
the summons began a new repeat. Almost at once she
could hear mounting steps on the stairs outside, heels
clicking on each separate tread. They had an angry sound
to them. They were very firm. Trembling, Madge jerked
open the door which had been her sole protection.

"Good morning, Mother."

Her guest, striding inside, looked a dozen years younger
than the mother Madge had seen off to Ireland. She was
wearing her hair, at the moment hatless, in a new and
more becoming style. Her makeup was more carefully
chosen, more deftly applied. This was a woman who cared
about her appearance; who had been convinced of her own
attractiveness. Shaara's doing, obviously. He had woven
his web with great skill, the detestable spider.

"Madge McHugh, just what do you think you're doing?
Why are you so set on hurting me?"

They stood facing each other, a yard apart—both of
them tense, both of them miserable. The electricity crackling between them cut through the fumes of fresh paint like

a knife through butter. The thick-walled house, even the street below, seemed icily still.

"Well?" Bernadette demanded.

"I never wanted to hurt you, Mother, but I can't live under the same roof with that man. You've made your choice. But that's only for yourself. I don't have to share it."

"*That man,* as you call him, is my husband. What basis have you for making any such belittling judgment of him? You've never laid eye on him."

"I don't have to. I know what I know."

"You know absolutely nothing. He's been in America a scant few hours, so how could you know anything? Sight unseen, you've decided to damn a man who has made me very happy."

"A man scarcely Liam's age. You're old enough to be his mother."

The words were scarcely past Madge's lips before she longed to retrieve them. Unsettling though it was, the age gap between them was not the real matter at hand. If the detectives in Dublin had wired back a different sort of report on the youthful bridegroom, she and Brendan would have done their best to adjust to the wedding. Perhaps in time she might even have been able to build up some sort of pleasant relationship with Cornelius Shaara, since obviously he loomed so large in Mother's affection. But this was not what made anything but contempt possible toward the greedy, sly, unscrupulous creature.

"So that's it," Bernadette breathed. "I'm too old for a new chance at happiness."

"It's you who's being unfair, Mother, not me. If you really believe I don't want you to be happy, you've never understood all these years how much I really love you. If I *didn't* love you, I wouldn't despise that walking worm as I do. I wouldn't care.''

''Kindly remember you're talking about my husband, Madge. About the man who means so much to me that I married him, very simply because I couldn't bear the thought of living without him. Whatever else, I won't tolerate your insulting Cornelius.''

''A person can't insult men like that. Whatever you say of them can only be a fact. A fortune-hunter with no scruples at all trying for three rich widows before he caught you!''

The older woman facing her seemed to turn to stone, as if she just had met the glare of a Gorgon. ''Who told you any such thing about Cornelius?''

''Why, I've heard it on good authority. I'm not mistaken. It's every word true.''

''You've hired someone to spy on him, haven't you? Sneaking behind my back to try and spoil things for me! My God, how ashamed of you your father would have been!''

Tears stung Madge's eyelids. ''That isn't how it was at all. Of course I was uneasy when you cabled about the wedding. You'd written a lot before then about your Irish beau, and all of it sounded *wrong*. So, yes, I did contact people in Dublin to check him out. But not to make you unhappy, Mother. To try to save you from even more unhappiness.''

''These 'people in Dublin', my girl. Of course you mean private investigators. You're too inexperienced to know diddly-widdle about such men. Who found them for you?''

''They were my idea, only mine. But I didn't have much idea how to locate trustworthy ones, so I did ask Desmond Molloy for help in that. The firm he recommended is top drawer. They were very prompt and very thorough in tracing what I asked for.''

"Which was obviously anything to blacken Cornelius that they could turn over with their manure rakes. How admirable of you, Madge. And how efficient of them.''

"If you'd taken time to find out what sort he really is, Mother . . .''

"Do you imagine I'm such a fool that I didn't know the unhappy story before I had his ring on my finger? The night Cornelius asked me to marry him—it was in a tiny arcade pub in Sligo—he told me the whole brief history out of his own mouth. He *had* set his cap for me from mercenary motives. But then he truly fell in love with me.''

"What would a man like that know about truly loving anyone but himself?''

"I must say you take a lot on yourself, feeling you're fit to sit in judgment. I'd written you enough about his being a painter, like yourself, and terribly ambitious. But he was raised poor, Madge; bone poor most of his life. He'd sold a little work by the time I met him, so he had a few pounds in his pockets. But not much. There was only one way he could think to get the backing he needed before he was established.''

Madge stiffened. "With his body, naturally. I hear he's terribly handsome.''

"He is. My heart sings whenever I see him. But it wasn't anything underhand he intended. He meant to do whatever he could to make a rich wife happy, in return. He proposed to give her all the attention, all the companionship, all the sport in bed that she'd been lacking. As he saw things, it was a fair and honest exchange of benefits.''

"Was it indeed? What kind of man would say making

love to a woman he didn't care a penny whistle about was 'fair and honest'?"

"Not Cornelius. In spite of his earlier rationalizations, not Cornelius. Because he really did fall in love with me, Madge. Considering the chasm between our ages, I don't know why he did. But he did. He wanted everything between us straight and above board. So that night in Sligo he put all his cards on the table, before he'd let me answer."

"All his cards on the table, indeed! Can't you see what a clever little monster the man is, Mother? He knew you'd find out his history some day, one way or another. So he forestalled being ditched by parading this sham nobility and honesty. He duped you neatly."

For a moment the room was dead silent. They stood facing each other like graven statues. Then Bernadette's ringed hand flashed up. The crack of it against Madge's cheek was like the sound of shattering glass.

The door slammed. Bernadette was gone.

Brendan still felt wretched, pressing the bell of the Sutton Place duplex. He had been plagued by conflicting misgivings almost since the hour of his interview with the old Monsignor. There was little doubt the marriage entered into by his Cousin Bernadette was a grave mistake. The character of the unfitting young bridegroom, almost his own age exactly, was clearly contemptible. Still, they were man and wife. A priest had blessed them. There was no turning back, as his mentor had impressed upon him. Facts, however sour, were facts.

What to do, under the circumstances?

He had tried his best to reconcile Madge to what could not be undone. That she still clung to her hurt and rage, even to her wan hope that Desmond Molloy's promise

might by some miracle be redeemed, saddened Brendan
deeply. Hearing that she had moved out of her parents'
home, intending not to so much as speak to the intruder,
seemed to him utterly wrong. But his arguments, even
pleas, had not budged her.

There remained the undoubted grief and pain Madge's
decision would bring to her mother. Several wakeful nights
had pressed this knowledge deep into Brendan's mind and
heart. It was his duty—in fact, his hope—to bring Bernadette what solace he could

Finger on the bell, he steeled himself. The familiar call
would most certainly involve a meeting with the new and
undesirable husband. He meant to make what he could of
it—be at least polite, if at all possible even decently
cordial in his cousinly welcome. Any visible hostility could
mean only further pain for an already wounded Bernadette.

Awaiting the ring's answer, he made a silent but devout
prayer. "*God please help me bring what salve I can.
Please banish hate from me when I have to meet this man.
If there is any good in him at all, please help me to
discover it . . . for their sakes and for Madge. Amen.*"

The apartment door opened.

The aging woman in apron and black uniform who faced
him across the threshold was almost as familiar to him as
one of the family. Since he was in short pants, Marie had
been part of his elderly Cousin Veronica's household.
These last several years, inherited along with the furniture
and the fortune, she had been devoted to Bernadette and
Eamonn. Seeing him now, she beamed. The furrowed old
face grew radiant.

"Why, it's Mr. Brendan. Unless already I am to say
Father?"

"Not yet, Marie. But soon now, very soon. Is Mrs.
McHugh . . . Mrs. Shaara at home?"

"No, sir, she's not. I know she'll be sad to have missed you."

"I, too. Have the others been ahead of me to welcome her home?"

She understood, of course, whom he meant by the others. "Why, Mr. Jim and Missus Sheela were here right off, bringing love from you and Mr. Shane and Miss Norah. I think Mrs. Shaara much appreciated it. She was feeling a bit down that day."

Because of some sort of confrontation with Madge, naturally. Brendan understood that, without asking questions. Indeed, Marie would have been loath to answer them. For the first time, he realized that Marie too must have been undergoing her own private suffering. Cousin Eamonn had always been an open-handed employer. Marie had adored him.

"Miss Madge hasn't called yet, then?" He did venture that much.

"No, sir." It was all the answer he deserved. No details.

"Any idea when I should call back, Marie? I do want to wish them luck."

"No, Mr. Brendan, I really can't say. They left together for Bar Harbor, the very next day after they got here. Mrs. Bernadette's only other visotor before they went was Mr. Bewisk, her lawyer. Even him she sent for. Nobody else knew they was back, I guess."

Even him she sent for? Turning away, Brendan thought he understood exactly why. The lawyer's visit meant more bitterness ahead. A deeper split in the family.

But who could expect otherwise?

14

The family were all well aware of the disruption on Sutton Place.

Dreading their comments, Madge withdrew from seeing them as much as possible. As the O'Donnell circle had always been her chief source of companionship, aside from Barry Sullivan, this declining October stretched emptier than any she could remember. Even her eagerness for work seemed to have abandoned her.

She set up her easel dutifully in the now greatly diminished space still serving as a studio. But no impulse seemed to be nudging her to stand before it, brushes at the ready. The materials for a planned still life—a table-top covered with worn old paisley, a pair of gloves, a leather-bound book of red to bring the cloth alive—stood as she had arranged them, ignored. Day crept off after day.

Brendan came by the studio-apartment with word that

her mother and her stepfather had departed for Maine less than forty-eight hours after arriving in New York.

"But they can't have! Not this late in the season! Bar Harbor is no place to dash off to in . . . why, it's almost November, Brendan!"

"Marie is my source," Brendan said. "She tells me Cousin Bernadette was much upset."

Madge nodded unhappily. "I know. She and I had what I guess you could call a knock-down-and-drag-out. I told her the truth about her precious Cornelius. She wouldn't accept it."

"Surely you tried to be as diplomatic as possible? What's done is done."

"Some things you can't be diplomatic about. This is one of them. Mother slapped my face, Brendan. She'd never done that before in all my life."

After that, her misery only increased along with her loneliness. She tried shopping expeditions, but there was nothing she really wanted or needed that she didn't already own. She tried art galleries, but nothing that anyone else was painting interested her any more than did work of her own. She tried long walks across the Park, but there was a limit to possible destinations and a limit to the number of animal cages to visit at the zoo.

One evening, to her absolute astonishment, she found herself dialing Barry's old number on the telephone. Belatedly, she hoped he would not answer. But before she could hang up someone lifted the receiver at the far end.

"Hello?" It was a woman's voice.

"Is Mr. Sullivan at home?" Madge stammered. "May I speak to him please?"

"Sure." The voice receded a bit, as if its owner had stepped back from the instrument. "Barry, Baby? Some dame for you. What are you running here anyway? A stud farm?"

Then Barry's light, pleasant baritone took over. "Hello, whoever you are."

"I'm Madge," she just barely managed. "Madge McHugh, Barry."

"Well *hello!*" To her vast relief, he sounded pleased. "Golly, what a surprise! It's two months since you told me not to drop around again. How *are* you, anyway?"

"Miserable." And that was far too true to be lied about. "I miss you, Barry. More than I ever guessed I would. C-could you . . . ? If you're not too busy . . . ?"

"You bet I can. How does tomorrow night sound? For dinner?"

He was ringing her bell within five minutes of the appointed hour. When Madge pressed the buzzer to admit him, his steps on the stairs sounded eager. She had her inner door open before he could reach the landing.

He strode into the new living room and caught both her hands in his and looked down, searching her lifted face. "It's been a long day's wait, Madge."

"Long for me, too. I . . . were you surprised to hear from me, Barry?"

"Knocked off my pins. Something monumental must have happened to crack the silence."

"Something did. Something terrible has happened, Barry, and I need you."

His arms slid around her just as they always had, back in those nights when they patrolled together and he wanted to seduce her. "I'm here, Madge. Whatever you need me for."

She made him his favorite Irish-on-the-rocks and settled him into a comfortable chair before she would talk about

it. But then, avoiding his intent gaze because she felt so
ashamed, she spilled out the whole story. Barry listened
with scarcely an interruption, nodding occasionally as she
made a point but otherwise remaining immobile.

"So your Ma has signed on this sterling stinker and given
you the boot? That's it?"

"No, it wasn't that way. I did the walking out myself.
How could I possibly have stayed under the same roof
with that slimy toad? If Mother had really wanted me back
home, at least she'd have listened to what I was trying to
tell her. But I only enraged her."

"What about the guy himself? What's he like on the
surface?"

"I'm sure I don't know. I didn't propose to make small
talk with him, under the circumstances. I've never laid
eyes on the man. I *hate* him, Barry."

"Not without reason, I gather. But you can't keep up
this two-worlds thing after they get back in town, Madge.
You'll have to see him then. Mrs. McHugh's your *mother*."

"She's Mrs. Shaara now. And that's odd from you.
You were always the one dead set against all family ties."

"Different folks, different strokes. You're the nesting
kind, honey. That's what you and I always fell out about,
wasn't it? You'll have to make it up with Herself sooner or
later. She's all you've got, since you didn't want me."

"I did want you, Barry. I wanted you until I ached with
it. But not *your* way."

"At least my way isn't with one eye on the cash register.
You know that for sure."

"I know! You wouldn't marry a girl for her inheritance.
Nor for any other reason. Oh, Barry, I'd trade every dollar
Daddy left me if only things were different!"

Barry reached up and pulled her down onto his knee.

"Hasn't this business taught you anything, Madge? About you? About us?"

"I know I've been missing you so much I've been pacing the floor. I thought I'd go crazy."

"That's just what you *will* do, girl, unless you start looking life in the eye. Your mother seems to have done that. She let nothing stop her, once she knew what she wanted."

"She didn't know what she wanted, Barry. If she's seen what Shaara is *inside* . . ."

"If you knew what you wanted, you wouldn't be here alone tonight. And that's what you'll be, come midnight. Maybe you think weeping on a sympathetic shoulder for a few hours will make everything bearable again. It won't. I'll go off where I came from, because that's how you insist on it, and you'll be alone again. The hurt will still be there."

Madge held her breath.

"Maybe tonight I wouldn't send you away."

His fingers on her arm clenched almost brutally. She whimpered at the pain of this grip.

"Don't play games with me, Little Miss McHugh. Don't say things like that unless you mean them. My God, you've clawed my guts too long already with those Lady Purity ideals. I'm through being toyed with. Either say right now that nothing between us is changed and I'll go quietly and to Hell with you . . . or come to bed with me."

A long shudder ran up her body.

"I don't want you to go, Barry. I don't want to be alone."

For a moment time stood still while he studied her. "You know what you're saying?"

"I know. If this is what gives Cornelius his power over

Mother, it must be something that can conquer worlds. Something that makes any sort of folly or humiliation endurable. Maybe . . . oh, Barry, maybe you can make me understand.''

"I'll sure as hell give it the old college try," he said. He lifted her off his lap, rising with her, and swung her from the floor into his arms. "Where the devil is your bedroom? You've got this place so changed I can't find my way around here any more."

"It's that door over there," Madge whispered, and let her head fall against his shoulder.

Light inched between the slats of the blinds that she had installed in the bedroom. Madge lay very still on her side of the frilly bed, frightened lest the slightest move might wake Barry. He might want to take her again, and from the waist down she seemed to be one throbbing soreness. Her breasts hurt, too, as if in the night he had bruised them. She could remember its happening, but she didn't think he had meant it—the hurt. Everything else, he most definitely had meant.

Did Cornelius do all this to Mother? Rigid on the bed's edge, she fought against the unwelcome imaginings. Was this what melted Mother into a credulous, fawning fool?

Morning meant Barry's leaving her. He had a job to tend to in that world beyond the blinds. He'd have no intention of keeping her here beside him all through the day, taking her again and again, over and over and over. But last night it had seemed so. Last night, he hadn't been able to get enough of her. He had pinned her down like a triumphant savage, laughing deep in his throat with pure exultation as he rammed into her. The fear already rising in her as he carried her past the threshold, had changed to terror.

All the while he had been satisfying himself, she had lain with an almost certain sense that someone else was in the dark room with them. Someone with horns and a tail and a gloating grin. Someone prodding her with a pronged pitchfork—except that the pitchfork hurting so hideously was also a part of Barry's pumping body.

She sobbed, remembering, and the sound seemed to get through to him, despite her frantic effort to choke it back. He stirred, his head still dark on the pillow beside hers, and after a moment he yawned prodigiously.

His bare, muscular arms reached out for her, seeking.

"Where are you, darling? Madge, sweet little Madge?"

Because she could retreat no further without falling on the floor, Madge let the eager hands find her and stroke her. Barry was awake now, no question of it. Awake and wanting her once more. In a moment, all that would begin again. Oh, God! Please!

"No," she whimpered. "Barry, no, don't."

Instantly he was altogether free of sleep. Rearing up on one elbow, he lay staring down into her frozen face. It was still half-veiled by darkness, Barry's face, but she could read the changes on them as they came. First puzzlement. Then slowly dawning realization. Then pain, twisting his wide mouth and fraying his audible breath.

"If you don't want me to, Madge, of course I won't."

"I d-d-didn't mean to hurt your feelings." She despised herself. How juvenile she sounded! How ridiculous and inadequate!

Barry sat up slowly, the covers falling from him. The light, slowly increasing, seemed to caress every male line of him. This part of it was all right, in fact it was beautiful. She wondered if someday he might take off his clothes and let her paint him. But then he'd expect her to come back here with him and let him . . .

"You didn't like being made love to, did you?" He sounded sad.

"It was like being slammed around by a terrible thunderstorm. I kept remembering the one where the huge tree fell through Cousin Veronica's at Greak Oak."

Barry shook his head slowly. "That wasn't how it was supposed to be, Madge."

"But it was. I feel all torn and bruised. I've been bleeding."

"I thought, what I meant was," He stopped dead, then began again. "I'd waited for tonight so many years. I guess I was carried away. If I hurt you, I'm sorry."

"I know you didn't mean to." She touched his bare shoulder timidly.

"But I did hurt you, nevertheless. I've managed to screw it all up, haven't I? And I thought it was so fine, every minute of it. I was off on my own cloud, I guess, letting go."

"It was my fault as much as yours. Perhaps I just didn't know how."

"All these years of waiting, blown to Kingdom Come in just a couple of hours. I'll be going, Madge. Don't see me out. Just you lie there and rest."

It would have comforted her to watch him putting on his clothes again, exploring each ripple of a torso muscle, examining each stretch or bend. But Barry scooped up his discarded garments from the floor where he had flung them hours ago, and carried them neatly out into the living room. The door closed quietly behind him. Madge lay where he had left her, motionless.

After what seemed a very long time, she heard the outer door thump shut. Only then did she drag herself up out of the rumpled sheets and slip into a dressing gown and move stiffly out into the tiny kitchen to brew a pot of coffee.

Daylight had still only half arrived in the street outside. In another season, birds would be fussing in the tree below her windows, but in waning October even the birds had deserted her. A trash truck rattled by. A taxi disgorged a late homecoming reveler. Otherwise the world was dead.

Madge felt the weight of it on her, crushing her down just as Barry's flesh had done. The weight of the world—no, the weight of sin.

She struggled to cast off her depression, but it had taken a firm hold. What had loomed between them all the years when she had held Barry at arm's length loomed even more ominously now. She had given a man her body, and he had not even pretended to want to offer her matrimony. He had never promised it. The fault, the sin, was altogether hers. Knowing full well how wrong her surrender was, she had let her scruples blow away like brown leaves in the October wind. That shadowy figure in the bedroom, lurking—she had known all along who it was. And she had let Barry take her nonetheless.

The coffee scalded her throat as she gulped it, but she did not notice. Suddenly, she put down the cup half empty; put it down so hard that much of the coffee sloshed over. Clutching the folds of her robe about her, she ran through the living room and into the bedroom and began pawing clothes from the closet. Skirt. Jacket. Blouse. Scarf. Shoes.

Only a few people were plodding up the street as she burst out onto the pavement. A chill crouched in the air, nibbling with the fangs of coming winter. Madge scarcely noticed it as she stumbled along. The chill in her mind was sharper. The word had a rhythm somewhere inside her. Sin, sin, sin . . .

At the corner of Columbus Avenue she flagged down a taxi. The seminary where Brendan was approaching the final semester of his studies lay still further west and a

considerable distance downtown. The fountain plaza of
Columbus Circle spun away behind them. Crowded buildings replaced the park's leaf-shedding trees. She sat forward on the edge of the pseudo-leather seat, concentrating
on the back of her driver's head and his shabbily jaunty
cap, not really seeing either. Crosstown streets clicked
past.

Brendan was just emerging from early mass when a
folded slip of paper was handed to him, telling him that his
cousin was waiting in the dormitory parlor. As he hurried
in, he saw her huddled on one of the friezé-covered chairs,
hands clasped, rocking gently back and forth. At first he
doubted that she recognized him, although their eyes met
instantly.

"Madge! What in the world? It's still breakfast time!"

"I've committed a terrible sin, Brendan. I must pay
penance. I want you to hear my confession."

"Madge, dear, you know I can't do that. I'm not yet a
priest."

"But you're the only one. I've got to tell. I was wicked,
wicked . . ."

He crossed to her and took her clasped hands in his and
gently restrained her mindless rocking. Watching her closely,
he felt a flower of alarm opening wide within him. Dear
Heaven, she looked as unhinged as the proverbial Mad
Hatter! Whatever was gnawing at her, it had driven her to
the edge of true madness. An awful doubt about his own
abilities struck him with the force of an iced snowball. In
years to come, he would be facing a hundred such moments.
Could he handle them as God would demand?

"I want you to sit here very quietly for just a few more
minutes, Madge. I'm going to ask the Monsignor to see
you. He'll be able to hear your confession, and help."

"You, Brendan, you. I *know* you. I trust you."

"I'll only be gone for a wink. If you trust me, you know I'll be back with proper help. I want you to keep thinking about times when you and I were kids and went through all kinds of scrapes together. I won't fail you, Madge. So just sit quietly."

Monsignor Harrigan was still in his office when Brendan reached it. A hasty explanation from his badly shaken young underling had the old man on his feet before Brendan's plea was half finished. He was on his way to the confessional as Brendan wheeled to sprint back to the dormitory.

In the worn chair, Madge still crouched like a frightened animal. When he paused beside her she did not even glance up, but she knew he had returned. He could tell that by the way the distracted rocking eased a trifle.

"All right, dear, Monsginor's on his way. We're to meet him immediately in the chapel. So on your feet now. We mustn't keep him waiting."

Obediently, Madge set her shoes on the frayed carpet— unmatched shoes, Brendan now noted, although each of them was expensive and meticulously polished. Standing, she was within four inches of his height. When he reached for her hand she took his with no hesitation. The two of them had run this way, in years long vanished, through Alex's rose gardens at Great Oak. She seemed to be making the connection, taking comfort from it.

In the chapel, he had to leave her to the Monsignor's wiser ministrations. Closing the door behind him, he heard the experienced voice begin to speak.

Saying his own silent prayer, Brendan turned in at the office where Rosemary, the secretary, had her desk. She was a kind woman, motherly to the young seminarians and didn't mind when one or another of her young men imposed on her a little. He was not the only one who had begged the use of her private telephone for some special call.

The number he dialed was one familiar to every member of the O'Donnell family. It was for the apartment his sister Norah and his brother-in-law Dennis Gallagher.

Norah picked up the receiver at the end of the second ring. But her clear voice sounded oddly distorted. He could barely decipher its mumblings and knew that he would have to wait. Without a choice, he waited.

"Sorry." A moment later she was back, and this time unencumbered. "I was changing a diaper. I had a mouthful of safety pins. Oh, Brendan, it's you. Hello!"

"We have some family trouble, Norah. It's Madge. She's all worked up over some moral matter which seems to have her half out of her head. I've just left her with Monsignor Harrigan."

"Wow! I'm up to my tonsils in moral matters right here, this morning. Dennis, too. Have you by any chance caught the morning papers yet? We're front page stuff."

Brendan blinked rapidly. Certainly his sister and her husband were not front page material. Not in a thousand years. Yet Norah did sound worried. Her expressive voice, so popular with crowds on her recent band tours, reflected concern and tension.

"Norah, they don't give me time here to even scan a headline. What's wrong?"

"This twig of the family tree may be headed for the unemployment office and the bread line. Our boss-man is in durance vile. Buddy Diston has been naughty."

"He's absconded with the Starlight Serenaders payroll, you mean?"

"Nothing that venial. What he absconded with is the prettiest little sixteen year old boy you ever laid eyes on. And both Pretty Boy's parents and the police are taking a very harsh view. Buddy's in the hoosegow, facing a hearing on the obvious charges. There are laws against the corrupting of minors. If he's convicted—well, no more band.''

"I'm sorry, Norah. Is there anything I can do?"

"Not a thing. Not you nor anyone else. But thanks."

"If the situation's something a little political clout might ease, perhaps Desmond Molloy could be useful. I seem to recall he once eased Cousin Terence out of police trouble."

This time, what happened to Norah's voice was no matter of safety pins. It froze hard as diamonds. It seemed, even over a telephone, to glitter with distaste.

"If I were drowning in a sea of sharks and Desmond Molloy tossed me a lifeline, I'd throw it back at him. Do me a favor, Brendan. Never speak that name to me again." A small pause followed. Then, perfectly normal, the voice came back. "What's this about Madge, now? Half out of her head, didn't you say?"

"She's been going through a rough time, this past week. She and Cousin Bernadette have come to a parting of the ways. She left Sutton Place, cold turkey. Maybe you know?"

"Matter of fact, Brendan, I didn't. We were playing Cincinnati the day Bernadette and her young man put ashore. That lasted until this Sunday. Then Buddy handed Dennis a sheaf of new tunes he wanted arrangements for—you know the Diston style: have these ready for me day-before-yesterday. So I've been sort of trying to help Dennis out. We haven't invested a single thought in anyone but our own two selfish selves."

"You can only do so much in any day God gives us."

"Correct, but I still feel guilty, now that you tell me Madge may have gone off her trolley. Dad did mention last night that they'd called and just caught the honeymooners before they took off for Maine. But you know how close Madge and her mother have always been. If those two have been swapping harsh words, surely the dust won't take long to settle.''

"It was a little worse than words. A day or so back, Madge told me Cousin Bernadette slapped her face. That's never happened before. Madge has just come completely unstrung. And Cousin Bernadette must be pretty upset too, to dash off with her beau to Scrimshaw just when winter's setting in. A Maine November isn't like Hawaii.''

"How do you think we could help?" Norah asked thoughtfully.

"Right now, the ball's in Monsignor Harrigan's court. But Madge will be coming out in a few minutes. I'll be standing by to intercept. She may be calmer than when she went in to see him, but she's bound to still be feeling rocky.''

"And me? Look, I could slap on something presentable and be over there in, say, twenty minutes. Maybe a hen lunch with her female cousin could work wonders. In some quarters, girl-to-girl works better than girl-to-priest.''

"*Could* you, Norah?" Brendan's heart swelled with gratitude. "You're really aces.''

"Not to mention you, brother," said Norah. "Did I ever remember to tell you that I'm kind of glad you're in the family?''

15

Cornelius was discovering an unexpected affinity between his home county back in Ireland and the rugged persona of Mt. Desert Island off the Maine coast. More than he had expected, he was feeling at home in this playground of the American rich.

Not that the rich themselves were very much in evidence, and this, for Cornelius, was a good thing too. He needed time to acclimate himself to the notion of becoming one of the rarified toffs. This first acquaintance with his new wife's Scrimshaw and its environs was best made in comparative solitude.

Get the lay of the land, first off. Then, next summer when, as Bernadette described things to him, Bar Harbor's social lid blew off, it would be time to put his talent for ingratiation to work. He intended to rub elbows with these neighbor folk who could afford stiff prices for having their portraits painted.

The lay of the land was in itself intriguing. Mt. Desert was a large island, as he discovered on the long solo walks he began taking a day or two after their arrival. His bride was suffering a bad reaction from some unpleasantness in New York about which she was mysteriously unwilling to give him the details. She was taking heavy medication to calm her ruffled nerves and had begun spending afternoons almost comatose in her bed. Since they were alone in the house, the usual staff being seasonal, Cornelius was left largely to his own devices.

A paperback combination guide book and local history, discovered during an idle inspection of the stocked library Bernadette had purchased along with the house itself, became his constant companion. He fell instantly in love with Bar Harbor's quiet elegance—an ambiance he had dreamed of since the lean days of his childhood.

The place seemed all the more his own because it had been founded as a summer colony by another painter—the celebrated Thomas Cole who had created the so-called Hudson River School with their nature canvases. These, Cornelius had decided in student days, were overly sentimental and picturesque. Now, confronted with the actual scenery which had inspired those paintings, his opinions were changing.

Majestic Cadillac Mountain, the highest peak along the full length of the Atlantic coast, awed him from the first. Blue Hill and Frenchman Bays, with their quaint pepperings of smaller islands, made him itch for his own paintbrushes, still packed in luggage left behind on Sutton Place. The virgin forests covering many of the lesser hills bred a special aura of mystery. And then there was Somes Sound, that royal fjord cut seven miles back into the island—deep, narrow and walled on either hand by towering cliffs, penetrating to the very heart of the island as if some super-god had delivered a mammoth blow with an immortal sledge hammer.

How could an artist not fall in love, Cornelius wondered. Each day was jammed with fresh adventure, although no one shared his expeditions. It was almost a chore to return at sunset to Scrimshaw, where Bernadette would be rousing from her sleep.

On one particular morning he had chosen not grandeur but isolation as his objective. One of the myriad small inland lakes had struck him as so typical of the island that it deserved commemoration. He had bought a sketch pad and colored pencils at a Bar Harbor store, and he toted these contentedly as he hiked along.

His trail wound up a gentle grade through stands of pine which had taken on a tindery look. Maine had been enduring a long period of drought, and it was dragging on. The parched quality of the forest added a special fascination to it. He wondered if with only pencils he could manage to capture it on paper.

Once at the lakeshore, Cornelius found a promising boulder on which to squat and braced his pad against a lifted knee and went to work. The sky overhead was a metallic blue. No sign of the rain for which all fire wardens were praying. The late summer months had been wet and green in Ireland. Over here, climate matters had been an exact reverse. The wardens were shaking doleful heads.

But the lake scene was immensely sketchable.

His hand went into subtle motion. A replica of what he looked out upon began to emerge. A tall pine which seemed grandfather to all the others, the stretch of newly bared false beach brought into view by the water's shriveling, the rocky gap where in normal times a small waterfall would be shimmering. Detail after detail took form.

The pad was slapped out of his grasp so abruptly that

Cornelius gasped as he made an involuntary grab to retrieve it. From behind, a hand like a vise closed on his reaching arm and jerked it up and backward until excruciating pain shot through it.

Engrossed, he had not even been aware of the two men coming quietly down out of the timber. They might have been watching him for considerable time; or again, they might have parachuted down out of that arid sky overhead. The frightening thing was that suddenly they were there, on either side of him, both of them huge and ugly.

Somehow, they had a look which stamped them as outsiders. City suits, cloth straining over bulges of muscle. City shoes, dusty now from tramping dry trail detritus. City haircuts. A city look in their hard, cold grins.

"Didn't expect company, did you, picture boy?" the one who gripped his pinioned arm asked with a voice like unoiled machinery.

His companion joined in. "We been watchin' you for at least a half an hour. You been workin' as steady as if you had to earn your own livin', kid. Some laugh!"

"Who are you?" Cornelius gasped, struggling futilely to free himself. Daggers of pain were racing up and down his arm. "What do you want?"

"It's more like what we *don't* want. And what we don't want most of all, right now, is havin' you within a couple thousand miles of your rich lady friend. Get it?"

"What damn business is it of yours what . . . ?"

The one with both hands free slapped Cornelius across the mouth so hard he was almost knocked off the boulder. He felt blood seep across his lower lip. A couple of front teeth seemed loose. His eyes watered in agony.

"What damn business it is of ours, boy, is that we're a special committee appointed to usher you straight out of the lady's life. We plan to do just that. Catch on?"

"If you're talking about my wife . . ."

"Who else? Only you ain't gonna continue as no husband, see? The party's over. No more silver spoons in the mouth. No more Bar Harbor mansions. No more easy gigolo cash."

"Damn you, let go of my arm! You're hurting me!"

The bigger and beefier of the pair, although not by much, let out a laugh like the snort of a bull buffalo. "We ain't even begun to hurt you. That comes along about now. When we're done with you, you'll wish we'd been nice guys and merely killed you."

Down came a massive boot heel, finding the fallen pad and grinding dirt into the delicate, almost completed sketch. Cornelius saw the paper rip and crumple. His morning's work no longer existed. Fear stabbed him. Would he himself exist, an hour from now, or whenever they decided they were through with him?

"Please, look, you fellows, if it's money you're after . . ."

"Kind of generous with your old lady's bank account, ain't you? What good is that to us? After today you won't have a claim to none of it."

The one still pinning his arm jerked him roughly to a standing position. The other one slammed a piston-driver fist into his belly, just above the belt line. Cornelius doubled over, but the hand at his back jerked him erect again.

"Please," Cornelius whimpered, in torment. "Jesus, no . . . please . . ."

"Listen good, buddy," grated the voice nearest his ear. "What I'm gonna say now, maybe you'll live to make use of. A guy takes a bead on the tall pine and faces seaward, see, a couple of miles gonna bring him out on a little private cove that's down there. Big house all closed up for the winter. Not a livin' soul nowheres around. But at the boat dock, since just this morning, there's been a rowboat tied up waitin'.''

His companion snickered. "You won't be in shape for much rowin', kid."

"But you're gonna row, just the same, if you ever get down there. You're gonna row for the mainland and never once look back. Once there, you're gonna catch the first bus outward bound. And you're gonna keep goin' until your rich broad couldn't locate you with a geiger counter."

"This'll be your one chance, boy," added the other. "Try sneakin' back this way again and you've had it. Instead of a rowboat there'll be a coffin waitin'."

Cornelius stared back at them in terror and knew they meant exactly what they were saying. These were professional killers, no doubt of that. Cornelius Shaara would be buried, probably in small sections, before even one of his paintings had been hung in any of his coveted American museums. All the years, all the hopes . . . gone.

"Please don't kill me, chaps. I'll do whatever you want. I'll go and never come back. Just don't . . . *owww*, my painting hand . . . oh, Christ . . .''

The one who held him laughed again, a horrible sound. The other's massive knee came higher. It slammed like a house-wrecker's iron ball full into Cornelius's groin.

With a scream that ended in a gurgle, their victim went limp. The harsh blue sky turned black, as if those prayed-for rain clouds had suddenly gathered.

When he opened his eyes, he was sprawling on the dried mud bank and his tormentors were gone. He lay for a moment wondering if he were on fire, the pain twisting his body was so intense. He was wet to the touch; not from rain but from his own dank sweat.

Slowly, the full horror of the visitation seeped back.

Cornelius began to tremble. They were gone, but he doubted they would have gone very far. From the woods, earlier, they had watched undetected while he sketched. They might be there again at this moment, keeping him under surveillance, making certain their commands were obeyed.

Nothing in the world, nothing, was worth risking their return. The mere thought of it made him whimper. Let the money go. Let his marriage go. Let anything, everything go. If only he could get away. Far enough away so those two could never catch up with him.

Painfully, laboriously, he tottered to his feet. Surprisingly, they had not broken his legs during their nightmarish game. They had them so he could make it to the rowboat. Directions? Remember directions!

Tallest pine . . . face toward sea . . .

Instinct rather than any mental process put his bruised carcass in motion. He had to circle the lake's nearer end before he passed the mighty pine. Under his stumbling feet the land sloped downward. What he needed to find was the cove. Big house. Boarded for winter.

It was easy to lose count of the number of lifetimes passed in this tortuous descent through the close-crowding forest. The trees were so brittle that whole branches snapped off as he reeled against them or caught at them to keep from falling. Dry. Dry as the Sahara Dessert. Ought to be camels. Be a camel himself. They travel without water. He was thirsty. A haze like smoke shimmered before him, easing through the pines like a poisonous gas. Where the sweet Christ was the cove with the rowboat?

Have to find the boat. Have to get away. Never come back. Goodbye, Bernadette. They'd kill me if I ever—Ah! *There*, dead below! A glitter of still water. The massive outline of a shuttered house. The pier. The boat, riding like a bathtub toy.

Cornelius broke into a slow run as he sighted his goal. Twice, he fell to his knees and rolled a short way before he could struggle to standing position again. The pitch of the slope here was very steep. He could hear waves lapping. An inbound tide.

There was another sound, too, although he could not seem to identify it. It came from far behind him, up on the hill—a kind of crackle and chuckle combined.

Somehow he comprehended that the sound spelled danger, but he dared not turn around to look. It would have to be his tormentors, close on his heels. If they saw him wheel back they might misinterpret the movement as disobedience, and then . . .''

When he trotted out onto the pier, the world became level at last, although the haze was thickening. Wooden planks. Excellent condition. Bar Harbor money, then. Boat will be shipshape, too, a place like this.

Bar Harbor money. None for you any more, Cornelius. Doesn't matter. Get away!

He fell rather than clambered down into the moored little craft and groped for its waiting oars. Without really knowing what he did, he worked them into their oarlocks and crouched ready to wield them. As his head lifted, he faecd full at the hillside he just had descended.

Higher up, the long slope was one mass of wavering, surging flame. Good God, the whole damn island was ablaze! Faster than an Olympics runner, the crimson tide swept across the treetops, leaping gleefully from one to another, transmuting the dry forest into the very Gates of Hades. Stunned, he gaped up at the conflagration. It seemed a living curtain.

"Bern!" To his amazement, he was shouting her name.

"Wake up, Bern! It's moving in Scrimshaw's direction and it's coming fast! Get up, get up! If you make it down to our boat dock the fire can't touch you. Hear me, Bern! Hear me!"

He dragged himself back up the ladder cleats nailed to the barnacle-armored pilings. He raced back along the empty pier, heat from the inferno overhead striking full into his face.

At the land end, he swung in the direction the blaze was taking and sucked in air and ran. His lungs ached. His legs felt like jelly, but he ran.

"Bern!" he was screaming as he pounded the shore trail. She was a country mile ahead and too doped to hear, but he had to sound the warning. Somehow he had to make her get down to the water's edge in time. After that, let those sadistic man-mountains do whatever they had a mind to do to him. It wouldn't matter, just so long as he outraced the flames.

"Bern! Wake up! I'm coming, but for God's sake wake up! Now, Bern, *now*!"

The phone was ringing just as Madge unlocked her door.

Dropping the gloves she had worn to her novena on a handy table, she picked up the receiver. Probably a wrong number. These days calls generally were, unless Norah or Brendan were checking on her admittedly still flimsy condition. "Hello?"

"Good afternoon, Miss Madge. I hope I find you well? I called twice before today but there was no answer. I'd begun to be concerned, my dear."

Although the unctuous voice was completely familiar, today something about it raked her nerves like a file. "I'm well, thank you, Mr. Molloy. Just out at church."

"Ah, excellent. Young ladies nowadays are far too prone to skip their religious obligations, I'm afraid. I congratulate you on not being one of them."

"What was it you wanted to contact me about, Mr. Molloy?"

"Why, only to reassure you. Your uncle-by-courtesy hasn't forgotten his promise to you, my dear. In fact, I have just attended to it. You may rest assured that your worthy mother has seen the last of her Irish rogue. He will trouble her no longer."

Madge recognized that this was news to inspire rejoicing. Why, then, did a pang of alarm race through her? Her grip on the telephone tightened.

"But how in the world could you possibly manage such a thing?"

"A simple matter for a man with the right connections, my dear. I just wanted you to know that you have no further imposition to fear from the scalawag. Good day, Miss Madge."

Had Molloy expected effusive thanks from her? Crossing the room, Madge still worried the question. Probably he had a right to her appreciation. What he had indicated he had done was only what she had indicated she dearly desired.

But there was something wrong, something she could not quite put her finger on. The timing was off. Mother's challenge, on the day of her dreadful visit here, had been that before she married him she already knew all there was to know about Shaara's past. What pressure, then, could Molloy have brought to bear that would have so speedily sent the bridegroom packing?

"Has he somehow laid us open to a blackmail charge?" she wondered, freshening her makeup before the dressing table mirror. "Will Shaara drag us all into court?"

But what basis for blackmail could exist, if Mother really had known everything about those other women? Automatically, that cleared the decks as far as he and her money were concerned. Could the pressure which drove him off pertain to some matter quite apart from his fortune-hunting, then? Had he a criminal record back in Ireland? Had he some hidden and obscene disease? Was he an escaped lunatic? What, what, what?

She had a dinner date with Norah and Dennis at their apartment, and had in fact only stopped by the studio to leave off her prayer book. A quarter-hour later she was relocking her door and hurrying downstairs to find another taxi, still puzzling.

Like half the cab-driving population of New York, the man behind the wheel of the vehicle which took her aboard was magnificently of the opinion that his taxi was personal property and owed no consideration to a mere transitory passenger. He had a radio news program tuned in at top decible and saw no reason to turn it low.

". . . greatest fire in its history," boomed the loud-speaker. "Hundreds of dwellings as well as many lives already have been lost to the conflagration, which is still raging. Estimates indicate that before the blaze is brought under control losses will have climbed to . . ."

Madge had to lean forward and rap sharply on the glass partition between them to attract the driver's attention. When at last he deigned to glance across his shoulder, she made frantic gestures indicating that the radio broadcast was giving her a splitting headache.

The driver gestured back, expressing the opinion that women passengers were pain in a good many areas other than the neck. With an exaggerated grimace of martyrdom, however, he did turn the radio off. Blessed silence filled the car. When he unloaded her on the sidewalk before the

Gallagher apartment in the pleasanter reaches of the Village, her unwilling host-on-wheels did not thank her for his tip. But this silence, too, did not really ruffle her. She still was pondering Desmond Molloy.

Norah had observed her arrival from a window higher up. As Madge toiled up the second flight of carpeted stairs, the door to the apartment already stood open. Light spilled welcoming from the room beyond, but Dennis's wide shoulders all but blocked it out.

He caught both her hands as she moved toward him, but he said nothing. The sick look on his well-featured face might have warned her of trouble on many another occasion. But tonight she had something else on her mind, and failed to notice.

"I bought a Mickey Mouse for Tony yesterday, and then forgot and left it at the studio. So I'm arriving emptyhanded. Will he possibly forgive me, do you think?"

"Toys don't matter. Come inside, honey. Norah's waiting for you."

"My goodness, don't you sound funereal. What's happened? Has your boss been found guilty of that business about the young boy? Are the Starlight Serenaders disbanded?"

Dennis made no attempt to reply, simply applied reassuring pressure to Madge's hand as he led her inside. From the corner by Tony's playpen Norah flew toward her and enveloped her in a tight, fierce hug. For a moment Madge's breath was crushed out of her.

"Hey, Norah, don't break any bones. What *is* this reception? It's not my birthday."

Norah let her go, drawing back a step. "You don't know, then? Oh, God!"

"Know what? Has the world come to an end?"

"You didn't catch it on the electric sign as you came

down through Times Square? You didn't hear any radio bulletins? Oh, Madge, darling!''

Uneasiness moved in. ''What am I supposed to know, for heaven's sake?''

''About the fire. There's a terrible fire still going on up in Maine, on Mt. Desert Island. The worst fire they've ever had. The town of Bar Harbor has been evacuated. Half the big estates surrounding it have burned to the ground. The flames won't be under control for days, the Fire Warden predicts. A stiff wind is blowing and the forests up there are like matches waiting to ignite. They say the resort area will never come back.''

''Perhaps Scrimshaw isn't in the path of the destruction.'' Madge had begun to shake despite herself, yet she still spoke sensibly. ''So Mother needn't necessarily face losing the place. She has her sailing sloop. Even if flames cut off the point, she could get away by water. Mother is a splendid sailor.''

''Madge,'' Norah swallowed hard ''the sloop was put up in its cradle for the winter two months ago. She didn't expect to go back to the island until next summer.''

''B-but even so. Scrimshaw has a dock much longer than most. If she got out on the dock . . . She could even cut it adrift, if the flames threatened . . .''

''Madge, dear, oh, Madge! Well, the truth is she didn't.''

Madge's answering voice sounded very small. ''What are you trying to tell me?''

''Dennis has a friend in the Memorial Laboratory up on the island. As soon as we first heard a report Den called up there to ask if Scrimshaw might be involved.''

''And? Norah, *was* it?''

''Jack gave it to us straight. The house was already gone, burned right to its foundations. Even those are just an empty shell. Those trees that stood around like a congress of Druids are all gone. The dock burned. The whole headland is bare.''

''But, but Mother?''

''You've got to take this, honey. I don't know any easy way to tell you. Cousin Bernadette, it seems, was up in her bedroom taking a nap. She wasn't awakened by the sounding alarms. By the time help arrived from the water side, it was too late.''

The cheerful living room seemed to be on some kind of merry-go-round, turning slowly. Lights blinked, but there was no music. Madge stood erect at dead center of the pinwheel, tottering slightly, but aside from this motionless. What held her erect was a seething hate. It supported her like a steel rod run along her spine.

''What do you mean help? She had help with her. Cornelius Shaara was there too.''

''They found Shaara in time. Badly burned, Jack says, but still alive. He looked like he'd been through some kind of severe physical beating when they got him to a hospital on the mainland. It was a close thing, but Jack says he'll live.''

''The God damned son of a bitch!'' Madge spat between set teeth.

''Honey! Whoa! You can't blame the man for something nature did.''

''The hell nature did! Just a few hours before they took off for Maine, Mother called Mr. Bewick in to sign a brand new will. Marie was called in as a witness. Mother cut me out flat—not that I care about the money. She left everything to Shaara. She wanted to prove her confidence in him, she said. Her belief that he'd married her for something other than her fortune had to be proven. And look at what it's cost her!''

"Madge, stop it," Norah protested. "A fire that's devastated the whole area . . ."

"You think that stopped him? You think that stopped Cornelius Shaara? He didn't care about anything when he set that fire. Not what he'd do to Bar Harbor or anyone else. Only that Mother would die and make him a millionaire with no strings attached, just as he intended all along!"

In unison, both Norah and Dennis shot a startled look into their cousin's taut face and sprang into action—Dennis bolting to the kitchen for whiskey, Norah to the bedroom for smelling salts and wet towels.

Left alone in his playpen, small Tony set up a clamor for attention. Too much was going on here.

"Hey, Momma! Hey, Poppa! Back, back! Why Auntie Madge fall down, go bump?"

16

The house occupied a low mountaintop well to the west in New Jersey, two hours from Manhattan.

It had been built of stone and cypress by one of the few first-generation American multimillionaires. In the time of its original owner, it had been one of the handsomest French Country Manor dwelling compounds in the state. The deaths of both sons of the builder in the course of the late war, leaving him without heirs or any interest in the future, had prompted the sale of the property. It was now a jewel among small private sanitaria, highly recommended for their patients by all three of the metropolitan specialists who had seen Madge.

Refurbishment of both main building and outlying structures had been completed with no financial shortcuts. Perfectionists in their own way, the new owners had recognized that the fees they intended to charge would quickly reimburse them. And their plan had already proven itself flawless. Had Eamonn McHugh left his daughter provided for by anything less substantial than the trust he actually had set up in her name, she could not have met her bills for nine months—let alone the past twenty.

Aside from the main building, with its baronial fireplaces and vaulted ceilings and bulky exposed beams, Dogwood Dell boasted forty-seven fenced-in acres. Five of them, down slope from the summit, were dense with the flowering trees from which the establishment derived its name. From the windows of the main building, the view of rolling hill country was spectacular. The sense of peace the surrounding countryside bestowed played no little part in patient therapy.

Set among well matured trees, surrounded by velvety lawns, the lesser outbuildings gave the place the air of a tiny rural community. The stone carriage house had been transformed into a residence boasting four additional bedrooms, one of which was now Madge's own. The equestrian barn of yesteryear had become an exercise gymnasium, complete with indoor A white-water brook, leaping down the wooded hillside, fed the swimming pond where the "guests" ice skated in the wintertime. Riding trails twisted through the more distant timberland.

Guiding his father's well kept though second-hand Plymouth up the wide sweep of the approach driveway, Brendan took in the serene vista and for a hundredth time gave silent thanks. For almost two years now, God be praised, his cousin had been granted this place in which to weave together the tangled ravellings of her health and personality. At the time of his last visit, three weeks earlier, she had seemed visibly improved over the Madge of six months ago. Twice he had even been able to make her laugh.

She was waiting for him in the bright solarium, gay with its baskets of plants and its wicker and English chintzes.

She came toward him with both hands held out in greeting, her smile delicate and solemn but also steady and welcoming. They found chairs in a quiet corner, their only intrusion that of a beady-eyed cockatoo chained to a perch.

"You're looking well, Madge," Brendan said. "Haven't you put on weight?"

"Almost two pounds. If I keep on like this I'm going to need a whole new wardrobe. Or Norah will have to find me a dressmaker to let out the old things."

"There are enough clothes in that closet back on the West Side to outfit an army."

She laughed, though it was not spontaneous or carefree, at least her laughter hinted at the return of her old sense of humor. "I doubt the army would approve of my old wardrobe. Don't they still cashier transvestites out of the service?"

"That question is both too bawdy and too worldly for me to answer, Miss McHugh."

They sat regarding each other, catching up in quietness on their separate kinds of isolation. Each of them let a small smile and glowing eyes bridge the entirely easy silence.

Madge was the first to return to words: "Speaking of fashion, I like the way you're outfitted these days. That Roman collar does become you, Brendan. And you always looked smashing in black. Romantic. I always used to imagine you as Zorro or Monte Cristo."

"Instead of a young, over-worked, under-recreationed assistant priest in a shabby small parish in threadbare Chelsea? I must find you a new crystal ball for Christmas, Madge. Your old one is growing dingy. Zorro? Monte Cristo? What would my Archbishop say?"

"Are you really happy, Brendan? I so often wonder."

"Most of the time I'm too exhausted to know whether

I'm happy or not. But yes, since you worry about me, I am. It's as far from what I'd imagined as Mars from the Moon. If you'd asked me the same question on the day we met with the Archbishop to receive from him our formal assignments, I'd have growled at you. I was raw with disappointment.''

"That was soon after your Ordination, wasn't it? They still wouldn't tell me very much about what was going on in the family, back then. It was supposed to be bad for me to brood. They were right, of course, but I hated them for not letting me out to watch you being consecrated and taking on God's responsibilities.''

"It was a very quiet ceremony. Very little pomp. But it meant more to those of us being ordained, I would say, than any other moment in our entire lives. We were priests from that moment, and forever. The great service we'd undertaken was fixed on us.''

"I'd love to have been there. You've always been my real brother, Brendan. More than Liam.''

"I know," he said. Briefly, their eyes met again.

"If you were so happy at the Ordination, why soon afterward was it a disappointment?''

"Because I hadn't yet learned to bow to higher authority. I'd prayed so hard to be sent to post-Ordination studies at Rome or Louvain, or even at Catholic University in Washington. That was my lifetime dream. And then, when we were handed our assignments, mine was only shabby old St. Cyprian's—to become Father Cullen's resentful handmaiden. I didn't realize then how I'd been blessed.''

Madge sat for a moment thinking. "Not much in the way of a blessing.''

"A very great one, I understand now. As priests, we ought not to care which furrow in God's field we are sent to plow. In one quick stroke, Madge, I learned more about

the priestly qualities of obedience and humility than years
of book study ever taught me.''

''I couldn't have taken it so philosophically. I guess I'm
not very strong.''

He touched her arm. ''Getting stronger every day, though.
You aren't at all the same person you were the night Bar
Harbor burned, close on two years ago.''

''I'm getting there. They've let me really get back into
my world again, Brendan. It used to bring on bouts with
near hysteria. They had to put painting off limits.''

''Why that hysteria? I often wondered, Madge.''

''Simple. Because Cornelius Shaara is a painter, too.
Merely thinking about him set me off. But I can handle
that now. I can paint! It isn't just occupational therapy,
either. Lately, my work has been fairly decent.''

''Good for you! You'll make it all the way, Madge,
that's for sure.''

Her slight smile flickered. ''If I don't, we'll have wasted
a fortune in Daddy's money. But I know he'd think Dogwood Dell has been worth it. He really loved me, Brendan.''

''The whole steamy family loves you, Dope. Every time
Liam gets back from whatever far spot his editor has shot
him off to with violence and riots to cover, the first thing
he asks me is 'How's Madge doing?' Norah phones me
twice a week, after she goes off the air. Dennis long-
distances from Hollywood.''

''Just to get up to date on me?''

''What else? Shane runs up half his private telephone bill
quizzing doctors at Dogwood Dell. Then he's right back
on the line again, relaying what he's heard to Mom and
Dad. We O'Donnells are what you might call a caring
conglomerate.''

''We O'Donnells.'' Madge seemed to hug the quoted
words against her heart. ''What an Irish stew we are, aren't

we? As different as night and day, no one of us really a
copy of any other—yet in some ways like peas in pod. That's
what Granny Veronica used to say to Mother; peas in a
pod."

"Give one of us a bit of trouble, and we close ranks."

"Too much, sometimes. Looking back, I can see how
wrongly I treated Mother. But at the time it was the only
way I knew. I wanted so badly to help her out of a mess. I
thought she'd leave him if I made her understand. But I
went at it all upside down."

"You were hurt, Madge. You felt abandoned. You were
just too young to handle it."

"Don't you dare say I meant well, Brendan. If you do,
I'll throw something."

On his stand the cockatoo continued pacing while he
made a raucous comment. His crest ruffled and his stance
was fierce. Looking across at him, both of them chuckled.

"A lot of the war-hawks Liam goes to interview must
look like that," Madge decided. "Oh, Brendan, I still
can't quite believe I have a half-brother who's a rising
foreign correspondent."

"He's going great guns at it, too. You'd been brought
up here before he really got started, with those South
Pacific pieces he began whipping to the magazines. But
it's turned out he has a real talent for it. You know how
violence always suited him."

"Alas, I do indeed," she said, nodding. "It used to
worry us, Daddy and Mother and me. Now it turns out to
be the cornerstone of his rise to fame and fortune."

"Liam has a long way to go yet before he's Ed Murrow
or Ernie Pyle, but he's on his way. Evaleen complains she
and Danny and Ambrose almost never see him. The kids
have to watch for him in news shots to remember what the
Pater looks like."

"The O'Donnells are on a crash course for greatness. Look at Norah!"

"That's always a pleasure, even though she is my own sister and I can remember her with wires on her front teeth. The radio program Martin Kenny has built up for her gets higher scores every time I read the ratings. Old Erin and her tunes are right up front there, no question about it."

"More because of Norah's charisma than for anything Old Erin contributes, in my opinion. They let me have my own radio, you know. I hear her every night."

"You'd better not let Great-Grandpa Liam's ghost hear you down-talking the Old Sod, girl. Or probably my own Dad either. You know how Jim is on the subject."

"He's too proud of you and Norah and Shane these days to pick any fight with me. I just love knowing that Shane and Agnes and their small fry are renting Mother's duplex. It was such a sadness, thinking of those beautiful rooms all empty and unused."

"They're loving it, darling. There's a good nursery school nearby for Brady and the twins. Regina and Ellen sit hours on end at the kitchen window, just watching the water traffic pass. They make up fairy tales about the garbage scows being treasure barges from whatever country it was that Cinderella became princess of."

It had been a good talk, better than Brendan had dared hope for when he first arrived. For the most part they had steered it at a safe distance from subjects which just a little while back might have brought on outbursts of irrational bitterness. But just as he was rising to go, Madge leaned quickly toward him.

"Brendan, I have to ask. You went to Boston last week, didn't you? I know because Cousin Sheela mentioned it in a postcard. Did you see Cornelius Shaara while you were there?''

He braced, but he would not lie. "Yes, Madge, I did."

"I've sort of sensed that you made other trips before."

"I have. Several. The man's been lying on a hospital bed for a year and more. He's sort of left-handed family, however you look at it. I thought it would be wrong to completely ignore him."

He half-expected her to break out with a savage protest, and was both grateful and a trifle concerned when she remained quietly seated. He studied her pale face for signs of trouble but there were none that he could positively identify.

"He was badly hurt trying to rescue Mother, wasn't he? I'm far beyond still believing he set the fire to get her money. He wanted that, but he did try to save her."

"The rescue squad barely got him off the island alive, Madge. He actually fought his way back into Scrimshaw when there was almost nothing left of it. Cousin Bernadette was long past help, but he wouldn't accept the fact."

"Is he coming along?"

"They're still doing skin grafts on him all this while later. He was a very handsome man, almost beautiful you might say. But it's hard to believe that now. So yes, Madge, I do go up to see him now and again."

Instead of blaming him for disloyalty, Madge reached out to touch his cheek.

"You're a good person, Brendan. And a fine priest."

Word that Madge was coming home spread through the O'Donnell ranks as swiftly as, two years earlier, deadly flames had ingested Bar Harbor.

No one quite remembered who had first heard the news, but within an hour everyone seemed to be aware of it.

Rejoicing was loud and sincere. The family, despite its differences, was at bottom as close-knit as Madge and Brendan had described it.

Sheela took charge, announcing that a 'Welcome Home' was to be organized for Madge's first evening back in the city. Everyone was to attend and everyone was to contribute. Jim wanted to play host, but his bustling wife pointed out to him that so did every other member of the family and that he'd better soft-pedal his intentions. At this celebration, after poor little Madge's long ordeal, the host was to be *every* O'Donnell.

They were gathered like a flock of jabbering starlings in Jim's parlor as Brendan, who had driven to Dogwood Dell in the Plymouth to collect Madge, rang the doorbell. A tense silence fell. Then, as Madge herself walked through the entrance hall, pandemonium broke loose. Surging forward like an engulfing wave, the other O'Donnells embraced her.

It was the happiest family gathering Jim could remember. Everyone wanted to kiss the returning member. Everyone was determined to get in his or her own effusive welcome. Only Dennis Gallagher, off in Hollywood winning fame for the tunes he was composing for film musicals, was absent, and even he had sent an affectionate telegram.

"She looks wonderful, doesn't she?" Sheela found opportunity to whisper aside to Jim. "A bit pale, maybe. So much more like herself though, than on that other night."

But "that other night"—the one on which Madge had collapsed in Norah's living room and suddenly begun to shriek wild accusations against Cornelius Shaara—was not to be mentioned aloud. Not on this happy occasion. If it lurked at the back of each O'Donnell's memory, tonight it was to be obliterated. Looking at Madge, smiling brightly in their midst, one knew that her long stay at Dogwood Dell had wrought its miracle.

There were two small O'Donnells Madge had not yet met; Shane and Agnes's twins, Regina and Ellen, whom she gathered to her as if they were matched armloads of flowers and instantly made them her own. Looking on, the proud parents beamed.

"We've loved having Sutton Place's endless space to start raising them in," Agnes murmured at Madge's side. "But now you're home you'll want the condo yourself, won't you? As tenant if not owner. I'll start poking around for a new apartment for us tomorrow. Maybe you'll house hunt with me?"

Madge's eyes met Agnes's above Regina's dark curls. "Oh, no! Please! I'm planning to go back to my West Side studio. I'll truly be more comfortable there. I'd feel all wrong in Mother's place rattling around by myself. Please, you and Shane stay on there."

Agnes hesitated, then plunged on. "We've been paying our rent to Mr. Shaara's agent ever since Cousin Bernadette's will was probated. Even owning it, he hasn't come near the place. But the condo should be yours to enjoy. It's where you grew up. I'm sure the lease could be switched to your name, Madge."

"But I really mean it. I want you to stay on, if you're comfortable there."

"Heaven knows we're *that!* And of course it's an ideal base of operations for Shane, now he's well on his way up the political ladder. One of our 'elegant little dinners' there—that's what the columnists sometimes write them up as, lately—can do wonders for Shane. Even men much higher up are impressed. Not to mention their wives."

"Brendan's kept me posted on how well Shane's doing, while I've been away," Madge said, speaking the last few words quite naturally, making nothing special of them. "I'm so glad."

"If you're sure and certain you don't want to move back . . ."

"I wouldn't dream of it. And you must delight your absentee landlord."

Her half-brother Liam arrived late, direct from the airport. He strode across Jim's threshold like a returning conqueror, beret, khaki field fatigues and all. Pausing on his way only to bestow swift kisses on Evaleen, Danny and Ambrose, he headed straight for the guest of honor. His enthusiastic bear hug left its recipient gasping.

"You look like a cool million, little sister!"

"I ought to," she laughed. "Dogwood Dell charged me that for the beauty treatment. You've changed while I was away, Liam. I'm happy to see that your by-line is the hot one on front pages nowadays. You certainly look successful, though weary—if a relative might say so."

"I didn't have time for a nap or a shower. I came here right from one of those two-for-a-nickle little African republics. They're staging an uprising against the bastard at their helm, a man who doesn't seem to know the difference between 'President' and 'Dictator.' "

"And you had to give him a dictionary lesson?"

"No, only shoot home a few stories straightening out the facts, and then skip over the border before his goons could catch up with me. There was a government price on my head. An insultingly small one. I've done his regime enough harm to deserve better."

By the time a buffet supper was served up—everyone present had brought along an agreed upon contribution to cover the expense—the party had dissolved into typical easy-going O'Donnell hilarity. Perched about the front room, plates balanced on laps, they listened to Norah at the piano. Her songs had become popular with radio listeners clear across the country in the time since the Starlight Serenaders folded. Martin Kenny had brought her along very well indeed. The same rich warmth filled her distinctive voice, but nowadays there was a gloss and a polish to it. Norah O'Donnell was by way of becoming a household name.

It was all Irish tunes tonight, as was not unusual when family gathered. Everyone knew the old ditties, beloved of the first Liam from whom each branch descended. If anyone had not joined in when the program came around to *The Maid That Sold Her Barley*, he would have met cold glances from the others in the circle.

> "Its cold and raw the north winds blow
>   Black in the morning early,
> When all the hills were covered with snow
>   Oh, then it was winter fairly.
> As I was riding o'er the moor,
>   I met a farmer's daughter,
> Her cherry cheeks and sloe black eyes
>   They caused my heart to falter. . . ."

Out in the hallway a doorbell clamored. The summons was so unexpected, with every member of the family already gathered for hours, that the sprightly singing faltered like their winter rider's heart all around the group. Even the piano silenced.

Jim slipped from the room to answer, and was back within minutes bearing a ribbon-tied florist's box for which he had signed a delivery boy's receipt.

"Flowers for you, Madge, honey. Welcome home from another admirer, eh?"

Watching her loosen the silk ties, Madge's family beamed

tenderly upon her. She opened the box and drew out, along with an orchid corsage, the card enclosed with it.

Smile met smile around the watching ring. It would be Barry Sullivan, of course. Tactful about invading a family party, but still wanting to say he remembered her after her long absence.

Madge stood staring down at the little rectangle of paste-board. Her hand began to tremble. Her face froze, like a still pond icing over. Suddenly, unexpectedly, she hurled both box and orchids furiously across the room. A blurred, strangling sound tore from her throat. She plunged blindly past the stricken circle. They could hear her drumming footsteps mount the uncarpeted stairs.

Overhead, a bedroom door slammed violently.

"Oh, no!" Evaleen breathed, on the edge of a sob. "And we all thought she was so much better! Then just one tiny thing like a card . . . Oh, poor, poor Madge!"

Norah had risen quickly from the piano bench. She bent where the card had fallen, cast one quick look at the writing scrawled across it, threw it down again, and was off with the fleetness of a deer in Madge's wake. Those left slack-jawed in the living room were treated to a second tattoo of racing footfalls on the stairs.

Hilda made a distressed move as if to follow, but Sheela's lifted hand checked her. "Better not, dear. Let Norah handle it. You know how good she's always been with Madge."

Meanwhile Terence had again retrieved the twice re-jected card. He read through its brief message twice, forehead wrinkled as if he could not understand the words.

"What in blazes did Sullivan say to her?" Liam growled.

"It's not from Barry. And it's a perfectly polite, even affectionate, little message. It's from Desmond Molloy—

and I, for one, think sending flowers was damned considerate.''

"Read it aloud, for God's sake. To crack up poor Madge just when everything seemed . . .''

Terence obliged. "He says: *Remembering an old friendship and my slight service to you long ago, I want to be among those saying Welcome.* What the devil's wrong with that? He must have sunk thirty dollars in that corsage. Poor Madge has sure enough flipped her wig again, that's all I can say. Old Des was only doing something kind.''

The upstairs door was shut, but at least Madge had not locked it behind her. After a rap on the panel passed unanswered, Norah quietly let herself in.

In Sheela's reading chair off in one corner, Madge sat rocking. Tears streaked her cheeks. She looked up as the door closed gently. When she recognized who had entered, the rocking checked. But not the harsh breathing that meant a choked-back sob.

"H-hello, Norah. I t-t-thought it was you.''

"It certainly is.'' Norah crossed the room swiftly and looped her arms around Madge's shaking shoulders. "I read the card, Madge. I hope you don't object.''

"What right have I to object to anything? I thought I was cured, Norah, but I'm not. I'm still a crazy lady. I still can't control myself. Even a small thing can still set me off again. I'm going to ask Brendan to take me back to Dogwood Dell.''

"Easy, now. Easy, Madge. Just tell me, if you want to. What did Molloy do to you?''

Madge jerked her head desperately from side to side. "N-nothing. I guess he really didn't. But for so long I believed—it was one of my crazies about Bar Harbor . . .''

"I caught the phrase about some old favor. Was that it, Madge?"

"It was just after Mother came back from Ireland and brought Cornelius Shaara with her. I was awfully upset, Norah. I was idiot enough to call him one day, and he told me he'd see to it the man left Mother alone and never pestered her again."

"The Molloy power machine in action. I know quite a lot about that power. What did he mean to do, did he tell you? Of course, the fire took care of that for him."

"Maybe not. He telephoned me the afternoon the fire began, you see. I didn't even know yet that one had started. But he, he said he'd taken care of his promise. And he seemed to think I'd asked him to do whatever it was he'd done. If that was true, then—then I as good as killed my own mother, didn't I?"

Norah was down on her knees now, holding Madge close. "You've been living with that thought all this while, honey?"

"I didn't mean it to happen. I didn't even guess what he had in mind. But if he set that fire *for me*, if Mother and so many others were made to die *for me*, if almost a whole town was wiped out just to get at Cornelius *for me*. . . ."

"Hey! Cut it. In the first place, I don't believe even Molloy could try such a monstrous thing. If it ever became known, he'd be lynched. But the fire was a pure tragedy of nature, Madge. Tinder forests, a careless match, even spontaneous combustion, that's what was responsible. Right now, you shrug any other notion off your shoulders."

"H-how can I? There was something . . . oh, almost sinister about the message with those flowers, Norah. As if he were reminding me of a criminal act performed in my name because, now I'm home, he means to collect on the favor some way. Norah, I'm afraid."

''You needn't be.'' And for an instant Norah, usually so warm, looked cold as steel. ''Honey, I'm going to tell you something about Desmond Molloy that I've never until now told anybody. Terence doesn't know it, Shane doesn't, no one does but me. I want you to know it, too. Once you do, he could never have any sort of hold on you. You'll be free of him. You see, it was like this . . .''

17

She felt new again. Strong inside, and growing stronger with each passing day.

If the story Norah had told her was a crutch Madge still needed, at least she now had it to lean on. An awful possibility that had hung over her for many dreary months was erased. She now dared to think about her mother, as the crushing incubus of a false belief had been lifted from her.

"But there's still something I *don't* know," she told herself, more than once, alone in her small but increasingly attractive West Side quarters. "Until I learn it, where am I? Molloy definitely did *something* to rid me of a stepfather. If he didn't set the fire that killed Mother, maimed Shaara and practically wiped out Bar Harbor—then what? He certainly spoke on the telephone as if what he'd promised me had been accomplished."

Although she was no longer sickly haunted by it, the

puzzle still remained. Armed with the armor which had
been hers since Norah's revelation, she still had something
vital to discover. The answer well might lie in Boston.
Even if not, she certainly owed it to Cornelius Shaara,
however much she might still dislike him, to find out.

One early summer morning, she boarded a train to
Massachusetts.

Madge had visited Boston many times before. There had
been one three-day vacation with the family of a fellow
student at art school. There had been the funeral of a very
old relation of Great-Grandmother Edith, herself gone from
among the living for so long she was scarcely even
remembered.

None of these trips had done much in the way of
familiarizing Madge with the city but she had never been
much interested in Boston anyway. To her the town seemed
stuffy and rather dull. None of New England, in fact, had
ever particularly intrigued her. People said that it was very
different and dramatically paintable, especially in autumn
when the leaves were turning. Madge had pleasantly agreed
she really must check out the scenery. Now, as she looked
out her train window, she studied the passing landscape
from a different angle. Cornelius Shaara, like her a painter,
had chosen to remain here. With the money Mother had
left him, he might have roamed the world over. His decision to stay on, in a country where he was a stranger,
piqued her curiosity.

At the South Street Station she found herself a taxi and
gave its driver the address she had been careful to obtain
from Brendan two evenings earlier. Patriot's Peak, of
which her cousin had provided scant description, she assumed to be a Massachusetts equivalent of her own Dogwood Dell. The environs of the station were anything but

prepossessing. Certainly, she told herself, the city must have more attractive sections, and Shaara's hospital would, of course, be in one of them.

When her cab veered into the short cement runway ending in a round bed of saliva, the loud red of a fire engine, Madge leaned forward in alarm. She was certain that the man had misunderstood her directions.

This couldn't be the place to which Mother's husband still periodically returned for his painful and protracted skin operations. This ugly yellow brick pile, with its girdle of jigsaw-decorated verandas painted in cheerless chocolate? This steep, restricted scrap of lawn flaunting as much plantain weed as it did grass? These almost random towers and minarets, all roofed in unattractive asphalt shingles?

"You said Patriot's Peak, lady. This is it."

Sure enough, the words were repeated in austere gilt letters on a sign installed above the main door. The driver wasn't mistaken. She paid her fare plus a decent tip and climbed the wooden steps, still more or less in shock.

Mr. Shaara was indeed in residence, so the colorless but efficient matron on duty at the reception desk informed her. Madge followed her directions along a corridor paneled in shiny, serviceable bird's-eye maple toward a door leading to what was evidently some sort of rear porch. A faint memory of New England Boiled Dinner hung in the air. The odor of cabbage predominated. Gigantic roses in the carpeting urged her to look away.

The porch, when she reached it, lay in shade. The sun had moved on around the building, perhaps in an effort to flee the cheerless structure altogether. At irregular intervals along the sturdy wooden platform, solitary figures occupied woven rush chairs. She turned to the nearest one, whose face showed more bandages than flesh, and cleared her throat to attract attention. The man looked up, pushing back a slouch hat which had been shielding his eyes.

"I beg your pardon, sir," Madge said. "Could you point out Mr. Cornelius Shaara for me?"

"I'm Cornelius Shaara." To her surprise, the voice was deep and musical. It hesitated only for an instant. "And you, unless I'm mistaken, are Madge McHugh."

"How in the world could you possibly have guessed that?"

"It was more than a guess. You're very much like your mother. It isn't hard for me to remember how Bernadette looked, short as our time together was."

She could think of nothing to say in the way of an answer to his comment. Having schooled herself to be gracious and polite no matter how she disliked this man, she found herself instead literally speechless. There had been something in the tone, however well disguised, which betrayed an underlying longing.

He arose from his chair and with a courteous gesture invited her to occupy it. He himself sank down at the edge of the high stool and let his legs dangle carelessly. The way he moved, despite a certain stiffness, was innately graceful. She found herself picturing him as he must have been in the Sligo heather where Mother had found him.

"I'm sure you must wonder why I've come from New York to call on you, Mr. Shaara, after this considerable time. I've been in hospital myself, until recently."

"I'm aware of that. Father O'Donnell has kept me more or less up to date with your progress. It was a long siege, wasn't it? I'm happy you've come out on top at last."

His eyes were green, green as the best grade of jade, and they kept looking up at her in a most disconcerting manner. Madge glanced hurriedly away. Suddenly she could imagine the appeal of them when they were not framed in surgical gauze. Small wonder that Mother . . .

"News of the fire at Scrimshaw," he cut across her halfformed thought, "must have been a ghastly shock to you, Madge. Look here, I hope you don't mind. But I'm going to call you Madge. Bernadette always did. It's the way she trained me to think of you. If I offend you, forgive me."

"I'm not offended." It astonished Madge to discover that this was true. She had not come here intending to encourage the slightest degree of informality.

"Then please call me Cornelius. After all, there's at least a technical connection between us. It troubles me to have anyone who looks like Bern 'Mr. Shaara-ing' me."

"Do I really resemble Mother so much, then?"

"You do," he said simply.

"I've come to Boston on a mission, Mr. Shaara," Madge said after a pause.

"Cornelius," he prompted softly.

"Well, Cornelius, then. Have you ever met a man named Desmond Molloy?"

This required thinking. "I'm sure I've never actually met him. But if memory serves, Bern mentioned him to me once. I seem to recollect she didn't much care for him."

"Neither do I!" It blurted before Madge could check it.

"If he's the same chap I'm thinking of, your mother told me that the O'Donnell ladies seem to harbor reservations about him. But one of you considered marrying him? Look, is this the one who's a big nabob in American politics? A mighty wheeler-and-dealer?"

"He's the one. Supposedly a good friend of the family—which he isn't."

Cornelius had not lowered those amazing eyes for a

second. "And why in the world would I have met him, the one day I ever spent in New York? Why do you ask?"

"Because . . ." Madge braced herself. "Look, Mr. . . . Cornelius, this isn't going to be easy. I don't quite know how to say what I've come to say."

"Try just spitting it out. I'll try not to rock in the backwash."

"I was very angry when Mother married you. Very hurt. I foolishly asked Mr. Molloy for advice about breaking up the marriage. He told me, all comfort, that he'd attend to it for me. Then, later, he called and said that he had done just what I'd asked."

"Did he, now? Fancy that! Was Bern aware, do you suppose, that she'd divorced me?"

"You don't understand. I'd never asked Mr. Molloy to do anything at all. I know I let him suppose I wished you were a million miles away from Mother, but that was all. He never told me what he later claimed to have done. I didn't want to hear. But if it was anything as despicable as starting the fire that burned up Bar Harbor and killed Mother . . ."

So far as its bandages permitted, a look of enlightenment was spreading across Cornelius's face. Abruptly, he lifted one scarred hand to silence her.

"I'm beginning to understand a lot more than you do, Madge. And your Molloy wasn't lying to you. If it was him who sent the strong-arm squad—and who else had a reason?—then he spoke true. I was on my way out. He had me on the run."

"You were going to desert Mother? But Cornelius, *why*?"

"Because I was young and not very brave and more than a little ashamed of myself. When those two sadistic giants turned up on Mt. Desert, the day the fire broke out, and started rearranging my bone structure, I was scared as hell. You bet I ran."

"You mean, two men you'd never seen actually turned up and . . . and . . .?"

"Oh, indeed they did. And they knew their man. I was still so jumpy about how Bern's folks must be perceiving me that every sneer about my rich wife cut deep. Who but Bern and I knew the truth about us? *Someone* didn't like me and sure as demons meant for me to decamp. Next time it was to be a coffin. I got the message loud and clear."

"I was the one. Only I didn't know that I was the one."

"Not you. Apparently it was this Molloy. The worst *you* did was mix up your signals."

Damn! She was crying. "You said you ran. But you were still there when the fire . . ."

"Slight correction. I was there *again* after all hell broke loose. I was snug in an escape boat, prepared to row clear to China, when I spied the first flames high above. Suddenly I remembered she was asleep in the house and wouldn't stand a chance unless I beat the fire to her. What choice had I? I happened to be deeply in love with her."

The tears increased, silent but stinging. "T-that's what Mother herself told me. I said she was being made a fool of, and she slapped my face. I-I never saw her again."

"Well, now. You mustn't take it too hard. We all have little spats with those we best love. You'd have made it up between you, peaches and cream, if time had allowed you to. Bern loved you so much. And I'm sure you loved her, as well. Both of you knew it in your hearts, and isn't that what matters? See here, I've made you cry. I'm sorry, Madge."

She stumbled from the chair, tormented with shame. "I

have to go now. I must. If you'd like me to, I'll come
again some time soon. To . . . to really apologize.''

"Apologize for what you never did? Try that, young
lady, and I'll put you over my knee and give you a slap
your mother never dreamed of. After all, I'm your stepfather.
I owe it to her to pound sense into you, if that's the only
way.''

"Do . . . do you really want me to come?''

"We'll refer that question to the Department of Blather.
Come when you can, and dress up in your prettiest. I'll
take you out for a day on the town. There's a lot you'll
enjoy in Boston. And as for me, I'll have the time of my
life just sitting and gawking at you. My Bern as she must
have looked when I was still in my nappies.''

"How could you possibly take me anywhere? You're in
a hospital.''

"Once, yes indeed. Nowadays, St. Patrick be praised,
only for little patches while they diddle with the ruins. I'm
told that inside a year or two I'll have to wear a mask
again on Halloween, instead of my own bare-naked face. I
won't frighten you too badly.''

From her return train to Manhattan she went directly to
St. Cyprian's.

Evening service there had just concluded, and a straggle
of the rather thin congregation was trickling down worn
stone steps and dispersing across cracked Chelsea sidewalks,
pausing to murmur dutiful good-evenings to Father Cullen
on their way. Back in the sacristy, lights still cast a
muffled glow. Madge paid her driver and headed toward
them.

Brendan met her at the door. Obviously, he had just
hung up his vestments and was on his way across the street
to the parish house for whatever further duties awaited him

there. But when he recognized her, he paused and bestowed his usual grave, beautiful smile upon her.

"Madge! What brings you here at such an hour? This isn't the grandest section of town for a young woman to be walking around alone in after twilight."

"I just this minute stepped out of a taxi and I'll take another home, but I had to see you for a moment. Have you the time to spare, or shall I come back later?"

"We can talk, of course." He motioned her to an end pew and sat down beside her, after first making his obeisance to the garnet light shining on the altar. "Is something wrong, dear?"

"Not wrong, exactly. But I'm so mixed up I don't know where to turn. So, as usual, I wind up on your doorstep. Don't you sometimes wish I had died in my cradle? Of some painless and very romantic ailment, of course. I'm certainly your resident pest."

"Not always. I can remember an occasion or two over the past twenty-odd years when you were actually almost a joy." His hand fell over hers. "So what is it now?"

"I've just gotten in from a trip, Brendan. A trip to Boston."

His face changed, or perhaps it was the glow from the chancel falling over it. "What you're really saying is that you've finally met Cornelius. Am I right?"

"I guess that's it. Anyhow, I most certainly have been to see him. Brendan, who is he really? You're the smartest man I know about other people. Who *is* Cornelius?"

"What am I supposed to say that you don't already know? He's thirtyish or a trifle older. He's a painter, or was one until his hands were severely burned in the fire. He was ambitious once, isn't any more, but well may be again if his wounds really heal. He was something of an opportunist until he met Cousin Bernadette. He fell in love. He still is, nostalgically. Enough?''

Madge smiled ruefully in the half-light. "Enough to give me plenty to ponder. But I need more. Do you think he *truly* loved Mother? Quite apart from her money?''

"Your best answer would be to watch his eyes whenever he speaks of her. The loss that shows there tells its own story.''

"But mightn't that just be . . .?''

"Camouflage? He had nothing more to win from her materially. She'd already made arrangements to make sure he got it all. She trusted him, you see. They hadn't known each other long. But I think they knew each other well.''

"How about you, Brendan? Do you trust him too?''

"What you're trying to find out is whether or not *you* trust him. I can't give you an answer, Madge. It would mean nothing.''

She sighed. "You don't make it very easy for me to pick your brains, I must say. Brendan, I've been so wrong about so much so often. It's myself I don't trust, maybe.''

"Then start giving it a try. Go back. See him again. Make a slow judgment.''

Madge began to smooth on the gloves she had removed just before their meeting. It would be unfair to detain her cousin longer. He had his work to do, just as she had her own. Just as perhaps Cornelius Shaara would have, if the hands he had destroyed trying to save her mother ever regained their old skill. *Find your own answer*, Brendan was saying.

Because it would be the only answer that could matter.

"You drive up to Boston often, don't you, Brendan?''

"Quite often. Whenever Cornelius is up for a new operation, I try to drop around and wish him luck. Luck, of course, being his euphemism for Another Thing.''

"Next time you go, will you take me with you?"

"It might do you considerable good if I made you walk. But yes, I'll take you."

As a mark of forced courage, however, the next time she went again to Boston she went alone. She had written ahead, a polite, almost schoolgirlish note suggesting that she planned to be visiting a friend in Lexington and perhaps he'd care to arrange another meeting.

His answer was back in her hand three days later, surely a record for the inter-city postal service. The lines were a trifle cramped, as though stiff fingers had held the pen. He wrote that he was no longer at Patriot's Peak and would not be there again for the better part of a month, at which time new tests were to be administered in preparation for another grafting. His present quarters were a hotel room at the Copley, scarcely a fit spot for a man to receive a lady, even granting he was her stepfather. But if she would meet him in the Merry-go-round Bar at half-past noon, if that were convenient for her, he would be delighted to buy her a lunch which ought to convince her that Boston was indeed a hub of excellence. The signature was a simple: *Cornelius*.

Madge arrived early for their appointment. So did he.

The food was all that his note had promised, but she barely noticed it, so engrossed was she in trying to live up to Brendan's suggestion. Had she made the mistake of her lifetime over this man who sat across from her and talked so easily and well, never once taking his eyes from her face? He seemed to be finding new things to see with every passing shift in their conversation. Was he really what he now seemed to her to be? Or was *this* Cornelius merely a false front concealing the one she had devoted

years to despising? Was he merely making over his surface
image as doctors were making over his physical features?

"Now what?" he asked, as they arose at last from the
table.

"It's your city, Cornelius. You lead. I follow."

"Then we'll start with the Common, I think. It reeks
with your American history. On that green, troops under
Washington rehearsed maneuvers between spells of hammering the devil out of British lobsterbacks, who numbered my Irish ancestors amongst them."

"Don't ever tell Liam that decent Irishmen ever con-
sented to fight for England."

"I'm not sure that much consenting came into it. When
you're starving, you go where the next miserable meal is.
But they did fight here, my people, one or two of them."

It was a short walk to their destination. Madge spent a
good deal of it in silent thought. Was this Cornelius's true
philosophy, the line he just had spoken so off-handedly;
that a man went where the pickings were easiest? If so, she
had learned all she needed to know about him.

But suppose what he said were a passing comment on
the standards of other, leaner times, and no more than
that? One which had no bearing on his own beliefs? Mere
conversation?

"I should have waited until I could come back here with
you, Brendan," she silently admonished herself. "You'd
know how to weigh the factors. Alone, I'm so at sea."

Go back. See him again. Make a slow judgment, the
bright afternoon sunlight seemed to echo. She felt swamped
by a tidal wave of inadequacies.

When they came out onto the Common together, passing through a very old corner gate and onto a shaded
diagonal walk, a microcosm of Boston lay spread before
her. School was out and children raced everywhere across

the grass, screaming at one another but not unpleasantly. Young people lay two by two in the shade of the great, ageless trees, arms locked about each other, bodies pressing close. On benches all along the walk, old men read their newspapers; some tattered, as if retrieved from not too distant trash receptacles. Near path intersections, a few ferret-thin characters were peddling something carefully concealed within cupped hands. Plump women who looked like nursemaids pushed baby carriages. Bicycles passed. Boston was Anycity.

As if reading her thought, Cornelius asked suddenly, "Is New York anything like this?"

"Very like it. Nothing like it at all. New York isn't even like itself from street to street, Cornelius. You saw it. Was Ninth Avenue like Sutton Place?"

"I remember I was stunned by the variety, the morning our liner docked, but I hadn't much time there to absorb details. Sutton is one of the choice bits, that much I can recall. I'm glad your Cousin Shane is living in Bern's duplex now. But do you miss it?"

"Not really. I'm happier where I am. But I do care about the place because it was Mother's and Daddy's, and because I was little there, I suppose. I do remember a lot that happened there. But I scarcely remember Scrimshaw at all. Even how it looked."

"Why should you want to? Bern loved it, but she owned it only a short while. It doesn't even exist now. There's just a bare, burned-over bit of headland."

Ambiguity again! "It was where you and Mother were happy together, wasn't it?"

"Where Bernadette and I were happy together," Cornelius answered softly, almost as if talking to himself, "was a hill drenched in purple heather. There's a cairn of rough rocks at the top, and under the rocks there sleeps a very

great queen. You can look out practically forever across
the farms and stone fences of Sligo, where many an
O'Donnell is buried. Far off is the sea. Nearer by, it's
mostly poetry; it's Yeats.''

"The Yeats who wrote about fairies dancing in moonlight and someplace called Innisfree?''

"The Yeats who wrote the signpost to our grand hill,
Bernadette's and mine. *The winds have bundled up the
clouds high over Knocknarea and thrown the thunder on
the stones for all that Maeve can say.* That's what he
wrote. I wonder if Bern still remembers Knocknarea.''

They walked along in silence after that. Neither spoke
until they came out on a large pond shaped rather like a
figure eight, where flocks of water fowl were parading.

Boats in the shapes of swans were making regal progress along the shoreline, each propelled by a boatman with
his foot paddle. Rows of passengers sat oddly silent but
visibly content, children enchanted, adults for the time of
their swan's passage magically divorced from landside
tribulations.

Their eyes met. Cornelius crooked an eyebrow question-
ingly. Madge nodded. Still without a word, they moved
out onto the landing pier. He paid their fares. They waited.

A swan drifted in. Voyagers clambered ashore from it,
and Cornelius's scarred hand helped Madge aboard. They
took places in the foremost row. Others followed.

It was all more a dream than a reality. The swan began
to float from the dock, its movement almost unnoticed by
Madge. Listless willows glided closer. She turned and
looked at the face beside her.

Scars and small ravished places showed clearly in the
unshaded light. At the corner of one green eye a livid line
pinned back the lid a millimeter and traced its wormlike
way through an eyebrow. Lines of long suffering etched

the mouth corners. It was an older face than the date
Brendan gave it. A destroyed face. If she came back out of
the shadows, Bernadette Shaara might not recognize it at
first.

Cornelius caught her studying him. "What are you
thinking, Madge?"

She answered quietly.

"I was just deciding that I trust you."

BOOK FIVE

SKYLARK ASCENDING

18

Norah could feel exhaustion begin to seep in as the excitement of the gala evening receded.

Whisking her away from the White House, her hired limousine seemed to purr approval of the invitational show just completed. President Truman had been flattering in his comments, which people assured her was a rarity since his beloved daughter was more or less a rival in the field. The songs had gone over well with a mostly white-tie assemblage of guests, gathered to celebrate the ending of the Berlin blockade and the signing of a finally-ironed-out NATO Treaty. She ought to be feeling on top of the world.

Instead, she wanted only to crawl back home, kiss Tony and Jenny without disturbing their dreams, rest her head on Dennis's shoulder and drift off to blessed sleep, sleep, sleep.

Stumbling blocks to the dream were manifold. For one,

she still had the long drive to the airport and a longer flight back to New York between her and the blessed apartment. For another, Marty, sitting at her side and looking very distinguished in his dinner jacket, had business to discuss with her. And for yet another, and most importantly, Dennis wouldn't be there waiting when she turned her key in the latch.

For so long now, Dennis hadn't been there.

The sleek car swerved into Pennsylvania Avenue. Lights twinkled at her in bewildering patterns. Sedate Government buildings peered at the passersby out of post-midnight shadows. If only she could close her eyes and sink back against the soft grey cushions and erase the world for a little while.

No such luck. Alert as he always was, and tonight even more so because her part of the program had been so well received, Martin beamed approval. Pride in her showed clear on his good-looking if not quite handsome face every time a streetlight shone across it.

"Never saw Harry and Bess give a bigger hand to a singer than you got tonight, honey. Except for Margaret, of course, and she's a special case. You're really up there, Songbird. Top of the tree."

"Top of the tree is where songbirds get to tuck heads under wings, isn't it? If they're lucky enough to be the kind with feathers? I could sleep from now till Christmas, Marty."

"The hell you could. You're booked for three weeks at the Copacabana, starting next Monday, remember? And now that the show is on TV, not just radio, we couldn't fake even one show by slipping in a few of your choice records. You've got to be the real McCoy."

"Amn't I always?" Norah struggled to sit erect again.

"Is there such a word as 'Amn't,' Marty? I'm too tired to remember. Oh, God, so tired."

"Peace. You can take it easy all day tomorrow. You don't have to be at the studio for rehearsal until five o'clock. Oh, sorry, I forgot. There's a costume fitting at three. Pussy says that gold lamé thing you were supposed to wear in the finale catches the lights all wrong. It puts ten extra pounds on you. He wants white velvet."

"You can take it easy all day tomorrow," she mumbled, staring at him woodenly. "Gee, thanks! We're already well into 'tomorrow,' Martin Kenny. Moreover, I'm in a strange city and hours from my bed. It'll be sunup before I possibly can tuck in. Jenny and Tony erupt at seven on the dot. My bed is their favorite trampoline."

"Those kids ought to learn to be more considerate. Don't they know how hard their little Mommy works to keep them in De Pinna wardrobes and plush nursery schools?"

"Kids have a vested right in their mothers. I can't lock my bedroom door against them. Even if I did, they'd only batter it down to get at me."

"That's because you're such a wow lady. Even babies know you're one of a kind."

"Soft soap will get you nowhere. You're sitting there in your corner cracking your blacksnake whip. And every aching bone in my body is feeling the lash. You don't fool me."

"Come on, Norah. Cheer up. You're the Irish Skylark, remember? Adored from coast to coast. Best variety show on the air. Ratings in the stratosphere. You've come a long, long road since I first signed you and Dennis with Buddy Diston, and you know it.

Norah shifted position wearily. "Poor old Buddy. Have you heard from him lately, Martin? I always felt so sorry for him, caught in that itch of his and able to do so little about it. Haven't you been able to find anything for him? Anything at all?''

"Buddy Diston is yesterday's roses, darling. People don't even much remember the Starlight Serenaders any more. But they do have a feeling that something nasty broke up Buddy's career. A stink of garbage is still in the air when his name comes up. I couldn't book him into a cattle show. But the poor bastard brought it on himself.''

"Do any of us really bring on the things that happen to us, I wonder? Or are the pitfalls all there in the path already, just waiting? Find Buddy something, Martin. Please. Couldn't we work him into a number in our Copacabana routine?''

"And have our heads handed to us by the management? Norah, Buddy is to show business what Bill Tilden is to tennis. Out, out, *out*. The public is just that way, comes it to other people's unzipped flies.''

"The public, who, of course, never personally sins. I'm still sorry for old Buddy. He was good to Dennis and me when we were starting out. He gave us chances.''

"Most likely because he had a greedy eye on Dennis's basket.''

"It wasn't that way at all. Dennis and I used to talk it over. Buddy never made a single pass at him, not even a verbal one.''

"That was because, for Buddy, Dennis was over the hill. He was old enough to vote and wear long pants. Not Buddy's style. But why are we wasting all this chatter on the has-beens? You've too much ahead of you to bother looking over your shoulder.''

"I don't know. Maybe it's because some of the sweetest things lie back there somewhere—over my shoulder. Dennis and I were always together then.''

"You could be again. Sure, your lad is raking in the

alfalfa out yonder in Beverly Hills, but he could do just as well in New York. It would only take me a couple of phone calls to land him with a Broadway show. We need tunes back east, too.''

''That's not the way Dennis sees it. He always dreamed of California.''

She turned her head and looked out the window. The limousine was gliding across a bridge now. Dark water flowed underneath it, reflecting an occasional scrap of light like a sewed-on sequin. She felt too tired to try to figure out which way the tide was running.

When she let herself into her New York apartment, grey light was beginning to filter across the city's skyscrapers like the dirty contents of a celestial slop bucket. Her windows were still dark, pocked with the lights of other distant windows, but there was a dreary hint of paling against the glass.

Norah shrugged off the fur stole she'd purchased especially for the White House jaunt, letting it fall half-on, half-off the first chair she came to. Pussy Clark had put together the gown that went with it—emerald chiffon, yards upon billowing yards of it, the color picked to underscore 'the Irish Skylark's' professional image. Passing a long mirror, Norah caught a glimpse of herself. She looked like a whole St. Patrick's Day parade.

''The O'Donnells are coming, the O'Donnells are coming,'' she began to hum, exhaustedly, to a tune best known among those familiar with the lifting of the Siege at Lucknow. Probably the warrior Campbells wouldn't resent a bit of larceny.

She sank, rag doll limp, onto the loveseat nearest the fireplace, fished for a cigarette in a silver box on the coffee table, and sucked in its smoke automatically.

Released, it drifted before her languidly, dissolving as she watched it.

Across the room, the telephone clanged suddenly.

At this outrageous hour? She dove for it, animated despite herself by the likelihood that a second ring would awaken the children. "Who in the world . . .?"

"Hi, Sweet!" the voice at the other end of the receiver greeted her brightly. "Safe home from Washington?"

"Dennis!" Her hold on the telephone tightened eagerly.

"I've been waiting to call until I figured you'd be back from dazzling the Mighty Moguls. How did it go? Were you the usual sensation?"

Weariness dropped from her like another discarded stole. "They liked me, I think. I did three encores. Finally cut them off with *The Good Old Mountain Dew*. I'd heard somewhere that the Trumans aren't drinking people."

"Who else was on the program? I'll bet you upstaged the lot, whoever."

"Greer Garson, reciting *The Charge of the Light Brigade* in that exquisite voice and making everybody misty-eyed. Fontanne and Lunt, playing a scene from their new show *I Know My Love*. Sono Osato doing one of her ballets. Pablo Casals on his cello. A mixed bag."

"But they liked my girl best, didn't they?"

She made small chiding sounds. "How am I supposed to answer that one? At least nobody shouted '*Get the hook!*' Oh, Denny, if you only knew how much I miss you. Catch a quick plane and get here within ten minutes and let me sleep on your nice, hairy chest."

"Funny thing, Madam. I was just about to say the same."

"Dennis Gallagher! I do *not* have hair on my chest, as you well know."

"I indeed seem to recall it from the dim past. But I didn't mean that. I was talking about catching planes."

"I can't . . ."

"Hush. Listen, I've been having a big day with a real estate lady. She's showed me a dilly of a place up one of our better canyons. Ideal for a man with a gorgeous wife and two fantastic offspring. When can you pop out for a look at it, Norah?"

She felt her heart sink like a lowering anchor.

"Dennis, darling, *please*. You know I can't just drop everything and leap. You of all people must realize how impossible it is to wangle time off from a weekly hour-long variety show. It's six o'clock here and I haven't even seen bed yet and I'll have to be downtown at three to have Pussy pinning yardage on me. I can't even take a few *hours* off, let alone several *days!*"

"Pussy certainly has the dream job, doesn't he? Why is it always the queens? Now if *I* were messing around, tucking up your bustline, flattening your fanny . . ."

"You're talking dirty, Gallagher. Pussy, thank God, doesn't give a damn about what he wraps up in his silks and satins. You ought to be grateful for that, too."

"Sure, at long distance. What kind of an act is this, anyway, Norah? You there, me here, neither of us getting any kind of a crack at marriage. We used to be together."

"We could be still. Martin and I were talking about that just tonight, on the way to the airport. He says there's a new Broadway musical coming up he can write you in to do the songs for if you'd just snap your fingers. I wish you'd consider it. I miss you so."

"I miss you too. Why don't you consider that? California's a marvelous place to raise Tony and Jenny, Norah. This sunlight ought to be locked up in Fort Knox. The air's straight out of Hans Anderson. They could have their own ponies."

"They can ride in Central Park, darling, when they're old enough. They both adore their nanny, and Miss Whittaker doesn't know there's an acre of America west of the Hudson. She wouldn't even *consider* a move for them."

"How about running Miss Whittaker up the flagpole? There are plenty of adorable nannies right here in Southern Cal. Good schools, too, for later, and maybe our offspring would figure the west has one other advantage. A real, live, breathing, loving Daddy."

"I'd have to leave my show. Just when Martin's hard work on me is paying off."

"You aren't married to Marty. You're married to me."

"If that meant as much to you as I once believed it did, Dennis, then you'd at least come back and give Manhattan another try. After all, you've built up a beautiful name in your field since our Buddy Diston days. Everyone's whistling your movie scores."

"That's because, take the Republic up one side and down the other, more citizens go to movies than ever set foot on Broadway. I know my public, Norah."

"Be fair. A good stage show . . ."

"Stage shows are one gut-wrenching gamble. Compose a couple of turkeys and you're as dead as the Duke of Wellington. Whereas, a big-budget film isn't *allowed* to fail. You toss a few names like Astaire and Rogers and Busby Berkley into the salad bowl and the studio damn well sees to it you're home free. I'm not a gambler, honey. I'm a songsmith."

They hung up politely, but with the usual undercurrent of mutual resentment. Lately, this had become more and more the pattern of each eagerly-begun long distance conversation. If there were a happy answer to it, Norah had yet to dream one up.

Each of them was right, she conceded, and each of them was wrong. Neither one was about to chuck a job which had been worked at and scrimped for down a row of prayerful years. Feeling bitter because he refused to listen to reason, she still was fair enough to understand that Dennis must have precisely the same reaction to her own answers to his wheedling. Life was a stalemate. And the years were dragging on.

She wanted her husband.

The family, one by one, were becoming increasingly concerned over the situation at 729 Park Avenue.

Their beloved Norah had moved uptown with the babies a bit more than a year after Dennis took off for the West. Obviously, the old apartment was outgrown with two children growing like weeds, and both parents well established and their incomes soaring. Obviously, too, Norah felt somewhat haunted in those more modest rooms where her marriage had started, but there seemed to be something more to her move than mere restlessness.

Now she had been settled into her unobtrusively elegant new apartment for two years.

On the surface the Gallaghers had little but dual success to plague them. Dennis flew east for a weekend, maybe once every three months. Norah reported frequent long-distance calls from California, so there didn't seem to be anything wrong. Still, things between Norah and Dennis just weren't the same.

Sheela was perhaps the most worried of the clan, being Norah's mother. "The young people miss each other terribly, but Jenny seems to have some allergy that does better in the

east. Norah just doesn't think it's right to take the baby
way out there to live.''

Terence's second wife, Hilda, had quite a different
explanation. ''I've read a good many gossip items lately
about some blonde Dennis is being seen around Hollywood with. Some say she's a rich Jet Set divorcée. Some
say she's a top talent agent. You don't know which to
believe, and of course, the whole thing may be just a
figment.''

Still a third possibility drifted along the O'Donnell
grapevine, woman to woman; this one from Evaleen. ''I
was having dinner with an old school friend at '21' the
other day, and who should be at a table across from us but
Norah with Martin Kenny. He's certainly been paying her
a lot of attention since Dennis quit town. Not that Norah
would encourage anything, but some men just won't take
no for an answer.''

''Little Jenny's never had a sick day in her life . . .''

''Dennis *adores* his wife. Why, just to see those two
together in the old days . . .''

''If Norah lunches with Mr. Kenny, it's strictly business.
He's her manager, after all.''

To each fabricated explanation of the nagging problem
at 729 there came an instant rebuttal. Norah was the family
idol and altogether beyond reproach. Dennis Gallagher had
been a popular adjunct to the clan since Norah first started
going out with him. No one wished either of them the
slightest scrap of trouble, even a sickly daughter. Still, one
did wonder.

Returning from two years of art study in Rome, Madge
was the first one to do anything constructive about the
mystery. She and Norah had cocktails together at a handy
if not chic lounge near the TV studio, and Madge came
away convinced that her cousin was unhappy. Since Norah's

prompt rallying to her defense at the party to welcome her home from Dogwood Dell, Madge would have lain down on a highway and let a truck run over her if it would in any way have benefitted Brendan's sister.

"I don't know what's troubling her and I'm certainly not going to ask," she told Shane's wife, Agnes, the following day. "But I do know Norah's unhappy and needs cheering up."

"How can we, when we don't know what's wrong?"

"Do you think I could give one of those old-time family parties?" Madge asked. "I've never done it before. But she always loved them. If you and Cousin Sheela would advise me about things . . ."

"It's what we've all been thinking, but never quite doing, Madge. A party, of course!"

So Madge laced in her courage and, with heart pounding nervously, telephoned her invitations. Not one of them was refused.

Terence thought it was very cute of the little family mouse, creeping out of her hole like this. Brendan offered a prayer of thanks for one more sign of his cousin's improvement. Shane—*Congressman* O'Donnell since Election Day the preceding November—took their call and accepted happily for himself and Agnes. It went without saying that Jim and Sheela would be present, and Evaleen was almost sure Liam would be back from his current field assignment before the appointed evening. All the children were to be brought along, so that no one need trouble about baby sitters.

The party for Norah was theoretically intended to celebrate Martin Kenny's just having negotiated a new contract which almost doubled his Irish Skylark's original salary, and was held on the evening following her current week's show. This way, she would be relaxed.

There had been discussion of including Kenny out of courtesy, but they decided not to. Everyone liked him well enough, everyone appreciated all he had been doing to advance Norah; but if there were any truth whatever in this rumor about his personal interest in her, she'd probably feel easier without him.

Just as the June twilight began to make itself felt, O'Donnells began to gather.

Madge's small apartment had, over her years living in it, taken on the look of what magazine articles on home decoration were apt to call "A little jewelbox." The little added touches she had brought back with her from Italy had already blended with her older belongings. A little Carrara marble cigarette box looked custom made for Veronica's olivewood butler's tray. The small but perfect Fifteenth-Century Madonna and Child discovered in Florence burned like rubies and sapphires against a pale ivory wall. There was much to be exclaimed over, and the compliments were appreciated.

If any among them were startled to be greeted by Cornelius Shaara at Madge's side, no one was sufficiently crass to comment. It had been generally known that before her departure for Europe Madge had visited him in some hospital in Boston, where he had been recuperating from the disastrous Bar Harbor fire. This had been regarded as a good thing, since it signified improvement from poor Madge's former erratic hallucinations. Still, to find him here in her apartment and even at her side . . .

"What a nest you've created for yourself, dear!" Sheela enthused. "Only a real born artist could have managed the lovely counterplay of colors."

"I had a lot of help making my decisions."

"Why, Madge, I didn't realize a decorator had been called in."

"None was, Cousin Sheela. My advisor was Cornelius."

"Really? I never heard he was with you while you were in Europe."

"He wasn't. Except once, for two weeks, when he managed to come over. Generally, he's preoccupied with his photography. Did you know he's getting to be a real professional with his camera? But once he came, and he showed me around the museums and shops. I got to understand a little about things he likes, and why. He's almost always right."

Because the party was a pleasant one, and because the family would have made it so in any event for Norah's sake and Madge's, things were flowing with a champagne gaiety by the time the long apartment windows grew dark. Terence glanced at his wrist-watch and eased up to their hostess, having decided that she needed mature advice on procedures.

"It's getting on for nine, Madge. I see the buffet's all laid out in the studio. The rest of us are only guests, you know, so a little sign from you is required."

"I've been worried about that myself, Cousin Terence," Madge answered. "I'd like to start people eating, but Shane and Agnes haven't arrived yet."

He glanced about the lamplit room. "Why, so they haven't. Very remiss of Jim's boy, I must say. He may be grown up and a Congressman, but his manners are still pre-Yale."

"Not usually, Cousin Terence. Do you think anything could have gone wrong?"

"With Shane? Not a Chinaman's chance! Notch by notch, he's been eased along by my good friend, Desmond Molloy. He's been shown the ropes by an expert. He knows the political view of punctuality. Tonight, he's no credit to his tutor."

As if on cue, the hall door opened. Agnes let herself in. A tenant two floors higher in the building had arrived in the street lobby simultaneously and she had not had to buzz for admittance. She stood now, facing the others, untidy and distracted.

Terence was first to notice her. "I must say! Here she is at last, but wouldn't one expect her to have changed to something more presentable? The rest of us did so. If she thinks this casual style is going to help Shane down in Washington . . ."

But Madge had left his side, crossing swiftly to the new arrival.

"Agnes, dear, we'd begun to worry about you. I'm so glad you're here."

As she moved a step forward into stronger light, Agnes was so visibly pale that all the others noticed. "I'm sorry I'm so late, Madge. And I'm sorry I look a fright. I didn't want to leave the hospital at all, but Shane insisted. He said we'd spoil your party."

Shane's mother cried out softly. "Shane's in a hospital? Why? Agnes, *why?*"

"He's all right, Mother O'Donnell. He wasn't very badly hurt. They tell me he'll be able to come home tomorrow. But he'd lost such a lot of blood, you see . . ."

"Accident?" Jim was suddenly alongside her. "A car, Agnes? A mugging? What the hell?"

"He's been shot." Her voice was low, almost inaudible, yet it seemed to reverberate in the graceful room. "Two hours ago, a man at City Hall tried to kill him."

Brendan, too, had crossed to her and stood at her side. She seemed fenced in between father-in-law and brother-in-law.

"Which hospital, Agnes? Perhaps I can be useful. If

he's lost blood, he may need a transfusion. We're compatible blood types.''

"He's at Lenox Hill," Agnes managed, obviously fighting off tears. "I got word at the apartment and met the ambulance there. B-but you mustn't all be alarmed. He walked to the Emergency Room on his own, leaning on me only a little."

"How can we not be alarmed?" Sheela shrilled. "Agnes, dear, my son has been *shot!*"

"The man responsible didn't do much damage, except for all that lost blood. They'd already removed the bullet from Shane's shoulder before I left the hospital. He said to tell you all that he survived much worse in the war and you're not to worry but go right on with the party."

"As if we could, after this!" Madge sobbed. "Oh, poor Shane! How horrible!"

Norah swept forward, chin lifted and steady.

"Of course we can. And of course we will. My big brother's not going to lie on his hospital bed hating himself for creating family grief."

"But if he . . ."

"Did you bring your guitar along, Dad? You generally do. You and I should sing a round or two together, even though Madge has no piano. Brendan, you run along. Give Shane our best. If there's any further news, bring it back. But he's right, he faced worse over in France. Mind you, he's to know we're all still enjoying a wonderful party."

19

Norah had sent flowers to the house, taking her brother at his word that he'd be leaving Lenox Hill within twenty-four hours. On her way from Madge's party, stopping at the little all-night florist's where she and Dennis had once bought single blossoms in more frugal times, she had almost succumbed to an urge to take them to the hospital in person and speed up their delivery. But then Shane would have known how worried she actually was—how terrified. And the whole songfest she and Daddy had instigated, last night, would have failed in its purpose.

Having telephoned Sutton Place before she breakfasted, Norah knew her brother was already on his way home. Agnes had ordered a chauffeured car and had gone to fetch him, which meant the poor woman was still too shaken to trust herself behind the wheel of her own Audi. Agnes would know it and Shane would know it, but neither of them would speak a syllable to underscore their fright.

I wouldn't have trusted *myself* to drive, so soon after, Norah thought to herself as she stood at one of her apartment windows overlooking Park Avenue's divided traffic. A gratuitous bullet! A slug popped off, maybe at random, at a respected government official!

Was it at random? Or had there been some gaunt purpose behind the attack? She wasn't sure she knew how to judge her world any more. Wherever she appeared in public to sing, applauding crowds converged upon her and all but drowned her in their love. But they'd loved Shane, too, last November. Look at the final vote tallies. He'd done nothing since then that she knew of that would rescind that approval. He was still Young Congressman O'Donnell, the shining knight.

Yet now some bushwhacker wanted him dead. Why, why, why?

She wished fiercely that she knew more about the background of her brother's near brush with death. Even the morning paper—Norah had sent out for all early editions—offered no explanation.

The Congressman had been emerging from City Hall after a conference on welfare scams with His Honor the Mayor. A man across the plaza was seated in a parked car, a green Hudson convertible with its motor running. As O'Donnell started down the wide steps, giving the driver a clear target, the still unidentified gunman had raised his revolver, fired one shot point blank and started his car in motion. Two witnesses identified the vehicle as it careened onto Broadway, but it had not been sighted again until found, two hours later, abandoned on the diagonal of Stuyvesant Street. Investigations proved the car had been stolen. It was the property of a thoroughly respectable, and thoroughly alibied, salesman from Yonkers.

The Congressman had refused interviews at Lenox Hill

Hospital, replying to questions only with a curt "No comment." A bystander, who'd been observed from a distance, had scurried from behind a City Hall pillar and bent briefly above the fallen victim, apparently to ascertain whether or not O'Donnell was still living. Having felt for a heartbeat and found one, the man had then raced back into the building in search of medical assistance. No such man had yet been found, however. Police, alerted by the gunshot, had summoned both doctor and ambulance. Informed by telephone of the attack, the Congressman's wife had rushed to Lenox Hill's emergency room. On the way, she listened to the radio reports, "Congressman O'Donnell is a brother of the popular singer, Norah O'Donnell Gallagher, a stage and television headliner billed as the 'Irish Skylark.' "

That was about all.

Cars northbound and southbound streaked past below her, divided by a narrow stripe of greenery. Norah found herself watching them closely, trying to isolate green Hudson convertibles. Ridiculous! The one purloined by the gunman had long since been fingerprinted and returned to its briefly publicized owner on the fringe of the Bronx.

Behind her the door to her private sitting room opened.

"Pardon, Mrs. Gallagher," Miss Whittaker said primly. "It's the telephone."

"Can you take a message for me, please? I'm not in a mood to talk just now."

"But it's your brother, Congressman O'Donnell on the line. I thought you'd . . ."

Norah was already past the impeccable nanny and half way down the hall. Breathless, she caught up the waiting receiver. "Shane! Where *are* you? How's the shoulder?"

"I'm home on Sutton Place where Agnes has just deposited me." His voice sounded strong enough, yet there was a disturbing quaver in it. "She's off now herding the kids to their school, so I have a chance to catch you solo. Listen, Norah, I've got to talk with you. As soon as possible.''

"You're talking to me right now, dear.''

"We're on a telephone. Telephones can be tapped.''

Her eyes widened. "Shane, you sound like some bit player in a Grade B G-Man movie!''

"This isn't a time for quips, Norah. I've got to see you. Right away.''

"Then I'm on my way already. Give me ten minutes to outwit traffic.''

"No. Agnes will be back before you could get here. I'm coming to you.''

"Are you sure you're feeling strong enough to—?'' But Shane had already hung up.

When he rang the doorbell, Norah was waiting to let him in. His call had already upset her, but one look at her brother's face started a genuine alarm bell clamoring inside her. His usual controlled calm had frozen into a granite mask. Only his eyes seemed alive, and they were not Shane's usual eyes at all. His grey pallor might be explained by last night's loss of blood; but that did not explain the involuntary twitch of a muscle high along one lean cheek.

She led him quickly into the sitting room and closed its door behind them. Only Miss Whittaker might have dared open it, and she had already departed for the park with Tony and Jenny. She looked up to find him staring at her. "What . . .?''

"I'm in trouble, Norah. Bad trouble. I don't know how to handle it.''

His words came out like the raspings of a buzz-saw.

They told her more than anything that the trouble was bad indeed. "Sit down, Shane. I'll fix you something."

While she poured him a neat whiskey at the cabinet bar, he was already blurting out the story to her back. "Somebody's trying to frame me. This could ruin my career, Norah, and like I said, I just don't know how to handle it. I can't discuss it with Agnes. It would just about break her heart. And I have to talk to *somebody*."

"Try me, dear." She handed him his glass, and waited.

"You've read the papers?" He waited for her nod. "Then you know about the man."

"The man in the green convertible?"

"Not him. The one who was lurking there behind a column as I walked out of City Hall. The one who was supposed to be feeling my shirt for a heartbeat, and then vanished."

Norah recalled that some such man had been mentioned by the press. He had seemed an unimportant detail of the reports. He had not remained long in her mind. But a vague impression did linger. Again she nodded.

It was all Shane needed to spur him on.

"When the police got to me, I was still sort of stunned. One of them ran through my pockets, looking for identification. A lot of them know me, but this one didn't. Well, in my breast shirt pocket he found the paper, already with blood on it."

"Slow down, honey. I've missed something. What paper are we talking about?"

"The one the guy who vanished slipped in there. I'd hit my head as I fell. I was stunned. I didn't get a good look at him. He was only bending over me for a couple of seconds. I felt him sort of tugging at my shirtfront, but I hadn't a thought what he really might be doing."

She said slowly, "He was slipping you a message from someone. Right?"

"Wrong. When the cop asked me to explain it later, you could have felled me with a feather. But now I can quote it verbatim: *Gross casino wins as of 7/18/56, $837,391. Casino wins less markers, $692,453. Slot wins, $57,994. Markers, $144,938.* All scribbled on a sheet ripped from a scratchpad letterheaded for the Garden of Babylon Hotel's gambling rooms in Las Vegas, Norah. This week's report to an undercover boss, telling him the figures his slice of the pie would be based on."

"So let me get this all straight, Shane. You're serving on some anti-gambling committee in Washington. I didn't know that. These were figures you'd need for your investigation."

"There's no such committee operative. And if it were, I'm not a member of it. But when the cop, who looked like I was trying to sell him the Brooklyn Bridge when I swore I'd never laid eyes on that paper before, when he turns it over to his superiors for a rundown, I'm mortally certain they're going to find it checks to the last comma with the week's Garden of Babylon gambling receipts."

"I still don't understand."

Shane winced. "Once this hits the papers, it'll be up before an Ethics Board and exit Shane O'Donnell. Congressmen aren't supposed to own gambling halls. Only the Mafia rakes in that kind of money."

"Shane, who could possibly believe such a wild concoction about you? You were elected because the public trusts you. No one would accept for an instant that you could—why, it's just absurd!"

"Since the O'Dwyer-Costello days here, honey, New York's voting public will accept anything that smells rancid.

After all, they've been educated. Look under a saint, find a worm.''

"But any Congressional ethics board surely knows you well enough to . . .''

"Maybe yes. Maybe no. In any case the voters won't, a year from next November, whether I'm unseated now or not. And, Norah, I don't even know who wants to ax me. I didn't realize I had this rough an enemy.''

Two plus two made four. "Look, Shane, there's got to be a connection between the man who shot you and the man behind the column. That second one was *waiting* for you, just as the gunman was. They had to be working together. What possible good could it do anyone to blacken your reputation after you were dead? You couldn't run for office then.''

"I don't think I was meant to die," Shane said heavily. "I was only a few yards away from that gent in the Hudson when he fired. I was alone on the steps. A perfect target. The bullet was just to wing me, and give the other guy a chance to plant his phoney evidence. But after yesterday, I'm just as good as dead.''

"Shane, honey, the point is that your fine reputation . . .''

"The point is, how am I going to face Agnes and the kids with this? Even if I resign from Congress with the usual crap about retiring to attend to private interests, *they* have to know. Whoever's after me isn't going to let me off the hook without a murmur.''

"Agnes loves you, Shane. She of all people knows how straight you are. The kids are only babies, they won't understand. But who would want to do this to you?''

"I guess I might find that out tonight," Shane murmured.

"Tonight?'' It seemed absured to echo his word. But she couldn't think of another.

"The call came through to my room at the hospital last night, after I'd talked Agnes into leaving for Madge's party. I was instructed to meet the voice on the phone at midnight, on a bench inside Central Park, just in from the Seventy-Second Street entrance. He'll tell me then what I'm supposed to do to quash the scandal and keep my name lily white."

"Then someone *could* quash the whole frame-up if you play ball?"

"I . . . oh, Christ, I suppose so. I've been in the game long enough to have seen it done. A Police Captain gets passed a white envelope, and *oops!* the figures with my bloodstain on 'em just disappear from the files before any step is taken. Desmond Molloy pointed out all the angles, years ago, by way of teaching me what to sidestep."

Suddenly Norah's breath caught, snagging like knit goods on a nail. "Desmond Molloy? Have you been to him about this, Shane? Did you phone him last night?"

"Not a peep. He's been my sponsor since even before I finished at Yale Law. Knowing all he knows about Tammany deals, he's pretty cynical. He for one will believe I've fallen. Another rotten apple from another tree. He'll be sorry, but he'll write me off."

"Shane, listen to me." Norah leaned forward. "You're not going into the park alone after midnight. You don't know what they may have in mind for you."

"Of course I'm going," Shane countered bleakly. "If they have a deal, it'll be a dirty one. I'd rather lie down with a skunk than play along, but at least tonight I'll have a chance to swing at somebody's jaw. Game arm or no, I can do that much. And it looks like that's about *all* I can do."

He set down the glass she had handed him on the coffee table with a small thump. He had not taken so much as a sip from it.

* * *

In the early afternoon, smartly suited, Norah journyed into Central Park, beginning at the Seventy-Second Street entrance.

Walks curved serpentine loops across soft grass and under trees. Nurses pushed baby carriages, or gossiped in pairs and trios while their charges tottered about on explor-atory adventures. Old bag women crouched in the sun picking through a day's ill-assorted loot. Squirrels scamp-ered. Dogs desecrated plantings. Elderly men, some of them ragged and others well-dressed, sat turning the pages of newspapers either first or second hand.

Occasionally, a word or two leaped at her from a wavering headline. *CONGRESSMAN! ASSASSINATION ATTEMPT!* Norah had headed south. By the time she reached the outskirts of the children's zoo she had a very fair mental picture of all approaches to the particular benches where Shane was expected to meet his nemesis. If her brother's impotent fury precipitated a scuffle, there were a dozen ways for the faceless enemy to melt away after weilding a knife or utilizing a gun equipped with a silencer—and no outsider and wiser.

She usually enjoyed a walk in New York. This one was a torment.

From that moment when Shane had spoken the name of Desmond Molloy, her thoughts had been following a path quite as tortuous as the one now underfoot. It could only be an automatic reversion to what she had known about the aging politician almost all her life, but more and more she kept zeroing in on him. Shane had suggested no shred of evidence connecting Molloy to what had happened yesterday. That very fact merely served to argue, to Norah, that some such connection could exist.

It would be typical of their alleged family friend. Were

he the one out to put pressure on his protégé, this would be his mode of operation, with himself far outside the picture. Norah hadn't a doubt but that Molloy kept competent and ruthless flunkies at his beck.

But his invisible staff would likely be as small as it was expert. A man with too numerous a squad of henchmen was risking a chance of including one who talked out of turn. Chances of personal entrapment were something Molloy avoided. She could recall as if it were yesterday what had happened on her own seventh birthday. Oh, Molloy took no unnecessary chances.

A thought drifted through her mind, hit a submerged shoal, grounded. Cornelius Shaara!

That afternoon when she and Madge had met for a quick reunion, her cousin had said something about Bar Harbor. Something about his being set upon by two roughnecks who simply materialized out of the pines, beat him into insensibility, and left him with instructions to abandon Cousin Bernadette forthwith. They had even supplied his means for flight—a boat left tethered to an inconspicuous dock.

Bar Harbor had burned to the ground that very day. Only the outbreak of the blaze had brought Cornelius racing back for the desperate rescue attempt which had left him seared and disfigured. Would his tormentors have figured him to be that sort of man? Certainly, few of his middle-aged bride's relations would have done so. Yet while the fire still raged, Molloy had contacted Madge to tell her he had done her a certain favor.

Norah's speculation crystallized into the next-door neighbor of certainty.

The patterns, save for details, were so strikingly similar, men with no traceable connection to Molloy whatever had emerged, done their work, and vanished, leaving only devastation behind them. In Shane's case, a ruined reputation. In Cornelius's, a dead wife he had loved and a talent he could no longer satisfy. No one could prove they had set the fire which still could inspire a shudder of horror on Mt. Desert Island. No one could identify them as responsible for yesterday's double hit, quick as a bolt of lightning.

"Why, the son of a bitch!" she said aloud, veering out of the park at the exit high in the Sixties. An ambling squirrel, startled by the intensity of the passing lady's tone, paused to stare across at her and flick his plume.

Once back on Fifth Avenue Norah made for the nearest available telephone. She dialed her Cousin Madge's number.

"Is Cornelius there?" she asked, when a light, familiar voice answered.

He met her, as she had requested, on the terrace at the Tavern on the Green. She made a very attractive picture, sitting in the dappling shade and sipping her innocuous claret lemonade. She reminded him instantly of Madge, as he made his way toward her. The O'Donnell women did have a look about them; the ones with Bernadette's blood in them, if not the married in-laws.

He eased into the second chair at her tiny table. "Here I am."

"And I'm grateful to you for coming, Cornelius. As I said on the phone, something's happening. I can't discuss it yet, but I more and more think it ties in with Bar Harbor."

He was not slow to catch her particular meaning. "The fire?"

"Perhaps, but more specifically, with the two men who attacked you by the lake that day. Madge has told me quite a bit about it. But that's second hand. Would you mind giving it to me in your own words? After all, you were the star. The victim.''

He looked at her sharply. ''What's this? A new act for your next TV show?''

''Please, Cornelius. I'm deadly serious. This may be terribly important.''

Without further evasion, Cornelius obliged. He had a painter's mind for descriptive detail. He brought the scene alive for her; for himself, no doubt painfully alive. When he sketched his two grinning assailants to her, she could almost see and smell them. She asked for a replay and Cornelius painstakingly gave one. It was as if four people were here together on the terrace, not merely two.

''But why are you so all-fired anxious?'' he asked, entitled to his question. ''It sounds almost as if you thought you'd have to recognize them if you met them yourself.''

''I think I may be going to meet at least one, Cornelius. Tonight.''

He half-rose from his chair in protest. ''No, Norah. I forbid it. They're killers.''

''I'm sure they are. And I believe Shane has an appointment with one of them. At least, it's possible. You've heard about a man we all know named Molloy?''

''Of course. I remember Madge suggesting at one time that he might have masterminded the attack on me—claiming he was doing her a favor.''

''Desmond Molloy never did another human being a favor in the whole of his life. I know him from the ankle bones up, and anything he does he does only for himself. I'm sure, considering his call to her afterward, that he *was* behind your beating. And now the same sort of thing is threatening Shane. My brother's no match for more violence at the moment, with a bandaged chest and one arm in a sling. I'm going to be there with him.''

"He mustn't let you, if there's any chance this man he's meeting might be . . ."

"Shane's not going to have anything to say about it. I've just gone over the ground around the spot where he's meeting whoever it is. I think I've picked out a safe cover. There's a small forest of forsythia directly behind the bench. I won't be seen."

"Norah, that Bar Harbor pair are animals. Big, ruthless animals. A slight girl . . ."

"A girl with her own gun, who knows how to use it," Norah corrected. "Prowlers tried to break into our old downtown apartment once, just after Jenny was born. Dennis was living on the Coast by then, so I had to take my own steps."

"What the deuce did you do?"

"I managed through my manager, Martin Kenny, to get a gun permit. Then I took lessons in how to handle what I bought. A small gun matches up pretty evenly against a big animal. I think maybe the odds are with me."

"I don't like this at all," protested Cornelius grimly.

"You don't have to like it. Shane is my brother, Cornelius, not yours."

Even in summer, the park grew colder by midnight than Norah would have figured it to do. Except perhaps for the increasingly infrequent pairs of lovers who passed in the middle distance and had body heat in their favor, the chilliness was uncomfortable. Well back in the bushes, and positioned so that a streetlamp cast its glow directly across the bench in question, she shuddered. The black gauze of an old stage gown dating back to Starlight Serenaders days concealed her almost completely, but proved no great barrier against a deepening chill. Or was it only her nerves that had a touch of the Arctic?

The bench was empty.

Somewhat earlier, a man had wandered up to it and dropped down to light a cigarette, but after a few puffs, he was back on his feet again and wandering away. She hadn't really worried about him anyway, after the first minute or two. He was medium tall and on the wispy side, which didn't fit Cornelius's clear description at all.

But then, of course, the caller who was to meet Shane might be someone altogether different. His pause might have been only for purposes of reconnaissance. He might return, once certain that the area was safe. Or after Shane's arrival. All she could be sure of now was that a man had paused, smoked, departed. In her flimsy black evening handbag the hard outline of her miniature weapon made reassuring company.

Now footfalls were turning in off the Avenue. They rang purposefully closer on the hard-surfaced walk, not sounding at all like feet out for a late stroll. Male feet, undoubtedly. Angry feet, Norah thought. She was almost certain to whom they belonged.

Sure enough, it was her brother who marched into the circle of lamplight. Reaching the bench, Shane stared at it for an instant as if in loathing. Then he sat down.

Clearly, the man he was meeting had been positioned somewhere off across the shadowy spread of grass. Shane was barely in position before the other one emerged. He was so like the description Cornelius gave that Norah as good as recognized him. There couldn't be two fitting so neatly an artist's word painting.

"Good evening, Congressman." His voice was low, the tone clearly taunting.

"How the hell do you know who I am?" Shane growled. "It's pitch dark."

"But the dark is light enough. That's the name of a big

Broadway show, Congressman. Couple of big stars playing
in it. Tyrone Power. Katharine Cornell.''

"What the hell do you want?" Shane demanded.

The big hulk eased down beside him. "I like that,
Congressman. No wasted time. Get right down to business.
Well, we have a little business to talk over. I'm told
you're the spearhead of a new special investigation down
Washington way. The one poking into these big high-
jackings of cigarette trucks in the tobacco states.''

"It's a dirty business, and one we're going to crack. If
you're involved . . .''

"Quick on the trigger, aren't you? Well, now, it does so
happen that someone I work for *is* involved. He doesn't
like your contrary plans, not one little bit.''

"If he's a highjacker, he's a criminal. If he's a criminal
he belongs behind bars.''

"Haven't you got that backwards, Congressman? It ain't
him, it's you that Congress is apt to be investigating. And
with jim dandy reason, eh? A lawmaker who's breaking a
dozen Federal laws out Vegas way, and who's number is
now just about up?''

A growl began low in Shane's throat. Alarmed, Norah
saw him rising off the bench like an incarnation of fury.
His good arm, unfortunately, his left, drew back, fist
clenched.

But for a big man his opposite number was a fast
mover. He was on his feet before Shane could even begin
the move so obviously intended. Something seemed to
leap from nowhere into one of the stranger's big hands.
She heard an almost inaudible click. He held a knife.

"Don't try to get fancy with me, Congressman. You're
as good as a dead man. I missed you yesterday at City Hall
because I was under orders. This time, I'm on my own.''

Norah started up from among the tangled branches,

clawing her small revolver out of cover. The two by the
bench had frozen like figures in a tableau.

More steps drew closer along the walk. They were
headed outward toward the Avenue. A man in tweeds with
a sloppy rain hat pulled low on his forehead tramped by
them. He was whistling whatever that tune was that Carol
Haney had danced to last season in *The Pajama Game*,
and whistling it very badly.

With scarcely a glance toward the pair he was passing,
he kept on his way. But he had moved close enough to
have had a good look at them, there with the lamplight
spilling over them.

After the footsteps had faded, the big man turned without a word to Shane and disappeared deep into the shadows of the park.

Shane stood alone, glaring after him.

But it was the passer-by, now almost lost to sight,
whom Norah's incredulous glance followed. Impossible
though it seemed, she knew that the man in the rain hat
was Cornelius Shaara.

20

After that shock of recognition in the park, she ought to have been prepared for anything, but the night was still capable of surprises.

When she turned her key in the Park Avenue apartment door, half an hour later, lights were burning in the living room, although the children were long in bed and Miss Whittaker retired to her own quarters. As she swept into the room, Cornelius unfolded from a comfortable Queen Anne wing chair by the fireplace. His one concern seemed to be that he might have alarmed her.

"Sorry if I'm taking you unawares, Norah. I know I'm not expected. But I beat you across from the park, I guess. You weren't here when I rang. A maid let me in."

"And left you just sitting here?"

"She was through for the day and making ready for a bath, poor soul. I explained that I'm a member of the family by marriage and didn't require entertaining. She

seemed delighted to leave me to my own devices. I rather
sensed she was afraid her tub was overflowing.''

"I'll have her head on a platter in the morning," grated
Norah angrily.

"Come, now, hired help are *supposed* to be pleasant to
the family. She was only doing her job. Once identified as
Miss O'Donnell's stepfather, I was in like Flynn.''

She could contain herself no longer. "What were you
doing at Seventy-Second Street? What right had you to be
butting in? It was Shane's business. And mine.''

"You wouldn't have a nip of Irish whiskey on the
premises, would you? Ah, thanks! And what a beautiful
sight it is, to be sure. I'd hate to be sipping it at Shane's
wake, my dear. And that's what was in the offing, with
the knife in play.''

"I was there. With my gun. I'd just started to burst out
from the bushes when . . .''

"I saw you coming. But what would have happened,
dear Norah, if you'd tangled your ankle in a root just at
that moment? By the time you were free and on your feet,
Shane would have only a hole for a throat and his knifer
would be safe in Jersey. He moves fast, that mountain of
muscle. I have personal reason to remember it.''

"Then . . .'' Her eyes widened. "Then I was right! He
is the same man who tortured you in the woods back of
Bar Harbor. The woods where people said the fire started.''

"I had a fine look at him. I'd know him anywhere. I've
never forgotten him.''

"It was Desmond Molloy who called Madge later and
as good as boasted about what had been done to you. It's
Molloy who's doing this to Shane, his own protégé. The
muscle man can't work for two employers, both out to
mess up O'Donnells.''

"What does the old shark have against Shane, do you suppose?" Cornelius asked.

"You weren't as close as I was, in the park. It was made clear. Those hijackers of truckloads of cigarettes that you read about in the news every few weeks—Molloy has some connection with them. He wants to stop Shane's committee investigation into their racket."

"Very interesting. Sorry I missed the dialogue. I was too busy taking pictures."

"Pictures? Dead of night and no flash bulbs? How does it happen that you even had . . ." Then Norah remembered. "Oh, of course! You've turned to photography lately. We were talking about it at Madge's party last night."

"I'm not so bad at it, either. I've peddled several picture essays to magazines, this past year. Even Liam likes my stuff. He's been suggesting lately that I go along on one of his foreign assignments and we do a sort of dual report job. But that's not the problem here. What's important now is that your man Molloy needs a bit of attention."

"Does he not, indeed?" Norah began moving restlessly about the room, picking up one small *objet d'art*, putting it down, reaching for another. She turned suddenly. "Would Madge give another party, do you think? And ask Molloy? And me?"

"Madge invite Molloy past her front door? I very much doubt it. She's deathly afraid of the man, Norah. She knows what he ordered done to me, and in her name."

"But wouldn't she if she knew it was a set-up? A will-you-step-into-my-parlor-said-the-spider sort of thing? I've wanted all my adult life to give that creep his come-uppance. I once told Madge why, too. Remind her of that when you ask her."

"So I'm supposed to do the asking? Right at the hub,

when I don't even know the scenario? Only this afternoon, I was out of play, thank you. Shane was *your* brother.''

"Don't be picky, please, Cornelius. I need you, you know I do. What's been holding me back all these years is that I had no solid evidence of what I knew to be true. That, and then he's never threatened Shane until now. If any of your pictures tonight show his goon putting the squeeze on our darling Congressman . . ."

"As a matter of fact, if it comes out I have a dilly. It should show them with Shane in defensive posture and the goon with drawn knife ready for a lunge. Shane's testimony to back it up would put Molloy neatly in a box."

"He'll deny, of course, that he's ever so much as heard of Mack the Knife."

"But good evidence says differently. I can identify the goon. Madge knows Molloy set him after me. Shane knows it's the goon who threatened him and admits having shot him at a boss's behest. Everything fits in, like bits of a jigsaw puzzle."

Norah, whose usual smile was warm and loving, smiled now in a way which might have sent chills playing tag along Desmond Molloy's spine.

"So it's up to you to talk Madge into it, Cornelius. If it weren't for my seventh birthday, and Shane, and what was done to you and maybe Bernadette, I could almost feel sorry for Friend Molloy."

Terence was delighted that, despite the City Hall event which had put a damper on Madge's maiden effort as a hostess, his reclusive little cousin was coming out of her social shell at last. Another invitation from her? And so soon? Bless the little mouse. She was really trying.

He and Hilda must make every possible move to assist her. After all, he was head of the O'Donnell family; its eldest male member. And the poor child had lost both her parents in a brace of tragic fires. Small wonder she'd had to be put away in that top drawer booby hatch—or whatever the proper euphemism was for Dogwood Dell.

When he heard from Des Molloy that his distinguished long-time friend had also been invited, his delight was doubled. This time it wasn't to be a mere family gathering, then. He was glad to know that Madge was overcoming that absurd aversion to good old Des which for so long had helped cripple her. Things were really going very well in that department. He wished dear Bernadette might be alive to take heed of her daughter's fine example. Bernadette, too, had in her day been a cross to bear on the Molloy front, utterly unreasonable in her dislike. And, my God, *her* mother too—old Cousin Veronica! What a batch of females to try to run herd on! Had any other head-of-family ever been confronted with such woes?

Molloy, for his part, displayed equal pleasure.

"I've always been fond of little Madge, Terry. In fact, not long ago I was able to do her a small service, but that only seemed to make her draw back from me more. It's saddened me, until now. I want all Delia's family to know I'm their friend. This soiré on Thursday sounds delightful. Ah, you don't suppose Norah will be present?"

"I hadn't thought of it. But her TV show airs on Fridays. Won't she be rehearsing?"

"Perhaps so. And just as well. She's a dear child, and of course she's Jim's daughter and Shane's sister, but somehow she and I just don't quite seem to gel."

"Speaking of your professional ward, Des, how's Shane shaping up in Congress? If you Tammany people hadn't staged his campaign, I doubt he'd have been elected."

"He's a fine boy, Terry." Although Molloy's eyes went a trifle blank, he was careful not to let Terence notice it.

"Perhaps a mite too ambitious for a Washington freshman, though. He's the spur for some dubious committee probing into cigarette thefts down south, I hear. The lad should hold back until he's better oriented. Crusades ought to wait for later."

If Madge had been nervous about her family party in Norah's honor, she was triply so about the approaching Thursday. Cornelius had carefully explained to her what was to happen. Since he approved, she had agreed.

But inside she felt like nothing but a mass of ropes all tied in complicated knots. She longed for Friday, when the whole frightening business would be over. Then Cornelius would be rewarding her with a promised gala lunch.

Came Thursday.

By seven, the baker's dozen guests all had gathered in Madge's charming if not overly spacious livingroom. Even so small a group seemed to tax the area. There was occasional overflow into the adjoining studio, where a set of small flower paintings Madge had just completed stood ready to be inspected.

As Terence was first to note, tonight was no traditional O'Donnell reunion. Aside from himself and Hilda, oh, and Brendan, looking rather subdued for some reason, there wasn't a single family member to be seen. Terence tended not to include Cornelius Shaara as family, although of course the fellow had once been briefly married to Bernadette.

No, this was a congregation best described as miscellaneous. Acquaintances of Madge's from various art schools, mostly. One obscure young Italian poet she had run into somewhere, possibly in Rome although the chap spoke passable English. One fledgling actress, not pretty enough

to bother with. One earnest female church organist, probably acquired by way of Brendan.

Surveying the assemblage, Terence for his own part put
them down as a medium dreary lot. No one in view was
either important or particularly decorative. Some of the
nonentities were clad in jeans neither new nor even particularly clean. Hair tended to straggle. Voices seemed overly
strident. Not a Paris frock nor a London jacket anywhere
on display.

Yet for some reason Des Molloy, who had accompanied
him and Hilda, having stopped by first at their own
apartment, seemed pleased with Madge's party cast. After
one quick glance about as he crossed the threshold, his
previous slight tenseness seemed to evaporate and he moved
from group to group with his customary glossy geniality.

Terence scarcely could fault that initial tinge of caution.
After all, Madge had until then behaved very standoffishly
with their good friend. Her good intentions had to be
established. With that hurdle passed, Des was being even
more democratically charming than usual. One would hardly
take him for a long-term member of the backstage coterie
who really manipulated the city's puppet strings. Considering that Des never personally ran for office and therefore
need not cosset mere voters, he seemed to be doing
handsomely by Madge.

It was Des who presently paused at Terence's own
elbow. Having just thrown together a weak martini for
Hilda at the serve-yourself bar in one corner, Terence was
in a mood for a moment of more robust companionship.

"Your young priest seemed a little off his feed, I thought,
Terry. So I pressed discretely for a reason. Poor fellow, no
wonder he's not in much of a party mood."

"What's wrong with Brendan?"

"Hadn't you heard? It seems he's a devoted admirer of

his superior down at St. Cyprian's—old Father Cullen.
This past year, the good man's been ailing. Cancer. Today
the doctor confided in Father O'Donnell that his boss
probably won't last out the month.''

Terence considered, his smile spreading. ''Then Brendan
will soon be in for promotion, won't he? I'm always glad
when things go well for one of the family.''

''I don't sense that Father O'Donnell is particularly
elated by the prospect.''

''Ah, that's the priesthood for you. Hearts in Heaven,
heads often in the clouds. But we must be practical, Des,
mustn't we? The old have to step down to make room for
the young. Father Cullen should have relaxed the reins two
years ago. I must remember to congratulate my nephew on
his . . . *Damn!* Hilda just spilled her entire drink! That
dress she's wearing cost me a mint, and the material never
really dry cleans.''

Someone from the Village had toted a guitar uptown.
The owner began to strum and a few untalented souls
nearby him drifted into song; not the sweet or rousing Irish
numbers Jim worked on and Norah interpreted so angelically,
but modern garbage that sounded more like hiccoughs and
belches than like melodies. The lot of it, in Terence's
view, should be dumped into the East River. One thing
you could say for proper O'Donnell gatherings, a song was
a song.

Across the room, he saw Cornelius Shaara take Desmond's arm and murmur something in his ear. Apparently,
it was a reminder that Des had not yet gone into the studio
to properly admire his hostess's latest creations. At any
rate, the pair of them started moving toward the studio
door. Cornelius kept chatting amiably. Obviously he'd
been wised up to Desmond Molloy's importance and knew
which side his bread was buttered on.

The room did not seem less overpopulated than before the two men's departure. In fact, no one else appeared much aware of it.

After one disgusted glance toward Hilda, who was agitatedly mopping up her dressfront and mumbling in anguish to the lady organist, Terence returned to the bar to make himself another highball, stiffer than his first. This social event was definitely a dud, but one must be sympathetic and understanding. Little Madge did try.

The studio door shut gently. It might as well have been slammed.

Standing alongside the largest of the flower paintings, faced quietly toward him, Norah watched the old politician stiffen as he recognized her. At the man's back, Cornelius reached out and turned the key in the lock. They would not be interrupted.

"Good evening, Mr. Molloy." She did not trouble to pretend that she really wished him one. "Nice of Madge to include you in her party—as we asked her to."

Molloy made a small, frustrated gesture and for an instant looked as if he would like to run, but he recovered quickly. The genial smile returned in all its practiced brilliance.

"Well, well, now isn't this a fine surprise! Terry assured me you'd be off practicing for that fine new show I've been hearing about. It's the talk of the town."

"I'm playing hookey. I just couldn't miss coming here."

"And how very charming for the rest of us that you've managed. Perhaps you'll be favoring us all with one of your beautiful numbers? I must say it would be a mercy after that caterwauling we've been subjected to, out yonder."

"No songs for tonight, Mr. Molloy. I'm more in the mood for a murder."

Molloy winced, but then decided to take it as a jest. "Ha, ha, ha! You've always had the rare O'Donnell sense of humor, haven't you, my dear? And the beauty, too."

"I'm often assured I look like my Cousin Delia's reincarnation. Do you agree, Mr. Molloy? I didn't look much like her way back on my seventh birthday."

It was an odd thing about Molloy's eyes. They seemed able to set and harden much like an aspic in a refrigerator. They were doing so now, Norah noticed. He sensed what was coming.

Yet his tone remained jovial. "Well, that was a birthday party, wasn't it? I still recall it happily, although you were such a tiny tot I'm surprised you retain many memories. The ride on the merry-go-round, perhaps? The ice cream and paper hats in Delia's dressing room?"

"All of that. And almost everything else that happened, too. On one's seventh birthday, one very seldom runs up against rape."

"Whatever can you mean by that? It's a very ugly word, my dear."

"It's a very ugly experience. Not that I actually had to undergo it, thank God. I was a lucky one. Delia missed me in time and came looking for me—to your fury."

"Norah, have you any notion what you're implying?" Molloy asked icily.

"Oh, yes, a very clear one. You were a much younger politician then. Only a little up the ladder from where my brother Shane is now—although your ethics, I'm afraid, don't much resemble each other's. Like Shane, you had an influential sponsor. What was his name, now? Lucius Cassidy? He was in a position to make or break you, wasn't he?"

Molloy glared at her, the glare of a hating beast in a cage. "Lucius was a very influential friend, yes. I'm surprised you remember him, Norah. He's been dead so long."

"I remember him only because of that nasty little affliction of his, Mr. Molloy. That unwholesome predilection for virgin children. Years later, when I was old enough to understand, I looked up the word in a dictionary. He was a paedophile."

"Look here, now, that's very ugly language to use on a poor old . . ."

"You don't have to say it again, Mr. Molloy. I've already done that. So there we were at the theatre, in Cousin Delia's dressing room. Ice cream, streamers, noise-makers and all. My parents were out of town that weekend on business. They'd left me in Delia's charge, knowing how much she loved me. In those days it didn't much worry anyone that she was friends with you. You were supposed to be respectable."

"Look here, young woman, I've listened to just about enough . . ."

"So you were third guest at my after-the-matinee celebration. And when you offered to take me for a little walk while she caught half an hour's nap before her evening performance, why should she have suspected anything wrong? She trusted you."

"As well she might! If you are trying to imply . . ."

"I'm not trying to *imply* anything, Mr. Molloy. Quite simply, you took me, hand in hand, to a dark place at the south edge of the park. Your master, Lucius Cassidy, was waiting there. If I screamed, which I did until he jammed a handkerchief into my mouth, nobody would hear. And you? Conveniently, you vanished."

"That's outrageous! Why, anyone who'd abandon a little girl to such treatment . . ."

"Yes indeed, there's a name for *that* kind, too. It fit

you like a second skin that birthday evening, Mr. Molloy.
Old Man Cassidy had seen me a couple of times before.
To put it coarsely, he had the hots for this virgin child. So
he told you what you were to do. And like his obedient
jackal, you did it. What plum had he promised to pay you
for pimping, I wonder?''

"Damn you, Norah! Not one word of this is . . .''

"I wouldn't have been a virgin much longer if Cousin
Delia hadn't gotten there, would I? When she awakened
from her nap and her theatre maid told her there'd been an
impatient call from Lucius Cassidy, asking what was delay-
ing you, she understood. You'd mentioned his habit to her
once or twice before that, never expecting his next yen
would be for me. Delia flew out of the theatre still half-
dressed, and frantic. Even after she found me in time—
thank God, the park was the first place it occurred to her to
search—she was hysterical. I guess I heard things said that
little girls aren't supposed to hear. She never again let you
come near her.''

Malloy's fleshy face had gone from crimson to corpse
white. Only his eyes seemed alive. They fixed on Norah as
if they were claws which could destroy her.

"Listen to me, Mrs. Gallagher, and I advise you to
listen good. You couldn't make a court of law believe one
word of these fantastic lies, not if you swore to them on a
stack of bibles taller than the Empire State Building. Breathe
a syllable of this filth and I'll have you up for libel before
you can spell your name. I'm not without influence.''

"Are you, now?'' Norah smiled coldly. "What else is
new?''

"For you, girl, what's new may be a jail cell. You
haven't one shred of proof of these ravings. Who'll back
up a kid with sick fantasies who grew up to be an hysterical,

neurotic, vicious female? Who'll take her word against a well respected pillar of the city?"

"Some might. I do have a modest following."

"You haven't even a witness. Not one. Delia's dead. Mary, the theatre maid, retired soon after and disappeared to New Zealand. Lucius Cassidy is with the angels. So my advice to you, given freely because I've so long been a family friend, is that you see a doctor. If poor little Madge had to be put away for a spell, you'll need double therapy."

For a moment the studio lay oddly silent. Molloy's apoplectic breathing was the only sound to mar the stillness. Then Norah laughed, a shocking trill after all the thunder.

"How right you are. That's precisely why I've hated you in silence since the day I turned seven. I knew how things would turn out—my unsupported word against yours. So I bided my time, and now my time has come."

His jaw worked, but he said nothing. His eyes said things for him.

"You know quite well what I'm talking of, so let's not bluster. You meant to frame Shane and get him under your thumb, for whatever you wanted him to do. It was Cassidy and Molloy all over again, with Molloy and O'Donnell. Only Congressman O'Donnell doesn't happen to be a pimp. So the screws had to be tightened, to get full cooperation on the quashing of the cigarette hijacking investigation."

She stood very straight against the delicate acrylic of lilacs and pansies.

"This time, there's proof," she continued after a brief pause. "This time there are living witnesses. Once I make my formal charges, Mr. Molloy, we'll begin with the cigarettes. I've been inquiring since the first of the week with a few of my own friends in high places. I do have a few."

"You'd better, if you hope to save your hide!"

"A hood named Benito "Benny' Terranova seems to be heading the hijack operation down south. But I find ten thousand new vending machines have been installed around town since April, and with licensing arranged directly by you. Now even a girl of seven could figure the profits on those, supposing the material to stock them all was obtained absolutely free."

"You fucking little bitch, I'll . . ."

"No, Mr. Molloy. I don't believe you will. Please show him those park photographs, Cornelius. And tell him how you can identify the man holding a knife on Shane. After that, we'll get down to the real business at hand. Which is, Mr. Molloy, the complete clearing of my brother's name."

"What have I to do with . . .?"

"Shane assured me that in this far from simon pure community, it is possible for a man with strings to pull to make a certain paper vanish from a file as if it had never existed. Once you've attended to that . . ."

Ten minutes later, the studio door again unlocked, and Norah crossed Madge's party-cluttered living room on her way back to rehearsal. Startled to see her, for he had not realized she was in the apartment at all, Brendan moved hastily to intercept her.

"Norah, listen, can I beg a favor?"

"To the half of my kingdom, sir."

"Father Cullen is dying. He may not last the week. He's always loved listening to your shows. Says your singing puts him in mind of his village in Ireland. Could you possibly squeeze half an hour for a visit?"

Norah smiled back at him brilliantly.

"Why not, little brother? I'll stop by before the show tomorrow and sing whatever he loves best for the dear old gentleman. After all, I haven't done a kindness for anyone in my family since I don't know when."

BOOK SIX

THE FLAMING HARP

21

When the last Friday run-through ended, clocks through-out the studio all agreed the dinner break was well past due. Three hours later the whole cast, a large one, would have to be back on stage, made up and in costume.

Norah thought of Dennis as she wiped away the last vestige of cold cream from her cheeks. She remembered what it had been like when they were just starting out together—excited and happy with Buddy Diston and his Starlight Serenaders. She thought Martin was probably right when he said the public wouldn't much remember the old outfit these days. Certainly they'd had a good many years that were better forgotten, yet it was surprising how much seemed to have happened just yesterday.

Her cheeks were quite clean, but she continued to rub them as she felt her hot tears stream down from her eyes. Just as she flipped the crumpled tissue into her wastebasket, someone rapped on the door.

"It isn't locked," she called without turning her head.

In the well-lit mirror before her, Martin Kenny's attractive reflection appeared. "Decent? Listen, I'm taking you to dinner. Ready?"

"Ready but no time for table service. I promised Brendan I'd stop by St. Cyprian's before show time. I'll catch a sandwich on the wing."

"Put Brendan on ice until tomorrow. I've got to see you. Important."

"Sorry, Martin. I don't dare put dear old Father Cullen on ice. He's dying. I said I'd drop in and sing for him. It's important."

"What I've got to talk about is important, too. Please, Norah?"

"Sorry. No." But Kenny's face in her mirror looked genuinely distressed. It was truly important, then. "I tell you what. Come along with me now, and we'll split a ham-on-rye on our way back. There'll be a lunch counter somewhere close by St. Cyprian's. It's that sort of neighborhood. I've gotten to know it well, since Brendan's Ordination."

Martin groaned. "Would it help me if I told you this is Life-and-Death?",

"It *is* death, Martin. Father Cullen's. I'm on my way. Are you coming?"

Once their taxi was headed downtown and westward, Martin reached for her hand. Norah let him hold it without giving it much notice. She was thinking of the frail Father Cullen, who had done so much to help Brendan in his effort to become an effective priest. It seemed a small favor to bring him music and a smile. She wished fervently that she was carrying a real gift to his bedside. Life, for instance.

"Norah, things have gotten so I just can't take it another

day," Martin said, breathing heavily beside her. "I tried again last night. I begged. I pleaded. I offered her every dollar in my bank account. She just kept shaking her head. Alice won't divorce me."

Norah turned from her view of a passing warehouse street. "You're still so eager to divorce Alice? I thought maybe that had cooled a little."

"God!" Martin looked as if she had taken a butcher's cleaver to him. "Don't you even *listen* when I'm talking to you? I've been trying to get through to you for months. I love you, lady. I want to marry you. How often do I have to say it?"

"But you can't marry me. You're already married, and so am I."

"That, Norah, is why I've been begging Alice for a divorce. Dennis will give you one, won't he? If he still felt all that gung-ho about his marriage, he'd be back on your doorstep like a shot the minute you told him you wanted out."

"But I've never told Dennis any such thing. We've never discussed divorce."

"High time you did. All you two have left between you is a transcontinental truce. Your kids know Daddy so slightly they'd probably call him 'Mr.' Gallagher."

"Martin, dear, you of all people ought to know show business. Our jobs just keep us one America apart, that's all. He can't quit his. I can't quit mine."

Alarm flicked in Martin's eyes. "You don't *want* to quit yours, do you?"

"Of course I don't. You needn't worry about losing all you've invested in me. I just signed your new two-year contract, didn't I? So stop fretting."

"Is it just the contract that keeps you in the East,

honey? Nothing else at all? I'd sort of gotten to hoping that
at least a little bit of it might be because you—''

"Here's St. Cyprian's," she said quickly, cutting him
off. "It's such a down-at-heels old pile, isn't it? Like a
one-time glamor girl who can't afford her beauty treat-
ments any longer. But for some reason I love it anyway.
So does Brendan. I hope they let him stay on.''

"Isn't that sort of a foregone conclusion, once the top
job here is empty?''

"Nothing in life is ever a foregone conclusion. Come,
Father Cullen's waiting.''

The parish directly across the pot-hole pocked street was
a twin to St. Cyprian's itself. Lace curtains at the windows
were immaculate, but had been starched so often over so
many years that they were more like wood than linen.
Peeling paint suggested the advance of irreversable decay.
The five stone steps were chipped and hollowed. To fancy
that once upon a time both buildings had stood pristine in
country fields, with an infant city still well to their south,
was to stretch imagination beyond reason. Yet it was true.
Brendan had shown her old sepia photographs.

Brendan was waiting now in the lobby, with its grim
suite of Eastlake furniture and its shiny-clean linoleum.
"He insisted on being out of bed to receive you, Norah.
Nothing I could do would dissuade him. Hello, Martin.
This way please, both of you.''

"Is he in much pain?'' Norah whispered as they mounted
the sturdy stairs.

"So excruciating that I can't think how he stands it. But
when you see him you'll probably decide I'm lying. There's
never been one like him, not that I ever knew.''

They entered a room which, except for a single bed off
in an alcove, had been arranged as an office. The wallpaper had clung to the walls for so long that it was difficult

to figure out what color it was. Its out-of-scale tulips
seemed like brown carvings rather than flocking. Seated in
a plain kitchen chair which had been arranged so that the
light was at his back and a shadow hid his face, Father
Cullen held up a thin hand in a gesture of blessing.

"Welcome, dear child. How kind it is of you to come
all this way."

"I came because I wanted to, Father. What's this I hear
about your being under the weather? All us O'Donnells
have known you from our cradles, and you've never seen a
queasy day."

"Just a case of the One-Hoss Shay, I'm afraid, dear
girl. I need a few new bolts to fasten me together. I've
ordered some. Now your brother here says you've come
prepared to warble. And what a sweet, clear sound that
voice is, to be sure. Small wonder you shine."

Crossing the space between them quickly, Norah bent
above the seated figure and brushed a kiss on his sparse
white hair. Then she stepped back to her original position.

"I wasn't able to bring a brass band with me, I'm
afraid, Father. This will have to be *a cappella*. What
would you like me to sing for you?"

"Anything, Norah. But I hope it'll be something out of
Ireland."

"Let's see now. You were born and raised in Kerry, if
my father Jim told me right. How would you like to hear a
bit of *The Kerry Recruit?*"

"It's been a long time since anyone's sung me that one.
Let's have it, then."

Norah threw back her head. With Martin and Brendan
looking on, she began filling the room with the brisk
melody. After a verse or two, Father Cullen began tapping
his feet in rhythm. His weak hands clapped together,
keeping time.

"About four years ago I was digging the land,
With my borgues on my feet and my spade in my hand.
Said I to myself, What a pity to see
Such a fine strapping lad footing turf in Tralee.
So I buttered my brogues and shook hands with my spade
And I went to the fair like a dashing young blade,
When up comes a sergeant and asks me to enlist.
I says, Sergeant a grá, put the bob in my fist. . . ."

After a verse more, a low strangled sound came from
the old priest. With a scowl of alarm, Brendan raced
forward, but the small figure in the hard seat was still as
erect as the Kerry recruit himself. His foot was still tapping.

They had not lost him yet, and with scarcely a break,
Norah kept on singing. The music, regardless of the words,
had become Father Cullen's jaunty last farewell to his
homeland.

They had little time left for a sandwich, once she and
Martin left the rectory, but, true to her promise, Norah
guided him around the nearest corner to a diner half-filled
with truckers and longshoremen. Here the style was nil,
and the provender hearty.

Eating, with one eye on the clock, Martin resumed his
pleading. "I've moved out of the house in Scarsdale,
Norah. I'm staying at the Gotham until I find an apartment
to suit me. Alice and I are through."

"Then I'm sorry, Martin. You two have been together
eleven years."

"Ten and a half of them were bitter years. She knows
it, I know it. There's nothing you could call love left on
either side. There are no kids to be considered, but she still
hangs on. Pretty much like you and Dennis."

Norah caught herself looking about the shabby, per-

versely cheerful place almost as if she expected Dennis to
stroll in out of the gathered darkness outside. Had she
become like Alice Kenny? More habit than anything else?
Drifted away so far from what they had once shared that
their separate boats were unlikely ever to sight each other
again?

People all around her laughed and talked back and forth
and perused dog-eared menus. The clock hands kept up
their spastic inching. They were in the kind of neighborhood place where everyone seemed to know everyone else.

"Partly, I guess, it's the Church. Alice has always
bowed to every rule and edict in the book. Say *Boo!* to her
and she's scuttling off to light a candle somewhere. I
wasn't raised that close to the manger. To me, a divorce is
only what you write at the end of a story that's played out
every possible nuance. Ours did that long ago."

"It's getting late, Martin. We ought to head back to the
studio."

"I've still got things to say to you, Norah. Things that
can't wait any longer. You know when I first fell in love
with you? It was at my office, the day I called you and
Dennis in to sign your first Buddy Diston contracts. There
you were, sitting in a chair across from my desk, eyes
shining, fresh as an April crocus, cute as a button. All of a
sudden, looking at you, I said to myself 'What's this?
Martin! Hey!' It's been like that for me ever since."

Norah avoided meeting his earnest gaze. A sense of *déjà
vu* all but overwhelmed her. It seemed so like that first
time things had clicked into place with Dennis. She had
been there before . . . or had she? Certainly, the waves of
feeling pouring toward her from the far side of the table
had the same intensity, the same ring of truth.

"I can't ask you to marry me, Norah. Not until Alice
does an about-face and sets me free, but you're all I've

wanted. All these years I've been faking our scene about my being only your business manager. We belong together. For keeps, Norah.''

"You must have said that to Alice, Martin, once. Didn't you mean it?''

"I was young. I may even have believed it, but only for a while. With you, it's gone on now so long there can't be any question. What I'm asking you, darling, is this. Will you live with me until we both have settled the formalities? Will you let me start trying to make up to you for all you've been deprived of these past several years?''

"You want me to be your mistress, you mean?''

"I guess that's the technical term, but what I'm trying to say is a lot more. I want to spend the rest of my life with you. I want to give you everything I am. We'll find a way to put the final ribbons on it somehow, I swear we will.''

For an instant Norah felt dizzy. "You forget, Martin, that I have Dennis's children.''

"You and I have a child, too, don't we? Your career. I'm certainly its father, I was its genesis, I've raised it and given it fatherly council and eased it over the rough spots. It's yours and mine together. What more can a father do?''

Dear Lord, was she about to cry? She lurched to her feet and stumbled from the drab booth hurriedly, as if in flight. "I don't know about you, Martin, but I'm going to get back to the studio. T-there's only h-half an hour left before I g-g-go on.''

From the make-up table in her dressing room, an envelope sat staring patiently at her. It had been there ever since she had returned from lunch.

She had a choice between ripping open the creamy flap or pondering those whirlwind moments in a booth with

Martin. If she did that, however, there'd be no smile to
give the rows of dim faces. Her throat would tense and
she'd blow the first bars of her opening number—*Will You
Come To The Bower?* She reached for the envelope.

She recognized Madge's innocent schoolgirl writing.
Puzzled, Norah tugged a single sheet of note paper from
its nest. Evidently, her cousin had been to the theater
while she was returning from St. Cyprian's and had left
the message for her. Cause for concern? Madge had been
keyed up last night at her party, until it seemed that strings
would snap. If this had happened, Norah Gallagher would
feel guilty. After all, it was she who had dreamed up the
scheme for the party.

> *Dear Norah: Cornelius and I will be out front
> tonight. We'll come backstage directly after. Please
> save us an hour, even though you may have other
> plans. Thanks. Madge.*

Not much to go by. It could be a cry for help. It might
equally well be a casual invitation to a wind-down drink at
Sardi's. The lines were probably not cryptic by intention,
but they contained no easily decipherable clue to a deeper
meaning. One must therefore be ready for anything. All
their lives Norah had felt a responsibility for Madge; more
as if they were sisters than mere cousins. Poor Madge was
so vulnerable.

Brisk knuckles rapped on her door.

"One minute, Miss O'Donnell! You're on!"

The actual performance seemed as usual, much like a
down-hill ski on a medium to difficult run. Moments
on stage flashed past like scraps of frozen scenery. There
was breathless attention from the audience, who sat so
still there was seldom a rustle. She had to concentrate

on the lilt of her own clear singing, the support of the show's orchestra rising under it, and her movements.

> *"Will you come to the land of O'Neill and O'Donnell,*
> *Of Lord Lucan of old and the immortal O'Connell,*
> *Where Brian drove the Danes and St. Patrick the vermin*
> *And whose valleys remain still most beautiful and*
> *charmin' . . ."*

There was a roar of delight when each song was over. Then there was the white-toothed smile of the M.C., gesturing her back from the wings to take yet another bow, and the stubborn refusal of the demi-train on the blue satin 'second-appearance' gown to reverse itself as she beamed and bowed low and backed gracefully from the mocked-up footlights. Hands reached out of nowhere to tug at her zippers, whip away satin, smoothe sparkle-garnished rainbow silk sleekly over her hips for the final. *"Brava! Brava!"*

She hurried back to the dressing room, forcing a preoccupation with Madge's letter for fear some errant thought of Martin might slip in. It would take them several minutes to reach her dressing room. Norah was expert at the last quick change, from costume to street garb.

When they knocked tentatively, as visitors from an audience always did, she was ready. She opened her door, smiled and prepared herself for gaiety or commiseration or even a quick leap into whatever required action. One look reassured her that it was a happy visit. Madge was blushing like old Cousin Veronica's rose garden at Great Oak, so fondly remembered from their childhoods. At her shoulder, Cornelius looked tall and smug. As recently as yesterday, Norah had become very fond of Cornelius. When she greeted him with a kiss, it was entirely genuine.

Sardi's, he inevitably suggested. And Sardi's it was, for
the whole family knew the light supper was Norah's last
event of any working day. Shown to the choice table the
Irish Skylark always rated, they sat overshadowed by a
phalanx of caricatures of famous faces, a hum of post-
theatre celebrations swirling about them.

"Well!" Norah beamed upon them, paving the way for
whatever they might be intending to announce. "This is
delightful. I was so pleased when I found your note,
Madge."

"We want you to be the first to know," Madge blurted.

A phrase as old as the announcement of the world's first
marital intentions. It was almost as traditional as a bride's
tremulous "I do" at the subsequent wedding rites. Yet
tonight it took Norah by surprise. Her evening certainly
had been comandeered by amatory declarations, but this
was its first old-fashioned Valentine.

What would her radiant host and hostess think if she
countered with her own, "I want you to be first to know,
too. I'm considering becoming Martin Kenny's mistress.
A fallen woman, I suppose you'd say. A bad mother. An
unfaithful wife. A smasher of wholesome skylark-type
images."

Instead, she divided a warm smile between them.

"I guess I wasn't quite ready for this, darlings. How
lovely! When did it all happen?"

Surprisingly, Madge took the initiative. "It was at lunch
today. Cornelius promised to treat me to a glamourous
feast as thanks for doing the party. He chose '21.' "

"And for glamor couldn't have chosen better."

"I hadn't been there often, actually only once or twoce
before, so it was splendid. Don't you dare laugh, Norah,
but as we were walking up to the door I could actually feel
some special welcome just for me surging from the walls

and the fancy lace. Those iron jockeys lined up along the outside stairs all seemed to be smiling for me alone.''

"Perhaps they were. Well! Tell me more.''

"Actually, I've been leading up to this a long time," Cornelius said. "Ever since my quick trip to Rome, last year. Since even before that, I suppose. After her very first visit to Boston, I couldn't seem to shove her out of my mind. At first I thought it was because she seemed like a young, unfinished version of Bernadette. Then, under that surface duplication, I began to grasp a little of the person she really is.''

"It's someone I've known and loved since we were babies together," said Norah. "And just lately, I've been discovering you, too, Cornelius. You've been quite a surprise. Well, I'm truly very happy for you both. God bless!''

"You're sure, then, that I'm not just marrying Madge for her fortune?'' It seemed that a touch of bitterness underlay his query, or perhaps it was only a fading, rueful memory.

"How could he be?'' Madge challenged instantly. "He already has what Daddy left Mother. He's raking in photography commissions at every turn. Cornelius needs more money like a porcupine needs pyjamas, thank you. The poor don't lunch at '21'.''

"Nor sup at Sardi's, not too often. Please let me order up a bottle of champagne.''

It was later than any of them had planned when her two escorts dropped Norah off at her doorway. She invited them up for a nightcap, of course, but they declined, preferring to be alone together although neither was impolite enough to say so. Norah rode up alone in the elevator, fishing for her latch-key.

It seemed unfair, even illogical, that Madge and Cornelius had left her with a faint yet identifiable pang of envy. After all, she too had been proposed to in the course of the evening. The circumstances, however, had been vastly different; almost as different as the setting. She hadn't the faintest idea how she was going to cope with Martin.

The apartment, so simple and expensive and charming, was her own creation. Dennis had been no part of it. Actually, Martin *had* been; the odd suggestion here, the small but exquisite gift to enhance it there. Martin understood her. In a very real way, he had invented her. There would be no ruptures in the fabric of living with Martin.

She began a random tour of rooms, moving quietly so as not to disturb Tony and Jenny in their bailiwicks or Miss Whittaker in her more remote ivory tower. Each familiar doorway she passed through led her to things she studied with a new eye. How would it seem when they breakfasted together at her favorite round table in the front bay window? How would the big porter's chair by the sitting room fireplace look, with Martin reading his newspaper in it? How would the wide but lonely four-poster bed accommodate itself to the hollowing of two bodies instead of one? The visions came, but they were tentative.

On the bed's smooth comforter, almost as if to accent the theme of singleness here, a long large manilla envelope had been positioned where she could not fail to see it.

Norah stared at it before reaching to claim it. Her daytime maid was an unquestioned jewel. Abandoned years ago by her own man, the girl had almost extra-sensory reactions. Any incoming mail bearing Dennis's California return address was always left here, without comment, awaiting prompt recognition.

Her hand shook as she ripped at the flap. Thick, folded sheets tumbled out. Music, hand-scribbled. The look was familiar. A few years back, Dennis's workroom wastebasket downtown would have overflowed with copies of these papers.

Across the top sheet he had scrawled a line: *Most of them nowadays are for the quick buck. This one's just for you—again.*

Her hands began shaking, harder and harder, so that the pages rattled.

"I'm sorry, Martin," she heard herself saying. "Sorry. But it just wouldn't work."

22

HOME IS THE HERO, the banner stretched over the archway to the parlor announced.

The lettering was a trifle crooked, young Ambrose having been out the night before on the first real bender in his eighteen years—chaperoned by his more sophisticated older brother Danny. But the sentiment was healthy. To him, his father had always been a hero, a St. George whose typewriter slew the world's most formidable and fearsome dragons. Ambrose had long ago learned to couch this sentiment in other terms, however, while in his father's celebrated presence—St. George being the holy patron of England and Liam O'Donnell being the widely acclaimed journalist who all his life had breathed Ireland's dragon fire at the British.

There were those who took offense at Liam's stand, and they had the temerity to flaunt foul beliefs that the English had a perfect right to be on Irish soil, protecting the miscreants who'd set up a three-penny Republic in Belfast. In the course of Ambrose's public schooling—especially of late, when he had reached a pre-college level—he had come home more than once with black eyes acquired in his endeavors to set straight the politics of classmates whose fathers' favored London.

More than once, he had asked to be transferred to the parochial school where thinking among the student body was more level-headed. If Pa were around the house more often, he believed, there was little doubt the demand would have been met. But Liam was off to one of the remote corners of the world, writing his by-lined news accounts of the latest mess mankind had managed to get themselves into. The job of raising Danny and his younger brother, Ambrose, had been left to Evaleen, whose conviction it was that every dispute had two sides to it, and that her sons should be exposed to both. Public high school it had been, despite Ambrose's objections.

Danny, never one with much of a chip on his shoulder, had accepted this decree with what Ambrose considered a despicable indifference. Danny was more interested in such matters as America's recent sending of an astronaut, Alan Shepard by name, into outer space. Science was his true love. The glorious homeland of their great-grandfather, whose name Pa so proudly bore, interested him almost not at all, at least so far as Ambrose could tell. All you could do with such a buffoon, he thought, was remember that he was a senior, star tackle of the football team and a veritable mass of muscle. With that in mind, scorn of Danny's attitude was prudently omitted from any brotherly conversations.

"I'm the son like Pa," Ambrose long ago had proudly decided, and he revelled in every Liam O'Donnell report degrading the English anywhere around the globe. Alone and singlehandedly, Pa could win Ireland back her sacred independence and drive all her foes into the sea.

Today being a homecoming day, and therefore to be reverenced, Ambrose felt it unjust that he should have to attend classes. His joy and duty was to be waiting on the family doorstep with a brass band ready to trumpet Caesar's return. Even the band might have been managed, if the description could be stretched to cover a four-piece teenage combo in which Ambrose himself whacked the drums.

But Ma's edict on the subject had been firm and irrevocable. She, and she alone, was to taxi out to LaGuardia to see Pa's plane from Africa set down. She, and she alone, was to escort him back to Brooklyn Heights. Liam's two sons and heirs were to carry on exactly as usual. The unfairness of such a proclamation was manifest. But to attempt to argue down Ma was like trying to out-debate Gibraltar. A fellow was licked before he started.

The two young O'Donnells raced out of school as soon as the dismissal bell was rung.

For once, Ambrose had completed all the night before's homework—this had been dutifully attended to even before he set out on the unexpected but exciting expedition Danny had invited him to share. For a Sophomore to be included in Senior revels was unheard of and Ambrose vaguely recognized that Danny was trying to make up to him for the frustration of Ma's cruel decision. Yet avoidance of any possible school detention for a make-up study hail period took precedence over even his admission to grown-up dissipations. Those, alas, had left Ambrose with a shaky hand.

Homeward bound, however, Danny had preferred to walk Rosemary Carey to her folks' place on Pineapple Street instead of taking the shortcut to the O'Donnell house on Remsen Street. Genuinely horrified, Ambrose put it

down to last night's debaucheries. Whiskey must have
rotted what poor old Dan regarded as his brain. Not to be
waiting at home for their father's homecoming was akin
to burning the flag, in his opinion.

When the younger O'Donnell brother loped up the front
steps, however, the cab from LaGuardia had already come
and gone. Pa's trench coat and shoulder holster lay tidily
deposited on the hall chair all but directly below HOME IS
THE HERO. Spilling from the parlor came not a duet but
a trio of congenially conversing voices. Ma and Pa had
company with them.

As Ambrose entered the livingroom, he saw his father,
sprawled comfortably in his favorite chair near the front
windows, long legs thrust out before him, muscular frame
relaxed, hair only a trifle thinning and peppered with grey.
The bold face was tanned visibly darker than Ambrose
remembered.

"Well look who's here!" Liam observed, looking up.
"My God, you've sprouted at least two feet since November!
What's your mother been feeding you? Manure?"

"Wheaties," said Ambrose, and let it go at that. As
usual, he felt a little tongue-tied in the August Presence.
Only after his father had been back in the house for a day
or two did Liam's second son ever loosen up his larynx
enough to ask questions. But then the floodgates opened.

"How's school been going, Ambrose? Still out for the
track team?"

"Yes, sir. I've a good chance to make the high hurdles,
and Coach says he may develop me as a sprinter. I have to
get my grades up first, though."

"What's wrong with the grades, Ambrose?"

"Only a C-Minus average last term, sir. Ma says if I
don't improve within the next six weeks, I'll have to give
up playing with the combo until I make a B."

Enough for parental duty. Liam turned back to the third member of the trio Ambrose had walked in on. He was a medium-height man, maybe ten years Pa's junior, with sandy hair and pale eyes the color of sherry. At first glance, he looked skinny. After that you began to notice the sinews like steel cords revealed by his rolled-up shirt sleeves; the oddly icy personality, although the man was free enough with a smile.

"Francis, this is my younger boy Ambrose. Ambie, pay respects to Mr. Francis X. Boyle, who's to be our guest here for a while. He's been with me these past couple of months covering the fireworks in Wambambi. We've developed a friendship under fire."

Boyle nodded negligently. Ambrose sensed that something a bit better was expected of himself.

"Pleasure to meet you, Mr. Boyle. Welcome to Brooklyn Heights." What more could you say to a grown-up stranger?

"Mr. Boyle was covering the same assignment I was, for the Dublin Gazette." Obviously, Pa was furnishing the information for Ma's benefit as much as for Ambrose. After all, to her as well, the Irish writer was a stranger. "We've talked America a good chunk of the time since we met. Francis wants to start the preliminaries for applying for citizenship."

"I'm sick to my stomach at living where the stink of Englishmen pollutes the air," said Boyle, his voice on the rim of harshness. "Not until Ireland's a free place, like your United States, would I want to return there. It's enough to twist a man's heart.

The words had instantly won Ambrose's own heart completely, but aside from an eager lighting of the eyes, he ventured no reaction. Best seen but not heard, had always been Pa's theory about children. That his sons were no longer exactly children had not yet occurred to him.

However, Ambrose had an odd impression that Francis X. Boyle had not missed his silent response. His pale eyes remained fixed on him an instant longer than indifference merited. The instant passed, and Boyle turned back to Pa.

"What's this speech you're to be giving, O'Donnell? The one your wife made mention of just before your son came in? I didn't know you were an orator."

"Did you ever know an Irishman who wasn't one?" Liam laughed. "No, seriously, I'm asked now and then to give a little talk here or there about my latest tour abroad. If it's an organization that advances the Cause, I hate to refuse. This invitation for next Tuesday is from the Five Boroughs Hibernian League. We stand to raise a healthy purse for our brothers in the I.R.A."

"A fine thing surely, to be able to make the contribution you do, O'Donnell."

Liam shook his head, half-modest, half-amused. "It's far short of what I used to dream of doing when I was the age of young Ambrose here. For me it was the front-line trenches or nothing. Blast the tyrants! Blow up their Parliament! That was my tune in those days."

"What deterred you, then?"

"I wound up in other front-line trenches. Only mine were dug out of sea waves over in the Pacific. And not meant to slip the skids under England, either. You were too young for that war yourself, Francis. It was a good one. I learned a lot."

"Begging Mrs. O'Donnell's gracious pardon, I've a question for you. Why haven't you been putting that fine knowledge to a more effective use, these years since?"

It seemed to Ambrose that his father suddenly looked embarrassed.

"A man grows older, Francis. He settles into a mold. A family man with responsibilities, that's to say. Machine guns and grenades don't much fit in. Evaleen here would have had the hide off me if I'd come back from Okinawa still set on sharing Irish violence. That doesn't mean my views have altered, understand. You've read my columns, you've read my books."

"That I have. And fine, fiery words are in them, too. But for me, hack scribe though I am, it's a struggle that can't be fought at a typewriter. I have to tackle it my own way, and my own way tends to letting loose some British blood."

Clearly, it was going to be exciting having Francis X. Boyle right here under Pa's Brooklyn roof.

Two blocks away, on busy Montague Street, there stood a popular bar called *The Flaming Harp*. Men from all over the area, and a few women, often gathered there.

Knowing his house guest as intimately as he did, Liam felt certain Francis would enjoy the patrons of the bar. Evaleen, moreover, was very receptive to the notion of the younger man's making new friends. After a few weeks, she showed subtle signs of restiveness. She disliked having someone constantly underfoot who was always spouting violence. Liam scarcely could blame her.

So he began now and then to usher his friend to *The Harp* to share a convivial pint. Francis did have the grace, while out among the Philistines, to soft-pedal his pronouncements until he made certain how the wind lay in any particular corner. All to the good, considering he'd be needing sponsors aware of his good character when the time came to petition for citizenship.

Two or three such evenings had passed pleasantly enough before the one on which Francis first made the acquaintance of Geraldine Donoghue. Geraldine was a regular at *The Harp*, and Liam had known her slightly in days before his departure for Wambambi.

To his taste, the girl was a mite too strident; not the soft-spoken angel he himself had married in his Evaleen, but there could be no denying she was handsome. She was taller than most, and had the strong features of some Greek statue of Juno or Aphrodite. Her coloration, however, was straight out of Galway; flaming red hair, deep blue eyes, and a fine dusting of freckles. As to costume, she favored sweatshirts and boots and Levi's with silver-decked cowboy belts to fancy them up. She had a slender and shapely figure which her rather tomboyish wardrobe could not conceal.

That very first evening they met, it was clear to see that Francis was taken. The way she talked to him about the assassination in Dallas was intriguing if it happened to fit your own notions. Blowing a President's brains out, that was all well and good, but not if the President were a good Catholic with names like Fitzgerald and Kennedy attached to him. The ambiguous summing up was one Francis was bound to find fascinating.

The affair progressed at what Liam could only regard as express speed. Two weeks later, Francis was already popping in and out of a bed two miles across the Borough. When asked how Miss Donoghue was faring these days, his smirk was that of a cat at a mousehole. He no longer needed to be accompanied to *The Harp*.

"The man's settling in like a native," Liam told Evaleen. "You'd think he was born at *The Harp's* family entrance, begging a bucket of suds for his granny, instead of on a rundown pig farm in Tipperary. Geraldine is some kind of witch, that's my humble opinion.''

"Did she ever bewitch you, then, Liam O'Donnell?"

"You know better than to ask it, macushla. But she seems to fit Francis. And he her. It's too modern to call a romance, I guess. But it's sure a relationship.''

The next afternoon, Evaleen went to a Matinee with Agnes, and reported the amatory progress of their seemingly permanent house guest. At the Russian Tea Room, after the performance, they ordered, removed their gloves and awaited service. Agnes, so her cousin-in-law decided, was even prettier in her forties than she had been at that Sweet Sixteen party night when the family first laid eyes on her. As for herself, Evaleen felt a long rest from radical company might soothe out a few unwelcome wrinkles.

"But what can you do? The man's Liam's best buddy these days. I don't want to offend him by suggesting it's more than time he might consider moving on. Yet it chills my blood to listen how he rants before my boys, especially Ambrose.''

Agnes nooded, in understanding. "Maybe this sort of problem is the price all O'Donnell wives have to pay for being married to our special husbands, Evaleen. Shane's a darling, and I adore him, but being the wife of a United States Senator is not what it's cracked up to be. Most days, I feel as if I'm standing on my head. Sometimes I can't remember which reception or state dinner or committee meeting I'm putting on my war paint for. Maybe the earth *turns,* but I *whirl*.''

"How about Madge?" Evaleen said. "Keeping abreast of Cornelius must be a fast race, now that he's fully recovered and back at his painting again. His portrait commissions flow in like the waters of the Johnstown Flood. Poor Madge just wasn't built to tackle speed. Yet, breathless or not, she keeps trying. She's so crazy about him it's indecent.''

"And what about Norah, out in Hollywood!'' Agnes exclaimed. "God knows she and Dennis are in love, and now that she's signed for a new show that's based in Los Angeles she has all the work of her own she can handle. But her second love really was always New York. She misses it, Evaleen—how can she help it? She's so far from her family, even with Dennis and Tony and Jenny alongside. No O'Donnell takes kindly to that.''

"We all adjust,'' said Evaleen. "We do because we have to.''

"Of course,'' Agnes said. "But in the process, haven't you sometimes felt that each one of us girls—well, we *were* really girls when we started the spin—is dancing her separate waltz on the wind? That's what I often find myself calling it.''

Evaleen chuckled wryly. "That phrase! I know where you found it.''

"Did I? It's not original with me?''

"It's from one of those old Irish tunes Norah used to sing. She picked it up from Jim, who picked it up from Grandpa Liam. Do you suppose our menfolk get that dizzy feeling they're waltzing too, and can't find out how to slow the dance? Or is it just a female thing?''

"If we ask them, do you imagine they'll tell us?'' Agnes wondered. "Do you think they'd even know clearly what their separate waltzes are? I do remember the line, now. Something terribly Irish, about moonlit fields and Midsummer's Eve and prancing in a fairy circle. Father-in-Law Jim always loved it.''

"Why not? It's beautiful. But I do wish my whole household weren't reeling morning, noon and night on account of that man Boyle. He wants to drum up war between Brooklyn Heights and Britain. I'm mortally afraid that if he does my Ambrose might volunteer.''

"Just as I'm scared to death that Shane may want to run for a new term in the Senate once this present seven-year marathon is over. I'd give a million dollars, if I had it, just for one quiet year somewhere with Shane all to myself. And the voters be damned.''

"Yet you won't quit. I won't quit. Maybe neither of us really wants to.''

"Not so long as we're O'Donnell wives. Evaleen, what do we do?

"We keep on waltzing, Agnes. Waltzing and waltzing on the wind.''

Most of the time it seemed more like a tavern brawl than a waltz. If ever there were the least chance for a bit of family harmony, it was certain to be blasted by Francis X. Boyle's warlike fulminations. And there Ambrose would sit, listening wide-eyed with worship.

Boyle had sensed Evaleen's resentment of his flamboyant presence, much as she struggled to conceal it for Liam's sake. It seemed to her that Boyle secretly relished the discomfort he caused her. As he uttered one of his more outrageous curses against the dastardly English, he would again and again let his glance creep toward her— always mockingly.

It came as a benison from Heaven when he finally made an announcement at breakfast.

"I'm sure you'll be happy to hear I'll soon be moving on, Mrs. O'Donnell.'' It was still "Mr. Boyle" and "Mrs. O'Donnell" between them; she had assiduously managed to maintain at least that illusion of distance. "Miss Donoghue, Geraldine, has invited me to move in with her. So I'll be saying farewell to your guestroom.''

"I scarcely know what to say, Mr. Boyle." (It would have been unforgiveable to cheer.) "I'd been given to understand Miss Donoghue occupies a very small apartment. One room, in fact."

"Gerry has it in mind to be moving along, too. She and some friends have found a nice row house on Hicks Street. Renting it together will offer them many advantages."

"A sort of communal venture, Mr. Boyle?"

"You might thus describe it. A commune, yes. For certain, we are folk with a common interest among us. We'll be joined in a business venture beneficial to Dublin."

"And to all of you as well, I hope. May one ask its nature?"

"Ah, Mrs. O'Donnell, that's to be kept private for a small while yet. But it's merchandise for export, that much I dare whisper. Perhaps there'll be a position there to offer young Ambrose. I'd like to repay you all for your cordiality."

Evaleen spoke almost in a monotone. "How kind of you to think of Ambrose, but I'm afraid his taking a job at present is out of the question."

"And why would that be, now?"

"He has two more years of high school to complete, and after that, it's Liam's and my ambition to send him to college. Your venture should be completely established long before our boy is free to be considered."

"We'd like to have him, Mrs. O'Donnell. He's a bright lad, your Ambrose."

"Like any mother, I'm prone to agree. But my chief interest is in seeing to his proper education. I'm sure you'll understand. No side jobs until he's done with college."

"Aw, Ma!" Ambrose protested. Something about his expression suggested that he knew more about Francis X. Boyle's grand plans than did she.

"Let's not wrangle about it here, Ambrose," Evaleen said firmly. "I'm sure that would bore Mr. Boyle unmercifully."

"But I'm not a kid any longer, Ma. If I can help Mr. Boyle with what he's been telling me about, the reason they're renting their house in the first place . . ."

"I think we'll not trouble your dear mother about it now, Ambrose," Boyle cut in somewhat hastily. "Plenty of time to discuss jobs there a bit later."

The emptying and cleaning of the guest room, returning it to its once pristine state, would require hard work, but Evaleen didn't mind. She found herself jabbering of Boyle's departure whenever she chanced to cross paths with another member of the clan. She had looked a touch peaked for the past while, they all agreed, but now she was blooming.

"But won't the boys miss Liam's friend?" Madge wondered. "Such a dramatic man!"

"Danny's scarcely been aware of his presence in the house, he's so daft reading up on who'll be next to follow John Glenn into orbit. Ambrose is still young enough to be somewhat impressed, yes, but that will fade quickly, once Mr. Boyle no longer eats his three meals a day at our table. The young have memories like sieves."

Terence, who happened to be present on this particular occasion, saw this as an opportunity to lecture briefly.

"That very quality might have been observed, not many years back, in those of your own generation. You'll recall, Evaleen, how seldom the name of our mutual friend and benefactor, Desmond Molloy, is mentioned nowadays in our family circle. Since his sad death, who has the decency or the gratitude to cherish him? Only Hilda and myself, I fear. It's a shame to the O'Donnells."

Senator Shane O'Donnell, so highly respected these days in Washington, contradicted his aging uncle. "I'm afraid some of us have little to cherish, sir."

"You of all people! You couldn't have gotten started without Desmond. Look where you have climbed now! For years you owed everything you achieved to him."

"And for years I was indeed appreciative. But conditions altered, Uncle Terry."

"I wish I had the slightest notion how or why. I've never understood why dear Des took himself off to Europe so suddenly just a week after Madge's little party. And then, when he finally did decide to return to us, the tragic timing of his decision! Of all the ships he might have chosen, that it should have been the *Andrea Doria*—and on her fatal final voyage."

A moment passed in which no one said anything. Then, finally, Madge spoke, her voice thin but forceful.

"Maybe I shouldn't say it, but I always hated Desmond Molloy. I'm not one bit sorry that he's lying somewhere among the fishes. If divers never find the ship and bring up the bodies still aboard, I, for one, won't cry a single tear."

"My God, Madge!" gasped Terence, genuinely shocked.

Evaleen stepped in at once to try to prevent a scene. "Mr. Molloy is gone, and no divers or friendly wishes will bring him back. The same is true now, I'm delighted to report, of Liam's friend Francis X. Boyle. He's not dead, of course, but he's gone from Remsen Street. For which I raise a hearty Hallelujah!"

23

Evaleen's error in believing Boyle was gone for good out of her life soon became apparent through Ambrose. One evening, some two weeks after the liberation of the Remsen Street guest room, her younger son was three hours late getting home from school. Since it was not a day for track team practice, maternal questions were forthcoming.

"Gee, Ma, no sweat," he answered. Ambrose had come to an age when he hotly resented being treated as anything less than a grown man; but he was elaborately patient with his mother. "I've just been having a look at the house on Hicks Street, that's all. It's keen."

Evaleen felt a prick of uneasiness. "*What* house on Hicks Street, Ambie?"

"Why, the one Francis—I mean, Mr. Boyle—and those others have been making over."

Just as she had thought! "And how did you come to stop by over there, Ambie?"

"Mr. Boyle just happened to be passing at the same time school let out. He stopped me to ask how you and Pa were doing. One thing kind of led to another. He invited me in to see what they'd been accomplishing, so I went along with him. No Federal case."

If there was one thing Evaleen felt certain she had learned about Liam's Wambambi friend, was that Francis X. Boyle very seldom "just happened" to be doing anything. He was the most singleminded young man she had met in years, and she found his opinions both alarming and distasteful. Her own flat opposition to the man's hint at hiring Ambrose was evidently being defied.

"What's their place like, Ambie? What renovations are they making?"

For the first time in the conversation, Ambrose shied away from giving a full and honest answer. "Oh, this and that. Little things. A few new electric wires and like that."

"Not really fascinating enough for a three-hour tour, was it? Tell me more."

Ambrose exploded. "Cripes, Ma, do you think I was doing something *wrong* over there? Is that what you're digging at? You don't trust me? What do you think—that I was there, maybe, because they're running some kind of whorehouse or gambling den or are selling drugs?"

"I don't mistrust you, Ambie. I mistrust Francis Boyle. I don't like him."

"Who's asking you to? But, geez, this is supposed to be a free country. I happen to admire Mr. Boyle a whole lot. He's one of the greatest patriots in Ireland. He'd lay down his life and never think twice if it helped to rid the homeland from stinking old England."

"Your personal homeland happens to be the United States of America, Ambrose O'Donnell."

"Sure, sure, sure. For a couple of generations. But

O'Donnells were riding high in Ireland when the Danes were top dogs in England. That's *milleniums,* not generations.''

"Francis Boyle has been feeding you all this nonsense?"

"Nonsense? That's all *you* know, Ma. You ought to talk with Pa about it. You'd find out different. Why do you think he's making all these speeches, except it's to raise contributions for the I.R.A.'s great struggle?"

"It just could be he enjoys the sound of his own beautiful voice."

"Read some of Pa's articles on England. Then you'd wake up plenty fast. This is the Twentieth Century. Imperialism is dead like the dodo. We've got to make a new, free world—for all mankind."

"By blowing up the old world first? I've heard Mr. Boyle advocate just that, I can't count how many times. I don't want you going over there again, Ambie."

"God, talk about a slave state! Talk about living in chains!" Ambrose stormed up the stairs, white with fury, casting himself as foremost of the early Christian martyrs.

This interchange, insofar as Evaleen could later remember, was the beginning of the end of her son's habitual frankness and trust-worthiness. On subsequent afternoons, when Ambrose came in from school equally late, he was always equipped with a thought-out and almost convincing alibi. He had stopped by a girl's house to compare their homework in algebra. He had twisted an ankle after gym and had to wait to see the school doctor and make certain there was no sprain. He had been nominated for class secretary and was talking with some of the guys about organizing a campaign committee.

Hogwash, all of it. Evaleen was almost positive that Francis X. Boyle was at the bottom of whatever it was that Ambrose was really involved in. She even tried prying information out of Danny, but Danny had the inherited stubborn O'Donnell loyalty.

"Ma, what would I know? I'm a Senior, the kid's a sophomore. Two different worlds. We hardly even pass each other in the halls."

"You attend the same school, don't you? You must hear things. What is it you call your locker room gossip, Daniel? Oh, that's right—scuttlebutt. Isn't there any about Ambrose?"

Danny looked both uncomfortable and pious. "See no evil, hear no evil, speak no evil. Do you think I have nothing better to do between classes than bat the breeze, Ma? I'm not spying on Ambie, that's for sure. Mostly, I'm with Rosemary."

Her final resource was Liam. She broached the subject while they lay in bed together, lovemaking finished. "Darling, I'm worried half to death over Ambie."

"What's the matter with the boy? His grades are up these days, aren't they?"

"From C Minus to Straight A. That's just what's wrong. He just isn't that much of a student, Liam. Even if he worked his tail off, he couldn't achieve that miracle."

"But he's already *done* it, macushla. Report cards can't lie."

"Report cards can lie their heads off, if there's something *really* wrong. I'm almost positive Ambie's headed for trouble, and I don't know how to stop it."

Liam rolled away from her a little. "What trouble, for God's sake, Evaleen?"

With all these Straight A's, I never catch Ambie cracking a book these days. Somebody's turning out his perfect papers *for* him. But what's he doing for them in return?"

"Mountains out of mole hills," Liam answered, running a fond hand over her flanks. "Ambrose is a good boy. Always has been. So forget about it, and come over here and give your husband a kiss."

The streets near Manhattan's west side waterfront were as dark as the proverbial blind man's pockets. Looking uneasily about him, Ambrose figured this must be the loneliest place in the world. Uptown, downtown, across town, not a vehicle was in sight anywhere. The broken pavements were peopled only by shadows. Nothing living stirred, not even a stray cat.

"Here we are," grunted the slightly older youth beside him in the light van.

Ambrose could not quite recall his companion's name, having met him only in passing until tonight, but the acne pustules peppering his thin face were familiar. Larry—wasn't his name Larry?—had been around the house on Hicks Street two or three times before that day. Francis and Geraldine seemed to know him as well as they knew Ambrose. However, Larry was half a dozen years older than Ambrose—and a chem major at some Long Island college—and it was Larry they had put in charge of tonight's mission.

"There's the place, half a block east," the youth behind the wheel said, pointing.

Looking in the indicated direction, Ambrose stiffened suddenly in dismay. "Hey, that's my Cousin Brendan's church! He's the priest there, now Father Cullen's gone."

"The head honcho, huh? Well, that cuts no ice with us. What we're here for won't hurt him none. We'll be on our way before him or anybody else knows what hit 'em."

"Just what *are* we here for, Larry? Francis said you'd clue me in when the time came. All I know is, this envelope is to be left at the scene when we scram."

Larry sniffled and wiped his nose with the back of one dirty hand.

"Okay, then, here's the scenario," he said to Ambrose. "You know the church, so you must know the statue inside the gate, right? Some jerk bent down humble-like, ready to have his noggin axed off?"

"Sure, that's the statue of St. Cyprian. I've seen it lots of times, when the folks brought me over to hear Cousin Brendan preach. He was the first Christian Bishop to suffer martyrdom."

"Yeah? What was he, too dumb to scram when the heat was on?"

"He was a rich Roman's son who'd been converted to Christianity. His followers made him Bishop of Carthage. Then the Heathen caught him and beheaded him. All this happened just a couple of hundred years after Jesus lived." Ambrose felt rather proud of his knowledge, bestowed upon him years ago by his Cousin Brendan. Larry might be older, but he obviously didn't know a thing about St. Cyprian. "His full name, in Latin, was Thascius Caecilius Cyprianus. How's that for a mouthful?"

"It'll do if you got no chewing gum. All right, kid, this St. Whoever has been kneelin' there close on a century, Geraldine tells me. You look at that pose, you know he's been askin' all along to get it. Tonight, we give it to him."

"Huh? We what?"

"Once we smash up the statue, you stick your note in amongst the wreckage. We're back in the van and off for the Brooklyn Bridge before anybody can get to a window to take a gander."

"No," Ambrose whispered, shaking his head.

"What do you mean, 'No'? That's what Boyle sent us over here to do."

"I can't help you spoil St. Cyprian. It's a sacred statue. Anyway, my own cousin . . ."

"What are you tryin' to do, Shithead? Play general of the whole Rebellion, when you ain't yet a proper private in the ranks? You follow orders, that's all you got to do. The statue's too heavy for one man alone to turn over, or you wouldn't even be here."

"If Cousin Brendan knew I did anything as bad as this . . ."

"Get your bottom moving, Buster. We ain't got all night to whimper about cousins."

Leaving the van motor purring, Larry was on his way. Terrified that he was going to vomit and bring down even further contempt upon his head, Ambrose sprinted after his leader. They both wore sneakers. Their footfalls made no sound on the patched sidewalk. A moon like a chipped plate shone above them. No streetlight glowed anywhere.

"Larry," he blurted.

"Shut up. You want to bring a squad car after us?"

"No, but about this envelope Mr. Boyle shoved at me just as we left?"

"You got to know every little thing, do you? Okay, this once more I'll tell. Inside is a note, see? A note signed from some pro-British outfit, claiming responsibility for this outrage. Who else would vandalize a poor Catholic church with a devout Irish congregation? Only folks who hate the Irish. If we bust up the statue good and proper, that's gonna generate a lot of anti-British indignation. I.R.A. contributions will roll in like crazy."

Absorbing the brilliance of this plan, a Boyle creation, presumably, Ambrose trotted alone in silence. They reached the iron gate protecting the weathered statue of a kneeling figure. Larry bent above the old lock for an instant; something clicked and the gate swung open.

"All right, now. *Fast,* you little numbskull!"

They took St. Cyprian from opposite sides, putting muscle to their work. At first nothing happened. Then Ambrose felt the hunk of carved stone tremble, start to tilt.

"Harder, kid! Harder! Pop your guts if you got to!"

With a sound that was half-groan, half-scream, the statue began to fall over. As it slid from its base, Larry dragged his panting companion aside. "Keep clear! It's gonna fall this way! Get your envelope ready. Now drop it. Now *run!*"

Once more they were panting along the sidewalk, this time in reverse direction. They jumped into the cab of the van through opposite doors, slamming the metal doors behind them. The vehicle swung from its curb with a whine of tires, headed up the black block toward Brooklyn. Far in its wake came the clatter of a window being thrown open.

"Father O'Donnell! Father O'Donnell! The statue's been turned over!"

Neither occupant of the van's cab so much as glanced across a shoulder to make out what was happening. Larry's pimply face was set hard, like an ugly pre-Columbian stone mask. The van rocked as it turned a corner. It bumped twice—up curb, off curb—then faster!

To his sick shame, Ambrose discovered that he was crying.

Liam's second address to the Five Boroughs Hibernian League was going even better than the first one had a few weeks back.

The hall, deep in the Cobble Hill area, was too small by half to accommodate his original audience. That night the overflow being harangued by earnest request was not quite capacity, but almost. Another substantial haul for the I.R.A.'s war chest. Liam felt fine about it.

"So, ladies and gentlemen, the key factor upon which one keeps a steady eye is the contemptible tactic of Great Britain in fomenting this bloody uprising in the first place. Ostensibly, London set free this former vest-pocket colony and withdrew all interference with the young government being formed there. However, behind the scenes, the same Machiavellian forces were at work. England has no desire whatever to see the African Republic of Wambambi succeed. Frequently, during my journeys into Wambambi's back-country . . ."

They were listening, row behind row of them, as if to the proclamations of a Moses newly descended. Not a pin was dropped. Not a cough was coughed. Liam felt pleasure pour through him like the blood through his veins.

He'd always had a hand for stirring up readers with his writing, but his knack for doing the same from a platform still surprised him. He'd only been at it a year or two, but judging from tonight's awed audience, and from several other recent gatherings, he was a magnetic speaker. O'Donnell genes? Norah was the world's pet skylark, Irish or any. On stage, in her day, Cousin Delia had charmed her fans silly. Even Shane was a political spellbinder. Sure enough, it was a family magic. Liam licked the taste of it with pleasure.

". . . hungry babies at their mother's breasts, and the mothers with no milk to feed them. The livestock has been devastated by the recent drought. In reality, as future history is certain to prove, this shrinkage is the work of rustlers hired within walking distance of the River Thames. Everywhere, starvation. Everywhere, bewilderment. Everywhere, anger. Blame has of course been heaped upon the native regime. President Mojela is the victim of frequent

assassination attempts, each of them subtly justified by
British businessmen as a sign of Mojela's villainy. Yet
these enemies are permitted to carry on their undermining
tactics within Wambambi's borders. . . ."

A door at the rear of the hall opened quietly. Down the
center aisle, walking on tip-toe, came Liam's son Danny.
Danny with doom on his usually cheerful face. Instant
awareness flicked Liam like a whip. Something wrong?
He kept on talking as if nothing were distracting him.

"The parallel is too obvious to require underlining,
ladies and gentlemen. It is the pattern, repeated again, of
England's mistreatment of valiant little Ireland since centuries long gone. A small country ground down by a powerful one. A helpless hare in the jaws of a wolf . . ."

Danny had come to a dead stop at the edge of the
speaker's platform. He handed his father a folded piece of
paper. Liam reached down and took the message, his voice
flowing on as he unfolded it.

"In the fate of poor, disrupted Wambambi, read also
that of a crucified Erin! What served the British Throne
generations ago now serves it equally well in a tiny unde-
veloped nation deep in the African jungle. If Ireland is to
be free at last, my friends, the victory lies not in England's
heart but in America's generous pocketbooks . . ."
Abruptly, Liam's jaw bone tensed. A startled, questioning
glance darted in Danny's direction. He straightened.

"I thank you for your kind attention, friends, and im-
plore your future generosity. Good evening." He was
down off the platform before the enthusiastic applause
could even begin. Surprised stares followed him up the
main aisle as he ran for the exit, dragging Danny along
beside him.

Outside, double-parked but not yet ticketed, the family
Plymouth waited with motor running. As Liam slid under

the wheel, Danny piled in beside him. They started in a leapfrog-style jump and picked up speed from there. They sped directly for the Heights.

"All right, then, Danny. How do you know he's in trouble?"

"Because I found out what he was up to last night, Pa. That story about the smashed statue at St. Cyprian's that made all today's papers. Ambie was in on it."

"My son a hoodlum vandalizing a Catholic place of worship? Impossible! That's his Cousin Brendan's own parish, Danny. For the boy to do such a thing would be monstrous!"

"I wouldn't believe it myself, sir, if Ambie hadn't told me. When I tooled in from football practice, an hour ago, there he sat in the front room. The late editions were scattered all around him. You've read them? About St. Cyprian's?"

"I have. Outrageous desecration. What was Ambie doing?"

"Just staring into space, tears streaking down his cheeks. It had to have something to do with the story. When he saw me, he said, 'I did it, Dan'. He kept gasping at me, like he was drowning or something, and saying, 'I did it, Dan' over and over."

"Did he give you any reason for such an insanity?"

"After a while I could dig a little of it out of him. It was because Mr. Boyle had told him to, he said. So blame would be put on the English. That's supposed to goose donations to the I.R.A. Like folks who book you for lectures intend."

"Is Ambie still in the front room, Danny?"

"No, Pa. That's why I came after you. A car drove up outside and the bell rang and Ambie went to answer. He seemed to know who it would be. After a little, he called in to me saying he was going out with friends. I saw him climb into their car. It sort of scared me."

"Going out to help in some other dirty business like the statue?"

"I don't know, Pa, but I don't think so. The car was headed for Hicks Street."

"So are we!" breathed Liam, knuckles white on the wheel.

In the evening shadows, the house looked like a duplicate of the houses to its left and right. Row houses, all of them, the block's Edwardian structures seemed a painted portrait of middle class solidarity.

The single small difference about the house Geraldine Donoghue and her friends had rented was that on its street floor, curtains had been drawn to block each of the windows.

Liam was out of the Plymouth before he had properly parked. His footfalls on the granite stair treads had the solid sound of a one-man army. Having jabbed at the bell, he tried the doorknob—without success. A latch was in place.

Most callers might have waited for a decent interval, but not Liam. His beefy fist pounded on the panel as if he were a man inventing thunder. He was still at his hammering when the door swung open. Backlighted from the hall behind her, Geraldine stood facing him—a Cerberus in gaudy orange silk pajamas.

"Why, it's Liam O'Donnell. Hello, Liam. And what can I do for you?"

"For openers, lady, you can give me my son. I'll be taking him off your hands."

"Ambrose?" Geraldine looked down at him, and then at Danny directly behind him. "I'm not quite sure he dropped by to see us tonight, Liam."

"He's here all right. He was seen being driven in this direction. Now, unless you'd like me to request police assistance in hunting Ambie down, you'd best produce him."

The door opened wider.

"My goodness but you're sounding ferocious tonight, Mr. O'Donnell. Come right in, both of you, if you've a mind to. If Ambie's about, you're welcome to him."

Striding past her, Liam was already sniffing the air of the front hall.

This was the kind of dwelling which might reasonably be perfumed by cooking cabbage. Instead, the scent drifting near the bottom of a rising stair well was one that was equally familiar. Liam would have liked a dollar for every time during these past two decades he had smelled it in some hideaway where terror was in the process. His face set hard.

"Bombs, is it? So that's what Francis is up to!"

"Why shouldn't he be, brave son of Freedom that he is?" She stared at him blankly. "Who'd expect you to be the one to condemn him, Liam O'Donnell? A fine contributor to the Cause like you!"

"I don't play amateur games with explosives. And that's what you are all doing. Not one of you, if I list you rightly, knows anything about constructing a bomb that could travel from America to Dublin. That's work for experts, not hot-heads."

"You underestimate us," Geraldine said. "We have two lads in our cellar this minute who both hold Bachelor Degrees in Chemistry. So when you're calling Larry and Crofton amateurs . . ."

"Don't try to swap ninny chatter with me, woman. Is Ambie down in your cellar?"

"Thinking on it, I believe he might be. A loyal supporter like you doesn't have to knock down the walls to get to him, man. That's the way to the steps.''

He swung in the direction she indicated, jerked open an inconspicuous door, and yelled down into the lower cavern. His roar was that of a rutting bull.

"You down there, Ambrose O'Donnell! Get yourself up here on the double or by Jesus I'll crack your neck! You hear me, Ambrose? This is your father talking!"

From the dim glow at Liam's feet came vague scuttling sounds like those of oversized rats quitting a sinking ship. Wavers of light indicated some general sort of movement, but it was only one lone figure who emerged at last with obvious reluctance.

"Hello, Pa. I'm kind of busy down here. I'm taking a lesson.''

"I can well imagine in what! Get up these stairs, boy.''

"Look, Pa, I'm not a kid any longer. I'm an Irishman, big enough and old enough to fight for his land's liberation. Mr. Boyle says so, too. What I'm learning down here . . .''

"In the first palce, Ambie, you're an American of three generations standing. In the second place, big you may be, but you're not big enough to take what I'll dish out to you if you're not standing up here beside me on the count of three. One . . . Two . . .''

Up the cellarway Ambrose stumbled. Mutiny quivered in every line of his rebellious countenance. He had been dressed down before compatriots, and the flush of resentment burned bright in his cheeks. But he did not quite dare challenge his father's order.

"See here, what Larry and Crofton are teaching me to do is . . .''

"Not a word out of you. Not unless you want it slapped

from your mouth. Now *get out of here.* On the double.
Danny, take him along. And I want no arguments.''

Angry but limp, Ambrose allowed his brother to grab
his arm and steer him past Geraldine's technicolor presence into a quiet street. Feet planted well apart, Liam
glared after them as they went. A full minute passed, or
maybe longer, before he spoke again.

"Now, Geraldine, I'll converse with Francis. Sending
my boy on a vandal's errand against the Holy Church, is
he? Have him up out of that pisshole while I'm still in a
gentle mood. He's seen me otherwise over in Wambambi.
He wouldn't like an encore.''

For a long instant Geraldine's eyes glittered. Then the
orange shoulders shrugged.

"However you like it. But I think you ought to be
warned, Liam O'Donnell. These days, Francis finds it
prudent to tote a revolver. So my advice to you . . .''

Everything erupted in one shattering, deafening roar.

The walls of the neat little dwelling seemed to rise off
their foundations and waver in mid-air before they started
to close in. Timbers crashed. Glass shattered. Miss
Donoghue's bright raiment—or its color—spread and widened before him, until the whole night was orange.
Flickering. Crackling.

Overhead, a beam split loose and hurtled downward. For
Liam, everything went suddenly black.

24

The special service had been announced for five o'clock in the afternoon.

It was open to the full congregation, and a reasonable segment of them had begun drifting down the shabby street soon after four-thirty. Many were in time to watch the cars from uptown arriving. On any other Sunday, a few of these vehicles might have caused a discreet sensation, but it was widely known that Father O'Donnell's family had good reason to turn up *en masse* for this particular occasion.

First to arrive at the vestry door was a shining grey Packard so ancient that it sported running boards. A '35 model, most frequent curbside estimates agreed. Actually, someone else challenged, it had rolled from the factory's assembly line early in '37. Either way, it looked that day as though it had never before touched common paving.

Bits of its history emerged.

Veronica Tyrone-Quinn, its first owner, had cared for

the car well. Her chauffeur Tom had conducted a genuine love affair with it. Upon its owner's death it had reverted to her heir and daughter, Mrs. Eamonn McHugh. She in turn had passed it along to her distinguished-looking cousin, Mr. Terence O'Donnell. His craving for the vehicle was said to have been all but indecent.

Terence had put it into storage in a private garage up the Hudson, where it had remained for years. It was brought out especially for this occasion.

Terence O'Donnell got out of the car—spats, homburg, silver-headed cane and all—and limped majestically through the church gate. Behind him swept a sallow old female in a Lily Daché hat and Valentina velvet suit. The whispers crescendoed, then faded.

Within a few moments, a rented limousine from the airport glided down the block, and when its occupants were sighted, there was renewed murmuring.

Every man, woman and child with a television set knew Norah O'Donnell, and when the nice-looking man who accompanied her stepped out and solicitously helped her out of the car, a spontaneous clapping broke out. The crowd was thrilled to see the famous Irish Skylark.

"Did you hear she's flown east just for this service? Her Friday show originates in California now. It has for simply ages. It's topped the ratings even longer than Dinah Shore."

"She's still so lovely, too. You just want to stand back and gaze at her. And not just beautiful, *nice*. Who's the fellow with her? Oh, sure, her husband. You know, Dennis Gallagher, the composer whose theme music for *The Prisoner of Zenda* captured last year's Oscar. They still look so happy together."

The onlookers sighed.

An older couple, dressed simply but tastefully, stepped

from the limousine to join the others. Someone in the crowd recognized them.

"Norah's parents. There were family pictures in *Life* Magazine a couple of years ago. Those are Father O'Donnell's folks. He, Norah and the Senator are their kids."

Father O'Donnell himself emerged from the rectory across the street and moved among the crowd. His black cape stirred in the mild breeze as he greeted each person with a warm smile. It was mentioned that he was up for a promotion to Monsignor—a good thing, it was agreed. He had done a great deal to build back St. Cyprian's, and there wasn't anyone who didn't adore him.

Some wondered who it was in a wheelchair being unloaded from a checker Cab. They finally remembered that it was a cousin who had been blown up when a radical gang destroyed their own headquarters a year earlier. Standing near by was a nervous woman clinging to a tall, handsome man with a face that, up close, was considerably scarred. The last of the O'Donnells went inside the church just as the music began to play.

The sounds of the organ swept into the drab waterfront street in resonant majesty. People began drifting past the vestibule, finding places in the rows of worn but freshly polished pews.

A regular mass was conducted by Father O'Donnell.

The simple sincerity of his richly vibrant voice, repeating meaningful old rituals as if they were hymns of the heart, had become a special treasure to many of his established congregation. Men and women once of the neighborhood, whose destinies had called them off to other corners of the city, came back to St. Cyprian's when they could merely for the joy of listening to the familiar vibrance in the old building's reverant shadows.

But when the day's particular purpose had been reached, young Father Aurelio—six years out of the seminary, and Father O'Donnell's assistant for three of them—took over. It was understandable that his senior priest might feel a reluctance to continue.

Father Aurelio stood tall before them, not at the dim altar but under the stained glass window. His solemn and extraordinarily expressive Italian face was like that of some dark and youthful archangel, and as he began to speak, his black eyes roved from one member to the next of the family assembled in the front pews.

"The joyful business which today summons us all together would not be possible were it not for the kinfolk of our beloved Father O'Donnell. Few of us have been unaware of the empty pedestal just inside our entrance gates. For a century, perhaps for longer, the figure which belonged upon it stood there as a constant reminder of the virtues of humility and fortitude. Then a sudden toppling of our St. Cyprian, the work of a single night, brought grief to every member of this parish. . . ."

The family looked at each other with expressive eyes. In Evaleen's might have been found traces of dried tears; in Liam's, a residue of forcibly suppressed anger; in Ambrose's, silent shame. Most other faces reflected simply the silent pleasure of contemplating the completion of a good deed well done.

Norah had drawn them all a bit closer together with an affectionate little note each had received from her. The anonymous desecration of Brendan's church had deeply distressed them all, had it not? Wouldn't the replacing of his statue be a wonderful testimonial to their mutual love for him? She herself would christen such a project with her salary for a month of Irish Skylark shows. If any of the rest wished to join her . . .

"With sufficient funds so generously made available," Father Aurelio was saying, "the rest, as the saying goes, has become history. After careful study of the work of several possible artists, the noted sculptor Ivan Orlosky was selected by our vestry for the delicate task of restoration. Today we gather to celebrate the outcome of Mr. Orlosky's labors."

Everyone's gaze was fixed intently upon a bulky, hooded object at Father Aurelio's immediate left. Ambrose clasped his hands tormentedly together. He felt sweat ooze between them. He had been granted no preview of the repairs and he was worried that the cracks would show, or that the mended spots would remain like raw scars forever.

He would gladly have given his remaining years in exchange for the power to erase that one secret night. The sour taste of regret was likely to remain undiluted.

The bar in Brooklyn Heights where Pa still dropped by on the occasional evening was still called the Flaming Harp. Once, Ambrose had told himself the words were a symbol; a symbol of brave passions stirring the hearts of all true men with Irish blood flowing through them. No longer. The flame, whatever else it burned away, consumed too much that was dear and precious.

Seated here in this old church, Ambrose could call back how the house on Hicks Street had looked before the explosion. It had been a part of the neighborhood; a familiar presence on countless days when one passed by on the route to school.

However, for the past two years there had been little to see but a gaping hold where the house had stood. Someday, when property rights and zoning ordinances had been appeased and a wasp nest of pending litigation settled, something new would arise there, but to Ambrose, it would always remain a smouldering no-man's-land. From it, po-

lice squads had extracted the barely identifiable remains of
Francis and Larry and Crofton; scraps of orange silk were
all that was left of the lovely Geraldine.

To his last day on the earth, Ambrose would offer
grateful prayers to God's mercy that Pa had survived.
Condemned to a wheelchair, no longer roaming the four
quarters of the globe on the heels of glamorous adventures,
Liam was still The Hero. Nothing in him seemed more
heroic than the stoic generosity of his forgiveness.

A mist stung Liam's second son's eyes as he listened.

"The misguided enemies of Christ who are to this day
unidentified, and doubtless will remain so, may well feel
as grateful as do we for the generous spirit of the O'Donnell
family. When the great spiritual symbol which today re-
turns to us, and which shortly will be re-installed on its
proper pedestal, stands again before this holy place bearing
his name—then, dear friends, those faceless ill-doers well
may sink to their knees. Their violence is this day
obliterated."

Norah's eyes met her husband's, and they exchanged an
all but invisible nod of sharing. Madge's hand closed tight
over Cornelius's and clung. Terence registered approval
and, in passing, wished that his old friend Des might be
with the family to share its glory.

"Therefore, as I now exercise my privilege of unveiling
this outcome of reverent giving and painstaking skill, I
seek also to remind all those here present of the day's
profoundest Verity." Father Aurelio paused dramatically.
"Out of deepest darkness may come a new light shining.
This, not a statue alone, is our gift from the family of
Father O'Donnell, and this is the real eternal meaning of
Christ's glory."

An aristocratic hand reached out ahd whipped away the
silken folds of the hood. A soft gasp ran through the

congregation. The statue, which many of those present had known since childhood, stood before them unchanged.

If it once had lain broken to lumps, no lingering trace of the disaster was now apparent. A jeweler with a loupe might find it impossible to detect the slightest seam, or locate the least replacement. In Ivan Orlosky, the vestry had located a true genius.

A smattering of inappropriate applause was quickly stilled.

But on the old steps outside, in the shadow of a still empty pedestal, the clapping began again. "Thank God for Orlosky. Thank God for the open-handed O'Donnells." That was the theme of a fading afternoon.

From St. Cyprian's the family separated into different cars, only to join again at Senator Shane's duplex on Sutton Place.

On the terrace overlooking the East River, they sat with their celebratory draughts, or strolled from group to group with stemmed goblets in hand.

Seconded by Hilda, Terence had raised a dignified protest because the reunion was not being held in his apartment. After all, some notice should be taken of his position as the senior O'Donnell. But his protest had been overruled.

The duplex had been Bernadette's. Madge had been raised there and Cornelius had come here as a bridegroom. Eamonn, still so devotedly remembered, once had entertained them all in these same spacious rooms. And surely Shane, the tenant for so many years now, was head-of-family in the public eye. There had been much speculation as to the likelihood of his becoming the Party's next candidate for Vice-President, so the public as well as the family had to be considered.

"If it helps Shane," Norah had summed it up, "why not?"

"But it's really *us*, not how people who read about the service in their newspapers perceive us, that matters," Agnes murmured to Evaleen. "Who *are* we O'Donnells, really? Looking at us today at Brendan's church, all together, I couldn't help sorting out an awesome tangle of memories."

Caught by the question, Evaleen frowned faintly.

"We're just ourselves, Agnes, I guess. Each one of us a separate self—together sometimes as a sort of conglomerate self, but most of the while separate like everybody else. Remember that day at the Russian Tea Room? What was it we decided then? We're each of us dancing our own private waltz on the wind."

It seemed to them both that this little sermon was too solemn for a relaxed reunion moment. Yet perhaps it was a true one.

Beyond the open windows, Norah had been led to the piano. Her song drifted out to the terrace as songs she had sung for them down the years often had done, gay and just a bit bawdy, drawing them all together. Other voices began to blend in, one after another. Male and female. Young and old.

With the river shining behind them, the two women listened.

"The O'Donnell choir!" Agnes murmured. "It doesn't sound much like a waltz, does it?"

"An Irish jig, more truly."

Evaleen set her tray down on the stone railing nearest at hand. Her arm slipped affectionately about her cousin-in-law's still slender waist. Together, they moved indoors to join the others.